Gillian White, a former jo[...]
pool, lives in Totnes, Devon[...]
their two dogs. Their four g[...]
sons live near by. Three of Gillian White's ten novels,[...]
Deceiver, *The Beggar Bride* and *Mothertime*, have already
been adapted for BBC television. *The Sleeper*, her first novel
to be published by Transworld, is also available in Corgi
paperback and is shortly to be a major BBC TV production.
Her latest novel, *Veil of Darkness*, is now available as a
Bantam Press hardback.

CRITICAL ACCLAIM FOR GILLIAN WHITE:

'This dark, spooky psychological thriller, grabs you by the
throat and won't let go . . . not a book for those who suffer
from high blood pressure' Val Hennessy, *Woman's Journal*

'A first-rate psychological thriller – perceptive, literate,
witty and full of suspense' *Good Housekeeping*

'A dark, disturbing tale' *Sunday Telegraph*

'An excursion to Barbara Vineland . . . Gillian White
handles her gruesome ingredients with control and
intelligence' *Independent on Sunday*

'A well-plotted thriller' *Mail on Sunday*

'A complex psychological thriller which will fire your
imagination and fuel your fears' *Western Morning News*

'A novelist of the highest quality . . . an intense and vividly
written novel which takes you by the throat and won't let
go: a splendid book for those who enjoy a psychological
thriller with a deep and provocative story'
Independent on Sunday

'Bitingly brilliant . . . complex, witty and sinister'
Daily Mirror

Also by Gillian White

UNHALLOWED GROUND

Gillian White

CORGI BOOKS

UNHALLOWED GROUND
A CORGI BOOK : 0 552 14563 7

Originally published in Great Britain by Bantam Press,
a division of Transworld Publishers Ltd

PRINTING HISTORY
Bantam Press edition published 1998
Corgi edition published 1999

3 5 7 9 10 8 6 4 2

Set in 11/12pt Linotype Times by
Kestrel Data, Exeter, Devon.

Corgi Books are published by Transworld Publishers Ltd,
61–63 Uxbridge Road, London W5 5SA,
in Australia by Transworld Publishers,
c/o Random House Australia Pty Ltd,
20 Alfred Street, Milsons Point, NSW 2061,
in New Zealand by Transworld Publishers,
c/o Random House New Zealand,
18 Poland Road, Glenfield, Auckland
and in South Africa by Transworld Publishers,
c/o Random House (Pty) Ltd,
Endulini, 5a Jubilee Road, Parktown 2193.

Reproduced, printed and bound in Great Britain by
Cox & Wyman Ltd, Reading, Berkshire.

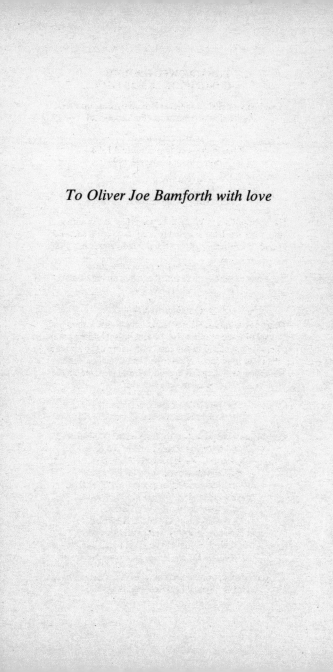

To Oliver Joe Bamforth with love

One

Once upon a time, it is said, the devil walked in this valley. His progress was marked by a straight line of hoofprints, black two-legged tracks on a light dusting of snow, over shippen and stable, stone wall and stile, through graveyard and frozen furrow.

No detours.

Legend has it that Millie Blunt, a silly wench, recovered his codpiece from the bough of an oak while searching there for mistletoe. The hapless girl spirited it home believing it held all manner of powers. She slept with it under her pillow one night – it must have been uncomfortable – when the moon flooded her attic room through her little casement window, and she never spoke another sane word from that day until she died, poor soul.

Though why the devil should choose a valley such as this for a survey, or a gathering of souls, was always far from clear; there were such few souls, even then no more than twelve, in the hamlet of Wooton Coney, and the few there were were undoubtedly Christian and safely hidden behind shutters on howling nights such as those. As pious and God-fearing a community as any. The church itself, and the graveyard through which the devil walked, collapsed way back in the seventeenth century, and only rubble and lichened old gravestones remain to mark the spot. At some unrecorded moment in history the weather-vane from the crumbled church spire was rescued from the debris, and for the last 200 years that bent tin cockerel has swung round on its rusty perch on the gabled end of the Buckpits' barn.

Centuries later, and Georgina Jefferson is as opposite in character to the blighted wench in the fable as it would be possible to get. Educated and cultured, she is sane, *she is sane*. Where Millie Blunt was free with her favours and considered something of a halfwit from the start (the preacher rapped hard on the pulpit and disclaimed her in church, called her child the devil's spawn), her teachers wrote in her termly reports that Georgina could go far. There is nothing melodramatic about her, unlike the troubled Millie with her wild tangled hair and her flashing eyes and her lies. When her child died she swore that the devil had come in the night and smothered it. In character Georgina is solid as a rock, not morbid or sentimental, not given to the flights of fancy in which so many of her friends indulge. So when she first heard this devilish tale it certainly did not unnerve her, although she did think, as a professional, that poor Millie's predicament would be more mercifully dealt with these days. She wouldn't recognize a codpiece if she saw one, she would probably think it was some piece of saddlery. Practical and sensible, Georgina does not over-indulge. She sits and watches while lesser mortals get rat-faced and make prats of themselves at parties, she is the one with tomato juice and a dab of Worcester sauce, the complete one, the one who drives.

Boring perhaps? A shade too cautious?

Certainly not. Not a bit of it. She is glad she is not one of these irresponsible folk; their lack of control shocks her, for she cannot bear to relinquish it, not in bed, not in the kitchen, and thus her meals (and her sheets) tend to be dry, with each taste a neat and separate daub on the plate. She would rather do without gravy, or too many dangerous spicy sauces.

So we can see that Georgina Jefferson, forty-two, slim, dark and attractive, who shops for her clothes at Marks & Spencer, sends Lifeboat cards at Christmas, is a solid, dependable person, concerned, right-thinking and busy. She knows who she is, believes that virtue carries its own reward and is satisfied with that.

And that is why it is such a worry for her to believe, like poor Millie before her, *that she is gradually going insane*.

And, like Millie, there's no help to be had.

It was autumn, a thick juicy one, when she first saw the figure on the hill. The air was rich with the smell of fungal decay and winter had started to breathe on her mornings. She walked straight towards him and frightened him away, or that's what she thought she had done.

Amused by her own curiosity, living where she did it was easy to forget the outside world and that everything wasn't strictly her business. She saw him through the softly stirring curtains of her opened kitchen window, through a blue pall of bonfire smoke, between the crooked branches of the ancient apple trees twisting and heavily hung with clumps of crab apples, bleeding with wasps.

A rural encounter.

At first she thought the Buckpits must have put up a scarecrow, so still and so stark did the dark figure stand. But hang on a minute, it was more substantial than a scarecrow, and why would they put a scarecrow on a small triangular flag of a field that was only good for grass, and poor grass at that?

Georgina stared on meditatively, inhaling watery lemon and her Marigold hands foamy with bubbles. A few towels flapped fresh on her line and tugged at her ears with the sounds they made, and the old wooden wheelbarrow, half full of logs, eyed her muddily from a tangle of grass, a reminder that she had not yet finished the first task of the morning.

Whichever window she chooses to look out of Georgie is forced to look up, because Furze Pen Cottage is down in a dip, a small coin dropped at the bottom of a coarsely woven patchwork purse, an envelope of moorland. Her skyline is unfailingly interesting, copses and boulders and low scudding clouds make vibrant colour changes and act as barriers against the outside world from which she has fled. Her horizons cast nothing but gentle shadows.

Has she fled? Everyone seems to think she has fled.

Or has nothing more interesting than fate brought her here?

Certainly, in her sensible, practical way, she was glad of the bequest when it came.

But back to the figure, this rambling will not do. It was the stillness of it which grabbed her attention. Nevertheless, she finished washing up, taking pleasure in the sparkle of the glasses . . . her life was solid enough, composed enough at that time to allow for pleasure from simple things, so that even changing the sheets on the bed was becoming a kind of sweet-smelling joy. She had been right about coming here. The effects of her rural retreat were already beginning to work.

Was it the distance which made him so dark or was he wearing black? It was rare for tourists to stray this far, mostly they miss the lane or see it and consider it far too steep, so they carry on along the road across the top towards the village one mile on, where they can have lunch at the Blue Bull Inn and peruse the slate etchings and metallic bird engravings in Mrs Morgan's gift shop. The lane, with its scatter of reedy grasses and its manure-splattered, rutted appearance, gives the impression that it leads to a farm, and people are nervous of finding themselves trapped by a pack of sheep dogs.

And what if the farmer is unfriendly?

The figure was not a Buckpit, not a Horsefield or a Cramer, because none of those would stand still for so long, and there was no gun on its back.

11

So Georgina went to the back door and sensibly slipped on her boots. She walked through her acre of rustic garden, ducking and bobbing to avoid the branches, ignoring the rush of her pecking hens. On reaching the fence at the end she hitched up her skirt and stepped over. Wading through her own small stream, looking back from her place on the boulder, she whistled softly for Lola.

The spaniel with careering ears, dewy wet on the fringes, outwitted once again because she likes to announce such outings by barking – she prefers to lead from the front – snapped at a few drunken wasps as she set off after her mistress.

There must have been something very wrong because the man had been standing for half an hour.

A diminutive figure, head down, arms crossed, Georgina started up the incline, no threat to man or beast, just a slender woman in a flowing skirt and a cotton smock with a hood. The sun was a hazy yellow as it filtered through the corn chaff. Every now and then she raised her eyes to check how far she had come. She'd grown used to climbing by then; wherever she goes she is forced to climb, and it had taken a while to acclimatize after living so long on the smooth flat streets of London. To climb properly and with purpose means adjusting the breathing so that it doesn't run out. There was no fear then – nothing to what came later – merely interest and a slight unease. A reporter who had managed, somehow, to dig her out of her hole? To expose her? To drag her back to the tabloid pages? The past sliding into the present? God forbid! Maybe he was lost and needed help. Maybe he was a hiker, or an artist, or a man from the Min of Ag come to do something about the water?

And yet she knew he was not.

Screwing up her eyes against the sun, Georgina felt the lines in her tanned skin pull and imagined she felt her age coming through. The figure (she could not see his face from here, no definable limbs, no neck, no hair) was no more than a smudge, a dark stunted tree trunk, and yet she could sense the furtiveness of him.

He must have been able to see her coming and Lola was charging about, driven wild by the scent of rabbits. She would be friendly and polite, she would ask him what he was doing.

That's all.

She stopped when she heard the sound of the whistle. It was soft, on two notes, like sailors piping a captain aboard, or how a shepherd might whistle to his dog. It was after she moved her eyes away, just for a second, while she eased herself through a crumbled gap in a wall, that she saw the figure had disappeared . . . into the copse . . . there was nowhere else. No other cover. No hiding place.

A feeling of outright panic gripped her. He must have moved very quickly.

An orange shadow came out of the clouds, swinging from one horizon to another and casting a horribly accurate spotlight over Georgina's fear. Because it was at that moment that she first sensed the violence, and yet pushed it away

13

from her consciousness – *Oh God, was she so in tune with violence that she could smell it from 500 paces?* Surely her reaction was nothing but imagination, and imaginations can become vivid when you live all alone, buried amongst such desolate, lonely countryside. Even for someone as sensible as she.

The shadow of a buzzard followed her home, and the sound of a distant tractor. Lola followed sorrowfully – the walk had been too short for her liking – and made an attention-seeking pass at a hen as they strolled back through the garden towards the silence of Furze Pen Cottage.

The incident was over. That first sighting was as strange and as simple as that. But frozen by the experience, for the first time since Isla and Suzie had left the previous weekend, Georgina wished that they were still there because she would have liked to discuss the matter. Isla and Suzie were the last of the summer visitors who were all kindly trying to put off the awful hour when Georgina must adjust to her new life and endure, alone, the oncoming winter.

'But I am not alone,' she used to tell them all, wearing that brave wooden smile of hers, attempting to reassure herself with that well-rehearsed argument: 'My neighbours live close by, almost within calling distance when the wind's in the right direction.'

'Neighbours!' Isla gave a derisive snort. Her lips curved mirthlessly. 'You might live next door to them, Georgie, but they're freaks, from some other planet. They are hardly going to provide you with the most stimulating company during the long evening hours.'

'Isla. This isn't fair. You're supposed to be trying to cheer me up.'

'I'm just wondering how you imagine you can depend on them, for anything.'

'They're polite enough.'

And here Suzie smiled in the same disbelieving way as Isla. 'Oh, yes, they mutter the odd miserable good morning when you meet face to face and there's no avoiding it.'

'Oh, that's silly,' Georgie snapped. 'They just believe in minding their own business; they probably think I don't want people nosing, prying into my affairs. They probably think I'm like my brother, a recluse, an artist, an eccentric who wants to be left alone. I bet Stephen bit their heads off in the past.' And she could feel that annoyance which itched whenever the conversation got too close for comfort. 'Anyway, what choice do I have? I've made my bed, as my mother would say.'

Isla met her stare, sifting through a dozen responses to find the most suitable one. In the end she said in a weak, troubled voice, 'You should never have come here in the first place. Out of the frying pan . . .'

'You think I'm a bloody fool, don't you?'

Isla looked away and picked up her drink. She lay on the messy sofa, surprisingly comfortable despite its amorphous nature, next to the crackling fire that winked on her overlarge tortoiseshell

15

spectacles. 'I think you over-reacted, yes. I think you are punishing yourself as usual. God said, "On all their heads shall be baldness and every beard cut off," and you, my dear Georgina, secretly want to be bald.'

Not funny. Georgie wound a curl around her finger and rubbed her sloppy socks together – curiously nervous gestures for her – as she stared thoughtfully into the flames. She suddenly felt an urge to lean forward and arrange a few untidy sticks in the enormous hearth. A cold draft spun down the massive chasm of a chimney. Crossly she reminded them both, 'There wasn't much time for thinking! Not then, dammit. This place felt like a refuge then, a friendly lair in a hostile world, *but why am I wading through this shit again?* You know how it was. You were there for God's sake. You know what it was like for me then.'

'It was bloody hell,' agreed Suzie, as frizzy-haired as a freshly gathered fleece, her complexion smooth as a china doll's with cheeks painted a soft pink and a cold nose bright and shiny. The evenings were already chilly and Suzie was almost entirely cocooned in a baggy, knee-length purple fleece. 'But even so, you could have used the cottage as a temporary hideaway and put it on the market in the meantime. Nobody dreamed you'd end up living at Furze Pen, Georgie, nobody thought you'd take it this far.'

No, neither had Georgina, but she'd never dreamed it would get that bad.

'If I'd put it on the market I would have had to be here all the time to show the punters round.

16

And I couldn't have faced all those strangers. I couldn't put that sort of false smile on my face or cope with anything so fake. Hell, Suzie, I couldn't put my mind to anything like hoovering or dusting or sorting out the garden.'

'That is ridiculous.' Isla, on the sofa, pounded the limpish cushions and rearranged them behind her back. A feathery aura of age and dust floated into the atmosphere. 'The solicitor would have sold it for you; you had an offer right at the start. They'd have had no problems selling this as a holiday cottage, bang in the middle of Dartmoor; it would have made a fortune, untouched, original beams, original windows, flagstone floors . . .'

'No central heating,' Georgie interrupted, shivering slightly as she crossed the small sitting room to the even colder, more primitive kitchen to add mushrooms to the stew. She felt like a piece of lettuce walking into the salad crisper. Perhaps she should not have chosen whitewash, a warmer shade might have done wonders. The cheery rugs did help a tad, and the paintings that covered the walls, of course.

From her place by the fire, Lola snored loudly and woke herself up.

'And we're just very concerned you're going to feel terribly depressed and lonely, way out of your depth, surviving like this in the winter,' Suzie called through the narrow doorway with a meaningful look in Isla's direction. 'All your perceptions of the world are fuddled. It's not as if it's too late. You could come back to London with us,

17

put this place on the market and start searching for something more practical.'

Georgie, chewing on her fingernails, watched the hypnotically floating mushrooms, allowing the steam to caress her face, enjoying the hot smell of the stew, taking comfort from the warmth and the feeling of something well made with love. Since she'd been down here her cooking had developed a wetter, more mixed consistency . . . so much free fruit, so many vegetables . . . it was easier to use only one pot because of the cramped kitchen. Home-grown potatoes from the farm and a home-made apple pie with fresh cream to follow.

Yet everything Isla and Suzie said made sense, while every argument she put forward fell apart full of holes. And if she was trying to prove something by standing out and being so stubborn, then for God's sake what was it?

She had been so frightened, so intimidated by everything. But most of all by the way she had, in a few short months, been so easily destroyed, shattered, all confidence gone, the confidence she had built up over forty-two years, melted away in a moment. Until she felt, as she lay in bed night after night weeping, that all the time there'd been nobody there, that Georgina Jefferson was a 'let's pretend' person from childhood, a face miming with nobody behind it. As unsubstantial as soap worn to a frightening slither, gargling off down the plughole.

Was she so naive as to believe that by enduring life on her own for a while, a hermit existence with only Lola for company, she would find herself again? Could she grow large and firm again as simply as that?

I will lay me down in green pastures. She wanted her soul restoreth.

Oh, I am a strong and sensible person . . .

Well, this was what she returned to her friends in the sitting room and told them. And they said, tipsily, that they did understand her motives, they saw how easily a person could be demoralized and torn apart under such attack from every quarter.

'Even people I'd trusted as friends turned their backs on me,' she wailed, tormented by an alien self-pity. '*Can you honestly imagine what that's like?* Ringing people up – oh yes, feeling bad enough about ringing people up – so damn needy, hands in a sweat, heart aching, so desperately wanting reassurance, and being told by quiet, polite voices that they weren't in, they'll ring you back, they were away when you knew they were not.' She played with Lola's soft ears as a child might play with a comforter. The dog opened one eye. It was soft and brown and liquid with love. 'And all the while, to add to the horror, the newspapers crucify you.'

'It could have happened to any one of us.'

'*Don't tell me that one more time!* I can't bear hearing that! I'm sorry, I'm sorry, I know it could have happened to anyone, but it didn't, Suzie, did it, *it bloody well happened to me!*'

And Georgie wanted to shout that, above all, she needed time on her own to mourn for the child with the wise grey eyes who had ended up in a grainy frame with shaggy hair on the front pages of all the papers. The child that had depended on her for its life. The child she had, through her own ineptitude, betrayed and allowed to die. But such a protest would have been unnecessary because Isla and Suzie knew that very well, and yes, as social workers, it could have happened to either of them, and it would happen, again and again as it seems to, every few years, and every time it would be equally terrible . . .

'What should I have done,' had become such a wizened old question that she had stopped asking it, even of herself. If only she could have taken time back. But what was the use of any of this? She had known there was violence at that wretched flat, it oozed out through that cold yellow front door with the thin metal letter box through which she had stuffed note after note, time after time, through which her lips had called so often. Hopelessly. Tiredly. Fearfully.

And back then, as she leaned forward from her sunken chair that even in late summer smelled of damp, wringing her hands and sharing her feelings with her friends, aware of her secret resentment, she would have liked to have screamed, And I am grateful for your continued friendship, can you sense that, dear God? Because that meant that their friendship, once on equal terms, once as honest as friendships could be, was flawed, even though they would have received this as an affront and answered, 'That is absurd.' Yes, that resentment, that bitterness, it was there now and nothing could alter it. And what would they have thought if Georgie had screamed across their cosy

20

pink drunkenness, as she longed to do, *This outrageous, diabolical thing did not happen to either of you, but my God how I wish that it HAD*. I wish it was me sitting where you are giving advice and sympathizing. *I wish I was you and that either of you were over here in my position*.

Yes, she was giving them too little and they were giving her too much.

She re-embarked on her train of thought. She said, 'I wish I'd been able to go to court and stand trial. It would have been fairer, and they were trying me anyway.'

Wretched. Despairing. *And guilty*.

'No, they were not. The inquiry never expected to find you guilty, Georgie. Nothing is that simplistic. You did all that was humanly possible. You are not a fortune teller. The inquiry found you blameless.'

'Blameless? *Jesus Christ!* A child is murdered and how can any of us be blameless? And I could have done more. It is always possible to have done more.'

Isla removed her dramatically circular spectacles and rubbed the lenses on the arm of the sofa, as if to polish them and study Georgie simultaneously. 'You can't stop dwelling on all this, can you? Punishing yourself over and over? I can see you doing it. One minute we're talking normally and the next you sink into yourself, clam up, your expression changes, you go miles away.'

During this terse exchange Georgie attempted a stoic smile, her teeth must have looked like false ones, clenched so rigidly, in a jar. She tightened

21

her hands in her lap. 'How the hell can I get this out of my mind? Five minutes is the longest time I've been free of it so far, and at night I have such nightmares about it.' She might as well admit it. Yes, yes, punishing herself over the smallest details, all those ifs and buts and if onlys, any device to add to the torture.

'What on earth is that rank smell?' Thank goodness the subject was changed.

'There must be a dead rat in the wall.'

'Last night, in bed, I thought I heard scratching. Maybe one of your more experienced neighbours could put some poison down.'

So you see how uncomfortable Georgie felt with her visitors, some of them colleagues from work, some old friends who went back to Toby, others picked up, like most friends are, while thumbing their way along the hard shoulder of life. They came in a steady stream, like memories, so that, incredibly, there had been no complete week from June through to September when she had been alone for longer than forty-eight hours. They kept her busy. They entertained her. But at the end of the day it did not matter how hard they worked with her on the cottage, it made no difference what fun they shared as they laboured in the sunshine repairing the fences, patching the thatch, turning over the rock-hard soil or unblocking the stream. It mattered not what picnics they shared or how many bottles of wine they drank, she could not overcome that grim stumbling block however hard she tried. They were the blessed, she the damned. They brought car-loads of supplies, they worked with a will, paying their way, but they overdid the kindness bit. Their visits were of condolence, of support in her hour of need, just as hers would have been if the boot was on the other foot. They pitied her and her sad predicament. They thanked her for her hospitality, they thanked her for their holiday, but they were being kind and *Georgie was grateful*. And that put something unpleasant between them, something she found hard to deal with. Poor old Georgina, psychologically standing up while everyone else remained sitting down.

Perhaps she was oversensitive, but she could suddenly easily understand why the troubled resent do-gooders so. And there's only so much support you can get before you see yourself as a cripple.

In some perverse way their well-meaning presences prevented her from healing herself. And yet, look at this, one week after their departure and already she wanted them back. She feared for the roots of her being. She thought she was going mad.

The shaking first started . . .

It was Roger Mace who broke the news that Angela Hopkins was dead. Over the phone for God's sake, a most personal call. The ringing woke her in the morning – a mental alarm in her head – she heard the freezing-cold news in a hot crumpled bed. 'Georgie. I'm so sorry. I wanted to tell you myself.'

She had to know, shoulders hunched to guard breathless conversation. 'How did she die?'

'They're not sure yet . . . a blow to the head . . .'

'When?' She hugged the duvet to her stomach. She could feel death's proximity. Her ankles were white as bleached bones, thin as a child's, thin as a skeleton's.

'Last night.'

'And Patsy and Carmen?' She spoke with deliberate, polite calm.

'There's a place of safety order, but no sign of abuse so far.'

'What will happen?'

'Well, I'm no expert, but the case will be given a high priority. There'll be an enormous public impact.'

Her hair fell forward to hide her face. 'I'll come straight to the office.'

'No, Georgie, stay where you are. There'll be time for all that later.'

A warning kindly given. A glimpse of the scalpel of scrutiny. She hadn't asked for an explanation. And then it was suddenly *déjà vu*, she'd always known this was going to happen and what would happen next. Oh God, let it not be true. *She had always secretly known and yet done nothing about it.* Guilty as that bastard, Ray Hopkins himself, the man with the bullet-shaped head and the earful of sleepers, who lived behind the yellow door and swore blind that his five-year-old daughter had fallen down the stairs.

She sank on all fours, her lips trembling, her eyes welling. She pressed one hand to her mouth and squeezed her eyes closed. And she thought, At least it was quick, dear God, at least the end came quickly. She would not let herself think more of the child, no, not at that time. She blocked little Angela out, and that was another small betrayal.

As if she had never known her.

And that's how the dreadful story began.

Two

Silvered with an impossible beauty, like view-finder slides of *Heidi*, and scented by her vanilla car-freshener, that was Georgina's first impression of Furze Pen Cottage. It was a chilling sort of beauty, sharp, more like a sound.

It was February, a pearly, tear-stained month, and Angela Hopkins had died that December. Christmas did not happen for Georgie, and nor did new year. All the horror was busy going on so the fact that her brother, Stephen, had died of liver rot added to her total destruction in a way which was quite irrational. Why such a traumatic effect?

Because she had never known him.

A healthy liver was horrible enough, even when dipped in batter, and Georgie imagined his gone brown like those in a butcher's window in summer. And to hear of such a tragic event in such an impersonal way, by solicitor's letter, seemed to reflect to Georgie the terrible sterility of her life.

Forty-two and what had she got to show for it? That was the way her thinking was going. It wasn't as if Stephen had left her the cottage intentionally either, a kindness perhaps, a last act of remembrance. No. He had died intestate and, as Georgie was his only family, the cottage and contents were hers if she wanted them. It was as cold and clinical as that.

She wept and then she wept some more.

Alas. Poor Georgina.

She felt bereft, as if something had been forcibly removed from her person. Confidences saved up for too long tend to turn to hysteria so, 'I never even met him,' she cried to Helen Mace, the social services director's wife, as she sat in their Victorian sitting room done out in wood and heritage paint, with paper by Laura Ashley. 'Stephen was twenty years older than me and nobody ever mentioned him. Black sheep and all that.' Georgie's hair stuck to her tears. 'I grew up believing he was dissolute, a drunkard who turned his back on society and became a recluse.' She sniffed, wiping her nose unpleasantly with the back of her hand. 'He ran away from home,' sniff sniff, 'when he was sixteen years old, and they cut him off, I suppose, mentally and financially. Anyway, he never tried to come home.' Sniff sniff. 'Contact with his family was the last thing Stephen wanted, that's what they said. I often thought about finding him and writing him a letter, but time goes by and you don't. I thought one day I might trace him. He might not even know I was born. And yet he was my brother,' she sobbed, 'and after Mum died my last surviving relative.'

How she detested behaving like this. So needy. So lacking control. So like poor Millie Blunt when they took away her dead baby. But at least she didn't stamp her feet. At least she didn't scream and yowl. She wasn't chained to the churchyard door, but you could tell poor Helen was taken aback.

'This is all you need right now,' she said kindly, looking anxiously at Georgie's blotched face, the exhausted, dark-rimmed eyes, the wet, shaking hands. This wasn't the capable Georgina she knew. 'And it's no good saying what's done is done, there's no point looking back and wishing . . .'

'But it's just one more bloody thing, isn't it?' cried Georgie desperately, kicking rhythmically at the chair leg. 'Just one more bloody thing I wish I'd done differently, but time gets between you and then it's too late.' But no words were sufficiently powerful to convey the distress she felt.

Cosy, comforting Helen, with the wooden solidarity and shape of a Russian stacking doll and the plummy public-school accent. Even the air seemed to move slowly around her, so calm and unflappable was the director's wife, a sporting product of Wycombe Abbey. She never panicked. She could balance two kids on her lap, feed a third, pot a fourth and conduct a sensible conversation all at the same time. Helen was a Grace Darling, the kind of heroic woman who might once have lived in a lighthouse. Helen was an oasis in Georgie's acrid desert of grief, to whom she went for comfort, humble as a kneeling camel with a large and trembling lower lip.

'Liking him or not liking him isn't the point. The point is I never knew him. I never knew my own brother.' And the sadness and self-pity of that last poignant remark collapsed her like a jelly taken too soon from its mould. 'Oh God, I do loathe feeling like this! Perhaps this is my nemesis for having life too easy. Perhaps I am facing The Truth at last.'

Helen was not the sort of woman to be dragged into that soul-scarring cul-de-sac. The Truth was not the issue here. Something more positive was needed or this discussion could last until dawn and reach no resolution. She buttered a toasted teacake, automatically spread it with Marmite, and handed it to Georgie who took it. 'Stephen was an artist?' she asked slowly and thoughtfully.

'Yes, that's what they said.'

Helen shrugged. She went straight to the heart of the matter, created a direction to head in. 'Well, in that case his paintings must be somewhere around.'

Georgie dabbed at her red eyes mournfully. She stared, perplexed, at the teacake before rotating it in its blackened butter. 'I have never seen any of them.'

Helen warmed to her topic, sensing a growing interest, a lull in Georgie's agitating brain. 'You'd probably find quite a lot down at this cottage in Devon. It might be too late to know the man, but maybe you could understand him, his pictures might tell you more about him than knowing him ever could.'

She clutched at this straw. Helen's words were an invitation. She walked restlessly to the window, hands cradling elbows. '*D'you think so?*'

Helen nodded sensibly. 'Yes, I really do. And you know as well as I do, Georgie, that if Stephen had a problem with booze then his inability to contact you was nothing personal at all, it was all part of his illness, poor sod, and by going along with his wishes you were respecting him, too.'

Georgie returned to her chair, fingers of warning tapped the plate. Helen gave her a napkin. The teacake jumped. 'Don't patronize me,' Georgie snapped. 'The reason I did nothing about him was because I never got round to it. There was no respect about it.'

'Just because you didn't plan it doesn't mean you didn't do right by him,' reasoned Helen patiently. 'You left him alone which was what he wanted. And now he's dead you can go and find him. A journey of discovery. A pilgrimage to Lourdes.'

'D'you think I should go?' Drained of all initiative, Georgie needed gentle prodding. In the state of mind she was in, a journey to Devon might as well be the moon.

'Why don't you go this weekend. I'll come with you, if you like. Roger can mind the kids.'

But if Georgie decided to go, she wanted to go alone. She began to view the venture as a kind of exorcism, holy, in a special way, and the more arduous the journey the better she would feel. For almost two endless months she had endeavoured never to be alone, the thoughts that came in were just too terrible. But this state of affairs could not be allowed to continue, and a journey might be the best way to get used to her own company again. Time was so hard to fill. Given leave from work meant long empty hours, and those which were filled were quick and dreadful. She felt like a prisoner in a cell listening for the torturer's footsteps. And they came unremittingly, to ask more questions, to listen to excuses, to take notes and make comments as again and again she told her side of the grim story.

The tabloid headlines shrieked out at her. HOW MANY MORE TIMES MUST THIS HAPPEN BEFORE THESE PEOPLE COME TO THEIR SENSES? And, TWENTY THOUSAND A YEAR TO CALL BACK LATER. MORE FATAL DECISIONS TAKEN. And outside her flat they were waiting, scores of men in black jackets and macs, with microphones, cameras and delighted eyes.

'Mrs Jefferson, this way, please, how do you feel about . . . ?'

'Will you stay in social work if you're cleared . . . ?'

'Why did you ignore all the evidence and take the fateful decision to leave Angela at home?'

'Is it true that you have no kids of your own?'

She faced them all with steely control.

To begin with, naive as she was, Georgie tried to explain, even though she'd been advised by the union to make no comment at this early stage. But she had to defend herself against the grotesque things they were saying, and why the hell should she keep quiet? They ought to be told how many children at risk she had in her caseload, the shortage of staff in the area and how many hours they put in. They had to be made to understand

31

the atmosphere of that tenement building at night, and what it was like to call back again and again when the vandals had put out the lights, discarded their dirty needles and the place was eerily silent save for the soft sound of TV sets, the occasional bark of a dog, the cry of a child, the curse of a man. They ought to imagine the impact on a child of being removed from home, what happens to the dysfunctional family and how easily mistakes can be made. Before they went on printing their lies they should damn well know that Ray Hopkins and his little wife, Gail, were convincing liars, convincing to even the most professional, and that violence was always a fearful thing and difficult to approach in the daylight let alone in the dark.

Violence.

Yes, the rat pack on guard outside her flat knew quite a bit about violence.

She spoke to them. She reasoned with them. She tried to explain.

They twisted her words and hurled them back like stones. Georgie had once watched a video which showed a woman in a biblical land on her way to be stoned to death. The horror of that had stayed with her ever since, she wished she'd never watched it, the way the victim clutched at a dagger as she passed a market stall and held it pathetically against her aggressors (she would probably normally go shopping for a nice bit of fish), so hopelessly and with such desperation, knowing the torment she faced. Daggers, words, what difference when your enemies were so determined?

They called her a woolly liberal, and wet, with flowers of ignorance in her hair.

But it wasn't like that. *She wasn't like that.*

'No comment,' came the official instruction. 'You see what happens. Don't say you weren't warned.'

There had to be a scapegoat. Everyone could see that Ray Hopkins was a totally inadequate slob, and it wasn't as if the authorities hadn't been told.

'Time and time again, I can't tell you how many times I've rung that emergency number in the middle of the night,' gloated a toothless neighbour in front of the cameras for *The Nine O'Clock News*. She was backed by a little coven in curlers. 'I dunno how many times.' But there was no record of her calls and when the police went round she refused to explain.

'The country's gone to the dogs. Too many bleeding dogooders if you ask me.'

Georgie began to get letters from people she'd never heard of. Vicious letters, mostly unsigned, and she was scared because somehow these fanatics had found out her address. They knew where she lived and they wanted her dead. They phoned her up in the middle of the night and breathed obscenities into the phone. *'Bitch.' 'Murderess.' 'Childkiller.' 'Whore.'*

And she wanted to scream back at them, 'There's no sodding point! *Can't you see?* You can't bring Angela back to life. I can't bring her back to life!' But she didn't scream, she listened, and she understood that this was part of a natural

33

reaction, a hopeless scream from an anguished and violated world. As if there was just no way of thinking about it gently.

Which there wasn't.

None of the support she was given could put up a strong enough barrier because no matter how often she was told she had behaved correctly, no matter how many times she was assured it could have happened to anyone, no matter how many people said she was the best social worker in the team, loyal, hardworking, caring, experienced, THE FACT was still achingly apparent, THE FACT no-one could take away, THE FACT the nightcallers knew very well . . . I, GEORGINA JEFFERSON, AM RESPONSIBLE FOR THE DEATH OF THIS CHILD.

It began to be intolerable. Georgie became intolerable. She could hardly live with herself.

She began to imagine, in a paranoid fashion, that people turned round and stared whenever she walked down the street, whenever she rode the tube. She began to imagine fellow drivers glared angrily through her car window when she waited for traffic lights to change. She glanced around her uneasily. To stand still was to be vulnerable. She breathed a sigh of relief when the green light released the cars. She fervently believed that shopkeepers served her deliberately slowly. The fellow residents in the flats where she lived edged away and cast their eyes down when she passed. And all the while she knew she was sick – she might be news but she wasn't notorious

– her face wasn't that well known. And yet, purely and simply, that is what it felt like.

But worse than that, and this was the reality, some of her friends distanced themselves. Oh yes. Of course they used subtle methods so it took some time to realize the truth, to absorb exactly what was happening.

Others, sweetly, came closer. But that was threatening in itself.

Of Angela Hopkins she would not think.

Because, quite simply, she couldn't.

Three

Georgina Jefferson was scared – how pitiful! Scared to be making such a journey alone. She wished she hadn't given up smoking. And why had she bothered to clean the car?

The hard shoulders and central reservations were chunky with wedges of old snow, tacky like badly set fudge. The countryside was the colour of her windscreen, spattered and grey. She was frightened when she first set out on so lonely a journey with no familiar end to it – no-one would kiss her, pour her a drink, show her her room, give her a towel. Like boarding school for the very first time and Mummy said, with a simplicity that was astonishing, 'Run along and make friends, Georgina.' Make friends? *How?* Everyone else had a friend. She was the only one standing alone. Had she missed something essential in her early development? The ability to make friends to order? Perhaps there was something wrong with her smile, perhaps it was too full of tears to count.

Oh for a best friend. She would have done anything to get one. She tried. In those days she tried too hard to please. Even when Georgie was one of the gang she never found anyone of her own, anyone special with whom she could whisper, giggle at night and swap secrets. She could flick from person to person with an ease that was shocking. How many faces did she have, and which was the real one? Perhaps the other girls at school sensed there was something odd about her, and distrusted her. Or perhaps it was she who was threatened by closeness.

She never could work it out.

So there she was, alone on the road. And then there was that weirdest of feelings, pulling into the services, that unearthly forecourt where she stopped for petrol, wincing as the cold metal pump burned her hand, the freezing wind tightened her face, and even her eyes went dry as she stared at the slow-moving needle. She kept her mouth firmly closed to prevent breathing in that petroleum ice.

Then the crazy warmth of the restaurant, clattering trays and the listless women who reluctantly collected them, looking as if they wore slippers, although a quick glance showed they did not. Where did they live, these creatures from nowhere? There were fields as far as the eye could see. Godforsaken. Soulless. Were they golems come forth from under some metal stanchion where they lived with their concrete men? And what would they say, these bravest of women, if they knew she was frightened of being here alone? Would the cardboard soles of their eyes crease and fracture as they recognized this fellow pilgrim, or would they shuffle away and ignore her, just another leaver of sticky wrappings, sugar-wet rings and tinfoil ashtrays?

Would their eyes tweak with interest if they knew who she was?

She took a steadying breath. There was no queue, but the effect of the place meant that everyone was somehow in one. They had come so far on their journeys that nobody could go back. These were committed travellers. And these fellow diners, these mild people dressed mainly in beige, could they possibly be the ones who, not five minutes earlier, encased in their steel chariots, had threatened her, overtaken her, chased her? Charging strangers seething by on a wet, straight road, exchanging sneaky sideways glances through shatterproof, dirty glass?

There was no real point in consulting her map, not yet. Not until she got off the motorway. Georgie stretched in her metal-framed chair and winced at the cramping of muscles held too long in one position. She sat in that restaurant and realized that this was the first positive thing she had done since Angela Hopkins's death; everything up until then had happened within the circle of it. No wonder there was fear to suddenly find herself stepping outside. In all the awful intensity she'd almost forgotten there was an outside, she had forgotten it was possible to step over the edge and into the void.

Toby was a best friend. Her first. She married him after a six-week engagement. She had not known such love was possible.

The last time she came to Devon Toby had been with her, so that must mean she hadn't been down here for the last ten years – incredible! Those were the days of hotels, the days of normal holidays, walking, exploring, riding, fishing and sailing. No children to think about, she smiled into her shiny white cup. The plastic spoon seemed to bend in the coffee, almost a Uri Geller illusion. Well, yes, they rode over that one, but not without pain. She could have them, he could not, that awfully unfair apportionment, deep swallows, meaningful glances and endless reassurances and no, she did not want to be inseminated with some student's sperm; no, she did not want to adopt; no, she did not love Toby any less or think him less of a man or fear she would spend the rest of her life mourning the children she never had.

Childlessness meant that they kept their careers, and they took more interest in other people's (children I mean, not careers). Godmother. Babysitter. Escort to the pantomime. Scourer of Hamleys at Christmas. It sounded rather sad put like that, a little pathetic when you looked at it, but it wasn't sad in any way, she and Toby had loved it. You could set off and spend, quickly, recklessly, enormous parcels, favourite things.

My God, my God. The toys she had carted round to the Hopkins's flat, not purchased at Hamleys, of course, but provided by generous well-wishers. (They had to sort through the tat that some people seemed to consider fair enough for the feckless poor.) Anne Stubbs's office was full well before the end of November, so that all Georgie had to do was go in and choose the appropriate gifts. Anne was so suitable, a female version of Father Christmas with frosty white hair and even the suggestion of fluff on her chin. She beamed merrily over all the proceedings with flushed apple cheeks and a paper hat. But she who cared so much, who organized the toy campaign with so much enthusiasm, never got to see the joy she gave. At the end of the day all she was left with was an empty office, a few tattered pieces of string, carrier bags and cardboard boxes. Ah well. That's life.

Yep, that's life. Heart attacks? Heart attacks were for old men on golf courses in the wind, or sitting around board-room tables, too much gin, too many veins, too much hard living. Heart attacks were irrelevant, they just did not apply to young guys of Toby's age who jogged and played squash and believed in low fat and high fibre. The disbelief, the unfairness of life almost throttled Georgie then, that, and the being alone again, nobody's favourite person. When a decent length of time had gone by, people (her mother) said, 'You are young yet. You will find another life, another man . . .' as if, without Toby she had died, too, flung herself on his funeral pyre, especially as they were without issue. When the point of her life was so illusive work became all important.

'Although why you work with those terrible people I'll never understand.'

'I know you won't, Mum.' Georgie met her eyes calmly. 'So there's no point in you trying.'

When she looks back on herself and Toby she marvels at how young they had been.

Work and friends became very important. But now Georgie had no work and felt uneasy around her friends, it was easy to think, once again, that without them she no longer existed. Death by proxy, like when Toby died. Especially here, in this motorway service area with the wind blowing blotchy sleet at the windows and the chrome hot-chocolate machine dribbling bubbles of hot froth.

Of course, when this was all over, when she was found to be 'blameless', she would be welcomed back into the fold. But it wouldn't be exactly as if she had never been away now, *would it*? There'd be a stain. No smoke without fire. The waters would be muddied and would never clear completely.

'Wasn't there something, some years ago, some tragedy, I seem to remember . . .'

She needn't return if she didn't want to. Survival would be difficult but at a pinch Georgie could manage on Toby's insurance if she pulled in her horns, left London, stopped spending on theatres, holidays and clothes, stopped ordering crates of wine and eating out when she felt like it. Huh. That makes it sound as though her life was nothing but one long holiday and that she was rolling in dosh. But no, she was what they call comfortably off because there was only herself to support and she worked long hours. She had worked very hard for her creature comforts, most weekends and quite frequently ten- or twelve-hour days.

When you whittled it down those creature

comforts amounted to a half-paid-for flat – a square box in a column of boxes, a three-year-old Vauxhall Astra, an Apple Mac, a fax machine and an old dog named Lola.

And that flat, that place she'd considered her sanctuary, that place where she went at the end of the day to escape from the world, that flat which was her private den in the centre of the whirlwind of life, that precious refuge was violated now by hate mail and vicious telephone calls. But that was not all. Almost worse than this invasion by strangers were the polite summonses to talks and discussions, the letters of consolation, all the paraphernalia of death, and the devious newspapers pushed through her door.

There was confusion over her future. Confusion over her past.

There was anger, terrible anger. She raged at herself and the system, at the self-righteous public and the way that men like Ray Hopkins found women like Gail to marry, have kids and refuse to accept another man's child. There was the fury, the childish resentment, at being singled out and hauled to the front to take the blame for the rest of the class. Oh yes, it could have been anyone, *but why is it always me?*

And why is it always Angela Hopkins? The child who clings and won't shake off?

'It's absolutely disgusting allowing women with no kids of their own to supervise other people's, surely that's a mistake! Surely only a mother can truly recognize the signs.'

Oh yes, Georgie listened to the radio discussions, such sensible voices in a vacuum, talking as if words couldn't kill. People on *Woman's Hour*, complacent experts she'd often heard and admired, with opinions she had respected, imagining that because they were on the radio or wrote columns in newspapers they were wise, they knew best. Appalled by her own naivety, she cursed the simplistic way her views had been formed in the past. They chatted on to fill the time, to fill the space, to fill the hour, and collected their cheques at the door with their macs.

Whispering.

Talking against her.

While she kept silent. Closed. Not permitted to speak. Defending herself. Controlling her grief.

And the PM listeners on Radio Four muscled in on their phones and faxes, castigating the uncaring world in which toddlers could be lured to their deaths in brightly lit shopping centres, women could scream and blow their alarms, and children could sob through the night and nobody would raise an eyebrow.

Community was dead.

It was dog eat dog.

Women ought to stay at home and unmarried mothers be punished.

Somebody must be punished.

Somebody must be made to suffer.

Where was God? Normally one could rely on him. For a scourge. For a famine.

Trial by rocking chair.

In contrast there was Helen Mace's incredible insight and kindness. 'We need you to babysit for us, Georgie. I've tried all round and there's nobody else, and Roger and I really should go. I feel bad having to ask in the middle of all this shit, but we could have supper afterwards, you could stay the night if you wanted.'

And her own intentional cruelty, hitting out against invisible critics. 'Aren't you being a bit obvious, Helen? I don't wield the knife you know. I am not a murderess afraid of being around children lest my control drops for a terrible moment . . .'

'Shut up, you paranoid person. You have distanced yourself from the kids, Georgie, and they miss you. That's all.'

She'd missed them, too. There was that extraordinary evening then, sitting in the rocker in the Maces' unruly sitting room, predominantly pine, the kids' artwork decorating the walls and the fire glowing softly behind the guard. Children in pyjamas spitting into recorders, making their hideous sounds. 'Look at me! Look at me!' Children in ladder-back chairs scooping sloppy cereal. 'Watch this! Watch this!' Children pressing transfers into scrapbooks and bringing her meals of plasticine. Trusting.

Olly couldn't sleep. Get him up. Nurse him. Bring him to the rocker and smell his hair. Story book flops. Rub the downy skin where his pyjama leg runs out, between there and his dog-eared rabbit slipper, because it feels cold there. Wipe his mouth where his dreams bubble over. Feel his breathing against your chest, quicker, more shallow than your own, and moist where your two bodies meet. Finally drop him back in his bed, unfastening from your neck his velour and gripping hands.

'Everything OK?' The astonishing bustle of adults arriving in a child-quiet house. Adults with an unquestionable right to be there.

'Everything's fine!'

But it wasn't fine.

Helen knew. Lots of people probably knew but turned away from it. To Georgina Jefferson, who would never admit it, it was mourning her own lost children for the very first time.

But back to the motorway services which smelled of pine and shepherd's pie.

She smiled up at a tired-looking family searching for an unoccupied table. Most were unoccupied, but they trudged on, searching, searching, nearer the window, out of the draught, a smoker, a table uncluttered and welcoming. Huh, some chance. So many choices and so important. They were all trying to co-operate. Travel was stamped on their faces, and they hauled their luggage after them like an extra problem, afraid to leave it unguarded in the car.

Could it only be two years ago? 'There's this new family. HOPKINS. We'll have to give it to you, Georgie, because Pat is beside herself already. Some concern from the school. Irregular attendance; they've noticed bruises, too regular to be got by playing. Not a lot known about the family. Two younger siblings, fine as far as the visiting NSPCC officer could see. Not old enough for school yet, but maybe we could find them some day care to give the mother a break. Case conference here at ten o'clock in the morning, check that the health visitor knows.'

The phone rang then. Georgie remembers the phone and how it had broken the flow. How could she take on another case? She could hardly cope with the ones she had. She never had time to voice her opinion because of that blasted phone. Angie might still be alive if she'd passed that file on to somebody else. She also remembers how she'd scanned the address on the top of the file and winced when she saw the familiar words, Kurzon Mount Buildings, because of the hours she'd already spent wandering round that soulless construction, peering for signs or directions or numbers, knocking on doors with no knockers. Ringing on bells which weren't working. Standing. Hopelessly. Looking down into the wretched yard, or play area, or clothes-drying area, or car-mending area, or dog-shitting area, depending on how you used it. A concrete, sunless, treeless base down between the square of buildings, the tier upon tier of mindless balconies, the maze of concrete stairways.

Buildings designed for rats not people because rats, being wise and resourceful creatures, could have burrowed their way out.

Funny how she remembered the moment when she'd been given that fatal file. She could not remember other such moments, although there'd been hundreds over the years. Had that been a premonition? *Oh dear God, had she known even then?*

Abruptly she got to her feet. A sad young man came to wipe her table with a dirty cloth. What the hell was he doing here? What sort of job was this? At his age he ought to be Godlike and proud, a brave young warrior with all the world at his feet. She suddenly felt such a surge of anger she almost grabbed his arm and asked him. How damn patronizing. At least he had a useful job. At least he wasn't going round killing children. She left the motorway restaurant and gave Lola a run. She fed the dog some biscuits and gave her a drink of water. She returned to her car and shoved in her favourite tape, Elgar's 'Nimrod', before driving off. She wanted to find Wooton-Coney before dark, and already the horizon was dimming. She had her duvet in the back and a small box of groceries: cheese, apples, a loaf, biscuits, coffee and tins of dog food. Lola spent the journey nesting in her favourite place, the blanket on the passenger seat. Our practical heroine had matches, too, and a paraffin camping light in case the electric was off and she couldn't work it out. The last thing she needed was to be stranded in a strange place in the dark.

Helen advised, 'Book in at a hotel for the first night for God's sake. Take some of the pressure off.'

'There's no need to rush back,' said Roger, reassuring.

At the time Georgie was resting her feet on Lola's soft back; the dog could get no nearer the fire except if she lay in the actual flames. 'No, I'd rather go straight there. If I leave early enough I'll have time to find it while it's still light.'

'But the weather,' said Helen. 'What if you can't get there because of the weather?'

'That was my excuse, Helen, if you remember! I watched the forecast and they don't give it so bad down there. There's only a scattering of snow on the moors.'

'Change your mind and let me come with you.'

'I want this to be difficult, Helen. I know that sounds daft, but I need to deal with this one myself. These are the kind of problems I should be able to solve on my own, and I want to get back to managing again. Solving something. Overcoming something.'

'You do sound crazy. Maybe you're not up to going.' This whole enterprise was Helen's fault. Had she been too premature?

'Leave her alone,' said Roger.

And Georgie felt an insatiable longing to escape from all this concern, human voices, telephone calls, accusations, sympathy, she felt an almost obsessional need for some kind of privacy again. 'Helen, if it looks as if I'm not going to make it I'll check in at one of those motel rooms, or a pub, somewhere Lola's allowed. Nowhere's going to be full at this time of year.'

But all that positive thinking happened before

she'd started out; that was at the planning stage when it all felt quite exciting. An adventure. That was when there were maps to peruse with neat printed names, not endless motorways and ill-lit signposts half hidden by road grime and slush.

She would have liked to have someone as comforting and comfortable as Helen with her then.

Four

Just as, between shafts of light, God peers hairily out of his heavens, so a February sun pierced an incredible sky and illuminated Georgina Jefferson's first sight of Furze Pen Cottage, and the unreality of it, the sheer unlikelihood of the sparkling, snowy scene, put her in mind of the most fantastic pictures in her illustrated Children's Bible.

The white light of exultation.

Noah glorying after the flood.

Even the cobwebs were frosted, like tracery upon silence. She felt her presence misty as a ghost's.

With her heart in her mouth and sweat prickling under her arms, she had skidded down a final meandering lane to get here. Don't panic. *Stay calm*. And Mark's 'always turn into the skid', Mark the responsible, Mark, the man voted by Helen to take Toby's place in Georgie's life. The rest of the roads might be clear but, despite the weather forecast, there *was* snow on Dartmoor and the last hour of hair-raising driving wore Georgie out. And here in the valley, where the sun doesn't shine until late afternoon, the snow lay virginal and thick on the ground. The earth was corrected of every flaw and made perfect at last. She let her car remain where it was, at the end of a skid – she couldn't have moved it – and, hanging on to the door for safety, she got out and gazed around, incredulous. Beyond the snowy verge was a stream with icicles dripping from fronds of bracken and stepping stones the size of boulders plodding regularly through the water. Beyond this was a wicket gate, and the sign, 'Furze Pen', hung slatternly from a crooked nail.

Come on, come on then. Dare you to cross!

'My God.'

The path that led from the stream to the door was invisible, the door itself winked out from under an eyebrow of thatch. The whole impression was a hairy one, the long, low cottage almost obscured by the mass of thatch that roofed it, like a child in an overlarge hand-me-down, and all the windows appeared to be shy and at ground level. One witchy chimney gestured to the sky like a thin arm waving, but even that had a hairy stack tangled with snow-covered ivy. She imagined the cottage in summer, beds foaming with Michaelmas daisies with tall sunflowers nodding above them and the manifold stars of the clematis clustering over the small stone porch. Granite mushrooms were dotted about with wild indiscrimination, leaning, tall, short, thin, stunted, a cultivated crop of pure white fungi.

'This is unreal.'

Was that a robin on the roof?

And the whole was dazzled by a coating of frosted icing, so bright you had to screw up your eyes, so glittery it was breathtaking – a Christmas cake iced by an overactive child or an inebriated housewife.

Georgie had arranged to collect the key from Lower Wooton Farm, so, with Lola still asleep in the car, glad of her boots and sinking into the depths of her duffel, she made her unsteady way further down the road, over a cattle grid, up to a barely flowing ford and towards the front door of a farm directly on the road. No garden.

She stood there, getting colder and knocking for a futile five minutes before she realized there was not going to be any answer.

Sod it.

But sensible and determined as ever she set off round the back, picking her way through clumps of steaming dung. She called out hello softly at first, then louder, afraid of giving someone a fright. They would not be used to visitors here. The farmhouse was long and thatched like the cottage, but five times larger, and it did not seem to hide away in the same cautious manner some-how. It declared itself and the life within with utilitarian pride – there was brown paper instead of curtains at some of the grimy windows, lids over eyes that will not look. Amidst the glorious snow lay snarled pieces of corrugated iron. A diesel tank, some inner tubes and orange bundles of baler twine stood out in defiance of the beauti-ful scene, fists raised and ready for blows.

Hell's bells.

Seeing a light over the back door of the house

Georgie headed hopefully towards it. Finding no bell or knocker she rapped on the open door and waited, huddled and cold, in a porch full of piled-up newspapers in bundles, so you had to squeeze between to get through. She knocked a second time, then a third before calling, 'Hello!'

The woman arrived out of total silence, her hair a lifeless grey, stick legs implanted in stained and moth-eaten slippers. Brown socks crumped down over them. She pulled her shrunken cardigan round her, stared hard out of beady black eyes. 'Yes?'

'I'm really sorry to disturb you but I am Georgina Jefferson, Stephen's sister, and I'm here to collect the cottage key.'

The woman drew in a breath which exaggerated her thinness. The brown and cream dog-tooth skirt was clipped round her waist with a safety pin, and a pink wool jumper and brown cardboardy cardigan hung off her skeletal frame. At no time did the hostile black eyes unhook themselves from Georgie's face.

She felt impelled to go on and explain. 'The key, the key to Furze Pen Cottage. I am Stephen's sister.' And she even began to search in her pockets for the solicitor's letter, for proof of her identity, for an excuse for this invasion, but she had no need because the woman finally nodded and said, 'Wait there, I'll go and get it.' No smiling introductions. No kind enquiry about her journey. No commiserations over the death of a neighbour who had lived on her doorstep for at least twenty years. No offer of a cup of tea.

Curses.

After a minute the woman returned with a sealed brown envelope. The words, 'Furze Pen', were printed in bold on the front.

'I have left my car on the road, I'm afraid. I hope it won't be in anyone's way. I must have slid the last quarter of a mile . . .' She tailed off feebly. Damn her, if she didn't want to talk, well, Georgie felt the need after her solitary journey, after the last terrifying half-hour. Perhaps she expected some sympathy, some crumb of comfort, but her swarthy-faced neighbour wasn't having that. Reluctant to leave, no matter how unwelcome she felt, Georgie looked up at the sky and tried again cheerfully. 'D'you think there's more snow on the way?'

'Who can say,' snapped the woman, pulling stiffly at her cardigan again, her face a still, dark tarn of distrust.

'You must be Mrs Buckpit.' Georgie's voice was overfriendly, lubricated with goodwill, compensation for the frost between them. If only Helen was with her now. How laughable this would be, how absolutely laughable.

The face before her narrowed with suspicion, as if knowledge of her name revealed some terrible secret. Half turned away she said sourly, 'I am, yes.' And then she snapped, 'You'll be wanting milk.'

Georgie had her own milk, but she said, 'Oh, that would be nice,' in another attempt to be neighbourly. 'Perhaps I could come and fetch it in the morning?'

'No need. You'll find a pint on your step.'

'I am slightly worried about things like water and electricity. I wondered if there was anyone who might come with me to show me the ropes.' She stood on one frozen foot, then another.

'Nothing's been turned off. Everything's been left as it was.'

'But the solicitor mentioned something about a water pump.' She was making a nuisance of herself, Mrs Buckpit made that quite clear.

'It's only a matter of pressing a button. You'll find it in the shed.'

By now Georgie's irritation was rising. There was, after all, a limit, and this woman's disagreeable manner verged on the downright rude. She caught herself from snapping back, Oh, of course, how silly of me for not knowing that, when the woman softened enough to say, 'There's kindling and logs in the woodshed to the right of your back door. The key to that's in the envelope, all tagged and sorted.'

She wouldn't be damn well undermined by those nasty, fluffy-toy, bead-button eyes.

The electric came down the lane on wires strung to miniature pylons, splintered, temporary, rustic structures like lines of ancient crucifixes. Thank God for the power of man. The telephone wires took another route, staggering drunkenly over the fields. As yet there was no connection to the cottage; they passed it and strode on.

As she made her unsteady way back to her car, Georgie noticed the other two dwellings which made up the hamlet of Wooton-Coney. Opposite the Buckpits' farm, on her side of the lane, was a much finer building, a traditional longhouse in the same style as the others, but far less decrepit. It looked as if it had been done up, the stone work had been pointed, and even with the snow on top the thatch was newer and neater. There were bushes in the garden, whoever owned this house cared. Up the hill, further on from the ford, was a fourth house, another cottage but larger than Stephen's. The lights at the windows reminded Georgie that it was already dusk.

The stepping stones, the only possible route to the gate, were white and treacherous with frosted water. She crossed in a crablike motion, half crouched, dragging poor Lola by the collar. In daylight she would have looked ridiculous, but in this half dark nobody could see, and why would they want to anyway? Georgie cursed to herself as the hem of her duffel coat trailed in the fast flowing water that bubbled up under jig-saws of ice. The key was more suited to the keep of a castle than a humble cottage. It was loose in the lock and hung heavily in her hand. She turned it, patted the spaniel encouragingly, and went in.

Stephen had clearly died without giving a toss as to who might come later.

The light – she hadn't realized that switches like this one still existed, round and painted – at least the light went on. And with the light rushed the smell of neglect and decay, of damp and ancient stone. She left the door wide open when she crossed the stream precariously once more and emptied the contents of the car out onto the grass. She was glad of the interior light, which cast soft patches of yellow on white.

How much more fun this would be if somebody else were around. Even Mark the responsible would have done. Concerned as ever, he had asked to come with her, but Georgie had refused. She blinked away the pitiful sight of the hurt in his eyes, she had more than enough to contend with already. But still she muttered to herself, 'I'm sorry, Mark, I'm sorry.'

I can't love you, I'm sorry, I can't.

Then, like a ferryman, it was backwards and forwards across the stream; the bedding was particularly cumbersome, she couldn't see where she was going, and in the end she flung it across on a wing and a prayer. By the time she'd finished, Georgie was sweating hard from her exertions and from the awful thought of missing a step and falling into that freezing-cold water. Her breath, where it hit the air, froze in white balloons. She was desperate to get inside and close the cottage door behind her, no matter what comforts it lacked.

Her voice was winded and weary. 'Don't look at me like that, Lola. OK, OK, we should never have come. But at least we're out of the car, and I'll get the place warmed up in a minute.'

For a sensitive man, for a man who presumably spent his life devoted to art, Stephen was remarkably unaffected by his spartan surroundings: there was no ordered harmony here. The lampshade which hung from the central beam of the long low sitting room was of yellowing-white plastic imitating raffia, and long-dead flies were stuck to the flaky rim. No efforts towards homeliness had been attempted. Beside the blackened hearth was one dowdy armchair in a loose, ill-fitting brocade. Someone had piled papers and magazines upon it: a half-hearted attempt to clear up? A limp rug of mottled purples bobbled across the uneven stone floor, and to one side of the room stood a gateleg table, heavily lacquered and chipped. On this, where the piles of books did not meet, there were layers of dust. Two upright chairs were pushed neatly up to the table and Georgie could only wonder who had met and talked here, or eaten here, and what sort of food would be served at a table which lacked such charm or style. Frozen beefburgers and chips?

No vases. No lamps. No personal trinkets, ornaments, photographs, floor cushions. No, not even a clock to mark the passing of life.

No life.

What did she want from him, dammit, a note? I must put up with it. I'm here now and I don't have to stay long. This is what she wanted, wasn't it? Punishment, harsh and severe?

The door to the staircase creaked uneasily, otherwise the house was utterly hushed. With Lola lopping along behind her, Georgie climbed the threadbare stairs and arrived straight in a bedroom which must have belonged to Stephen. The bed was bare, the mattress rolled up to expose the springs, and a folded candlewick

58

counterpane. She moved it slightly, the single stained pillow was striped and uncased. A simple rug lay beside the bed, and thin unlined curtains hung from tiny windows that looked out back and front. Other than these, and one small chest of drawers, the room was empty. No mirror. No bedside table. No bedside light.

Oh, did you die here at night, Stephen, in this very room? Night after night, is this where you lay in your drink-induced unconsciousness? Did your bloodshot eyes stare at this very ceiling, or were you too pissed to get this far? Did you lose your fight with gravity and collapse downstairs in the chair by the fire?

Mutely wallpapered with a garden trellis design, the second bedroom connected to Stephen's but was more the size of a boxroom. Here there was no furniture at all, no curtains at the tiny windows, not even a shade on the light bulb, but there were myriad paint stains on the floor, vivid stains of the colours an artist might use, not for house decoration. So this is where he must have worked. The smell of oils mingled in here with mouse droppings and old fruit. Georgie touched the paint smears gently with the tip of her boot and thought that the colours she saw on the floor were the nearest she might ever get . . .

She pictured him then, her stereotyped fantasy brother, wild-eyed and manic in his smock and hand-sewn boots. A rude and intolerant man with the kind of passionate energy she'd always wished she had possessed, brawling in the local pubs, a bottle to his lips, a man with a flaring temper, not interested in pleasing anyone. Not concerned with the importance of image.

A wolf of a man who howled at the night, but honest, at one with the world, which he would see as wonderful, miraculous, awesome, astounding, outrageous. Impatient with the small comforts and boring inconsequentials with which Georgie seemed to surround herself.

A few confrontations with the media probably would have amused him. Disgrace would have ricocheted off him.

She pursed her lips. How pathetic he would think his sister, frightened and furtive, with nowhere to put her passion. She was angry with Stephen. Terribly angry. And morbidly miserable.

To fight the depression and the feeling of letdown after she'd found the courage to come here, she retraced her steps, passed through the kitchen, unbolted and unlatched the back door, seeking the woodshed with a flickering torch. She had no need, for the light in the small stone building went on and she busied herself with armfuls of kindling, followed by a washing basket of logs. She pressed the button her neighbour had mentioned and heard the whirring water pump. Eureka! She sat before the fire place on the cold thin carpet, breathing heavily as she arranged and lit it. The comfort which came with the instant warmth might be the fire or her satisfaction – perhaps the combination of both.

What an overwhelming relief.

Georgie shivered as the warmth returned to her hands and feet, burning. She shared the rug with

Lola, who sat beside her and watched the flames, the same glazed look on their faces. She would sort out some food in a minute.

But what sort of man would chose to spend his life here, hidden away from the world and contented with the most meagre of comforts, without the reassurance of family roots or possessions, not even a radio, TV or books? But his paintings, his easels, his brushes, where were all those? *Where was Stephen?* Most people leave at least some ghost of themselves behind, and Helen had suggested, quite reasonably, that Georgie might find the brother she'd lost.

But this was the home of a squatter. Abandoned save for the most basic essentials. As long as she sat by the fire and wondered, noticing every bulge in the wall, every nail, every empty socket, she began to realize with growing concern that he had never lived this way at all. She knew without doubt that somebody had been here before her and taken his things.

Hey, what's going on? Because you don't knock nails in your walls unless you're going to hang something on them. You don't paint carefully round your sockets unless you intend to plug something in. And what was that aerial socket doing poking out of the skirting?

What is more, if you have a large open fire like this you are forced to own some sort of poker, and a basket in which to carry the logs.

If someone had stripped Stephen's cottage after his death, then who? And why hadn't she been told? And where did they put his paintings?

You could easily go mad living here, sitting, listening to the cold north wind. She unwrapped a Kit-Kat and ate it. This was all wrong, nothing like she'd imagined. She should not be worrying about the minutiae of life, she should be celebrating her new-found solitude.

But who the devil . . . ?

The solicitor must have the answers, Georgie told herself, fighting down her concern. That's if it doesn't snow again. That's if she could get out in the morning.

Five

That first fatal night she stayed at Furze Pen, as she heated up her tin of baked beans, grated a little cheese and rattled the grill to hurry it up, Georgina thought about Stephen. He was always disappearing.

She still remembered the shock she'd felt on being told she had a brother. She'd been lying to the girls at school – she lied about everything in those days, lying came almost more naturally than telling the truth – finding it so intolerable to be a boring only child, no-one to blame or admire or laugh at as most of the others did. She prayed that her parents might divorce so she could be more interesting. She'd found an awful old picture of Daddy when he'd been a boy, dated and faded, a brown and pink carefully posed picture with a rubber plant setting the scene. How had she ever believed she could really get away with her lie? Her father's hair was slick to his head, stuck there with varnish, and that wide brow, those round staring eyes, that touch of colour they'd applied to the cheeks to give the figure some semblance of life. Well, they stopped taking photos like that years ago.

She had packed it at the beginning of term, hidden it away in the cheesy-smelling newspaper at the bottom of her school trunk, ashamed of it as well as of what she was doing. So pathetic. She'd been writing to this imaginary brother for a couple of terms now. 'Tom is at Cambridge,' she bragged to Gloria Butts, her catty, slant-eyed friend who came from a family of six. 'I went to the student ball in the hols.'

Well, other people made up boyfriends so why should she be denied a brother?

'Why does he never write back?'

'Oh, Tom's always been like that. He doesn't have time for writing, he's so busy playing rugby and rowing . . .'

'So why doesn't he come to visit?'

'*He is coming*. After half-term.'

Why had she compounded the lie, knowing she had trapped herself in a net which would lead to more complications and eventually, probably, the most humiliating exposure? The fear of that alone was dangerous and exciting. And what is more she kept up the bluff until it wasn't just Tom who was coming but a group of his friends as well. 'They'll take me out for the day, I should think. Lunch at a pub by the river. Maybe a ride in a punt.' Those who believed her were impressed, those who did not nudged one another. She would have given everything she owned, even her right arm, in order to make this dream come true. The photograph of Tom she kept on the locker beside her bed, third by the door in the spartan dorm, next to the compulsory double-framed parents and the family pet. And if there was some vague resemblance to Daddy, well, why not, the boy in the gilt

64

frame was his son, so no-one should find fault with that.

Half-term. Georgie's bags were packed and she waited at the large double doors in the hall for Mummy to come and collect her, hanging around with her friends, all of them eager to be gone before embarrassing introductions, dreading those awful stilted questions which other people's mothers ask. Ashamed of their families.

'You've forgotten your dressing gown, it's waiting at the end of your bed,' announced Miss Hiller, the matron, at the very moment Mummy came rushing from the car. Kisses. Too many kisses, and fussing, and 'I'll come with you darling, I've forgotten what your dormitory looks like . . .'

'Please don't bother, Mummy.' But Georgie was anxious to keep Mummy in tow, to stop her loitering round her friends.

'What on earth is this quaint old picture of Daddy doing beside your bed?'

Gloria Butts looked up, she must have forgotten something, too, her eyes were slyer than ever but her voice dripped sweetly when she said, 'Well, Mrs Southwell. How strange. Georgie told everyone that was her brother.'

'How very peculiar, darling. What a very odd thing to do.'

Driving away, Georgie looked back to see Gloria Butts in deep and giggly conversation with Hannah Murphy, watching the back of the car as it went.

'Why did you tell them that, darling? Why on

earth did you tell all your friends that Daddy was your brother?'

It was painful to speak about something so deep and shameful, a secret need which she couldn't express and certainly could not discuss with Mummy. She did not want her mother to know, and Mummy, despite the questions, did not want to know either.

Scarlet-faced Georgie changed the subject. 'Is Daddy home?'

'Yes, and he's looking forward to seeing you.'

'I could have spent the weekend with Daisy.' It was half a threat, half a plea.

'You spent your last half-term with Daisy. You can't always be at Daisy's. And why don't you bring your friends home for a change?'

She hated her mother then, she'd refuse to discuss the photograph. But Sylvia Southwell, unperturbed, clicked on her indicator, peered right and left at the junction and pressed on. Then she announced very coolly, 'You had no need to invent a brother, Georgina, because you already have one.'

She stared at her mother, startled and embarrassed, not liking the guarded tone in her voice. 'I don't know what you mean.'

'You had to know one day, I suppose. Daddy and I both knew that, but it has always been so difficult to judge the right time. It was always important we waited until you were old enough to understand.' In the heat of the freezing-cold moment Sylvia's perfume cloyed the silence.

The spray on the road rose like steam. The

wheels hissed along. Georgie's legs were stuck to the seat and she let them stay stuck, shifting them only a little, she liked the oozings of her own skin. On a layer below the perfume, on a subterranean layer deep down, her mother's fur coat smelled of stale cupboards and formal outings, disliked places and difficult times.

Sylvia Southwell gave a short laugh. 'His name is Stephen.' She closed her lips round the statement. 'Or we christened him Stephen, Lord knows what he calls himself now.'

Georgie stared rigidly before her. She did not comment, afraid of this secret they were sharing. To her, Mummy was a stranger. She played more games with her mother than she ever played with her friends. Aloof and unapproachable, the only place where Sylvia unbent was on the telephone, as if the wires distanced her from the words she was speaking. But if Georgie approached this human face a spare hand would come up, and a frown, as if to say, 'Stop right there. Don't come any nearer, you are too real. Don't you dare come near and disconnect me.'

Off the phone and Georgie knew that Sylvia spoke about nothing real.

'He is twenty-one years older than you. He left home at sixteen.' But she spoke in the tone of voice she used for the ill-bred and the vulgar.

And Georgie was eleven, so that meant Stephen was now thirty-two. Not even exciting, not a dashing young man with which to impress her friends but an adult, a fully grown man, more of an embarrassment. With a toe-curling name like

Stephen. She stared angrily out of the window. Her mother had shared the secret but not given her daughter her wish. And that would explain why Georgie's parents were so much older than everyone else's. But why had they waited so long to have her? Twenty-one years was a gap too wide. But she supposed they only wanted one child, and they waited until they lost that one before deciding to try for another. This made sense. Sylvia Southwell did not like children.

She cast around in her mind then, searching for all the clues she had missed – pages torn from a photograph album, old tin cars buried in the garden, careless references to times and events, the sudden frown, the unexpected silence covered by a cough. But she could remember none of these things. They had covered the secret absolutely and not one glint of it remained.

'Why didn't you tell me sooner? What did he do?'

Sylvia's words were beaten out harshly like twangs on a musical triangle. 'He caused Daddy and me all sorts of terrible grief, and when he left home it was merely the end of a long and anguished period for us. From the beginning he was a difficult child, we lost him long before he went.'

'Don't you ever hear from him?'

Sylvia's lips tightened. She changed gear with a black-gloved hand and Georgie saw the bulge in her sleeve where she kept her white lace handkerchief. Mummy was always immaculate, with her pearl stud earrings, black patent leather bag and shoes, a shade too perfect perhaps? She must have been pretty once, before she got lines on her face, with her slim figure and her gracious smile, with her brown hair shot with expensive gold. 'We are grateful for his continuing silence.'

'And you never tried to find him?'

'We heard once, from an acquaintance, that he was an artist living in London doing quite well for himself. That he lived alone and had no interest in contacting us or renewing the relationship.'

Georgie hesitated. 'Perhaps he might want to know me.'

Sylvia gave her a sharp look and the car swerved slightly. 'I doubt that, darling. I doubt that very much.'

Georgie squirmed on her seat. She didn't want to ask questions, she didn't want to appear too interested, but fascinated as she was, she badly needed to know. 'But what was he like, Mummy? And what sort of trouble did he cause?'

Her voice was artificial and strained. 'It is painful for me even to remember, let alone discuss it with you.'

'It might have been better if you'd never told me.'

'You had to know, Georgina. You couldn't have grown up not knowing.'

'Why? Why couldn't I have?'

'Because you have a right to know. It would have been very wrong for you to find out from some other source.' Whatever the cost, the rules of life must be observed.

'But only so much and no more?'

'He was dark. Dark like you, dark like your father.'

'But tell me what he did wrong?'

Sylvia Southwell took the top of her tongue round her lipstick to lubricate a passage for the dryness of the words. 'He was wilful and moody from the beginning. Stephen was never an ordinary child, never placid or amenable. Every single thing he did was either for attention or to cause trouble.'

Sylvia seemed to surprise herself, to stumble over the possible discovery that she had never loved him.

'I'm amazed that you took a second chance after that. By having me.'

'We had no say in the matter, Georgina. You came along unexpectedly.' And then she added quickly, 'And we were thrilled to have you.'

A lie.

They drove along in silence then with thoughts too thick to penetrate. Eventually Georgie was forced to ask, 'So you don't know where he lives now?'

Mummy cleared her throat delicately. She answered her daughter with cold dignity. 'No, and we have no desire to.'

This was so unsatisfactory. 'Why are you still so angry with him?'

'Because Stephen is still hurting me. You can't lose a child and forget. Even a child such as that.'

'You made a good attempt at it.'

'There is no need to be offensive, Georgina. You know nothing about it at all. You are still a child, too young to understand, I see. And already

I am regretting the fact that I told you.'

The conversation was just too awkward. Neither of them could cope with it.

Tall, dark conifers, their heads oddly detached in rows behind the high garden wall. Symmetrical. A square lawn. Chimneys, also detached, and everything in shades of brown. Even the house was a brown one, and the chips in the driveway were fawn.

A house in uniform.

Through the brown study door and into a totally brown hall, banisters leading up, wooden floors with matching rugs, a tall brown settle next to the telephone, and a brown umbrella and hat stand full of walking sticks and brown macs.

When the sun shone through the landing window that overlooked the hall, it glowed russet.

Immediately she entered Georgie wished she had gone to Daisy's, but the fact was she hadn't been asked. Not again. Not a fourth time. But what would she do all alone for three days, here, in a house which was full of things, and hung with pictures of her father's father? And how could she possibly invite her friends?

Mummy was wicked to suggest it, knowing how impossible it was.

She knew every stair that creaked in that house, she knew every giving floor board. Born in it, she was one with it, it and its smell of pipe smoke and polish, and she hated it. She would have half an hour to go upstairs and familiarize herself once again and then it would be four o'clock and the gong would go for tea, splitting the silent house with its summons. She would have to come down for tea, that brown interlude of tea and paste sandwiches and moist fruit cake. Fascinated, she wondered which of the five bedrooms had been Stephen's. Perhaps this one? Perhaps this very bed she lay on with her arms behind her head, perhaps this had once been his and all his things filled the cupboards?

Georgie could well understand why Stephen had fled. She had always sworn she would leave herself the moment she was old enough. She imagined a wild boy playing in the garden, messing it up, pulling up the flowers and scattering the petals about, cutting the square lawn into circles, smashing the panes of greenhouse glass.

Bravely. Gloriously and mightily. Not in the cowardly way she had broken the flower pots and hidden them afterwards.

An artist in rebellion against the sordid values of everyday life. Free from the tyranny of property and praise.

If Stephen lived here for sixteen years then he must have gone to school. It was awkward for Georgie to raise the subject again, difficult and embarrassing. She could see that, as with the facts of life, once her mother had raised the matter, it was dropped and done with for ever. But over tea, alone with Mummy after Gwyneth the maid had gone, she tried to press her once again.

Sylvia eyed her crossly. Her daughter was breaking the rules. She poured tea from the silver pot and her handkerchief trailed from her sleeve like disappointment. She answered Georgie's question abruptly, and the bitterness, it was almost hate, crept back into her tone. 'Stephen went to Grantly House until he was thirteen, and then he was sent to your father's school, Stoyle. At both schools he disgraced us. I'll say no more than that. They only kept him on because of the family traditions, but in the end he was too much for them and he was expelled. Of course, that nearly killed your father.' And she patted a pin-curl into place.

Family tradition! Family name! Georgie was tempted to laugh. A military family until it came to Daddy with his poor eyesight and his hip. In spite of family tradition the Army refused him. And yet photographs of men lined up glowered from the walls of Harry Southwell's study, jutting chins, ruddy faces, ranked in military or sporting rows, which did not matter. Guns replaced cricket bats, khaki berets replaced caps with a smooth indiscrimination. Yet Daddy had not inherited those fat shiny knees, those tuberous thighs or those clothes-hanger shoulders. Oh, he had the rigid stance, the love of discipline, the yearning for rules. Daddy was a walking moustache, twitching and twirling at the edges. Routine. Order. Duty. But courage and medals and mentions in dispatches don't make for money. Not a generation later they don't, and the worn leather chairs and the threadbare carpets said as much. It was years before Georgie realized that her childhood was spent in genteel penury.

Daddy, working permanently at home, dealt in stocks and shares not terribly successfully. Sylvia,

73

with her respect for worldly position and wealth, called his projects hare-brained schemes, told her friends he was empty of enterprise. But the lady of a house never lifted a duster, never plugged in an iron, these were the jobs of the live-in maids, and they came and went back to their homes in Wales in regular succession, probably because of the surfeit of work. Sometimes they could light fires in the autumn, sometimes they could not, depending on the market. Cauliflower cheese, bubble and squeak, rice puddings, meat rissoles, brisket and fish pie were regulars at the table, all well browned on top. School uniforms came second hand and Georgie suspected her fees were paid by some kind of military trust. Trimming the sails and making ends meet were constant irritations, but Sylvia kept accounts at all the best local stores while bitterly resenting her restrained circumstances. Such mortification. She had a real horror of poverty, of eventually having to sell the house and lose face in the neighbourhood.

Oh yes, at all costs, the image must be preserved.

So on that first night at Furze Pen Cottage, pouring her baked beans over her toast, Georgina Jefferson shivered. She had escaped from all that eventually, but not quite soon enough. She wished she'd had Stephen's determination.

She decided to drag the mattress downstairs and sleep beside the fire tonight, next to Lola. She needed warmth. She needed light. But the most disconcerting thing was the silence.

Georgina desperately needed sound.

Six

Please be patient. We must proceed slowly and
with caution because of Georgie's frail state of
mind.

So, she was housebound. It was no longer a matter
of strolling up the street to collect the dreaded
papers, far from it. She looked upon a snowy
world spangled with winter sunshine and saw the
pint of milk on her step, as promised. And that
slim white bottle was the one firm thing which
gave her a sense of contact with this new and
extraordinary world.

Melting snow dripped off the thatchy over-
hangs. The tall tufts of grass in the garden turned
asparagus green at the tips. Birds flashed from
branch to branch between statuesque apple trees,
and she prayed that the thaw would continue so
she could get out tomorrow.

Her radio was a life-saver. Plugging it in and
turning it on made Sunday familiar again. She
fixed some breakfast on the mean, cream cooker
in the starkest kitchen imaginable and opened the
stable door to let Lola out. Slowly. Slowly. To fill
out the time. To adjust to this new pace of life.

Apart from electricity the cottage's one concession to the twentieth century was the tiny shower

in the whitewashed bathroom, an outhouse stuck to the side of the kitchen. You squeezed yourself small to get inside, but merely to see it in this freezing weather raised goose pimples everywhere. The frosted window, an odd gesture to modesty here, was fortified by rusty iron bars. It looked as if it hadn't been used for the last fifty years, and so did the stained lavatory, and Georgie gave a gasping shriek when a splosh of water fell on her head straight after she tried the chain.

She banked up the fire, which was smouldering nicely. If Stephen's liver had rotted away where were the empty medicine bottles? Someone had cleaned up the cottage, whoever it was had removed them, too.

The solicitor's letter had been brief and to the point, and the telephone call she made to the firm had not thrown much light on the subject. It seemed to be a matter of coming to see for herself, and 'we will be here should you require assistance'. But the letter included the phrase 'house and contents', so presumably there were contents once worthy of the name.

'How did you trace me?' she'd asked Tom Selby.

'From his birth certificate, Mrs Jefferson. That's all the information we had.'

'It was lucky my parents lived at the same address for so long.'

'Yes, that was helpful. And so was the fact that the present occupants knew where you worked. We traced your present address from that.'

'My mother only died four years ago and that's when the house was sold. I met the people who bought it, I suppose I must have mentioned my work during the brief conversations we had.'

'Mr Southwell was a sick man for many years.'

For a second Georgie was thrown, believing he referred to her father. Flustered she replied, 'We didn't know him, Mr Selby. He cut himself off from his family years ago. Nobody knew where he went. There was no communication between us.'

'Ah. An obstinate man. I believe he refused all advice in the end and refused to go to hospital. In fact, he declined any help he was offered.'

So he had died at home. Where? Something made her ask, 'Who found him?'

'There was an inquest, of course.' She heard Tom Selby rustling his papers to find the answer to her question. 'A neighbour,' he eventually replied. And then he read in his dusty old voice, and Georgie imagined his thin-rimmed spectacles, 'A Mr Horsefield of Wooton House. It gives no more information than that. He was found soon after his death, Mrs Jefferson, you need not worry on that account, he was not left mouldering for days.'

And did she sense a tiny barb of accusation? Or was that her guilty conscience speaking? Because her only living relative had been so needy and she hadn't known, hadn't bothered to find out? But any guilt Georgie felt was soon replaced by anger, anger at time, at life, at the world, but above all anger towards Stephen, who had gone and died without giving her time to get in touch, or the chance to be near him in his hour of need.

And what was worse, she might have been able to love him.

She gazed around while she ate her breakfast, sitting erect at the gateleg table with a pile of damp magazines piled haphazardly before her. All the magazines – she'd taken a look last night – had a passed-on look and the name Horsefield was scribbled on the corner of each: *Horse and Hound, The Devonian, The Country Landowner*, an impersonal mixture of taste that managed to give nothing away. So Stephen had died somewhere in here, maybe in this very room, not three months since. She could only assume that Mr Horsefield of Wooton House must live in the most imposing of the four Wooton-Coney dwellings, the house with the newly pointed walls and the fresh thatch she had noticed last night opposite the farm.

Could it be this Mr Horsefield who removed most of Stephen's belongings? Could he have been a friend of Stephen's, a fellow boozer, a regular caller? There was some sense of community, then, here in this peculiar valley, in spite of her frosty reception at the farm last night. Silly, but she had half expected a visit from someone because, hell, apart from the smoke from the chimney, her car parked outside on the road, all sorts of pointers would make it clear the cottage was occupied again.

And how could anyone live in this tiny insular

hamlet and not be aware that a stranger had arrived?

The morning slowly meandered by, and she, who had grown to loathe the phone, wished there was one in this house. She smiled wryly when she realized she was already talking to herself; it was more of a little hum she supposed, just to relieve the silence. She took Lola for a short walk, but turned back, puffing and out of breath, unable to cope with the slippery hills. She must be well out of condition. She'd done far too much sitting around and moping miserably of late. There was no point in drying the dog, there were no carpets to be ruined, no piece of furniture she could jump on and make damper than it already was. So, blowing hard on cold fingers, Georgie shut Lola inside and firmly resolved, despite some qualms, she set off down the road to call on Stephen's friend, on the man who had found his body, on the man who could be the last person on earth to have seen her brother alive.

The sunlight glittered on crests of snow as she tramped determinedly up the path. A miniature bridge had been built over this section of the stream that dissected the house from the road, so much more sensible in light of the struggle she'd faced on arrival at Stephen's cottage.

She pressed the bell, half expecting to hear nothing, suspecting she would be forced to raise the fox-head knocker, when she heard an encouraging soft burr echoing through the house. She composed her face and waited.

The door was opened softly by a long, straggling, powerful man with the face of an undertaker, gaunt and pallid. Well over six foot six, he stared at her morosely, and his eyes, sunk deep in his head, were almost obscured by his low-hanging eyebrows. The original Mr Munster. His thick tweed jacket was stained and his voice was deep and sepulchral.

'Yes?'

But before Georgie could answer, the tall, burdened man was pushed aside by a quick-moving, spinning creature aged around sixty and dressed in trainers and a tracksuit which bagged badly at the knee. There was a fiery light in her eyes. 'We thought it was being sold on. We thought you would sell it, didn't we, Horace?'

'Mr and Mrs Horsefield?' asked Georgie nervously, not knowing which to address.

'We kept an eye on him, you see. He knew he could count on us, did Stephen. Didn't he, Horace?'

Horace looked down on his coiled-up wife fondly. While she talked she plucked at herself and no part of her very rouged face was still. Was this St Vitus's dance? She seemed to be wearing a hairnet, her grey hair was so flat to her head, but that was the way she wore it, so cropped, so short it seemed it was netted. But her features were free and made the most of it, wrinkling, twisting and contorting as she went on.

'Yes, yes, we used to pop in. I made you call on him, didn't I, Horace? Well, it wouldn't have been fitting for me to go, what with the way he was and that, and nearing the end it was three times a day. Sometimes four or five. Oh yes, and I sent little treats, even when he sent them back saying he didn't want them. Not a friendly man, your brother, Miss, no, a troubled soul, I would say . . .'

The inside of this house wreaked of Glade air freshener. It reminded Georgie of her childhood home after Daddy died. Those mornings Mummy spent cleaning the silver, brightening the medals and trophies, rubbing, rubbing, rubbing. If she rubbed hard enough, sprayed hard enough, they might go away.

'I am his sister.'

'We guessed as much, didn't we, Horace, when we saw your car and you called at the farm. But Selby, the solicitor, said he thought the place would be sold. Nobody much interested in keeping it, he said. We never expected anyone to come looking, we never expected anything like this, did we, Horace?'

These were not farming folks, or locals, that much was clear. Nor were they the kind of people you'd expect to find in a Dartmoor valley. For all his staggering size – his slippered foot would do justice to a carthorse – Horace Horsefield was a mild sort of man, his wife had only to push him aside and he moved without a trace of annoyance. He merely suggested, 'We ought to invite the young lady in, Nancy,' which caused his wife to pause, straighten up on a sharp intake of breath and mutter, 'Of course, of course, what am I about? Oh dear, you can see how unused we are to having visitors living down here. Come down in the world, and you'd never know now that we always lived such an active and sociable life,' and she rushed off, soon out of sight. It was left to Horace to stand aside, Georgie followed him in and he closed the door behind her.

Nancy Horsefield knelt by the fire, a pair of bellows in her hand. She twitched now and then like a wounded sea bird, glancing over her shoulder lest she miss the slightest movement. 'No, no, Horace, not there, move those magazines, she must sit in the chair by the fire. It'll blaze in a minute. It's this wood, it's too wet, not nicely seasoned as I like it.' And then Nancy Horsefield stood up. Extra daubs of vivid colour had been applied to her powdered face, a clumsy smear of lipstick, some of it stuck to the sand-coloured cardigan over her navy tracksuit. She brushed her knees, wiped her hands on her trousers and Horace said, 'Would she like a cup of tea, perhaps?'

'Would you, dear? Would you like a cup of tea?' Her eyes glittered brightly in her tiny head. Already bent and ready for the off, ready for the race to the kitchen, her overlarge trainers, that made her feet look huge, were tied with bright-red laces.

At once Georgie agreed to the tea because Nancy was so keen to make it.

Horace eyed the departing back with sad, half-closed eyes. He lowered himself into a sofa-sized leather chair opposite Georgie's. She felt lost in hers. Her hand looked very small on the arm. He made his excuses. 'She likes to keep herself busy.

She always has, keeps the place like a new pin. My wife has so much nervous energy.' But his tone was a pained one. And with Nancy gone from the room the atmosphere became peaceful, as if a machine had been turned off.

Every single thing in the house was neat, tidy, pleasant, but not the kind of furniture one might expect in a rambling old house. An Indian carpet covered the floor and an Indian tablecloth over-hung the small upright piano. Apart from this the room had the modern bungalow touch, or that of a house on a new estate. As if he could read Georgie's thoughts, Horace said, 'Nancy can't abide old things. She likes everything new. She does her buying from catalogues, you see, she'll spend hours over a catalogue.'

Georgie had expected an old country family, retired, perhaps, children gone, country folks who decided to spend their retirement tucked away in glorious seclusion, or city people retired down here, walkers, bird watchers, shooters and fishers. Apart from that contradiction, the couple did not fit together at all, for while he could be a retired bank manager, or even a vicar, or a doctor, then Nancy would be his housekeeper.

Or was that the effect of the drifting cardigan, hung behind her like a broken wing? Or maybe the missing hairnet?

But at least this reception was more welcoming than the one she'd been given at the farm last night.

'You were lucky to make it at all,' said Horace darkly, 'given the conditions yesterday.'

'It wasn't easy.' And Georgie added, 'But I was determined. And by the time I met the snow it was too late to turn back.'

'Oh yes, of course.' Horace, regarding her gravely, appeared to understand.

'I was surprised to find the cottage so empty apart from a few basic essentials.'

'Stephen never was a man to attach great importance to personal possessions. He never ate properly, either. Always thin as a rake.'

'I realize that, but even so, there is an aerial beside the chimney but no TV set, and I could have done with a television last night.'

The Horsefields' own TV was enormous, one of those you see in shops, almost the size of a cine screen. It stood on an imposing stand with a video recorder beneath it, obviously state of the art.

Horace sighed and turned his long sad face to the fire. 'That'll be Cramer, then. If anything's missing, that'll be Cramer.'

'Cramer?'

Horace inclined his head and grimaced up the road. 'Further along, lives with his girlfriend, Donna. Not much better than a pigsty. That's where you'll find Cramer.'

'And you think this person, Cramer, came and removed Stephen's things?'

'Well, I didn't actually see him, you understand. But then Cramer doesn't make a fuss, he'd have gone early in the morning. If it was him,' he added dourly, and Horace Horsefield's eyes sank even further into his head.

Now Georgie was totally confused. From the

kitchen across the hall they could hear cups rattling, plates being stacked and dropped. And was that an egg being beaten? 'Did Stephen, did my brother tell this man, Cramer, that he could take his things?'

Horace rasped his large hands uneasily. 'We all thought it would be sold on. That's what everyone thought. Even old Tom Selby. So Cramer must have believed he could get away with it. If you want them back you'll have to tell him.'

'I certainly will.' One small problem solved. But Georgie wanted more from Horace Horsefield, she wanted to know more of Stephen. She was keen to explain the reason for her presence. 'I wasn't sure whether to come to Wooton-Coney or not. I made the decision on the spur of the moment. I never knew my brother you see, Mr Horsefield. He cut himself off from his family many years ago, and when I was growing up I wasn't even aware of his existence.'

'Well, that's what we all thought. We didn't think there was any family.'

'Did you know Stephen well?' She had the feeling she needed to hurry. She wanted to dispense with any sensible questions before the excited Nancy came back. 'You see, part of my reason for coming here was to find out more about him.'

'He was a very sick man at the end. Very sick. But he wouldn't let anyone help him.'

'But you went in. You gave him your old magazines.'

'He never wanted to see me. And even the

85

magazines, they were Nancy's idea. Stephen would have been happier left to himself. He never encouraged people. He preferred animals and children.'

'He was an artist, I understand?'

'Cramer must have the paintings,' said Horace, crossing his long legs dispiritedly. 'You ought to ask for those back. He was a good painter, no-one can take that away from him.'

'Don't worry, I intend to ask for them back,' said Georgie, straightening up. And then, out of politeness, she was a stranger here after all and might be boring him with her problems. 'This is a lovely house. How long have you and Mrs Horsefield lived here?'

Horace stroked his long grey chin. His eyebrows wound their way over his eyes. 'We've been here twenty years, since Nancy had her breakdown. We didn't mean to stay to start with, but the place grew on us and now she's terrified to go out. She won't go back. I wouldn't want to go back now, not even if she wanted to.'

Something about him seemed so lonely. She knew she'd be beside herself stuck with just the few oddballs in the hamlet and Nancy to care for all day. 'I've only met Mrs Buckpit briefly, and you've said enough about Cramer, Stephen didn't seem the sociable type, so don't you find you miss company in such a small community?'

'Sometimes,' mused Horace with a shrug of his shoulders. 'We don't have visitors. We have no other family, you see, none that we're in touch with now. But Nancy does tend to get so excitable round people and that's not good for her condition, so all in all it's better that we don't see many.'

Oh, the poor man. Given up so much for his wife. In her social-worker role Georgie had visited several carers, and had always worried that she, unlike them, would never be able to deny herself, endure such hardship, day after day, night after night, with no respite and little complaint, had she ever loved anyone enough to do that? She hoped she would never be tested.

'Where did you come from?' She wore her official socialworker face and smile, immediately assuming they were needy. The fire glowed neatly beside her feet, the wood was arranged in neat little piles and the flames licked them obediently. Everything in this house was obedient and neat save for the wallpaper-sample book out on the floor, where someone had been choosing some appropriate pattern. So poor Horace Horsefield had buried himself away twenty years ago to look after his sick wife. Looking round, meeting Nancy, it was obvious she was still sick. Is this what had given him, over the years, this stooped and miserable air?

'We came from Preston originally. That's where our roots are. I still have some family up that way, but we've lost contact now. I was in the biscuit-packaging business. Small family firm. We sold up. Had to because of poor Nancy.' Georgie thought he winced when he said, 'A child, you see, it was over a child. A dear little girl. Very sad.' He drew a deep and sonorous breath, 'Luckily it was a good time to sell, as it turned out.' Horace looked round the room and nodded in satisfaction, the first sign of pleasure he had shown. He cleared his throat and became more positive. 'Yes, we invested the money well and we live quite comfortably on it. And there were stocks and shares inherited. Yes,' and he stretched when he heard his wife coming back, 'we live well enough. Nancy and I.'

Georgie breathed in and settled her shoulders. She dropped a sigh heavier than his. Dead children. Dear God. Was there nothing in the world except dead children?

On fast squeaking wheels the afternoon tea came into the room on a hostess trolley. 'I like a challenge,' said Nancy, wrapped in an enormous white apron. The silver-plated cake stands were made pink with doilies, and the little round cherry cakes sprinkled with hundreds and thousands were clearly home-baked. The sandwiches, on brown and white bread, had their crusts cut off and were cut into triangles, small and neat, while Nancy, crouched above the trolley said, 'There's sardine or tomato paste, or there's sardine and tomato paste with cucumber.' And her eyes darted this way and that.

She handed Georgie a plate with a napkin folded on it and a terribly modern knife with a red plastic handle. 'I do so like having people,' she murmured contentedly, smacking her lips together, 'although, just recently, I have become a drudge to this house and we have been reduced to living this creeping existence.' And when Georgie took a sandwich she knew that Nancy watched to see how she was enjoying it, or if she dropped crumbs. The certain knowledge was that the minute she had gone Nancy would fetch a dustpan and brush and clean out the chair she was sitting on, fluff up the cushions, go round the carpet with a sweeper. She raised sympathetic eyes towards Horace, but he sat giving nothing away, tugging on a sandwich of his own.

Christ. Not only did this poor defeated man have Nancy to contend with, but, until recently, he had heroically coped with Stephen, too.

Nancy did not sit down. She stood beside the hostess like a waitress after a meal in a restaurant, pointing out the desserts with pride. No sooner had Georgie finished than Nancy was there with that plateful of sandwiches, urging just one more.

'I can't,' she confessed after three. She patted her chest. 'I'm full up. But they were lovely, Mrs Horsefield.'

'But you're going to have a cake? Surely?'

Georgie was firm. If she took one cake where would it end?

'Egg white is the secret,' declared Nancy Horsefield triumphantly, freed to sit down at last, but her hands remained restless on her lap. 'Poor, poor afflicted man. It was the drink that did it, of course,' she said sadly, her eyes brightening. 'The drink that defeated him. But then, of course, he was an artist. Look!' she suddenly cried, remembering, and went to stand by a picture on the far wall of the room. 'He put it in one of those old wooden frames so I had to take it out. It wouldn't have suited a room like this. But look, Mrs Jefferson! Your brother painted this!'

She beamed at Georgie. She beamed at the picture.

Georgie stared in amazement. The picture was heartbreakingly beautiful. Something had led her to expect Stephen's work to be modern, slashes and daubs and wild impressions of colour. Uncanny and unnatural? The kind of painting she might have done? But this painting was nothing like that. It was gentle. It was of a child's face lit up by a strange blue candlelight, and all manner of fears lay beyond the flame. She sat by a tree with her toys half obscured by a tartan rug, but such a yearning was in it, such an understanding of innocence and hope that Georgie gasped. The frame was an awful ornate gold, too heavy, it swamped the picture and tried to squeeze the innocence out. It could not.

And Georgie felt such a stab of pain, it was more like jealousy, when she recognized the fact that Stephen had found a way to cry out while she . . .

'Yes, it's a sight to behold, really, isn't it?' Nancy, palpitating and muttering, watched her visitor's expression with pleasure. She shuffled about in her bag, a red rucksack, obviously new, and pulled out a dainty handkerchief. She dabbed at her nose as if in sorrow, the first sorrow Georgie had seen in regards to her brother's death. 'He gave it to me, Stephen did, for altering his jacket. Remember, Horace, that old black canvas jacket of his? Personally I wouldn't have bothered, I'd have thrown it away or used it as a duster. I said it's no trouble, Stephen, but he insisted on paying me and that's how we came by the picture, and it's one of my most precious possessions.'

Perhaps the picture reminded poor Nancy of the little child she had lost.

Before Georgie left their house, after a third cup of tea, she knew that, whatever else, she must find the rest of the pictures. She must find out all she could about the artist who spoke to her so clearly. So simply. And so directly. As if she had always known him.

Seven

Sunday teatime, the most wretched time in the world for the lonely. But Georgina Jefferson was not lonely was she? She had made her bed and must lie in it.

That first weekend was a long one, with a Sunday lunch that consisted of brown bread and cheese, quickly eaten in the early evening, sitting as close to the fire as she could without squashing Lola.

This was silly. She would have to sell the cottage, this was not the sort of place in which she felt comfortable, in this lost valley with the surly Mrs Buckpit and the vague and defeated Horse-fields, some jerk up the road who assumed it his right to raid his dead neighbour's house and nick whatever he wanted. Georgie did not possess the funds to renovate or maintain a holiday cottage and, if she got back to work, she wouldn't have time to visit it regularly. As for moving here permanently, the thought never crossed her mind.

Not then.

Not yet.

Had Stephen actively chosen to stay here, or had he somehow got himself trapped?

She would call on the shifty Cramer, collect Stephen's pictures, attempt to get out on Monday morning and visit Thomas Selby. Then she would return to London and await the sale of Furze Pen Cottage. All very positive and sensible.

London. She sighed. The internal inquiry into the death of Angela Hopkins was due to begin next week. The inquest was over, a slow and merciless exposure, indifferent and formal. The verdict was one of manslaughter, and Ray Hopkins protested his innocence loudly when taken into custody later. Everyone hoped that while on remand his fellow inmates would give him hell. Even better if the devil could be thrown to the crowd to deal with as they wished. Raymond Peter Hopkins, suddenly the most friendless man in the world.

The post mortem report seemed such a defilement of innocence.

And why did everyone have to be told that the child was illegitimate? Shit, what relevance did that have?

Georgie gave her evidence with professional calm, as did everyone else, as if they were discussing a car which had gone wrong, trying to discover the dodgy parts of the engine. A kind of leaden resignation helped her through the dreadful day, it blunted some of the pain. She wielded her weapons well. God helped her to set her teeth, clench her fist and hold herself together long enough to finish the job. No blame would be apportioned here. That would come later, depending on the coroner's verdict. Even so, Georgie felt she was under sentence of death.

The coroner, a little bright-eyed old man – no

aura about him suggested a career presiding over a range of deaths from sad to unspeakable – made his points very slowly and quietly and described the child's death as monstrous. 'The last cruel act of a man who has undoubtedly made the last two years of Angela's life a misery.' For the record he added with sorrow, 'But in the circumstances, I have to add that, save for the social services living on the premises night and day, there were no steps that could have been taken that were not taken. There were no justifiable or legal reasons why this child, registered at risk, should have been removed from her home. Indeed, it is hard to see how any court, given the circumstances, would have agreed to a place of safety order at that particular time.'

Georgie listened to the proceedings with a kind of dull, glum interest, all feeling stunned and stilled. Oh God, oh God, oh God. She leaned forward to hear, her hands clasped over her knees as she tried, by concentrating, to understand precisely what had happened and how. A large square hall, lit from above, packed with people to its cream-coloured walls. A handsomely carved door, surmounted by the royal arms. And there was Georgie when it was over, exhausted, desolate, sitting at the back of the court, wringing her hands and almost weeping when Roger Mace squeezed her hand.

'You see,' he said, outside on the steps, 'what more can be said to convince you? The coroner had no need to add that opinion. There is nothing you could have done to prevent Angie's death,

Georgie, nothing. And yet you continue to torture yourself.'

But the media, howling for headlines, did not take the coroner's view. And even then, standing on the steps with her name virtually cleared, they swarmed towards her with their microphones and their notepads, jostling and shouting so that Roger had to put his arm round her and hurry her away to the car. Like a criminal. She might as well have worn a blanket over her head. She heard the hisses and jeers of the idle and the curious, and assumed a kind of carelessness as if they really didn't interest her. And that same little huddle of crones was bunched on the courtroom pavement eager to get a look at her, faces ugly with hate, waiting to attack, made sick by their own twisted perceptions.

'Blast them all,' muttered Roger, frazzled.

Right out of the blue the thought sprung on Georgie of how appalled her mother would have been to see her pilloried like this, to read the cursed newspaper comments and realize they were maligning her very own daughter. Neighbours would know. The places where she shopped. The man at the garage, the mobile librarian. Her fragile image would break into fragments. Far from providing any support, Sylvia would have slapped her down with, 'I told you it would end in tears, if you will work with people like that. Associate yourself with those types, Georgina, and what on earth can you expect?'

As bad as refusing to pluck her eyebrows. 'No, I'm sorry, I wipe my hands of you.'

Sackcloth and ashes.

There were more abusive phone calls that night, but Mark stayed with her, so he took them. While Georgie's hands, trembling badly, curved round a glass of brandy.

Oh, there were so many echoes. Whenever Georgie closed her eyes her head turned into a cave and they came. The utilitarian, chilly conference room in the social services building, with its apology for a carpet and its scrounged softseated chairs. The metal blinds, half pulled, were slotted with a weak, dust-seeking sun when they held that first case conference. 'She is a lovely mum,' said Judy, the playgroup leader, plump and woolly in the Fair Isle patterns of childhood. A young hopeful with little experience of life and a face angelically healthy. 'Patsy and Carmen are always beautifully dressed, pleased to see Gail when she comes to pick them up, mostly with some little surprise, a cheap toy or some sweets.'

'It's not Gail we're concerned about,' Georgie remembers insisting. 'Does Ray ever pick them up?' The scars on the laminated table top cried out to be traced with the tip of a pen.

'Oh yes, and me and the other helpers have often seen him give piggy-back rides to the other children. And I've always said how much better we'd be if all the fathers took part like he does,' Judy continued bouncily, her cheerful face and her bright-blue eyes avid with absolute honesty. 'All the kids adore him, and I must say we like him, too.'

Miss Parker, the class teacher from Angie's infant school, told a similar tale, but with a frown in her wary brown eyes. 'There is definitely something the matter. It's not what Angie says or how she acts, no, it comes out in her drawings. And, of course, we are particularly worried because of the weeks she's off school. But there's always a convincing reason given. Ray was working away from home and Gail was in bed with flu, couldn't get up to bring her, no neighbour available, didn't think we'd mind as it was only a few days, but then it dragged on.' Miss Parker, intense and nervous with the thinness of a very quick knitter, shuffled her notes, but the action was more to do with sorting out her thoughts. 'The burn on her right wrist was the result of cooking fudge. Gail Hopkins told the school nurse that the child was being supervised, that Gail only turned away for a second and that Angie tried to test the consistency by dripping the boiling hot stuff on a spoon. Angie's story matched this exactly. The child did not sound as if she was lying.'

'And the bruise on her foot?'

'She told us quite happily that she'd stepped on some sharp farmyard pieces that the younger children were playing with. She said that Gail told her off for going round the house with bare feet when she should have known the toys were all out and that she might hurt herself. We'd never have seen that bruise if one of the kids hadn't got a verruca and we decided to check the whole class. But Angie didn't hang back. If I remember, she was first in the queue.'

'But the cut on her head, that needed stitches. The doctor was involved, I believe.'

There was a note from the family GP. Georgie read it out to the meeting. *'The bruising around the wound was accounted for because of the weight and the speed of the swing on impact. This was quite conducive to the kind of lesion that would be caused by such a common accident. I chatted informally to Angela while I sutured the wound. Angela Hopkins gave a clear and precise account of how the accident had occurred and her version of the event matched that of her mother's. She is a bright, attractive child, and likeable, and I am satisfied that she told the truth. However, naturally I will keep a close check on any further incidents which might occur in view of the concern expressed.'*

Barbara Brightly, the health visitor, was also uneasy. 'But that's mainly because of the times I've called and been unable to get in. Although I've been absolutely certain there was someone there. Of course, it's impossible to say whether the door was kept closed because my visit was inconvenient, maybe Gail considered the flat was a tip, maybe she hadn't got herself dressed, maybe she just had a headache and didn't welcome a call from me. That's understandable.' But Mrs Brightly frowned. She who was usually so sure of herself disliked the uncertainty she felt about this. 'It's happened so many times that I have to admit to the feeling that all cannot be well with that family. In view of everything else.'

Georgie asked, 'And Angie's attitude? The way she responds when you do get in?'

Barbara referred to her notes. 'Always alert. Always happy and chatty. Clean. Well dressed. Hair brushed. Runs to the door to meet me, drags me into the room, shows me the pictures she's been crayoning, offers to make a cup of tea.'

'The perfect child then,' observed Georgie dryly. 'Never grumpy, never naughty, never teasing her siblings, never out of sorts with Gail, never in any trouble.'

'Exactly.' Barbara Brightly closed her file and stared straight ahead with worried eyes. 'It doesn't make sense.'

Barbara Brightly's experiences inside the Hopkins's flat mirrored Georgie's own. Calling at number 108 Kurzon Mount Buildings was always a harrowing experience, and the door was rarely opened on the first visit. It took a note, a warning of a return in the afternoon or on the following day, to insure success. And then, entrance gained, the visits tended to follow a formula. But whose formula? And how could a five-year-old child be forced to play such a difficult part?

High up on the third landing there was only a slither of flaking concrete to separate the front door from the carpark below, a slither of concrete and a tall yellow wall too high for kids to fall over, even a small adult had to stand on tiptoe to see down.

Inside, expected as usual, into a narrow hall and turn right into the sitting room. Square, and one wall made up by double-glazed windows, and a French window onto a 'balcony' large enough for a pot plant, but nobody at Kurzon Mount Buildings bothered to put a pot plant there; one had a dog tied up on it, a dog that barked pitifully all day. So the balcony was bare save for a puddle and a pile of old leaves. A beige and white striped put-you-up on splayed wooden legs, nearly paid for, filled the room, it took up most of the longest wall. The two matching chairs beside the gas fire slanted slightly to face the telly. The adults ate off plates on their knees while the children knelt at the glass coffee table, but no drinks were allowed in here in case 'the kids fuck up the carpet'.

Pert, pretty like a pixie, Angela Hopkins, with her huge grey eyes and her curly hair, her small elfin face. She had the paleness of a child who lacked enough fresh air, and the drawn features of one allowed to stay up way after bedtime. And she fiddled too much with her hands. She might look clean and well cared for, but her nails were often uncut and there was no quiet around her. She was not the sort of child, the kind of victim, to ask for abuse, not smelly, not dim, not rude, and her manners, for her age, were near perfect. Her communication skills were good. Was she genuinely pleased to see Georgie, to bring her a cup of tea, to turn from the TV immediately without needing to be told, without any fuss?

The pictures she showed Georgie, once she got used to her, once she understood why she came, the pictures she laid on Georgie's knee were meant to be proof of her happiness. And Georgie

felt that Angela brought them to her triumphantly, as a defence lawyer might place his
evidence with a slap on the bench of the court.
They were crayoned, pictures already printed in a
colouring book. Neatness was the criteria. 'Look,
I haven't gone over the edge, not anywhere,' said
Angela Hopkins in her crisp little way, aged five.

And Georgie smiled gently at the child in the
tartan pinafore with the neat white socks.

The playdoh pots were rigidly the same. Bowls
made from snakes rolled together. Some tall,
some fatter, but pots, useful pots to put things in,
not an animal, not a flower or a tree or a nonsense
of any sort, not a little mud hut or a human being
among them. There were no handles on Angela's
pots and they were painted either red or black.

Never both.

And meanwhile the toddler, Carmen, would
be cruising the furniture, wobbling dangerously
towards them. When she reached out a chubby
little hand for Angela's precious crayons, prior to
sweeping the lot off the table, Angela would
scoop them up, saying firmly, 'No, Carmen, no.
You can't have these, they'll make a mess or
you'll swallow the tops and choke.' Reasonable.
Caring. Repeating the words of her mother. No
sign of natural childhood anger, not that time and
not ever. Angie hugged her little step-sister
and left her pictures with Georgie. She started to
thread some blocks on a spool, entertaining the
baby.

'There's a good girl,' Gail would say from her
place on the sofa, and smile.

Patsy, aged four, would be sitting on the floor watching something on the TV, following the flickering pictures, unconcerned with the lowered sound. Good as gold.

'We are rather worried about Angela,' Georgie explained the first time she called, following up a visit by the educational welfare worker, Mrs Carlyle. 'We are concerned about her absences from school, and anxious about the causes of the bruises on her legs that seem to appear with such regularity. Concern has been expressed . . .'

'That cow up at the school,' snapped Gail Hopkins, inviting Georgie in, but seemingly un-surprised.

'There are teachers who are worried, yes, and for several reasons. So I wanted to take the opportunity to talk to you about . . .'

'You won't tell me which bitch has complained, but then you don't need to, I know. It was her, it was that Miss Parker, wasn't it? Stupid cow. I know because of the way she's started nagging on about Angie. And then she asks sly questions about Ray. Oh yes, I know. Angie comes home and tells me all about it. There's nothing wrong with any of my kids, Mrs Jefferson. They'd bleeding well say if they was unhappy.'

And it did look as though Angie would say. During those visits she seemed more in control than her mother.

'Why do you think Miss Parker at the school, and myself, why do you think we are so con-cerned, Mrs Hopkins?'

Gail did not hesitate. Her face, free of make-up that morning, was pale, the skin as fresh and pink as a child's. Skinny as her eldest daughter, she wore black leggings and a thigh-length sweater, hand-knitted. Her arms and legs were tightly crossed and she shook a baby's rattle in the hand that was free, shook it to emphasize her points. 'Because I think it's the way everything's going today. Let a kid get a bruise or a cut on the leg and it's, Oh yeah, let's get the bastard, all hell breaks loose. When I was a kid not a day went by when I didn't fall down or scrape myself. My legs were forever covered with bruises. And then there's where we bloody well live. You lot, you think because some of us have to live in dumps like this that we behave like animals. Well, some of them bleeding well do, it's true, smashing up the landings and breaking glass, even if it's been reinforced, they still manage to break the doors. Dealing quite openly. But not us, Mrs Jefferson. We're not bloody well like that. Ray and me care about the kids, and you might think we're bloody inadequate and thick because we live like this, but we're not.'

Gail Hopkins came to a breathless conclusion with sharply protruding brown eyes. They were sharp and knowing. She was no fool and nor was her daughter Angela.

'You can talk to Angie all you want,' she went on, unwinding and lighting a fag. 'Take her off and question her if that's how you bleeding well feel. It won't worry me and it won't worry her. You'd tell the lady the truth, wouldn't you, Angie?'

It was disturbing to have the matter discussed so openly in front of the child, but, from the moment of Gail's defensive response, there'd been no simple way of avoiding it. The minute Georgie said what she'd come for, Gail made it her business to include the child deliberately. There were times when Georgie, sitting there being entertained in the Hopkins's third-floor flat – that's just what it felt like, as if she was sitting there observing some carefully rehearsed performance – wondered what she was doing harbouring such dark suspicions, such narrow concerns, especially when there were so many others who needed a visit: the pensioners, the handicapped, the debt-ridden, homeless people who were eager to see her and let her in.

Money was short for the Hopkins family, but not worryingly so, they scraped by. There wasn't much left out of Ray's pay packet by the time the bills were paid; they couldn't run a car, much as they'd like to, but they stayed ahead with their rent and the club book, they paid the electric by key meter, and even the TV licence was paid for on a monthly basis. 'And now that Carmen's started playgroup I can think about getting out to work again,' said Gail, who used to work in a betting shop. 'That'll make a big difference.' No, the Hopkinses had no need for that sort of practical help, nor were they under that kind of stress.

And as far as coping with the kids went, as Gail quite sensibly said, 'Every mother goes barmy once in a while, with the shopping to be hauled all the way up here, no bleeding lift and two small kiddies. And there's nowhere decent to hang out the washing. They've stopped us using the balconies. Said it wasn't decent, said people don't like to see it. What crap!'

When Georgie asked about punishment, Gail laughed. 'Of course I whack them now and then, who doesn't? And since when has there been a sodding law against it?'

Georgie didn't tell her that would soon come.

'And what about Ray?' Her question sounded sly. 'Or does he leave the kids to you?'

'Of course he doesn't. He's here in the evenings. They're up and playing around him then. Sometimes he gets annoyed, of course he does, he's only bleeding human, when he's trying to watch the telly and they're making a racket. We're all crammed in here like bloody sardines and sometimes it does get on your nerves, but we can't let Angie play down in the yard with all the dog shit and hooligans. Ray's not the sort of man who goes out all the time and comes back pissed, Mrs Jefferson, if that's what you're trying to make out. We're not all afraid of the bugger, you know. Not like some I could name.'

'And what sort of relationship does Ray have with Angela? Was it easy for him to accept another man's child?'

'Ray's fine with Angie. If anything it's her resents him. Plays us off against each other. She's quite a jealous little cow, you know. She likes her own way does Angie. She likes the attention, don't you, eh?'

Angela Hopkins gave an overbright, gappy-toothed smile and continued to play on the floor with the baby.

'Does Angie see anything of her own father these days?'

'Nah. The bugger pissed off before she was born. Isn't that in your file, Mrs Jefferson? I thought you lot had it all in your files?'

Georgie waited till she left the room before asking Gail, 'Do you think that Angie would feel she could tell you if Ray lost his temper with her? Something like that? Hit her a little harder than he intended? Does she confide in you, Mrs Hopkins?'

'Angie would tell me. Ray would tell me. We are a close family, Mrs Jefferson. And a few bloody cuts and bruises, a few days off school, don't prove otherwise. You want to go and look elsewhere, there's plenty round here you should be bleeding visiting if that's what you want, I can tell you.'

But then came Angela's broken arm and the specialist's suggestion that the injury could have been caused by falling out of a tree, but he would have expected more scratches and general bruising if that were the case. The specialist was suspicious. Angie was quieter this time when Georgie visited the hospital, shy. 'It hurts,' she said aggressively, looking smaller than ever in the hospital bed with a huge, wild-eyed rabbit tucked in beside her. 'When are they going to let me go home?'

'I'm sure it hurts, Angie, they say it's a nasty break. Has Mum been to see you?'

'She's coming tonight. She rang up. D'you think they'll let me keep this?' With her good arm she flopped the rabbit up and down. 'I'd really like to take it home.'

'With Ray?'

Angela's eyes were glittery bright, but the child had a broken limb not a fever. 'Nobody did this to me, nobody!'

And then Georgie knew for the first time, without doubt, that Angela Hopkins was lying. The longer the child could be kept here in hospital, the better. She might be drawn to confide in one of the nurses, or one of the cleaners might be able to encourage her to come out of herself. Georgie sat beside her bed and read her a story. She drew some pictures, they played squiggles, with Angie trying to draw with her left hand and giggling with the effort of trying to lean over with that clumsy sling and her new plaster cast. Georgie scribbled the start of what turned out to look like a fish, the head of a fish and one dorsal fin. Immediately she saw a goldfish pond, lily pads, sunlight on water. She handed the paper to Angie. With an immobile smile on her face the small girl took the black felt pen and filled the page with the shape of a black and menacing shark, a cavernous jaw and serrated teeth. And then she scribbled it over, in black. And handed it back. Still smiling.

'Angie,' started Georgie gently. 'What happened to your arm?'

The little twist of expression could be just a secret sigh. 'I was lucky I didn't bust my head. I was quite high up, you know, when I fell. And I didn't yell or make a fuss. The ambulance man said I was brave.'

'And there was nobody else in the park at the time? No-one who could have seen you?'

'No,' she said defensively. 'I was all on my own.'

'Playing in a tree all alone? And the whole of the park deserted? Do you often go to the park alone?'

'It was early,' said Angie quickly, lisping. One front tooth was already half grown, the other was just a bulge in her gum. 'I like to go out early before there's anyone about. You can get a go on the roundabout and there's no bigger ones to push you off or make it go too fast so you get dizzy and fall off.'

'What do you do when the bigger ones come and push you off?'

'I don't hang about. I see them coming and I'm off before they can catch me,' said Angie lightly, licking at the slight chapping around her lips. 'I keep my eyes peeled when I go to the park, like Mum says, 'cos there's not just big ones, there's filthy men, too.'

'It must be quite frightening to go there and play if you're always on the watch like that.' And Georgie scribbled aimlessly while she talked sympathetically, neat little patterns on the paper.

'No, not when you're used to it,' said Angela Hopkins bleakly. 'I can look after myself.'

Five years old, yet the barrier she had set round

108

herself was as thick and white and protective as that plaster cast that encased her skinny right arm. It held the bone together, kept out the knocks so the body beneath could work its own healing.

Georgie drew a long brown line on the page and Angie followed it in black, a line so straight it could almost have been drawn with a ruler. The thin blue lines going across the page formed a simple cage. Bars. Healing. Simple. And no-one else on earth was going to be allowed in.

Oh, dear God. *Had Angela Hopkins known all along that nobody could help her?*

Eight

Georgie started obsessively watching . . .

Sunday was a quiet day, little movement outside the cottage, hers were the only footprints outside on the snowy road. A tractor driven by a red-necked bullock of a man with a balaclava hiding his face rumbled by on several occasions bearing a link box packed tight with hay bales. Around about mid-morning the same vehicle, this time carrying a portable milk tank, spluttered out of Wooton Farm and disappeared up the lane with the same driver in the seat and a gangly, more meagre person hanging dangerously off the back, fag between his lips. Two foxy collies with their ears well back tagged along behind. The tractor slowed in order to pass Georgie's car – yes, you see, she was watching closely – the two men stared at it and made some comment before going on, leaving caterpillar tracks in the snow.

She set off for a second visit, not eager for a confrontation but prepared to have a go if necessary, to the cottage of the unsavoury Cramer, who had so discourteously nicked Stephen's worldly goods. A delicate matter, Georgie was not quite sure how to broach it, and how could she be certain that the accusations made by the melancholy Mr Horsefield were true?

Dusk. The only lights she could see came from the Horsefields' house. The rest were in darkness. The sun was a golden moon surrounded by a yellow-green light. To either side of it the hills, massive and overwhelming, turned a deeper and deeper purple as it sank. The sun's rim dipped behind the hills, stayed for a minute, then disappeared behind them as she watched. The world gurgled water. The sky was defrosting with drippy kitchen sounds. The stream was full and flowing fast, but the icicles that clung to its fraying edges were melting quickly.

Down the road determinedly went Georgie Jefferson, passing the farm on her right, the Horsefields' house on her left, through the rushing ford she paddled, and then up the hill until she reached the only other habitation to make up the hamlet of Wooton-Coney. A rustic response to Mount Kurzon Buildings. More ramshackle than Furze Pen Cottage, the melting patches of snow left a grey unhealthy shade of thatch, tufted and tattered and clumped to the roof. The front door was a scarred and multi-nailed affair, the tiny garden neglected, overgrown with briars and brambles, dead now, of course, but straggled messily across the white grass. In summer it must be hard to pass through what would surely be a riot of undergrowth. The one fruit tree to the right of the path was dead, strangled by a cruel skirt of barbed wire that someone had wound round its trunk in its infancy, and its gnarled, misshapen branches dripped with accusing, tortured tumours.

'My name is Georgina Jefferson, I am Stephen Southwell's sister.' She smiled. And she nodded behind her to show the slatternly girl which way she'd come. 'I'm down here for the weekend, so I thought I'd pop over and introduce myself.'

The girl in the blue jeans was in her early twenties, muffled against the cold with a long purple scarf that twisted round her neck like lagging and tied round her back like a halter. It was tangled in several places in straw-coloured, lustreless hair. The hairy sweater that drowned her slight frame was outsize and heavy, and sore red fingers spidered out from fingerless mittens. The several pairs of socks on her feet gave her movements that dragging sound.

'Oh?' she said, her blue eyes startlingly bright. 'Oh?' And her hand would have moved to her mouth, except that she restrained it. 'We never thought anyone'd come down.'

'Who is it, Donna?' growled a voice from within.

'Hang on a sec.'

She must get in. This was important. Georgie asked quickly, 'Did you know Stephen? Only, if you did know him, I wondered if you'd give me a moment to ask a few questions, because I never met him and this is my only opportunity to find out more about him.'

Her words sounded pathetic, verging on the needy. And she felt needy, too, standing there like a fool on the front doorstep of a stranger, confessing to what felt like carelessness. 'I've been round to the Horsefields, I called round there this morning, but talking was difficult because Mrs Horsefield was rather flustered. She's not very well, is she? Your neighbour?' She attempted to make conversation.

'You'd better come in then,' sniffed the girl.

If Donna had been a child you would have said she was sulking. Georgie followed as she shuffled through the dark and airless passage, and Donna grunted, 'He's in there.'

The room was similar in size and shape to the one at Furze Pen, and almost as spartan. The man who sat beside the fire was lanky and leathery, with large angry hands and a thick mat of dirty hair. He looked up when Georgie entered but carried on cleaning his gun, rubbing oil along the barrel, rooting through the tube with a frazzled pipe cleaner. 'I suppose you've come about his things?'

She hadn't imagined it would be this easy. The girl had taken the only seat, the moulded plastic chair on the other side of the fire; the sofa, the only alternative, was covered with a filthy old cover. No wonder the girl seemed cold, the air in the room was damp and freezing, and Cramer's answer to the arctic conditions was a coalman's leather jerkin and a blanket like the one on the sofa thrown round his shoulders.

Georgie stood uneasily, and at last the girl, Donna, got up from her seat with a small gesture of annoyance and squatted on the hearth's limp rug. Georgie felt an instinctive dislike of the man with the uneven teeth and the stubbled chin, the man so absorbed in his weapon, as she took the uncomfortable chair so grudgingly offered. Cramer himself enjoyed the one armchair, stained and filthy though it was. 'Ah, yes. Mr Horsefield suggested you might know something about Stephen's furniture.'

'There weren't much.' And as he spoke the tiny roll-up in his mouth moved sullenly with his bottom lip.

The faded curtains were drawn. The icy room was lit by one bare bulb. Crumpled tins of extra-strength lager and plates containing half-finished meals, tomato sauce gone hard and the odd cigarette stubbed out in the mess, littered the floor. The mean piece of rug round the fire was charred and criss-crossed with old burns, bald and blackened like a burned field of stubble. This cottage was certainly no contender for *Homes and Gardens*. 'It's not so much the furniture that interests me actually, I'm sure there must have been paintings.'

Cramer continued his poking and rubbing while eyeing her craftily. 'Yeah?' He spat his fag end into the grate unpleasantly.

He thought she was after money!

With gathering annoyance Georgie continued, 'I never knew Stephen, you see. And that's why these paintings are so important to me. But I would like to know if you did remove the stuff from the cottage, and why you felt you had the right to do that.'

'The legal blokes had finished with it. That

bleeding stuff was worth nowt, they'd have thrown it out if I hadn't got it. I don't like to see things go to waste.'

'He's got a stall, see,' chipped in Donna in her reedy, catarrhal voice while starting to roll a fag of her own. She licked the paper with deep concentration and poked at the flakes of tobacco sticking out of the end with a match. Her flaxen hair touched the floor and she peered up through it. Every so often she delved into the box for a tissue with which to wipe her peeling nose.

'They wouldn't have brought me owt, hardly worth the bleeding petrol.'

'But it might have been more prudent to wait. To get permission, perhaps. It was a bit premature.'

Cramer raised one dark eyebrow. 'As I said, I thought it was bleeding done with. I didn't think there'd be anyone.'

'But have you still got the furniture or has it already gone? Have you got anything I could look at? And what about the pictures? What has happened to those?'

'They're all out in the bleeding shed. I hadn't got round to loading it all up. What d'you want me to do then? Cart the bleeding lot back? Like hell.'

Georgie wasn't sure until she'd seen it. Outraged to be made to feel such a nuisance – a right pain in the bleeding arse – Cramer was making out she should accept without question his right to Stephen's belongings, should be almost grateful that he'd gone in there and removed almost every

115

last stick. There was nothing in the man's attitude to suggest shame or guilt. No, only annoyance that she'd come asking.

'Chad's got his own business, see,' said Donna with a snuffle of pride, striking a damp match several times on the chimney in order to light her cigarette. 'That's why he needed the stuff. But you'll hear nothing good about him in this bloody hole. He doesn't get on with them at the farm, nobody does round here. He rents the cottage off them, pays them the rent each week, and that's as far as it goes. They want him out now,' she added, puffing hard, 'that's why the place is going to rot around us. They want us out so they can do the place up and let it for grockles at fancy prices.' She dragged the smoke deep into her lungs and threw the match onto the fire. The flame from that tiny piece of wood almost outdid the fire itself. 'We keep telling them the damp's coming in, but that old cow don't take no notice. Serve them right if the place falls down.'

If they took some small trouble themselves they could make quite a dramatic difference. They could clear up the rubbish for a start, they could hang the dragging curtains back on their hooks. They could wander outside and pick up any number of broken branches to make up the paltry fire, but they'd rather sit here and freeze with their grievance. Georgie was glad she had kept her coat on. But she wasn't here to criticize. Just as important as his belongings was any information that might be gleaned about the elusive Stephen. She might as well ask immediately in case she got thrown out. 'And what about my brother? Did you get on with him? Did you know him?'

'He kept to himself,' muttered Chad Cramer. 'We all do round here,' he accused Georgie with a thrusting, bristly chin.

'But Stephen must have had some friends? Did nobody ever call on him here? Did he go out anywhere local?' And she wanted to scream, *Did nobody know him for God's sake?*

Donna rubbed her chilblained fingers. 'I only moved in with Chad last year, so I dunno what went on before that. But since I've been here I never seen anyone visit that cottage 'cept old Horsefield with his bleeding magazines, nagged into going by batty Nance. And I dunno that Stephen was that grateful or friendly with Horace.' She flicked ash onto the grate. It added to the pile there, along with the hundreds of old dog-ends. 'Was he, Chad?'

Chad shook his head while continuing to rub the barrel of his gun. He cocked it and stared down the barrel with one dark eye.

Donna went on, 'And he was ill, see, so he couldn't go far, could he? Not in the year that I knew him. If he did go out it weren't for long and it was only to do his painting. Well, there's sod all else to do round here unless you're into hunting, like Chad.'

'But he must have gone somewhere to sell his paintings.' Georgie had to know. She couldn't go home with nothing, dammit. 'And if he didn't do that then he must have gone somewhere to claim

117

his benefit, even Stephen couldn't have existed on fresh air,' she wheedled. 'And what about a doctor? Didn't the doctor ever visit him? Towards the end? When he was so ill?'

Chad Cramer's contribution was grudging and unexpected. 'He didn't hold with no doctors an' I wouldn't know about his bleeding dole. That hag, Buckpit, might know more about that. She might have cashed cheques for him. It was her who fetched his shopping. But you won't get much out of that bleeding bitch.'

'But . . . what did Stephen look like?' It was more of a plea. If nothing else, his reticent neighbours could surely tell her this, soften her childish vision of the moody, wild-eyed artist who couldn't give a toss for the world or the people in it.

Donna brightened up to be asked such a simple question. She sniffed, 'He looked exactly like you, you know. Scruffier. Bigger. But you. There was nothing odd about him. He was just quite normal. There's a self-portrait he did somewhere with all the junk in the shed. Isn't there, Chad?'

'You'll have to look for yourself,' said Cramer, casually leaning forward and claiming Donna's half-smoked fag from her fingers. He dragged on it himself. 'I don't take no bleeding notice.'

Donna asked disinterestedly, 'What will you do with the place? Sell it?'

'A nice little scoop,' leered Chad.

Georgie ignored him. 'I think I'm going to have to. There'd be no point in me keeping it up. I wouldn't be able to use it enough to make it worthwhile.'

The girl blew her nose sorely. She enquired, between tissues, 'You wouldn't want to live here then?'

'I couldn't,' Georgie admitted. 'I work in London.' And please don't ask me what I do. I don't want to talk about that. I don't want to think about that.

'I don't blame you,' said Donna with a painful wheeze. 'Who'd wanna end up in a shit hole like this? It's the end of bleeding nowhere. The arsehole of the world.'

'You were keen enough on it once,' said Chad unpleasantly. 'You couldn't get enough of it once.'

'Huh, there wasn't much bleeding choice.'

'You didn't say that then. You was all pleading and begging then. And you know what you can do if you feel that bleeding way, you can piss off. That's what you can bleeding well do.'

Donna softened immediately, her voice turning into a wheedle. She stretched herself out and tried to reach Chad's knee with her hand, but he pushed her off roughly, having none of it. 'It's just that we never go anywhere, Chad, and it's so bleeding cold.' The girl gave an exaggerated shiver and adjusted the serpentlike scarf. 'You could maybe move into town somewhere and use a garage for the stuff, or a yard. Save on petrol.'

'You know bleeding well why we stay. To leave here now'd be playing straight into their hands.'

Georgie felt uneasy, the atmosphere between them was hostile. She would have to remind them why she was waiting or these recriminations could well go on all night. 'Well, maybe I could take a look at the bits you've got while I'm here. I go back to London tomorrow so I'm afraid this just can't wait.'

Chad nodded to Donna, who huffed and puffed as she got off the floor, tucking in bits and pieces of clothing, pulling her socks over her knees as if preparing for some expedition.

'I could give you a few bob for the stuff,' said Chad Cramer gruffly as Georgie got up to follow Donna out. 'Save you finding somebody else. Some bugger had to clear it.'

Some chance. She gave a frosty reply. 'I'll have a look at it first and I'll let you know before I leave.'

He was a nasty piece of work, and what was the miserable Donna doing living here with this oaf of a man? A girl her age? She'd do better to hitch herself up with some travellers, from whence it looked as if she'd come. At least she might be treated with some semblance of respect. At least there might be a decent fire and some lively young company. Cramer might sell furniture, he might get the pick of the goods on his stall, but as Georgie followed the girl's stooping figure through the hall and out to the outhouse, she eyed the patches of seeping damp, the depressing, un-carpeted passage, the miserable, unshaded light bulbs, and thought it strange that the fellow did not use his scavengings to improve standards in his own sorry home.

It was almost as sparse as Stephen's and there was no love in it.

Nine

The more she heard the more Georgie came to believe that Stephen was no angry young man after all. More of a timid mouse. More like a woman, as if he had discovered a gentle way of screaming.

The old railway carriage, minus its wheels and embedded in earth, sat in the corner of scrub which made up Chad Cramer's land, a weed-entangled, final siding. Donna, shivering with cold, shoved the door with her shoulder. This precarious shed was so crammed with books, furniture, mattresses and bits of scrap carpet, so stuffed with pots and pans and electrical appliances, that it took a while to notice the windows were painted over in white. This, along with the cold, gave the impression that Chad's small warehouse was more of a long, low tunnel of ice.

At once Donna, with her scarf trailing behind her, began to climb a hill of soft furnishings. Her bootlike slippers were already soaked from their short trek through the garden. Cushions and rugs fell down like scree behind her and she called back over her shoulder, 'The bleeding Buckpits don't approve of Chad using the premises for what they call business purposes. They're saying they never gave permission for it to be used as a business. But the truth of it is they don't like to see anyone else doing well. They want him out. They're just bleeding jealous.'

Jealous? Of this? The climb was fairly hazardous, with a very real danger of sinking into the mess of soft furnishings.

'How long has he lived here?'

'Oh, years. Ever since he arrived they've wanted him out, but he's got rights on his side, see. If they go to law it'll cost them an arm and a leg. He and the Buckpits don't get on. But then, no-one who lives in this valley gets on. It seems like a condition of residence: you have to hate your neighbours.'

'But people seem to have tried to help Stephen. Mr Horsefield, for example . . . even Mrs Buckpit . . .'

'They only did what they had to. Chad only stays here 'cos he's an obstinate bastard. He'd be far better off in town with a garage and a market stall. If the Buckpits'd leave him alone he'd go like a shot.'

Over the first mountainous pile and then they reached the floor behind and the going got easier. They reached the narrow passage through a ceiling-high collection of junk. The smell of mould was pungent. Unpleasant outcrops of fungus massed along some of the rivets and frost made elaborate patterns on the insides of the whitewashed windows. All the exertion made them breathless, but Donna managed to pant between breaths, 'Most of this stuff's not decent

122

enough to flog, that's why it's still here. Every so often Chad has a fire and gets rid of most of the crap. Now where did he put Stephen's stuff?'

Georgie felt her annoyance growing. Stephen's belongings were piled high at the furthest end of the carriage, awaiting transportation through the double doors at the end, under the battered exit sign. 'It would have been easier to come this way but the doors bolt from the inside. The whole thing's a pain in the arse,' said Donna, her breath hanging whitely in the stale, dead air. 'You can never find anything you want in this bloody lot.'

So these were Stephen's bits and pieces. Perfectly adequate. Nothing fussy, but nothing particularly objectionable either. Georgie sorted through as well as she was able. A nicely scarred pine table which would fetch a bit at auction, a couple of easy chairs and a dresser, an over-stressed sofa and a put-you-up that must have been used as a spare bed. The lamps were good ones, a selection of well-worn Turkish rugs which would have done well on Cramer's stall, a few eye-catching blankets and cushions along with two gigantic vases. With this collection of odds and sods the atmosphere at the cottage would be totally different, and Georgie felt a dull sense of sadness that she would never see it this way. And by not claiming it now, by allowing Cramer to keep the lot, she felt she was handing over something, something precious she needed for herself.

'Well, whaddya think?' Donna viewed her activities with a lack of interest and the odd wet sniff. 'Whaddya gonna do then?'

'Some of it's quite nice,' said Georgie, 'it won't sell for peanuts.'

'It won't make a bleeding fortune either.'

'Storing it here's not going to help.'

'The TV and the fridge, like the radio and the heaters, will be over there with the rest of the electrics. Chad needs to check them before he takes them out.'

Yes, he probably removes all the plugs to sell separately. 'Safety conscious, is he?' asked Georgie sharply.

But Donna began to unfold a chest-high package of blankets. 'These are some of the pictures, but I think there's more upstairs in the house. Chad says Stephen never sold them for much, bread-and-butter paintings, he calls them.'

Well, he would say that. She looked at them with interest. None were framed. All were in oils, some so fresh they looked wet. There was no space in the railway carriage to step back for a good impression, and from close up they looked oddly childish, daubed even, with little thought, done on impulse, in a terrible flurry of urgency lest something be overlooked or forgotten, some quick emotion lost in the terrible staleness of life. Staring at them so objectively felt like prying.

Georgie was suddenly too close for comfort.

A little sob jerked in her throat uncontrolled. Why did she think about Angela Hopkins? What aspect of these pictures took her mind straight to that? Donna looked at her curiously.

'Let's get them out of here,' said Georgie quickly, and this proposed plan of action suddenly felt so absolutely urgent that she stifled the urge to hack out a route through the junk in order to let these feelings of Stephen's get to some space for breath and light.

It was something akin to panic.

'We can unbolt the doors from here,' explained Donna, climbing on a rickety pile of kitchen tables to reach the locks.

'It might have been helpful if Chad had come, too.' The thought of that surly good-for-nothing stretched out by the fire, toying with his gun while they worked so strenuously out here in the cold to undo his lawless actions, the thought of this drove Georgie wild. So it was then, out of sheer frustration and tiredness, that she suddenly decided, 'Damn it, and I want the furniture returned, too, put back in the cottage exactly how it was. But I have no intention of doing it myself, that's up to Chad.'

'He'll be well pissed off to hear that,' remarked Donna matter-of-factly, still puffing, stacking the pictures beside the rusty carriage walls on a piece of cardboard packaging to protect them from the snow. Georgie handed them to her carefully one by one.

'Well, that's just too bad I'm afraid. Even if I do decide to sell the cottage immediately, it will look more attractive fully furnished, just as it was, and the buyer should have first option on the contents. I don't see why I should accept some handout from Chad on the strength of his opinion of its worth. And I certainly won't let the pictures go.'

'You'll have to tell him,' said Donna uneasily.

'Oh, I will.'

'It'll be a right piss-off for him to have to return all this. For nothing, too,' added Donna, wiping her nose on her overlong sleeve. 'Rather you than me.'

'Maybe it'll teach him a lesson.' Georgie climbed down from the carriage doorway and started to count the pictures. 'There's twenty here, now let's go back inside and see what there is upstairs.'

Donna was more uneasy than ever. 'Oh, please don't tell him I told you.'

She might be afraid of Chad but Georgie couldn't care less. 'I'm sorry, Donna, but I have to. This is my property and I want it back. All of it.'

'I shouldn't have sodding said anything,' wailed the red-nosed waif, her sparkling blue eyes watering badly.

Georgie ignored her. This was between her and Chad. 'Now, what can I put these pictures in to get them safely home?'

'There's the wheelbarrow.' And Donna eyed the Christmas card, snow-lumpy barrow that stood, unprotected, on the grass. All it lacked was a robin on the handle. 'If we cleared the muck out, that would do.'

The prospect was all too much. And why the hell should Georgie be slaving outside here in the cold when the man responsible for this nuisance was taking his ease and, no doubt, laughing at her behind his grimy hand. 'Let's get them back indoors and think about this later.'

After much toing and froing across the slippery back garden the pictures were finally stacked safely in Chad Cramer's hallway. By this time the material of Donna's inadequate slippers was soaked. The girl was pinched and frozen, on the brink of hypothermia, and the small fire in the sitting room would not come close to thawing her out. You couldn't help but worry about her, she seemed so pitiful. 'Why don't you change into something dry?'

'I'm already wearing three pairs of socks and I haven't got any more.'

'Well put some dry shoes on at least.'

'The ones I've got are all soaking wet.'

The girl was a pathetic dead loss. She stared helplessly back at Georgie as if pleading to be cared for and looked after. What was she doing buried away here, living with this coldly dishonest and wicked bugger who didn't care a jot if she stayed or went? How had she got herself in this mess with nowhere else to go? Georgie led the way back to the sitting room to find Cramer lolling by the fire as they'd left him, but this time his gun was on the floor and now his eyes were closed. He was snoring lightly, mouth open, exposing his yellowed uneven teeth. Georgie had no compunction about waking him up.

'I have looked over my brother's belongings.' She was gratified to see him jump into wakefulness. His ferret eyes narrowed as they focused upon her, and one grimy nail rasped on his bristly chin. 'And I have decided that I want everything back, put back just how it was, and as quickly as possible.'

'But there's nothing frigging worth . . .'

'Really? It might be worthless in your eyes, Mr Cramer, but in mine it is all extremely important,' said Georgie sternly, wondering how he would take this arrogant tone.

'Ah, that might not be quite so easy,' he started to say, pulling himself out of sleep, aware he might be losing out.

In their absence Cramer had allowed the fire to die back dingily to a few sad puffs of smoke. 'I don't see how returning my rightful possessions could prove more difficult than moving them out in the first place. They're all stacked up out there quite neatly, apart from the electric gadgets. It would be a simple matter to load them onto the back of a trailer and drive them back over. We are only talking about a few hundred yards after all.'

Donna, still with chattering teeth, trailed into the room behind her. The man was a bully and Georgie could sense the girl's nervousness.

'I'll have to see what can be done,' he growled ungraciously, and his eyes whisked over her, mean with temper.

But Georgie remained standing there glaring down on him. 'I want the job done today, Mr Cramer, while I'm around to supervise.'

He smiled then, a thin-lipped smile full of pleasure. 'That won't be possible, I'm afraid. It'll be bleeding dark in a minute.'

Georgie drew herself up, hands on her hips. 'If the contents of Furze Pen Cottage are not

128

returned to me today, and all of them, then I shall report them missing to the police at Bovey Tracey in the morning.'

Cramer pulled himself as high as he could from the depths of his unsavoury chair. His eyes darted over Georgie, testing for sincerity. 'That's being bloody stupid, that's well over the top.'

'That might well be. Good,' said Georgie. 'Just so long as you realize that. And there must be more pictures than the few I saw outside. I know that Stephen was prolific, there must be more paintings about somewhere. The police, no doubt, could also help me solve that small problem, Mr Cramer.'

She could feel that poor Donna, behind her, was holding her breath with tension. There would be all hell to pay if Chad discovered her gaff. But Georgie could not spare the girl, if necessary she would say what she knew and she would insist on searching upstairs. Cold, tired and irritated now beyond endurance by the attitude of this surly scoundrel, Georgie had taken enough. She was not prepared to play his games, or be intimidated by the man, by his size or by his insolence; she was sure he enjoyed abusing women. Georgie, with no intention of coming to live here in Wooton-Coney, didn't give a damn if she fell foul of this disagreeable neighbour or not.

Luckily she was not forced to betray Donna's thoughtless indiscretion because, unsettled by the word 'police' and speaking with lazy indifference, Cramer said, 'You'd better show her the rest of the rubbish if she's so bleeding determined.' So

129

they left the room to Donna's palpable relief, and the girl led the way up the twisting stairs to the freezing cold of the bedrooms.

Stephen's paintings were stacked in piles, up-ended along walls, balanced against broken tea chests, in a bleak, distempered bedroom with nothing else in it save packing cases and cardboard boxes. There must have been fifty pictures in all. With Donna's help Georgie counted, and some were good, very good.

'You stood up to him back there. That's daft. He can be wicked, can Cramer. And he carries grudges about for years.' She sounded like a weak old woman, tired, dulled and defeated.

'What do you suggest I do? Let him get away with it? He's a bully, Donna. There are lots of men like him, leftovers from the old days. Dinosaurs, really. And some can be flesh-eaters, can't they?' But Donna, blinking blankly, looked as though she couldn't possibly be held responsible for anything that happened in the whole of her life.

'He wasn't a monster when I first knew him.'

'No,' Georgie smiled. 'They never are. But I can't see Cramer as a Mr Wonderful.' Out of her habit of caring, perhaps, or because she was merely interested, Georgie asked, exasperated, 'How did you get mixed up with him, Donna?'

'He's OK most of the time. And it's a home.' There was little expression in the girl's voice.

Georgie looked round her and crossed her arms against the bleakness she saw. 'Not much of a home. Not many comforts to write home about.'

Donna brightened and looked through the cracked window into the gloomy daylight. 'I might go this summer. I've been thinking of pissing off out of here for a while now. I've just got to wait till the time is right.'

Georgie knew she wouldn't go in the summer. She wouldn't go in the spring or in the autumn either. Donna would not leave Cramer until he decided to chuck her out and move on to the next sad cow, and even then the lamentable Donna would probably beg to return. Georgie had seen too many Donnas in her day, damn the job, it soured too much of the world. Too many victims to remember and far too many to count.

And yet Gail Hopkins had not been a Donna, she was far too sparky for that, and Ray Hopkins had not, on the surface, in spite of his gruff hostility towards the social services, been a Chad Cramer either. How easy it is to set up stereotypes just because it is simpler, no, to hell with it, let's be honest, without stereotypes nobody could survive. At the end of the day it is simply a way of sorting the unacceptable, the unspeakable, out.

There were no words of wisdom Georgie could say to the girl with the bright-blue eyes, this overgrown child who stood so inadequately, so hopelessly before her, but she tried all the same. Once a meddler always a meddler. Maybe a good discussion with somebody with her welfare at heart might spur her on to take action. 'Perhaps, after Chad's moved my stuff back, you'd like to come over and have a drink and a chat, help me

131

sort the place out.' She hesitated, afraid she might sound patronizing. 'I need a friend.'

Donna, filled with dismay, explained, 'Oh, I daren't, Chad wouldn't like that.'

'No?'

'He doesn't like being bested you see, especially by a woman.'

'No, I understand that.'

'Perhaps tomorrow, when he's gone out.'

'I won't be here tomorrow, Donna. I'm leaving in the morning. I have to get back to London.'

And then Chad was calling from below. It was a cup of tea he was wanting and Donna hurried down to oblige, apology in her backward glance, an appeal for understanding.

When Georgie had finally finished she went downstairs and confronted Cramer. 'The sooner you make a start the better, while there's some light left. I'll expect the first load in about . . . what? . . . An hour?'

Cramer did not look her in the eye. He glowered into the fire, one eye closed against spiralling cigarette smoke, then he answered sourly, 'That brother of yours couldn't paint a bleeding fence, not with a brush and a tin of whitewash. The lot together aren't worth fifty.' And he spat the dog-end angrily into the hearth.

'The canvas alone is worth more than that, as well you know, Mr Cramer. So, as I said, I'll be waiting. And there might be a few bob in it for your troubles if you're lucky.'

He missed the insult completely for he was a man without shame. If she'd slapped his face he'd have understood. And Georgie heard him cursing some clumsiness of Donna's as she briskly and triumphantly showed herself out. In these difficult circumstances, she congratulated herself, she thought she had done rather well.

Ten

Not only was Georgie aware that Cramer was slyly eyeing her departure, but that several other hostile stares were following her from the other two lonesome habitations that made up Wooton-Coney. She looked for the twitching curtains, but saw only vague reflections on glass. Not a woman given to dramatic imagination, nevertheless she could not dismiss the certain feeling that her every move was being watched and had been watched, carefully watched, since the moment of her arrival. But why?

At the cottage she fed Lola, then sat in the damp, distressed chair waiting for the devious Cramer to arrive with the first load. It might be inconvenient for the slob to leave the comfort of his miserable fire, it might be unreasonable to expect such exertions in the snow and in the dark, but there was no alternative. Georgie, determined to get her belongings back, was quite clear in her own mind that if the villain did not return them straight away she would go to the police in the morning.

Cramer was no lovable local scoundrel. The cheeky poacher. The colourful rustic. Georgie disliked him intensely.

Half an hour later Cramer arrived. He did his

work with sullen efficiency, Donna tagging mutely behind to help him hump his load. The caterpillar tracks left by the Buckpits' tractor meant that the battered old Land Rover and trailer had no real difficulty grinding their way up the road. Cramer cursed darkly as he worked, grim reluctance in every movement. He was rough with Stephen's belongings now they were no longer his for the taking, and Georgie watched him nervously while she traversed the awkward stream, backwards and forwards, backwards and forwards, making sure the breakables, at least, reached the house in one piece.

Total darkness overtook the horizon and fluttered the valley like a fan. A tawny owl hooted and the churring note of a nightjar tore the stillness of the night. Quite alone with nature in the complete stillness between Cramer's deliveries, it was easy to think her strange and hostile, busy with her own life, indifferent to the needs of men. Georgie's tautened hearing meant that the chattering stream flowed more swiftly and small animals moved in the snow.

It took Cramer four journeys to finish the job, and by the time the Land Rover rattled away the night sky was pitch-black. She had looked at the mess Cramer had left and decided not to tip him. It was a relief to close the door and make a start on sorting it out.

Already the cottage felt more comfortable, began to breathe real life. The battered yet comfortable sofa and the second, more reputable, armchair removed the vacant feeling of space. It was a relief to be busy, absorbed in something positive, removed from her normal relentless problems. Already Georgie was aware of the gulf that divided this life from the other. She positioned the lamps and turned them on. Some of the old horse harness she hung on the obvious hooks. She laid the rugs down over the carpet and the eerie echo went out of the place. She wiped Stephen's books and stacked them in the bookcase, not a great deal to be learned from those, mostly classics, collections of poetry, books about painters and the history of art. She tried the archaic TV and was surprised to find that it worked. She filled the little walnut dresser with bits and pieces from boxes: a portable typewriter, a chess set, music tapes, again mostly classics, a clarinet in a case, a silver cigarette lighter, a camera and several photograph albums filled with nothing but views. And there's nothing so bleak and empty as a photograph of a view.

Even the kitchen was slightly improved with the bright selection of tins on the shelves, the bread board, the mat on the floor, the vegetable rack and the small kitchen cupboard.

Tired by now, she went upstairs where Cramer had thoughtlessly dumped the furniture and boxes of art materials. She tried to sort the bedroom out to look as though someone had once slept there. There were clothes in the chest of drawers, more in the blanket chest. The sweaters and shirts and corduroy trousers, mostly old and unfashionable, the rolled-up socks and underwear, did not smell of Stephen, after their sojourn in that damp old carriage they smelled of decay. And the brown flying jacket was in the process of growing a white and unpleasant coating of mould. Ugh! She would have liked to have made a 'studio' out of the second bedroom again, but was frustrated by ignorance. How had Stephen arranged his things? So she left the paints and brushes in their boxes, and only when Georgie was satisfied that she'd done as much as she could did she go downstairs where the paintings were waiting for her excited perusal.

But along with the ashy smell of wood, now there was something else, something underneath, and pervasive, hard to pinpoint save to say that the smell had not been there before. And then she suddenly had it: the sickly sweet smell of gin gone sticky. It came to the house on her brother's things and touched her like a troubled hand.

Savage. Primitive. Breathing on her as she backed away.

There were many times, after the tragedy, when she'd started out to the Hopkins's flat to visit Gail and offer consolation on the death of a child, to offer a shoulder to cry on, to try to share the grief in some way, to find out how to do her own mourning. Yes, many times she had started out only to return to her flat, daunted by her own inability to handle her feelings and by the vast impossibility of grasping exactly what had happened to Angie, to Gail, to herself . . .

Eventually Georgie chose evening, certainly not the happiest time for a visit to Kurzon Mount Buildings, but a time when she would probably

137

find Gail in. She stood at the familiar door, the door she had waited at so many times, she held her breath as she pressed the bell. She didn't know what she might find, and she wasn't at all sure what she would say. She was unprepared for the angry reaction.

'*You!*' It was a hiss.

Gail? But so different. No longer the lazy, easy-going veneer; stripped of that lethargic good nature, now she was lean and predatory, her cheeks thin and hollow and her red eyes ringed with tiredness and grief.

'I thought we might talk,' ventured Georgie, already aware she had blundered badly.

Gail Hopkins recoiled with revulsion. 'Me? *Talk to you?*'

Embarrassed, bewildered and forgetting why she had come, yet still unable to walk away, Georgie tried to explain, 'I want to tell you how sorry I am, and how much I am sharing your pain . . .'

'Piss off, you bitch.' And yet Gail did not attempt to slam the door in her face. She seemed to actually be gaining strength from this hellish encounter. Her face was thin and hollow, her eyes stared brightly as she spat, 'You! *You interfering cow*. You don't give a toss. You make things happen with your poking and your prying, all your vile suggestions and your bleeding filthy minds.' She spat on the floor, a bitter taste. The spittle sizzled. 'You dirty everything up. None of this would have happened if it wasn't for you and your sick mind. Angie fell down the bleeding stairs!

But no, no, you won't have that, will you! You went and bleeding told them all, you filled their heads with your filthy lies and now they think that Ray did it. You've taken my kiddie and they've locked up my bloke.'

'But Gail! *Surely you can't believe . . . ?*'

'And now you have the nerve to come here and tell me I'm wrong . . . as if I don't know my own husband, my own kids . . .'

As woodenly unhappy as she could ever remember feeling before, Georgie pleaded, 'I didn't come here to talk about this. I came here because of Angie and because I was so fond of her, and I wanted to let you know . . .'

'Yeah, yeah!' Gail's face screwed up, knotted with a defiant rage. 'You came here for yourself, you bastard. Because of your bleeding guilt. Because you know bloody well what you've done to me!'

Despair blocked every route of thought. It clogged the channels of speech. Georgie's head worked from side to side as she fought a battle with desperate tears, and she would never know if she won it or not. Everything she said was hopeless. 'If I'd known this was how you were feeling I wouldn't have dreamed of coming here, Gail, and making this any worse for you.'

Gail stabbed her with her eyes. 'But I'm glad you came! I'm glad you gave me this chance to tell you how it bloody well is. D'you really know what's happened to me? D'you know what's been going on with me and the kids? They can't go out to play in the yard and they're too upset to go to the playgroup, people are so bloody vicious. They tell them their dad's a killer. The other kids, yeah, that's what they say to Carmen and Patsy. I've had insults daubed on my sodding door. I've had broken windows. I've had shit shoved through my letter box, and all the while this crap is going on, while I'm breaking my heart over Angie, *where's Ray*? You tell me, Mrs fucking Jefferson. *Where's Ray in all this?* He's shut up inside, that's where he is. And if I get one half-hour with him a week then I'm lucky, if I can get someone to mind the kids, 'cos I'm not taking them to that place . . .'

'Gail, listen! Perhaps the social services would be able to help you . . .'

And then Gail Hopkins threw back her head and laughed in Georgie's face. Patsy, a tiny figure in a dressing gown, crept shyly along the passage and tugged nervously at her mother's hem, then backed away into the room on the right. Gail's laugh grew more hysterical, shaky. 'Oh, that's right! *That's right!* Say what you've been trained to say. Come out with all your glib answers. Move us? Is that it now? D'you think there's a place left in London where they won't soon know who I am? The wife of the killer! The mother who let her kiddie die! She did it! She did it! That's what they're really saying and that's what they're really thinking.' Gail stopped laughing suddenly and tried to pull herself together. 'If you honestly want to help me, Mrs Jefferson, if you really came here with good in your heart, then get down to that bleeding nick and tell them that Ray never touched her, that he's never touched a child in his life, that he was a good and caring dad and that Angie fell downstairs like he says . . .'

'But, Gail, you know if I truly believed that I would have said it long ago . . .'

'Oh no, oh no you wouldn't. Don't give me that shit. You and your lot, sick, suspicious, spreading rumours, telling lies.' Gail rammed her hands on her hips. 'Tell me this! Tell me, is this how you get your sick kicks, Mrs Jefferson? Ray says it is. Ray's always known what this is about. Prying. Spying. Can't have kiddies yourself so you have to nose about other people's. Other people's lives. Reducing them all to pieces of paper. Your fucking library of files. *At risk!* At risk my arse.'

She was reduced to begging. '*Please, Gail*, let me come in.'

'To watch me crying, you mean? To gloat, you freak? To make notes about me and take them back to your bloody office for all your mates to see? To make sure that I'm coping properly and the other two aren't at risk now? Like Angie? Is that why you are so sodding eager to get back in my house? You want the others, is that it? Well? Is that fucking it? Oh no, you cow, the next time one of your lot sets foot in here is over my bloody dead body, and I'm telling you that for fucking nothing.'

Georgie gradually realized she was no longer alone on the windswept landing outside the Hopkins's flat. A small group of neighbours had gathered round to listen. They had come out onto the landing quiet as ghosts, and their faces were white in the dirty light. Little yellow pools in

doorways told her from which flats they had
come. There were no men with them, just the
women, for this was women's work. One held a
dustpan and brush. One had a baby under her
arm. Georgie stared about her in alarm, but they
held their ground aggressively, the judge, the jury,
the just.

'You're the cunt, aren't you?' growled a woman
with a long nose and darting, sneaky eyes. 'I've
seen your bleeding picture. You're the bitch in
charge of this whole bloody mess, the one supposed to be taking care.' And Georgie noticed
Gail Hopkins quietly closing her door.

'Should be inside with the bastard himself.'

A small woman in rollers and slippers wiggled a
thin forefinger and her eyes flashed with menace.
'And I hope you're bleeding satisfied. We knew
what was bloody going on. We knew. No fancy
education, no bleeding letters after our fucking
names, but we knew what was happening inside
there; we heard the kiddies crying and yet you did
fuck all about it.'

They were right, dear God, they were right.

All she wanted was to escape. Georgie was
surrounded, a drop to her right, all the way down
to that black asphalt. The crowd hostility was so
extreme, the eyes so full of blame, she was terrified. She could feel the hate on their breaths, she
tasted the bitter heat of their words. 'I only hope
one day you'll be able to forgive yourself because
you're just as much to sodding blame as that bitch
in there.'

'More to blame if you ask me . . .'

'Murderer!'

'Cunt.'

'You sodding bitch.'

'You've got the front to come round here . . .'

Quite unable to face them, unable to cope with any of this, trembling and shocked, Georgie backed away. They called out their sickening insults long after she'd pushed herself free and negotiated the corridor, and she could still hear the echoes of their screams as she stifled her tears and careered blindly down the dark concrete staircase. Her body blundered on but her mind stayed to take the blame. Her own shadow loomed and terrified her as she floundered through the series of alleys that made up the estate. White and shaken, she longed for the security of her car and its central locking system, a tiny slither of silver to keep her attackers at bay. Were they coming after her with hard stones of righteousness in their hands? It took two hours of agony, she had read, for a woman to be stoned to death. Dreamlike, she seemed to be moving so slowly. And if this angry posse had been waiting for her, how much worse must it be for poor Gail every time she went out with the kids. For Gail, flight was impossible, although Georgie's super-ficial escape only led to self-torture. The minute Georgie got home, *if she got home, please God*, she would ring Helen, Roger, Suzie, Isla, even Mark would do, any number of friends and colleagues who might understand and calm her down.

Tell her she was not guilty.

But no-one could take the pain away, however sympathetic they were, *no-one could make her feel better*.

In her agony of confusion and despair Georgie had not considered that this might be Gail Hopkins's attitude. She always used to deny Ray's violence, so why should she now, when faced with this terrible reality, change her mind or lower her defences? And yet Georgie had not considered the possibility of such deliberate obtuseness.

Was it conceivable that all the experts were wrong and that Gail Hopkins was right? Was there the remotest possibility that Angie had fallen downstairs? No, not in a million years. Not with all those professional opinions . . . Georgie corrected her crazy thinking. She gripped the steering wheel in her trembling hands. She dreaded, in those days, that she might lose concentration, that her car would skid off the road, that she would be involved in an accident and kill a child. *Another child*. The terror of that, at one point in time, had almost stopped her from driving.

Georgie stirred from her stillness, sighed and forced herself to bank up the fire. She would sleep in Stephen's bed tonight and hope for a comfortable, more satisfying sleep than last night's uncomfortable vigil beside the fire. She hugged herself as she moved into the cold kitchen to make coffee. The chinking crockery inside the house contrasted with the soulless screeching of an owl somewhere outside. Made nervous by this splitting of the night, she searched for something stronger than coffee. If the wily Chad Cramer had removed Stephen's empties he had not brought them back, and there was no sign of any bottles unopened. Christ, she could do with a drink. But she calculated, probably correctly, that Cramer thought he could get away with a few crates of booze.

And then Georgie steeled herself for the half longed for, half dreaded unveiling of Stephen's paintings; she would have to decide which ones she wanted and which she was willing to leave behind. She would probably never return to this place. Once the cottage was on the market she was sure it would sell fairly quickly.

A self-portrait somewhere, Donna had said. And there he was, her brother, Stephen, a ghostly apparition in oils staring innocently from the canvas, lost under a large Panama and too-long khaki shorts. All those years ago Sylvia had said, 'Fancy making up a brother. How very peculiar, darling. What a very odd thing to do.'

And the shame of her lie was deep and lasting.

'He caused Daddy and me all sorts of terrible grief, and when he left home it was merely the end of a long and anguished period for us.'

But now. A reunion at last. Stephen's smiling, genial eyes stared opaquely into her own, the deep crevasses in his face were painfully, deeply drawn, but the mouth was wide and generous. She noticed his badly bitten nails, and from this she could deduce he was given to times of secret thinking. Such a sad and crooked smile. He carried a light canvas bag with what looked like a

145

folded easel and an artist's stool strapped to his side. She could almost see him breathe in and out under his collarless shirt, so realistic was the likeness. *Speak to me, Stephen, speak to me.* And if he resembled her, as Donna had suggested, Georgie could not see it. Stephen was the kind of man she might once have fallen in love with, and she remembered how common this reaction was when parted siblings were introduced. Georgie leaned forward, hands gripped across her knees, a determined look on her face. She fully intended, by concentrating hard and letting her imagination take her away, to understand and keep her lost brother with her for ever. In the quiet she experienced a peculiar peace. She kissed him on the forehead and wept. Too late. Too late. Just another little stone on the mounting cairn that buried the past.

Eleven

Surely this is the witching hour. Four o'clock in the morning comes secretly and in great quiet. Soon the world will arise out of darkness. More people choose to die and more innocent replacements are born at this hour than at any other in the twenty-four. It was Lola, scratching at the door, who alerted Georgie to the noxious smell.

After she'd dragged herself down the stairs, fuddled and confused, Georgie realized with relief that the smell was coming from somewhere outside.

Wide awake now, nerves on edge, she opened the back door and was knocked back by the foul vapour that billowed straight from the woodshed. Corrosive. A chemical fire? But how? And she was certain she'd closed the shed door last night after she'd brought in the last load of wood.

At home she'd have rushed back indoors and dialled the fire brigade. Onlookers would have gathered by now, there'd be a crowd in the street. But here, in the back end of nowhere, what the hell should she do? Tearing down the road for the neighbours would be a waste of precious time. There she was, this capable woman, shivering on her back doorstep, tearing at her brain for the options. *Fire! Fire!* But there were none of the crackling sounds that come from leaping flames, just a slow and steady smouldering, oozing a noxious yellow. Perhaps whatever it was in there could be dealt with. Perhaps she should take a look. Cautiously, holding her breath, she snaked her arm round the open door and snapped on the light. Her eyes stung as she peered inside. She was right, there were no flames – as yet – and the pungent cloud was spiralling out from the far corner that was full of junk. The logs were piled from floor to ceiling at the opposite side of the shed, and thank the Lord there were no sparks or the place would go up, an inferno.

In fact, the smoke was more like the sickening belching that came from industrial chimneys, reeking of solvents and chemicals, poisonous to the system. Georgie dashed back to the kitchen, tearing her hair as she waited for the slow flow of water to half fill the galvanized bucket, gritting her teeth, cursing, peering out of the door at the gathering, billowing cloud. She snatched up the bucket and covered her mouth with her free hand, but by the time she stumbled the few yards to the woodshed her eyes were smarting.

She neared the source of the vicious vapour. It looked like a pile of old clothing, rags, discarded overalls, paint-spattered and torn. In spite of the light this corner was dark, and she kicked aside a worn-out floor mop, a mouldy square of carpet and a washing-up bowl with a hole in the bottom. Not knowing if this was a fatal error, if water would make matters even worse, she dashed it onto the smouldering pile and the smoke hovered, still for a moment, before the fumes continued to billow, but weakly and more blackly. Thank God she had made some sort of progress. Back she rushed for more water, muttering tensely under her breath. Again she soaked the heap of rags, a third time, then a fourth, until from lack of breath and exertion her face was a boiled red and her breathing came in frantic gasps.

But, thank God, the fire was out. And then, underneath the burning came the stench of household cleaner, so something of that sort, not petrol, must have been used to start the fire. *There'd been nothing accidental about it.* Georgie's skin crawled. Fear pricked under her arms and she gave a sudden shudder. She swallowed quickly to clear her parched throat, because hell, who would do something like this? The fire, had it spread, could have been lethal. If the wood had caught the cottage could have been razed to the ground, with her and Lola sleeping upstairs, rendered senseless by the fumes. Christ. God. *Who would do something like that?* Surely even Chad Cramer was not that ill-intentioned. Surely even he would not be so mindlessly evil?

She could think but she could not feel. Reason told her that everything that had happened was simple and straightforward. This was not an attack. This was an accident. The night was passing. A little while ago the gutters had been overflowing, but now the flow had become just a steady drip. Apart from this an audible silence enveloped the house. Some sensible instinct made Georgie search the ground outside, something to

149

do with tell-tale footprints, but the snow lay in puddles and patches and she could find nothing. Maybe, because of the time of night, she was building this whole thing up into something far too sinister. There was a possibility that something self-igniting had been left behind in the mess, some tin that, reacting to the freezing temperature, had cracked open; substances can be volatile, especially if they are carelessly abandoned. She really knew very little about exposure and evaporation. Rust, thought Georgie logically, could possibly cause a reaction.

With an old curtain rod she found on the floor, Georgie poked at the dormant pile. Carefully and slowly she moved what looked like an old pillow case, a filthy face flannel, a sleeve torn from a shirt; she pulled the layers off the top of the mound, going about the job so cautiously she felt like a surgeon removing dressings, approaching the crux of the matter, the wound. The stench of solution grew stronger as she delved, as did the mildew smell of age.

Oh dear God, no. The doll's plastic face had fallen in with the heat, but its eyes were wide open and its cherubic mouth stayed smiling. The fire-blisters on its concave cheeks looked like tears turned into plague sores. With dawning horror she sensed that she and her bent curtain rod had been disturbing the creature's bed. The bits of rags she'd assumed were rubbish were what it had been wrapped in, lovingly and with care. But it was these rags that were soaked in the acid solution. The give-away cylindrical tin lay close by the doll, like a terrible hot-water bottle, leaking over its legs and onto the blankets around it. What was left of its hair was charred, but the residue showed it was near-bald anyway. There were tiny rashlike holes in the plastic skull where the hair had once been, and it looked as though it had suffered from some incurable nervous affliction.

Georgie searched. There was no sign of matches.

She left the doll just as it was, maimed and burned. She did not want to touch it.

From horror to horror. From the unspeakable to the fantastic. From Angie Hopkins and the stuff of the untouchable to the terrifying fabrications of fiction.

She had chosen a doll because she had never seen one among the toys in the Hopkins's flat.

So was it coincidence that Georgie had found the burning doll, so similar in size and shape to the one she had chosen from Anne Stubbs's office high up on the third floor of the social services building only three months earlier? Coincidence or not, it was cruelly significant, especially in the middle of the night when the brain is so suggestible, when there are so many dark thoughts which daylight holds at bay.

A doll called Mandy in a cellophane box with a neat little case full of its own clothes. She did not take toys to the Hopkinses because they were needy, she took each child a toy merely because it was Christmas, and as a visitor she should bring gifts. The doll was for Angie, of course. For Patsy,

151

aged four, she had taken a Noah's Ark full of colourful animals, and for the youngest, Carmen, she'd chosen a clockwork frog for the bath.

The visit before Christmas was the last time she saw Angie alive and, unusually, Ray was home. As normal Georgie had expected the door to stay closed. She had planned to call, leave a warning note and return that same afternoon, but it was Ray who opened the door. She'd been scrabbling in her bag for a pen, that is why she looked up at him, at the quietly opening door. There was surprise and some confusion.

'Oh, it's you,' said Ray, devoid of any expression.

She had met him on one previous occasion. She smiled and held out her hand. The handshake was cold, the flesh hardly meeting. No grasp, the grasp was done quickly with the eyes. Unlike his wife's Ray's eyes were a pale, cold blue and his wheat-coloured hair was cropped close to his hefty bullet-shaped head.

She bundled into the flat with her parcels, following Ray Hopkins through.

'Day off today?' she asked him casually, and he grunted a reply she couldn't catch.

Gail hurried in from the kitchen and took up her position on the sofa in haste, slightly irritated, thought Georgie, as though she'd been caught on the hop, ill-prepared.

'Don't let me interrupt if you're busy,' said Georgie, taking her usual seat in the armchair to the left of the telly. Ray stepped in front of her to turn down the sound.

'No,' Gail shook her head. She tightened the rubber band, twisting it round the knob of hair that stuck from the back of her head in a stunted ponytail. As usual she wore her patterned leggings and a long, knee-length jumper. 'No,' she said, 'it wasn't important.'

'No sign of the children?' Georgie asked her easily. 'I thought they'd be on holiday.'

'Patsy's asleep upstairs, and Carmen was tired so I put her down, too. They get fed up,' said Gail, suddenly annoyed, probably by Georgie's unscheduled visit. 'The holidays are too bleeding long. Especially when you're stuck up here with no bleeding space.'

'And Angie?'

'Angie's running messages,' said Ray Hopkins.

'That's a shame. Perhaps she'll be back before I go. I've brought them their Christmas presents.'

'There's no need for you to do that,' said Ray aggressively, so much younger than his wife, with a face unlined and fleshy. He had chosen the other armchair, and now he sat in it lazily, his long legs stretched across the carpet so that Georgie had to pull hers in. 'They get enough without needing charity from the social. They get enough rubbish at Christmas time.'

'I'm sure they do,' she agreed with him. 'But this is not a charity visit.'

'What? You went and bought them yourself, did you, with your own bleeding money? Nah. Don't tell me that. What sort of visit would you say it is then, Mrs Jefferson?' He held her eyes as he asked her this question, laying emphasis on her name to make it sound slightly absurd, as if she amused him, as if he was sneering. His wife sat watching from the sofa, silent, still fiddling with her hair.

'This is one of my regular visits, as Gail will tell you, to make sure that everything's going OK. To give you a chance to discuss any problems, to give me a chance to talk to Angie.'

Ray Hopkins's eyes did not shift. 'But Angie's out.'

'And to deliver my presents to the children.'

Gail sat forward suddenly, the wariness in her eyes like a skin. 'Would you stay for a cup of tea, Mrs Jefferson?'

It was something to do with Ray's belligerent, challenging attitude that made Georgie accept, while truthfully all she wanted to do was leave and come back when Angie was home. She could not allow this man to believe that his presence had driven her out. There he sat with his long legs splayed, a T-shirt tucked into blue jeans and huge trainers on his feet, the laces untied. Both his head and his feet looked disproportionately large compared to the rest of his chunky body, his neck was too thick to support his head and his thighs were almost chubby. Something about Ray's fleshiness suggested corruption. Gail left the room to turn on the kettle, and the silence that settled was just as intrusive as the pictures that crossed the TV screen, the pictures that pull your eyes all the more when they are without sound.

But small talk, in these circumstances, would be inappropriate.

'I hear Angie had a brilliant report.' Yes, she had to speak to break the silence.

'Yep. Not the sort of thing you'd expect from a battered kid.'

'Nobody's saying that Angie's been battered, Mr Hopkins.' Georgie sighed. 'You know yourself we are only acting in her interests based on the concerns of several professional people.' But the words sounded weary. She'd had this same conversation with Ray the first time they met.

'And that's enough, is it? That's enough to make you feel you can push your way in here and come prying and nosing about, making us feel like God knows what with your nasty bleeding suspicions . . .'

Georgie leaned forward, difficult with her legs tucked in, but Ray's were still taking up half the floor. 'I do wish we could clear up this antagonism and take a more positive attitude, Mr Hopkins. I have no choice but to come here, it's my job, and if it wasn't me it would be somebody else. You know what the specialist report suggested when Angie broke her arm, and all the other numerous instances when she's turned up at school with bumps and bruises, falling asleep at her desk. Surely we don't need to work through this again . . . ?'

'I just wish you bastards would get off our backs. How long does this nosing go on before you're convinced? Months? Years? I'd just like to know how sodding long . . .'

'Until we feel satisfied . . .'

'Until you feel satisfied, you mean . . .'

'All right then, yes, until I feel satisfied . . .'

'Tell me this then. What would satisfy you, Mrs Jefferson?' And his voice was laden with contained fury, but on his face was a smile.

At this point the door was pushed open. Georgie looked up, relieved, expecting Gail with the tea, but it was Angie, still in her nightie; it looked as if she'd just woken up. Confused and nervous, one finger between her lips as if she thought she'd done something wrong, she crossed the room and sat down on the sofa, one eye on her father. In a low, subdued voice she said, 'I didn't know there was anyone here.'

'I thought you were running errands,' said Georgie, glancing at Ray Hopkins.

'If we hadn't bleeding well said she was out you'd have gone and disturbed the kid.' His anger was more visible now. His face was hard, the baby chubbiness seemed to have left it. 'And the kid's tired out. She needs her sleep. She was late to bed last night.'

Bewildered, Georgie shook her head. 'But why didn't you just tell me that? Why lie at all?' Was the man speaking the truth? And if not, what was the point of his lying?

'And would you have let her sleep? Or would you have gone interfering upstairs?'

'Oh, it really doesn't matter.' How Georgie hated the way difficult discussions in this house took place in front of the children. They were all sitting there with flushed faces, eyes sliding sideways. She could see the concern on Angie's face, the way the child twisted her hands, tormented, as she turned her head to her mother's husband and back to Georgie again, trying to work out what was happening, aware of the tension, afraid she had caused it. 'It doesn't matter in the least. It's just good to see her.' She turned her attention to Angie. 'When you're woken up properly, or when I've gone, whenever you like, you can open your parcel. Patsy's and Carmen's are in the bag, too, perhaps you can give them theirs when they wake up, later on.'

Angie rested her questioning eyes on Ray Hopkins.

'Go on then,' he told her roughly. 'Open it. Mrs Jefferson's brought you a present. You might as well open it.'

Reluctantly Angie slid off the sofa, her long nightdress trailing at her heels as she approached the bag. The atmosphere was toe-curlingly awful, but there was no way, now, that Georgie could turn it round. When Gail arrived with the tray she rested it on the coffee table and resumed her place on the sofa. Angie, the present in her arms, went to snuggle up beside her.

The child unwrapped the parcel with an oddly neat precision, finding the joins, removing the Sellotape, folding it after her, making no mess. All the while she licked her lips and occasionally glanced at her mother for reassurance. Georgie sipped her tea and attempted to make conversation, to take the spotlight off the poor child, but the other two adults in the room refused to respond. They just continued to stare at Angie, watching her every move, and when she pulled the doll from the wrappings she took control of the whole situation with her broad smile and her exclamation. They were all back to acting again. And little Angie was taking the lead. No-one was more aware of the fact that it was important she do well.

She did.

She became engrossed in the unpinning of the clothes from the case, laying them, one by one, on her knee, admiring every outfit while she rocked the doll in her arms. At one point she held up the doll for general admiration, and Georgie's heart sank when she noticed the doll's expression matched that of the child: bright, pert and moulded in plastic.

Just like the smouldering doll in the woodshed.

The whole incident was so disturbing there was no sleep for Georgie that night. Even Lola stayed awake and alert. Dawn seemed a long way off and she wished she had a phone; it was five thirty in the morning but she longed to talk to somebody sane.

Her fear subsided and Georgie built up the fire, made a comforting hot drink and took some final decisions as to which of Stephen's pictures she'd keep. She was tempted to keep most of them. Either it was the effect of the booze as it gradually warped his brain, or Stephen had been experimenting with a new and primitive style, but a few of his paintings were quite inexplicable. Angrily done, in a chaos of colour, it looked as if the paint was applied with the heel of a hand or a fist daubed with oils. These were unnerving to put it mildly. They were messy, with no centre, no beginning and no end; it was hard to know where to rest the eye without that feeling of riot in your forehead.

Although Georgie didn't want these, she felt she ought to take them. Because if, at some point, this was Stephen's message to the world, then she, as his sister, should take them on board, and not reject them because they were worrying.

Despite a search she'd found no personal letters. Not one. Just the usual bills and receipts, a menu from a Chinese restaurant, mail-order catalogue forms for paints and canvas from a company in Exeter. There were odd shopping lists which he must have given to the sour Mrs Buckpit, and there was a sheath of order forms, spares, which he'd obviously used for his generous monthly supplies of gin. All these she had sorted out earlier, boxed up and put beside the dustbin for eventual collection.

She was glad that someone related had done this.

There was nothing among his personal effects that Georgie wanted apart from a few books and tapes. She wished she did, she wished there had been something she could have felt fond of, some ornament, some jar or lamp which might have meant something to Stephen and which struck a chord with his long-lost sister. Sadly there was nothing like that, nothing that would go in her flat.

So when, later that morning, Georgina Jefferson left Furze Pen Cottage with her weekend case and a bootful of paintings, she left the memory of the burning doll firmly behind her. She had no intention of ever returning. She thought she would never see Wooton-Coney or Stephen's cottage again.

Twelve

As Georgie drove away a pale-blue sky stretched over the valley and a low sun lit the boggy moorland and wrapped it in mother-of-pearl. A brief joy jumped out of nowhere and swamped her. What is the mischief of the gods, she thought, that throws us these moments of promise? Or is it not a promise at all, more like the blooming of a flower, merely its own justification?

She approached the solicitor's ill-lit, Dickensian office with a swing in her stride and was astonished to hear his news. 'We have received an extremely generous offer for the cottage. Unfortunately it arrived on Friday, so there was no way we could contact you.'

How very peculiar. 'But, Mr Selby, it's not even on the market.'

The gnarled old man with the manic white Einstein hairstyle, stretched out a palsied, papery hand and passed the letter across. The threadbare office held the faintest smell of cheese and beer, or did that come from Mr Selby? Bespectacled and earnest, he sat at a large roll-top desk littered with yellowed papers and files. The marks on his face, the age marks, were like ink spots used by psychiatrists. Georgie settled in a worn leather chair next to a spluttering gas fire that did little to raise the temperature. The walls were hung with sporting pictures with stale jokes underneath, as stale as the office itself. 'As you will see, this document fails to tell us who the prospective purchasers are. For some reason they do not wish to declare their interests at this stage, thus they are working through solicitors themselves. But it must be someone who knows the cottage, and knows it is about to be disposed of.'

But who on earth would possess such knowledge? She had only just decided herself. With frozen hands Georgie leafed through the letter. Old Tom Selby was right. The offer was generous and she would be a fool to ignore it. Mr Selby wheedled home his message, his wheezing voice crackling like paper. 'In the distressed condition the cottage is in, and the amount that would need spending on it to bring it up to scratch, there is little doubt, Mrs Jefferson, that you should consider this offer very seriously indeed. And, as you see,' he pointed with a restless forefinger, 'the interested party would like an answer fairly quickly.'

'Perhaps we should start the ball rolling.' After the weekend she'd just experienced Georgie agreed wholeheartedly with the wizened old man in the dusty old suit.

'I will put the matter in hand immediately.'

His face cracked into an uncomfortable smile and it was obvious that Thomas Selby was eager to get the whole business concluded.

'It would certainly be much easier to sell it like

this rather than go through the trauma of adverts and viewers.'

'Yes,' he agreed, rubbing his hands, which must have been as cold as her own. 'A most convenient offer. I wish all my work was as simple as this. A most satisfactory conclusion to the whole rather sad affair. As we have already discovered, the residents of Wooton-Coney are rather eccentric and cannot be relied upon, indeed, the lady of the farm, Mrs Buckpit, was even reluctant to hold the key. We could not have expected much help from that quarter.'

'Well.' Georgie sat back, relieved. 'That's settled then. And with the recovery of the furniture I think I can say that the whole weekend has been extremely constructive.'

'An unsavoury business.' Mr Selby's reaction to Cramer's untimely removal of the furniture had been grave. 'And one, of course, of which we were completely unaware, I hope you understand.' He spluttered his disapproval and waved his arms like a tired swimmer.

Georgie wondered if she should mention the fire. Naturally it still worried her. Not only the fire itself and whether it was deliberate or not, but the bizarre discovery of the doll – not the sort of item which Stephen might have inadvertently picked up with his other bits and pieces. As far as Georgie knew there were no children in Wooton-Coney. It did not feel as if the place had ever had children . . .

But what was the point of mentioning it? Mr Selby could hardly offer twenty-four-hour protection of the place when she'd gone, and the police were unlikely to make regular calls on so isolated a home. There was no sign that an arsonist had attempted to torch the place before, and Georgie tried to put it down to one of those inexplicable incidents that happen in life without reason. She was going back to London. She had more immediate concerns on her mind. It was important to keep things in proportion, and she was glad to be relieved of responsibility for Furze Pen Cottage, visiting at awkward times, showing people round . . .

So she left the key with Tom Selby and set off on the long journey home, with Lola asleep in the passenger seat.

Selling houses. Sale agreed. Sold. Four years ago, and selling her childhood home had felt like selling her past. All the hiding places went with it, the dens, unseen, unlabelled in the particulars, so many hidden things excluded from the brochure, not just the rising damp.

And she had found herself closing her eyes in certain rooms, as if the smartly dressed couples with the critical eyes could somehow sense an atmosphere, ghostly conversations seeping from the sepia walls, quick footsteps, voices hard with hate, hard smiles. All the furniture was still inside. Well, Georgie herself didn't want it, and it was all exactly the same; in all the years they'd never changed a thing save for the odd renewal of curtains and covers. Even in this new adult role Georgie was still the child in this house, controlled, hidden, polite, smiling with her hellos and goodbyes and gagging on the mothballs.

And it was while she had waited there to show prospective purchasers round, alone in all that neat brown silence, that she'd felt the worst of the weariness that dragging house always gave her. The smell of pipe smoke still filled the house, not present as an actual cloud, but more like a ghost, a strong, stale smell. Black umbrellas, brown walking sticks and cream, lacy tray cloths – tight, formal things, so innocent in themselves, but they came together in that creaking house to make such a sad song. Even the rattle of the curtains took her back, the full feel of the banister underneath her hand, almost tacky with polish, and the slightly slippery rugs on the floors on long brown landings. All very Fifties.

The dining room was the worst place of all, and she realized that, in spirit, she had always loitered here at the door, unwilling to venture further. She had always seen this place from the threshold.

She could have been a courier on a coach, reciting the past as they drove through it all, waving a casual hand at her childhood. 'This is where they used to eat,' she could have told them abstractedly, as if her parents were long extinct, as if she was speaking of some rare and ancient tribe of man. Shining with wax, the dining room table was monarch of the room and everything else subservient to it. 'At all other times of day they spoke to each other and saw each other no more than necessary. They were polite and passed. But not so in the dining room. This is where we were summoned by a gong, the one you passed in the hall earlier. Breakfast. Lunch. Dinner. Human suffering amid the mahogany. We all emerged from our private dens and here, at the door, we put on our faces, collected our voices before we sat down. See that chair at the side of the table, well, that chair was mine, while Father sat at the top and Mother at the opposite end. I, as you appreciate, sat between them. Sometimes I passed their words, at others I passed the salt.'

The silence was violence.

Conversation was ominous.

'Food was irrelevant but we had to eat it. I can never remember being hungry. I wanted something but it wasn't food. Brown gravy in gravy boats and brown slices of meat which Father carved with that same knife there, the one with the brownish, ivory handle.'

Georgina could have gone on and said, 'Look, there's my old silver napkin ring with my name inscribed on the side. It was given to me by an aunt at my christening. I wonder if she gave one to Stephen.'

Dear God, those endless meal times. The general comments were safe, and most of it was general comment interspersed with chewing. But when three or four pieces of comment were strung together to make conversation, that is when the going got tough, the jaw began to ache, looks were exchanged, throats were cleared and the sound of silver scraping on crockery grew unbearably loud.

'My mother would dab at the corner of her mouth with a napkin, she did it so much there were sore places there.' This was not the room they thought they saw. 'And her green raffia bag from Madeira was invariably placed beside her feet, that side of the chair. By the end of the meal the handkerchief which she kept up her sleeve would be out, creased, sweaty and tattered.'

This is how it would go:

'I met Isabel Evans in town today. We had coffee. She asked to be remembered.'

And Harry Southwell would lift his eyes from his plate to murmur, 'Oh yes.'

'They're moving to Bath, apparently.'

'Well, his family come from there.'

'They've always been a close family.'

This irrelevance would be digested.

'I have ordered the logs. They are coming to-morrow,' her father might announce.

'So someone will have to be in,' Sylvia would say, brittlely, dabbing at her mouth.

'I just assumed that somebody would be.'

An angry flush flew over her cheekbones. 'It might have been nice to have been consulted.'

A heavy sigh from Harry's end. 'I cannot consult you on every damn issue . . .'

'It just would have been . . .'

'For Christ's sake, Sylvia . . .'

'And why are we still ordering logs from the Turnbills when there's that new man . . . ?'

'If you would like to order the logs, dear, then you must say so. I would quite happily delegate that responsibility any time . . .'

'Oh, do stop being so absurd . . .'

'Oh, I'm so sorry. I ought to have realized . . .'

167

'But you don't realize, do you, Harry, that's the trouble, you never have realized . . .'

Silence. The sounds of heavy digestion, and Georgie felt she was interfering, annoying them by just sitting there, as a morsel of gristle might annoy.

And then, 'When did you order the *Radio Times*? I told them at Buntings it wasn't ours. I told them we don't take the *Radio Times*, never have, and Mrs Betts said you'd been in and ordered it last week.'

Sylvia, plying her knife and fork with the utmost delicacy, said mildly, 'It's easier having the *Radio Times*.'

'And what is wrong with looking in the paper?'

The clock on the mantelpiece rang half-past one, its tinklings unnoticed by either opponent. From the lime trees outside came the chatter of sparrows and from behind the shrubbery the burble of pigeons. There was such a thin slither between the world of normality out there and this vicious ritual. If only the walls were of cardboard, Georgie could put out one finger and knock them down for ever. Some other part of her mind could see the radiance outside and faraway like a golden cloud. But these walls were solid and square, shutting the three of them off from every other soul in the world. 'I can never find the bally paper, Harry, that's the whole point. You always take the paper and disappear off with it, and then I find it somewhere obscure like the greenhouse.'

The light in Harry's eye was now as angry as his wife's. He worked his fork rapidly and vigorously.

'I take the paper because I know damn well you never bother to read it.'

'Well, I need to see what's on TV. That's why I ordered the *Radio Times*. So you don't have to worry about taking the paper away now, do you? If we didn't have such a dry, boring paper maybe I would read it.'

'It would have been more sensible, Sylvia, if you had ordered a paper like the *Sketch*, instead of the *Radio Times*. The sort of paper you might enjoy.'

'There is nothing wrong with the *Sketch*.' Sylvia's lower lip was thrust forward obstinately.

'Not if you enjoy scandal and overt pornography, no.'

A cold, silvery laugh. Sylvia had sharpened her stilettos and was determined to use them. 'Pornography! My God, Harry, you wouldn't know what pornography looked like if it slapped you in the face.'

'*For God's sake.*' His eyes lit up angrily. He slammed his knife and fork on the table.

Silence sat between them for a while and mingled with the smell of mint sauce.

'I don't know how much more of this I can take.' There'd be much scrabbling at the handkerchief. 'I've had it up to here and I really don't think I can carry on with all this . . .'

'You don't have to take it, Sylvia.' Although Harry spoke quietly his fists were clenched, starched as the cloth, and his mouth, under his fierce moustache, was a grim, thin-lipped straight line.

'Oh? *Oh?* And what is my alternative? This house is mortgaged up to the hilt, I have no means of earning a living, I have given my life to you and Georgina,' – there was never any mention of Stephen – 'and what do I get in return? No gratitude. No respect. Just a miserable existence cutting corners, having to manage this blasted mausoleum with only one maid in the house . . .' etc . . . etc. And when she had finished, she sat there panting while Harry chewed on the stem of his pipe, puffing its contents into furious life.

The voices were always controlled, never raised.

Silence. A much longer one this time. And Georgie might dare to chip in with, 'I might be going riding tomorrow. Sarah said if I helped her clean the stables this morning I could have a free ride tomorrow afternoon.' Her mind wandered and babbled.

But her words would be swallowed by quick sips of water as the battle subsided, as the contestants refreshed themselves ready for round two.

And then there were those tough little puddings: syrup tart, burned jam sponge, hard pieces of pineapple with bits in, blancmanges with leathery skins. And every time Gwyneth or Megan put her head through the hatch there was a stony silence, and every time that hatch was closed they'd be off again with some harmless comment that piled and flowed into conversation, thick and enveloping as the custard.

Georgie would have to explain to the viewers

that they'd always had live-in staff. 'This was their room, this mean little bedsit next to the kitchen, filled with ill-matching odds and sods: the old-fashioned telly, the glued ornaments, the Lloyd loom chair.' The staff never stayed long. Most of them came from Wales, and Georgie used to wonder why so many rosy-cheeked girls left their homeland and came to live and work here. Why would anyone choose to live here? The idea was incredible. No wonder they cried so frequently. She would come upon them all over the place, dusters in their hands and hopeless tears running down their faces. It was only when she got older she learned why they got fatter and fatter. They had their babies in the nearby mother and baby home, gave them up for adoption and went.

The girls got their keep, nothing more. This was just somewhere to hide their shame from the sad little valleys they came from. A charitable venture most convenient for embarrassed gentlefolk with large houses.

She might stop and explain in the hall. 'My parents loathed each other, you see, that's the musty feeling you can taste on your tongue. Their hatred. And I can't understand why they stayed together, but then people tended to do that in those days. Not like now.'

And then she might show them the drinks cupboard, sticky still, with the sort of stain you can't scrub off. No household cleaner is strong enough to take away that kind of stain. And her teeth might clench as the shudder passed through her and she saw the drunken eyes, smelled the sweet stench coming towards her, between the teeth in the dark . . . no wonder . . . poor Stephen. They say it is genetic. How come it affected Stephen, not her? A nasty little bequest. She demanded a key to her room in the end and spent her holidays at Daisy's.

How could she ever invite her friends there? Her mother was wicked to suggest that she could.

But in spite of all this, Georgie managed to sell the house to a nice respectable couple with children, who were not put off by the terrible brownness or the clinging of pain.

Perhaps they didn't even notice.

She thought about this as she drove back to London, dreading what lay in store for her there, the internal inquiry was starting tomorrow, but with the worry of selling the cottage off her mind, and with Stephen's paintings stacked in the boot.

She was looking forward to choosing her favourites and hanging them up round her flat. She would enjoy showing friends, especially the self-portrait. Discussing them. Exploring them. A family she could talk about at last, a brother she could display with pride.

And Wooton-Coney seemed far away, as unreachable as any fantasy world.

Thirteen

Her head felt as though it had burst right open –
at eleven thirty that night a brick came smashing
through Georgie's window.

After so many disturbed nights she was exhausted anyway, relieved to be back in her own
bed, just dropping off, reaching that dreamy unreal stage when she heard the explosion and
leaped up, heart bursting, dry eyes pulsing.

The first terror was that some madman had
broken into the flat. The screaming quiet after the
crash buzzed in her ears as she tried to listen.
Cautiously she got out of bed, slipping into her
dressing gown as she crossed the hall and entered
the kitchen. The draught drew her gaze to the
window. Jagged shards of glass strew the carpet
and a little drizzle dampened the place where she
stood. Timidly Georgie stepped forward to draw
the curtains before attempting the light. She trod
on the brick on her way to the switch. 'Jesus
Christ!' she shivered in terror, standing still while
she stared down helplessly at the crude, broken
weapon, clutching her dressing gown more firmly
round her for whatever protection that might
afford.

If she had been slightly less tired she might
have been able to summon some anger, because it

was there all right, a knot in her chest, bulging furiously, screaming to be unravelled and pulled to pieces. But she couldn't reach it and was left instead with the dry-mouthed, panicky cold of fear. Was the invisible enemy still out there watching, waiting to throw something else? Was their intention to frighten her stiff? Or were they after more than that, actual bodily harm? She thought about Gail Hopkins; these same attacks were happening to her, poor Gail had even had shit shoved through her letter box, impossible here because the flat was on the first floor and the front door was automatically controlled by the residents only.

Oh God, she prayed that one of the residents had not been careless tonight – it had been known to happen, somebody came in late, worse for wear, and forgot to click the door after them. Of course, she had never done that herself. Georgie has more self-control.

So how do you deal with this sort of hatred? 'You mustn't take it personally,' Helen Mace used to say. 'You have to understand, Georgie, there are a lot of sick sods out there who wriggle to life whenever there's an excuse for violence. These warped buggers aren't worthy of your attention. They are sick and they need help, and if you allow this disease to touch you you're playing straight into their hands.'

'But I'm the one who needs help, dammit. It's easy to say they are sick, and I'm quite prepared to give them, whoever they are, the benefit of the doubt. But it's me they are after, Helen! And bit by bit, no matter how ill they are, they are destroying me!'

'Only because you're letting them.'

'So how do I protect myself? How the hell can anyone dismiss such hostile aggression? You can't just smile and wave it away. I feel like a kid again, Helen, just as helpless as I was as a child.'

If only Toby was alive it would mean all the difference in the world. Georgie was all the more vulnerable because she lived alone, with nobody of her own to rely on, to hold her or make her better. What was the point of ringing up friends? Who would honestly welcome a phone call at one o'clock in the morning? She didn't come first with anyone. Feeling more lonely than ever, and drenched in self-pity, she whispered distraughtly into the silence, 'Who are you? *Who are you and why are you following me?* Don't you think I am suffering enough with a child's death on my hands? *Don't you think the fire was punishment enough?*' Holding herself together with difficulty she went to fetch a dustpan and brush, 'It's OK, Lola, it's OK,' and began, slowly and meticulously, to pick up every slither of glass. Tears of fear and self-pity began. The glass shone with rainbow prisms as she stared at it through her lashes, and she loathed herself. Her shame was total as she recognized the feelings – *resentment and blame* – resentment towards little Angie for allowing herself to die, blaming the child for her own predicament, and hatred, *yes, hatred*, because of her own unbearable unhappiness.

Who said Georgie was blameless? She was as

guilty as the murderer, more so, she was grotesque!

She ought to ring someone up, but just couldn't face those same old platitudes, apart from the fact that her friends must see her as a bore and a nuisance by now. So she sat to attention on the sofa with the light on and the kitchen curtains gently blowing. She tried to watch the TV, but it was some mindless American game show and the canned laughter was mocking. Anyway, that was no good in case she missed some stealthy movement outside. She was far too nervous to pick up a book, to concentrate on anything. The wet patch on the curtain was growing. She fondled Lola's ears distractedly. She couldn't stand any more of this. She would have to move, she would have to flee and let nobody know where she was so these maniacs couldn't find her. She wept, unable to control herself. In spite of her secret hopes, the weekend in Devon had been nothing but a small distraction. It had done nothing to help her, she was back in the same old purgatory again, right in the middle of the monster which threatened to gobble her up.

Mercifully, by morning, matters did not seem quite so desperate. The threat of physical attack was gone, but other monsters were lying in wait, devils of a different kind. The internal inquiry was starting today, and although Georgie did not fear the outcome, by its very nature it was bound to be unpleasant. This would be no informal chat with sympathetic colleagues, this would be more like the dock. This would raise painful issues: her part in the tragedy. She would have to put into words experiences and impressions so deeply felt they ached. As Georgie changed and showered she thought dully that she would have preferred to face today feeling fresh, no sleepless nights banging her ears or the dull inertia of weariness.

'So how was Devon? Tell me about the cottage. I wish to God I'd come with you. I've had a hellish weekend and I'd have loved a couple of days away.'

She nearly fell on Helen's neck.

'Helen, you wouldn't believe a place like Wooton-Coney still existed. So prehistoric, so primitive, and the natives, my God. Now it all seems like a crazy dream. It's just not possible I was there yesterday, mixing with those oddballs.'

'You make it sound more tempting than ever. I've missed out on something bizarre. And what are you going to do about it, have you decided?'

Helen's driving was quick and competent. Perhaps it was her largeness that gave off the feeling of total safety, complete control of the car. Helen had insisted on collecting Georgie that morning and she had needed little persuasion. She would have hated to face this ordeal alone.

'I've already had an offer and, of course, I'm going to take it. Helen, it was unnerving being there for one weekend, let alone a few weeks in the summer. Not good. Definitely. Bad vibes etc. And I need the money urgently. I'm going to have to move from my flat.' Relief flooded through Georgie as she shared the terrors of last night with her friend, the calm and confident woman beside her. She was comforted and commiserated with, and Helen's large and comfortable hand moved from the gearstick and patted her knee.

How important human touch was proving to be.

'But it's not for much longer,' comforted Helen. 'You've got to keep that fact in your head. Soon all this hell will be over, it'll start to feel dream-like, as if you've never been there. Things always happen that way, no matter how awful. Everything fades in the end, and that's why it's so important you don't do something impulsive. I mean, you love your little flat.'

'Not any more I don't. Not now it's been invaded. It feels as if I've been invaded, almost as bad as rape.'

Helen glanced over and caught Georgie's eyes in the mirror. 'I do understand, you know.'

But Georgie found herself wanting to scream, *You say you do, but how can you?* And she knew if their positions were reversed she would be mouthing the same damn platitudes in the same tone of voice with the same concern. She moaned, 'I seem to get over one obstacle and then there's something else. It's beginning to feel never-ending, and I'm tired, Helen. Really tired.'

'The sooner this ordeal's over the better. And then it's obvious what you should do: get away for a good long time, somewhere warm, with lagoons and palm trees.'

Easy! So easy. Helen made everything sound so simple. And Georgie felt a fierce pang of yearning for Toby.

Helen's voice was tinged with anxiety. 'You do look tired. Worse than usual. Are you sure you can cope with this?'

Georgie's laugh was a cold one. 'Do I have an alternative?'

'No, not really.'

'Well then.'

The massed and pulsing life of London. A medley of noises, woven voices, hazes of sound. Pushing and sweating people. With a startled heart, Georgie glanced at the news-vendor's headlines, would she be headline news tonight? But no, surely not, this inquiry was private. How infinitesimal one really was – a grain of sand – so much tossed spume created and driven by unseen winds. The morning rush-hour traffic built up around them, and Georgie, shatteringly nervous, wished she was one of those faceless people sitting in the bus, rumbling and swinging, with a certainty about where they were going and why. Taken along with the nodding crowd. Oh, for a ticket to somewhere calm. How she would treasure it. How she would value normality now.

Eventually Helen dropped her off and disappeared in the jerking stream, just one more atom in the mass of metal, suddenly very insubstantial, and the sense of comfort drove away with her . . . too distant to call back.

The smiles Georgie faced were bright or sympathetic, nothing in between. Everyone knew why she was here. Even the conference room felt different, probably because they had cleaned it specially and it smelled oddly of polish. With her heart leaping and scuttling she thought about school, only the rubbery gymshoe smell was absent at this assembly. Acutely self-conscious, her shoes actually squeaked on the floor as she went to take her place at the table. She opened her briefcase and removed the fatal folder, placing it before her neatly, straightening it up with nervous hands, which is what she would have liked to have done with every word in the document.

She must face this day and be positive, no negative whimpering. This was being done for her benefit as much as anyone else's.

Conducting the inquiry was Andrew Finch, indifferent, formal, but a pleasant man, chair of the social services committee. When he took off his jacket the shirt underneath was startlingly white and ironed hard like paper. Roger Mace sat beside Georgie. He said, 'OK? This'll soon be over.'

But she was more than disconcerted by the tape recorder placed in the centre of the table. She'd never approved of her own voice, thinking it unconvincing.

Strangers and colleagues. They filed into the room casually carrying cups of coffee. They took their places and opened their files. They all glanced quickly at Georgie, who was acutely aware of their stares and the carefulness of their eyes; the lights put a shiny gloss on the room although it was not dark.

So many times now. Dear God, she'd been over this so many times. And this would not be the last time because the trial of Ray Hopkins was still to come, but that was some time in the future and Georgie could not think that far ahead. The process began. When she spoke she held her hands behind her back, she grasped a wrist tightly to stop any trembling. They questioned her politely and listened patiently to her answers while jotting down notes of their own, and the tape recorder made no sound as it spun round mindlessly gathering its awful information.

Outsiders, summonsed to help, came and went, and gave their views while Georgie sat with legs crossed and eyes gazing into emptiness. They were thanked for their time and their usefulness. Mrs Brightly the health visitor, the policewoman who visited Kurzon Mount Buildings, Angie's teacher who first raised the alarm – she looked older, more strained, and sent a sweet smile to Georgie before she left the room. No blame. It was essential for Georgie to know that they apportioned no blame. All they could do was get to the truth and try to prevent such a tragedy ever happening again.

Some hope.

So impossible.

At coffee time Georgie stood beside Claire Bettison, an old friend she had not seen since university days. At first she was thrilled to see her, the chance to talk over old times seemed tempting, to get away from the present, however briefly. They had done the same course. Claire, bright and ambitious, was now an area director, just moved from Scotland to Kent. But she stirred her coffee without smiling. 'If we'd known the next time we met would be in these hellish circumstances, would we have acted differently d'you think?'

'Would I have chosen another career, is that what you mean?'

Claire, smoothly dressed, tall and slender like a mannequin and every nail filed and polished, every pleat in her skirt straight, said, 'Well? Would you?'

Georgie shook her head. 'I'd never go through this again. Not for anything in the world. Nothing else seems worthwhile any more. Every single thing I've done has been shadowed by this. Yes, I'd have chosen something else if I'd known this was going to happen.'

Claire's next words were so shattering that at first Georgie frowned, unsure that she'd understood them correctly. 'It was a terrible mistake to make. The worst. You should have anticipated it. You should have taken some action after that last visit, shouldn't you? Do you know why you didn't?'

Cheeks flared and steaming, she stared at Claire defensively. 'But no court in the land would have given a place of safety order on the flimsy grounds that existed after that Christmas visit. Claire, you know that! You've been sitting here. You heard.'

'I also know that you could have persuaded a judge, if you'd felt strongly enough, if you'd pushed hard enough.'

How dare she? So unimpassioned, so unperturbed, while Georgie was almost spluttering

182

with rage. 'Claire!' The coffee was suddenly cold and sour. She had to struggle to grip her cup, her hand was shaking so. 'But I didn't know! This situation was on-going! I hadn't the slightest clue that anything would happen so quickly.'

Claire Bettison raised two groomed eyebrows and asked quietly, 'Hadn't you, Georgie?'

'Jesus Christ, if I'd had the slightest suspicion I'd have acted immediately! *What the hell d'you take me for?* Why would I sit back and do nothing? You must be out of your mind.'

They stood to one side of the room. No-one could possibly overhear them, but Claire kept her voice low and said, 'Violence affects all of us in vastly different ways. There are some subconscious responses which can't be trained away, no matter how experienced or how professional we are there is always that something that undermines us . . .'

'I have dealt with violence before, many times.' She fought to keep her scream down.

Claire stared in surprise at her friend's discomfort. 'I'm sorry, Georgie. I've upset you and I certainly didn't mean to do that. I thought it might help you if you knew somebody else understood.'

What? *A kind of collusion?* With her hand shaking beyond her control Georgie put down her coffee cup. How peculiar it was that someone had bothered with such a white cloth at a gathering like this. How strange priorities tend to be. She stood straight, her arms at her sides, but her fists were clenched and her legs were weak as she battled with a white-hot rage. 'I don't think that

183

you *do* understand, Claire. I don't think you have grasped the situation at all. And I have to say that I feel badly hurt, even betrayed, by your suggestion. We knew each other years ago, so you know very well how conscientious I am and how sincerely I care. I don't do this job for the sake of it and I know that you don't either. I was fond of Angela Hopkins, she wasn't just a name on a file for me. Angela was sweet and I liked her. If I had had the slightest suspicion that anything was going on in that family that meant Angie should be removed, the very slightest suspicion, then I would have taken immediate action.'

'Then I'm sorry.'

But, Christ, that wasn't good enough. Georgie wanted to lean forward, grab Claire Bettison by the padded shoulders and shake the very life out of her. She hated the face that swam before her, so full of well-meaning and yet so undermining, so devious. How could she make such vile suggestions at such a traumatic time? How could she come here, so cool, so judgemental, when everyone knew the very same tragedy could have happened to anyone here?

'Perhaps we could get together afterwards, talk some more, have a drink.'

'No. I don't think so, Claire. I'd rather try to forget what you said. I'd rather we did not meet, and there's certainly nothing to talk about . . .'

'Georgie, just let me . . .'

But people were drifting back to the table and Georgie turned her back on Claire and strode purposefully away. By now she felt sick, she felt dizzy. They had turned the heating up far too high and she shouldn't have worn this thick jumper. Cotton would have done, the wool itched round her neck.

If that's what Claire Bettison was honestly thinking, then how many more thought the same, but were not prepared to speak up? She felt like climbing onto the table, screaming at every one of them, kicking holes in all those polite, caring faces.

As the day wore on and the room grew hot with human breath, it was obvious that this was not how the majority were thinking. It was certainly not what they were saying. They were firmly on Georgie's side, if sides could be taken in such dreadful circumstances. They were tactful and sensitive. They tried to be positive and helpful. Afterwards, with another day to go but the worst of the nightmare over, Roger accompanied Georgie to the door. Helen would be waiting outside. She would have managed to find somewhere to park against all the odds. Georgie ignored Claire pointedly, although she had seen her floating towards her with a velvet cape over her shoulders. 'They're all behind you, Georgie,' Roger said supportively. 'They are all reliving this horror with you. There was absolutely nothing you could have done, there was no way you could have known . . .'

But Georgie hardly heard his words she was so busy searching his face. It was mild and well-meaning and full of nothing but the truth. He was an experienced social worker, certainly no kind of fool. He was a friend who knew Georgie well, better than Claire ever had and yet . . . and yet . . .

They might as well do away with all this, put her in prison and throw away the key. The huddled women with their hatred were right, the arsonist at the cottage was right, and the person who threw the brick last night came closer to the truth than any official inquiry.

For Georgie that meeting with her devious friend proved to be the final straw.

Fourteen

'You are right out of your tree.' Helen Mace looked across sharply. 'Only yesterday you were telling me you wouldn't live there to save your life, a place where nightmares are made, and now you're saying you've changed your mind. You've lost it, Georgie, you have, seriously.'

'It wouldn't be on a permanent basis.' It was hard to argue when even she was so supremely unsure of her ground, just full of a desperate courage. But every morning she scanned the papers with a fear so fascinated that it was almost a disappointment to find nothing. Fate was offering her a quick way out, she would be a fool not to take it. 'I just need to get away from here.' Georgie longed for a cigarette. They were at the Maces' house again, supper was over, the kids were in bed and Roger was out at a meeting. They sat round the fire, toasting their feet on the fender along with damp socks that steamed on the safety guard, all colours and sizes of socks were threaded through the holes in the wire. It had snowed and the five little Maces had soaked themselves in the pure white joy of it. In the early evening Georgie watched them, in the grey snow-dark as the sun sank, as their footsteps turned to black, and her heart ached for just one tiny glow of their happiness, their innocence. 'I'm asking for a year's sabbatical. Whatever happens I've got to move, and I can't sit around doing nothing until all this horror is cleared up. The cottage is there already. It needs a hell of a lot of work. I can go there at once, hide away for a while and get to grips with this whole damn thing, get to grips with myself. Helen,' she groaned, 'I can't go on like this.'

'But what about the offer? Don't tell me you're turning it down. All that lovely money!'

Georgie shook her head. 'There'll be other offers, Helen, especially when the place is done up. It could be a dream cottage' – she put some enthusiasm back in her voice – 'with a tad of imagination and money spent on it. And while I'm down there I'll let the flat to bring in an income and pay the mortgage. After a year I'll sell them both, when I've finally decided what to do.'

'So. You've got it all worked out.' Helen remonstrated gently, aware of Georgie's frail state of mind. 'But you'll be so far from your friends, that's what really bugs me. And from what you've said there's no-one around in that spooky place who'll be the slightest use.'

Georgie looked at Helen directly, a listless stare out of dull eyes, oh yes, she knew what she looked like. And they both knew there was only so much a body could take before action was required, any action, and common sense rarely plays a part. Georgie said, 'Perhaps that might be a good thing. Perhaps I've been leaning too hard on my friends, maybe it's time I relied on myself. And I can't do that here, Helen, it's just not possible here.'

'Something has happened,' said Helen astutely, in her most businesslike voice. 'Something has made you change your mind and you're not telling me what. I don't like this haste, I don't like this panic. It seems like you're running away to hide.'

'What the hell is wrong with that? I've no intention of hiding for ever. I'm talking about one year, that's all.' And such a short while ago all things around her were ordained, considered and under control. Once all she cared about was getting her pine doors stripped. She chose to go into social work to help other people, dammit. A very proper ambition. Served Georgie right, how little is virtue rewarded.

Helen frowned and bit her lip. She stole a glance at Georgie's face, so pale with emotion. Georgie was in a strange mood, not looking well. 'Yes, and around about then it'll be time for Ray Hopkins's trial and everything'll start up again. You can't run away, Georgie, there's really no escape from this shit.'

'But I can build myself up, get stronger.' Georgie, with her strained face and her un-brushed hair, was sadder but no wiser. What games people play. She automatically spouted the first thoughts that came into her head, like repeating great chunks of *Hiawatha*. She knew the persecution she suffered could not be connected to the fire in the woodshed, nobody in Wooton-Coney knew who she was or where she came from, and none of the brick-throwing, phone-calling heavies would be able to trace her down there. So buried in Devon she would be safe. Sticks and stones may break my bones . . . the evil tongue of old Mrs Buckpit would be all she would have to endure.

'If it's work you want, I'm sure Roger can find you some research to do.'

'Now you're being patronizing, Helen, I'm going to Devon and that's how it is. Whatever you say, and I know you're worried about me, really, I have made up my mind.'

'But it's such a sinister place, Georgie,' said Helen, despair on her plump and easy face. 'Dammit, you wretched woman. You're only just back from there. You can't have forgotten already.'

'I know. I know. It's the weirdest place I've ever been.' What on earth is the matter with Georgina Jefferson? For the first time that evening she managed a smile, if a wry one.

Wise head shakings and gloomy prophesies. Everyone was against it, especially old Mr Selby. 'But we've even agreed a price,' he wheezed, 'we can't go back on our word. That would be most unethical.' She imagined him rolling his watery eyes at something so vulgar and distasteful.

'I know it's difficult, and I hate to back out of an agreement, but you must see that my circumstances are unusual and that this is a kind of emergency. This is a personal matter and I'm afraid I can't explain it further.'

'You won't get another offer like this.'

'No? Well, we will have to see.'

'The purchasers are not going to like it.'

'Well, as we don't even know who they are, I can't say I am too concerned about that. I'm sorry, Mr Selby, I really am . . .'

'This is not the sort of way to behave. You should have made this decision in the first place.'

Georgie groaned inwardly. She had not expected to be treated like a wayward child. He should be on her side. 'Circumstances have changed since then, I'm afraid, Mr Selby, and you must admit it was all being done in rather a hurry. I didn't have much time to make my decision. And we haven't actually signed anything.'

But it was quite clear that Mr Selby did not approve at all. And rightly.

And the more Georgie had to argue her case the more sensible it sounded, until she began to feel it was the only way out of her trap.

Isla was furious.

'Who's going to come to the theatre with me now? David won't. He can't stand it. Who's going to come shopping, play tennis, drive me home from parties? And we're all going to miss you at work, already this place feels odd without you. How can you selfishly seriously think of abandoning us like this?'

Georgie was in the flat showing Isla Stephen's paintings. The flat felt like a different place when there was someone else in there with her. But alone, it was unbearable. She went out at every opportunity, even just to browse round the shops. But were people really staring? Did they know who she was, even in a headscarf? Was Georgie ill? Was it paranoia?

Isla caught her breath as she saw one of Stephen's more crazed efforts. 'There's definitely something wrong here.' She turned to Georgie and said seriously, 'I think it's probably a good thing you didn't know this man. I mean, look at this. Don't you feel there's something wrong?'

'Disturbing? Yes. But he was an alcoholic, remember. He did drink himself to death.'

Isla propped up the picture and backed away, turning her curly dark head this way and that in an effort to make sense of it. 'But how old was he? Was he a schizo, on top of everything else?' she asked. 'Because compared to the others it looks as if someone quite demonic has taken over the oils.'

'It is odd, yes. Because the majority are so good.'

Isla went to sit down again. Gypsylike, with her beads and fringed scarf and her long dangly earrings, she was always boasting that some distant relations had once been Romanies. 'I think the others are excellent. I think Stephen could have made serious money if he was into that sort of thing, if he'd known the right people and the right places to go.'

'I'm going to try and sell some of them,' said Georgie. 'I'm only going to keep the ones I really like.'

'But no-one'll touch these crazy ones.' Isla poured more wine and her wrists jangled with

192

bangles. 'No-one'll touch them with a barge pole. They're far too harrowing, and ugly. There's something vicious about them. Infantile, even. A crazy baby. Bits of mouth and eye, broken limbs and blood . . . and all those screaming crimson faces.' Isla stared at the painting she had rested against the chair, perhaps it was more acceptable through the dull red glow of a wineglass. A gypsy musing into her ball, could she see something Georgie could not, so puzzled was her expression?

Eventually she shook her head, too bemused to take it further. She might as well say what she came for. 'So there's no point in arguing with you about this flight into darkest obscurity? You've made your decision and nobody's going to change your mind?'

Georgie nodded.

'For a true act of contrition, my child, you should go into proper retreat, or cut off your hair, sackcloth and ashes, or do a spell with Romanian orphans. Shelter would welcome you with open arms. Languishing down in Devon is such an easy option, nourishing the inner self and all that crap, so wickedly wasteful, I am very much afraid you will continue to dwell with the damned.' She noted Georgie's smiling complacence. She climbed down off her soap box. 'You always were an obstinate prat. Suzie told me it would be a waste of time, but I thought I'd give it a try.'

'But I'm going to need you to visit. I don't want you to forget where I am. And there is such a thing as a telephone, that's the first thing I'm going to arrange. And years ago, remember, people actually used to write letters.'

'You'll have to come up and stay with me and David.'

But Georgie made her point, straightening up to defend herself. 'If I need to keep coming to London it will mean that my plan has failed.'

Isla ignored her. She tried to put some hope in her voice. 'I know someone who'll be thrilled and that's Lola.' She touched the spaniel gently, the dog snored at her feet. Still avoiding Georgie's eyes, drumming her fingers on the table, she added, 'We haven't been much help to you, have we? We haven't protected you enough. Our support didn't work and that's why you're going. I've got an awful feeling that you won't be coming back.'

You always hurt someone. No matter what you do or how full of good intentions you are, you always bloody well hurt someone. What could Georgie say? Without her friends, without Isla's constant good humour, phone calls, outings, conversations, without them throughout these last few months she'd be in a mental home by now. But surely Isla must know that? It hadn't been easy for Georgie's friends, it hadn't been easy for anyone; so steeped was she in her own despair, Georgie hadn't given much thought to the feelings of those around her. To some people she had drawn closer, from others she had backed away, perhaps wrongly. But Isla had always been special.

They had been misguided to protect and support her.

She was guilty. She had fooled everyone.

Claire Bettison was right. She had known something was wrong and she should have done something about it.

When Georgie failed to reply it was left to Isla to say softly, 'Don't you think you've punished yourself enough without taking this step, locking yourself up and throwing away the key?'

'It doesn't feel slightly like that.'

'From where I'm sitting it does.'

'I thought you'd decided not to argue?'

Isla slumped. 'OK, OK. I can see it's useless. So when are you off?'

Georgie, relieved the heavy stuff was out of the way, was happier with practicalities. 'A local agency is letting the flat, you won't believe what they're charging . . .'

'Oh, I would.'

'And they say they'll let it easily. People are actually prepared to pay these exorbitant prices. So I've promised to be cleared up and out of here by the first of April.'

'An appropriate date,' Isla said witheringly.

Georgie raised her eyes and said tensely, 'Don't give up on me, Isla. Not after all we've been through.'

Isla gazed vaguely round. 'You're hiring a firm for the job?'

'No need. The cottage is already furnished. All I need are my clothes and a few bits and pieces. I'm locking my personal stuff in the wardrobe, so I reckon one car load will do it.'

'Are you going to let us come with you? Help you get sorted? If I followed you down in my car the whole move would be much easier.'

It was such a relief to laugh. 'You're just nosy. But OK, I'd love you to come.'

'Nosy and jealous,' said Isla. 'Don't forget the jealousy bit. Good heavens, I wouldn't mind a year off, burying myself in the country with a few crates of wine and some Fortnum's hampers. Think of the books you'll be able to read. Think how fit you'll get with all those long walks.'

'I'm going to be working most of the time.' Georgie smiled haughtily. 'But it would be really good if you could come down and help me out sometime.'

'Oh, I'll have to think about that,' said Isla. 'How about two weekends in the summer and a fortnight in September? But seriously, have you told Mark yet?' she asked with sudden anxiety. And she gave Georgie a confiding look.

Mark the conscientious. Mark the English gentleman. Mark the responsible. Poor Mark. 'I'm telling him tonight. But I don't think he'll be particularly surprised. And we've never been that close, you know that.'

'I'm not sure Mark sees it that way.'

'Mark's very laid back, and he's got his sailing and lots of friends. He's got that boring old car to work on.'

'You're always too busy to bother with him. Maybe this lazy year of yours will change all that. Who knows?'

'Mark will never be right for me. Stop trying to match me up. I'm more contented on my own, now that I'm used to it. I've missed Toby more just lately. I could have done with him around, but I don't see Mark as a substitute, never have.'

'Or any of the others who beat a pathetic path to your door?'

'No. None of them.'

'We shall have to see,' said Isla, refusing to admit defeat.

And so they relaxed, drank more wine together, made their travelling plans and managed to forget about Angie Hopkins for as long as five minutes at a stretch. Isla left before midnight. And after Georgie went downstairs to let Lola out she returned to a silent flat which felt doom-laden and uneasy. She had to take two sleeping pills before she felt safe enough for bed.

And that night she slept with the light on.

Fifteen

Isla persuaded her to buy the hens, acting out some country fantasy of her own, Georgie supposed. Given her head she would have filled the cottage with blue and white striped jugs full of primroses, but Georgie was happy to trail along because it was her fantasy, too.

She felt an odd stab of fondness and pride when she saw Furze Pen again, and she watched through her mirror as Isla, in her battered old estate, juddered to a halt behind her. In her short absence the cottage had changed, now it was quite mysterious, hidden there amongst growing things, damper, darker and tinged with green foliage.

'No clamping here then.' Isla climbed stiffly out of her car and exercised her shoulders. She'd insisted on wearing that broad-brimmed hat with the wobbly black rose and the full-length coat that resembled a curtain. Once again Georgie knew that although there was no sign of a soul, the hamlet could well be deserted, dozens of eyes were watching.

This time the cottage recognized her and sent a shy smile from under the thatch. 'Well?' she asked Isla. 'What d'you think?'

She badly wanted Isla to like it. She was glad that this time it was furnished, she was pleased there were lamps and rugs and coloured mugs on hooks waiting to greet them in the kitchen.

Typically Isla waxed lyrical. ' "I know a bank whereon the wild thyme blows . . ." '

'I've got my own bank,' said Georgie with pride, 'and it's covered with garlic and briar roses.'

'Aha. The garlic to see off the devil and the briars for your own special crown of thorns. No seriously, Georgie, this is absolutely incredible. Marvellous!' The black rose on Isla's hat nodded its total approval. She picked her way over the stepping stones, across the stream and to the front gate. She stroked a granite mushroom with awe. 'Wow! Unreal! What a setting! Harebells, thistles and real sheep droppings. How could you think of selling this? Done up, it'll fetch a fortune. It's a dream cottage, isn't it? They give them as prizes in the *Mail on Sunday*. But where will you go to get your hair cut? And how will you get your papers delivered?'

'Wait till you see inside.'

Some of the trees were still mauve with winter. A pigeon flapped across the sky. Everywhere was speckled with daisies. There were daffodils and forget-me-nots, and a faint warmth, heavy with the scent of greenery, rested on Georgie's cheek. Lola dashed ahead of them as if she'd never been away, as if the cottage was hers and she knew it. Was the burned doll still in the woodshed? This thought had nagged Georgie all the way down from London. In the weeks between she had thrust it aside and its importance had faded, but as

199

she drew nearer Wooton-Coney, as the roads became narrower and the stone walls higher, as the newly budding trees assumed that battered, shrinking shape and the grass grew thicker in the lanes, as the hedgerows flamed with wild flowers, the doll began to loom in her head, began to assume massive proportions.

So far she had told no-one about it. But some time tonight she knew she would have to tell Isla.

Isla sniffed. 'Something dead.' But her eyes sparkled with undisguised glee like they did when she made one of her famous 'finds' at the local flea market. 'Magic. All magic. If it wasn't for that repulsive smell. And surely underneath the paint that is a Jacobean chest. You nearly passed over a Jacobean chest for God's sake! Cramer would have made a fortune.'

'The smell is probably just the damp. It's been empty for so long.' And Georgie took Isla on a short tour of inspection, trying to remember to duck her head, trying to remember if everything was exactly as she had left it or if Chad Cramer had somehow gained entry again and removed some tempting item. This time she noticed the cottage was shabby and not very clean.

Bending to start down the stairs, Isla sniffed again. 'That's not damp. That's something dead.'

'Well, you should have seen it the last time I came, freezing cold, filthy and almost empty.'

Isla shuddered at the barred lavatory window with its stains and mouldy old drippings. 'I wouldn't fancy a shower in that. It has to be rampant with spiders.' She touched the rusty bars.

'They didn't mean anyone to break in, did they?' She fingered the torn and grubby shower curtain. The plastic was brittle, crispy and speckled like burned chicken skin.

'Years ago it must have been used for storage. Look, meat hooks in the ceiling. Gross.'

'Meat hooks. Ugh! Pig carcasses dripping blood on the floor, their smooth white flanks swinging. Are you going to leave them for atmosphere? If you were tall enough you could hang your towels on them I suppose.'

'It won't be so dark in here once the windows have been cleaned.' Georgie saw how the sun was trying to shine on the dusty floor. She moved back into the sitting room and frowned at the tinge of mould on the cushions. She wiped it off before sitting down, but the cotton felt chill on her back and it clung, slightly stickily. 'It'll all feel very different after it's been lived in again, warmed up a bit. Most of this stuff has spent the winter stored in Chad Cramer's railway carriage and it hasn't had a chance to air.'

'Let's light the fire before we unload the car,' said Isla sensibly. 'It won't be dark for an hour or so yet. No, no, you sit there and I'll do it. I'd love to do it, I don't get a chance with the central heating. Just tell me where to find the wood.'

Georgie sat stock-still after Isla left the room, lugging the broken log basket. She held a pose of absorbed contemplation for what seemed an endless time. She waited for the shout, or the laugh, some exclamation, as her friend noticed the pile of rags and the singed doll staring menacingly out from the corner. Even worse, there might be a scream that would jar the jangling nerves in her head. She was so strung up she actually winced as she waited for some reaction from Isla. But maybe, concentrating on the job, Isla would miss the little cameo; it was dark in that corner after all, and there was no wood there, just bits of household junk. Georgie twisted her hands in her lap, she sat there nervously biting her lip, she hardly breathed, and although it was cold in the cottage she was sweating.

Isla's laboured breathing overtook the baskety sounds as she came back through the kitchen, staggering under the load of logs. 'I'm not used to such heavy labour. Something's dry in this place anyway. This old wood's lovely.'

Georgie let her breath go and attempted to relax slowly. But it was no use, she couldn't play it like this, waiting for Isla to find it, she'd have to see for herself. If the doll was still there she would have to face it, but if it was gone . . .

She got up. She went outside. She forced herself into the woodshed.

She'd known it would be gone.

That's what the terror had been all about.

And the terrible bedding was missing, too.

So she described the doll and the fire, and after she had finished speaking her words still hung in the air like fog over water, haunting and gloomy. She was tempted to wave them away and start again, tell it differently.

'Shit. You are telling me that somebody actually started a fire the last time you were here?' Isla stared nervously over her shoulder as the kindling started to burn. Her shocked smile was uncertain. *'And you didn't mention it?* You didn't even mention it to that solicitor of yours, let alone the police?'

Georgie felt distinctly foolish. 'I didn't think I'd be coming back, did I? And I managed to convince myself it must have been accidental.'

'Perhaps one of your God-awful neighbours wanted to drive you out? It must have been that appalling man, Cramer,' she shuddered, 'with his looting. It must have been his revenge. God, he must be so damn sick.'

'He's foul. A bully and a cheat. But I can't imagine him doing something as childish as this. Such an odd thing for anyone to do. I just feel Cramer doesn't have that sort of imagination, you know, he's a sod but he's not that twisted.'

'Then who the hell?' Isla sat back, shaken, the leaping flames were some consolation. 'In the middle of the night it could hardly have been some passer-by. It has to be one of your neighbours.'

Deep in thought, Georgie tugged at her lip. 'Nancy Horsefield's barmy in a mild sort of way. She's lost her marbles, but she's not aggressive and she'd never be out alone at night. Horace is far too sensible, he'd never dream of such a thing. I've already dismissed Chad or Donna, and I don't really know the Buckpits. She was pretty surly and unhelpful, but they're hard-working farmers for goodness' sake, and Mr Selby told me their family has farmed here for generations. So why would they suddenly break out and do something like this?' She shook her head in bewilderment. 'They wouldn't. *They just wouldn't*. So it has to be an accident. Perhaps when I turned on the water pump the electricity shorted and sent a spark into that corner?'

'And what about the tin of chemicals?' The firelight flickered on Isla's cheeks, heightening her colour.

'Perhaps it was leaking anyway. Maybe someone dumped it there years ago.'

'But the doll's gone, Georgie.'

'Yes, yes, I know,' Georgie answered fearfully.

'And why would Stephen have a doll in his woodshed?'

Georgie wrestled in her head for an answer. 'Perhaps he used it as a model for his art.'

Isla answered wryly. 'That's complete crap. We've looked through all your pictures and there's nothing resembling a doll.'

'A passing tramp?' Georgie tried again. And then, annoyed with Isla for making her more nervous than she already was, she said, 'Well, it's gone now anyway and I'm moving in, so it's best we forget it and get on with the unloading. There is probably a simple explanation and there's no point in making a thing of it and getting upset. We're not going to solve it tonight so we might as well let it go.'

So they didn't refer to the doll again and spent the next two hours getting Georgie's belongings unloaded from the cars, sorting them out and putting them away. She hung up her clothes. She arranged the tiny airing cupboard. A product of her education, she made up the beds with hospital corners. She liked to be organized; she'd already made a list of repairs, mostly superficial, and various friends had promised their help through the summer. It is surprising what ordinary people can do in the way of plumbing, pointing, electrics, fencing, hedging and ditching. Once the subject came up the most unlikely characters seemed to nurture a secret skill and no-one needed much tempting. With common sense Georgie could do most of it herself; she would not need a builder. And next spring, when her year was up and the work was finished, she could seal the whole job by getting the thatch professionally done.

When Isla left she would have five days alone at the cottage before Mark arrived, for the weekend he had said.

How she dreaded those five days alone. *How she dreaded them*. And yet getting to know herself had been her prime reason for moving. What odd stories you tell yourself, Georgie thought, ruefully, when she waved Isla away two days later. What crazy scenarios seem normal when you are lonely and desperate. But hell, you don't expect to carry them out, fate normally intervenes and rescues you from yourself.

But not this time. Not now.

She had gone too far. This was it.

And if Georgie had secretly hoped that Mark would save her from her own stupidity and persuade her to stay in London, she was, once again, sadly mistaken.

'You must do what you need to do,' had been his first feeble reaction to the news of her departure. 'And I will support you. You know that.'

Why was he always so damn reasonable?

'But how do you feel about it? I will be away for a year.'

'Disappointed, naturally. But I assume you won't be in purdah. I will be able to visit.'

She wanted to kick him under the table. Shake his shoulders till he wobbled. They were dining at the Old Orleans; they always went there because Mark liked jazz, his reaction to jazz was the only emotion that really lit up his face and made it extraordinary. He enjoyed the informal atmosphere, the sawdusty floor and the jugs of ale, nothing romantic here unless you were into Western culture and the sight of a couple of guns turned you on. Why the hell did she bother with Mark? Why did she bother with anyone when all she felt, when she got home, was that hollow feeling of loss?

'You choose. We will go wherever you want, you know that,' Mark would say when he saw that look of distress cross her face. But Georgie didn't know where she honestly wanted to go. It wasn't the restaurant that distressed her, it was something much deeper than that, a yearning for something so beautiful, so agonizing, so lost to her that she couldn't express it to this pleasant-faced sandy-haired man with the depth of a character from Agatha Christie, who made love to her when she wanted him to, spent the night when she told him he could, smiled when she smiled and listened when she talked. Small talk. Nothing talk.

If he was a plant he would be a rubber plant. Tall, cheerful, stoical but dusty. So what would Georgie be? A sharp little heather with dry roots.

And sex with Mark was embarrassing, far from the familiar, practised gropings and peaceful, experienced murmurings of Toby. Almost foaming at the mouth, Mark went at it like a horse, with arched neck and flaring nostrils, buttocks pumping and veins throbbing in his forehead. She could feel all the bones in his back. Smell his medicated soap. Heaven knows it was hard not to laugh when he gave one of his piercing whinnies during his violent, muscular orgasm. She used to soak in a perfumed bath, she made herself smell very sweet to compensate for her sourness of mind.

When she was younger, so long ago she had been a small child, a child so used to repressing emotions, it was hard for outsiders to see she had any. There were times, then, when she'd held out her arms, in love with the world all around her. There'd been moments of pure ecstasy, so pure she'd been wading through it, and these intimations of infinity filled her inside so there was no room for anything else. There had been this secret place where she went, full of buttercups, where the sky was blue and the wind was warm. And when she breathed in she drank the whole world, her own small griefs sublimating into understanding and compassion. She had held out her small arms and cried when she realized she could not keep this mental intoxication, this intensification of life. Perhaps that was something you never found once you grew up and knew too much, once you had seen something of the world. Perhaps you just lost it. And some forgot it completely.

Sometimes Georgie felt she had spent her whole life searching for that experience ever since. When Toby died she gave up hope. She felt she would never find it.

Yes, she was more lonely when she pleased Isla and went out with one of her 'hangers on' than if she spent the evening alone with a book and her feet up. Unbearably lonely.

Everyone thought Mark was 'lovely'. She called him Brillo, he referred to her as Snuffles. Educated, charming when he chose to be, he was interesting, too, in a mild kind of way. He worked at the British Museum, was an expert on the ancient Greeks. His wit and his humour, his hair and his lips, everything about him was desert dry.

And she did like Mark. He was a decent man. The injustice of her own feelings troubled her, she was taken aback by her own malice because she was using him, pretending, giving nothing of herself, she, who had trained herself in compassion for others.

'I'll move in with you,' was his immediate and generous response when she had felt so threatened by violence in London, when she was so lost and afraid to be left alone in her flat. 'You shouldn't be on your own.'

But she couldn't explain the truth to him, couldn't tell him that sharing the flat with him would have afforded little protection, how could she say that in some odd way she would have found it more threatening to wake up every morning beside him and his big bare feet, to smell his peppermint, listen to him cleaning his teeth for hours like he did, and that damn gargling, to have to watch him hanging his clothes on the chair with such infernal neatness, just as he had been taught at school, so organized, so maddeningly sensible, even worse than she was. But it would be so easy to slip into this to answer a need for love.

'I love you, Snuffles,' Mark would sometimes whisper in her ear, mostly when he had drunk too much wine, marring an otherwise happy evening.

'I really do. I love you.'

And Georgie would try to reply in kind, try to soothe him, and try not to weep.

'You have been on your own too long,' scolded Isla. 'You're a dried up old walnut and you'll end up cracking, that's if you haven't already. Far too choosy. Too selfish. You want too much. Mark adores you, he would do anything for you. He would be a dog at your feet if you'd let him, if you weren't so bloody awkward.'

Sadly this was true.

'You need someone to help you fold your sheets,' Isla said. 'Everyone does. And someone to whip the cream when your arm aches, and support you in your dotage, if you play your cards right.'

So Isla had been gratified to hear that Mark was arriving in five days' time. She had that silly gleam in her eye and Georgie turned away in disgust.

Sixteen

It was painful to admit this, thought Georgie, even to herself, as she stared at the pendant Mark had given her for Christmas, as she fingered the greenish stone of archaeological interest, but Mark was an older, leaner version of Toby, safe as Toby, unthreatening as Toby. Yes, that is why she had married Toby, out of a need to be safe.

She had married Toby for two reasons, first because she loved him, and second because she was terrified that anyone else might see through her. How she detested her own vulnerability. If she had had children she might have been different, less afraid for herself, and more concerned about them from the moment they rose from crawling position to sway on their tiny feet. She probably would have been overprotective, far too worried to endure the fear that some monster might hurt them – a teacher giving a thoughtless report, a team leader picking them last, a friend forgetting their birthday. Her vulnerability made her inadequate, as inadequate as her 'clients', who, in the words of her mother, 'ought to be compulsorily sterilized'.

Mark was a person everyone talked to because he did not. Because he mostly stood around staring with one raised, interested eyebrow, more interested in abstract matters.

Perhaps that's why women slept with him, too.

It was Mark who built her that neat little hen house, and Georgie was glad he was with her when they went to fetch the hens because of the unpleasant business of pushing them into those dirty sacks. Their warm female bodies bundled in jute. Bump bump bump they went, their silence made a forlorn entreaty. 'Oh, they'll be fine,' the farmer assured them, 'they favour the dark, do chickens.' But the journey back felt endless and Georgie could hardly wait to get them home and tip them into the bright daylight of her orchard.

Mark wandered off to watch the milking at Wooton Farm on his first morning in Wooton-Coney. Funny how men can do things like that without being thought pushy. He brought her an early morning cuppa. Georgie peered at the clock to see to her horror that it was half-past six, but he said perkily, clapping his hands, 'It's a glorious morning, too good to be wasted, so I'm off to explore.'

So Blytonesque. So Julian.

He had arrived well equipped for the country with his new green wellies and his three-quarter-length Barbour. Georgie was already being nasty, she couldn't help herself around Mark, she regularly had these unkind thoughts and it didn't make her feel any better about herself.

There was a fishing rod in the back of his car, an

old MG, a collector's item, not too comfortable for the passenger, not when you're dressed for a night on the town.

But Georgie had been relieved to see him after her five days alone, when she'd found herself doing worrying things like pacing the floor, glancing at her watch and speculating that he might not find her because Mark was not the most practical of men when it came to making his way about, or making love either. He never quite managed to hit the spot, there was so much fussing with maps and lists . . . He would find himself somewhere else. Somebody else would take him home.

But she had no right to be so vindictive because it was with Mark that she went to the merchants and picked the items she would need to make a start on her cottage. And Mark's advice was good. Practical in some small ways, why should he be practical in all? Georgie demanded too much of Mark, she too readily lost patience, she rarely bothered to be civil, but he invariably came back for more with his damn tail wagging.

She dithered for days over whether she should put him in the spare room, Stephen's old studio, or if she should make it clear from the start that he could sleep in her bed? It wasn't even a double, it was that strange size in between, which meant that sheets never fitted properly and double duvets touched the ground. So, if Mark was to sleep with Georgie they would be close, extremely close. He would not get up when he had finished, he would fall straight to sleep with his mouth wide open and she would be squashed against the wall.

Oh no. Oh no.

In the end, after much contemplation, on that first night she made sure they finished their love-making downstairs, uncomfortable though it was. He would not have the strength or the inclination to perform a second time, and he hated to miss *Newsnight*. When the programme had finished she noticed some relief on his face when she showed him to Stephen's studio.

'It smells in here,' was all he said, wrinkling his freckled nose and dumping his Gladstone bag on the bed with such a thud that the bedsprings twanged. He had brought his Paisley pyjamas with him, he already wore his brown leather slippers. He had made love in his brown leather slippers.

He put her in mind of Prince Charles. Damaged by privilege. 'It's the damp,' she said encouragingly. 'You get used to it.'

Why did she let him? She never bothered to tart herself up, in fact, if anything, she dressed in her shabbiest, most-washed clothes in order to turn him off. For his arrival Georgie had worn torn jeans and a dirty old shirt, huge, like a smock. There were bits of old cobweb in her hair and she hadn't bothered to wash it. Quite a statement, one might imagine. But with Mark, sex was like saying hello. He arrived with the lovemaking question in his eyes, like a worry. You had to get the ritual over before you progressed to anything else. In bed, Mark was the theme tune to *Neighbours* as opposed to the *Planet Symphony*. Oh why, oh why did Mark Bamber-Jones force her to thoughts mean and unkind? Behaviour quite unworthy of her because Mark was a good friend of Georgie's and she never intended to hurt him.

She was downstairs cooking breakfast when Mark returned from the milking. He liked his meals at precise intervals, and his sleeping times to be regular. Routine was all important. 'They're a bit queer to put it mildly.'

'Queer?'

'Rustics, of the old-fashioned kind. Peasants, really, damn tricky to fathom out what they say.'

'Oh? So they actually spoke to you then?' Surprised, she turned round to study his face while her hands cracked an egg into the fat. It sizzled and spat, like Georgie's own resentment at the easy way Mark seemed to manage to slot himself into every situation. 'You've made more progress than I have. I went to order more milk when I arrived and got the same miserable reaction as the first time. I only see the men when they're passing by on the tractor, or high on the hills with the sheep.'

'Lot and Silas. The sons. The old man's long dead.'

'Really?'

'Quite horrid,' said Mark with a bit of a shudder and a nervous laugh. 'There's a filthy jar on a shelf, mixed up with capsules, detergent, syringes, rags and an old bacon sandwich. When I asked, they said it was the old boy's ashes. Apparently he asked for his urn to be put on the parlour shelf. They told me he died twenty years back. They didn't introduce themselves. I heard them calling each other. I wasn't addressed directly at all.'

Georgie was horrified. 'Jesus. How grotesque,' she said, wide-eyed. 'They must have been kidding you. Twenty-year-old ashes on the shelf? But they let you stay and watch the milking?'

'Naturally. They could see I was interested, and I kept well out of the way. Both somewhere in their thirties, I'd guess. You'd never imagine they were brothers, one a burly oaf and the other a nervy type with a wicked twitch in his eye. Both thick as shit, that's obvious.'

'I bet that mother gives them both hell. She's a foul-tempered cow. And they didn't even ask who you were?'

'Didn't seem bothered. Too busy. Both the silent, macho type. Can't put more than two words together. Probably both illiterate.'

'Of course they'll already know who you are. They might be thick but they don't miss a trick. Always staring. Whenever they drive by here they peer in, and if I'm out walking they'll turn their heads a hundred and eighty degrees. They've never been told it's rude to stare.'

'Well, you get all types down here, products of incest, sheep-shagging and God knows what else.' And happily Mark tucked into his breakfast. 'I'd rather do without the milk. They piss in the parlour along with the cows and I'm not sure that's all they do. There should be some law against it.'

It was good, it was warm enough to open the top of the stable door and they sat in the kitchen together using Stephen's scarred pine table with the morning sun streaming in. Georgie felt she could be in an advert with a packet of Corn-flakes on the table.

She had spent five long days cleaning. Not your ordinary sort of cleaning, it was scrubbing on hands and knees and on ladders, buckets of detergent slopping all over the floors. She scraped the grime off the windows with a pallet knife before she could see through them properly. She had washed all the blankets, chair and cushion covers by hand. Naturally there was no washing machine, and nowhere to plumb one in. No room in the kitchen anyway. But the sink was deep, made out of stone and back-breakingly low. The two huge draining boards were ample for dumping piles of wet washing. She had even made an attempt at turning over some ground for vegetables, but the ground was so heavy her hands got blistered before she could make much impression. Since Isla had left she had kept herself on the go every minute of the day, and she had dropped into bed at night exhausted. Her behaviour was obsessive, she hadn't wanted to stop, even for a second. Sometimes Georgie caught Lola staring at her with a worried expression on her soft, wrinkled face.

She was safe to slow down and relax a little now that Mark had arrived, and they spent his first day out in the orchard with him building the hen house and Georgie trying to assemble some sort of run. She asked him brightly, 'D'you think that tomorrow, after we've been for the hens, you could help me clear out the woodshed?'

Mark wandered over to have a look. 'Bit of a

waste of time, surely, as it's half full of logs.'

'I know.' She picked abstractedly at the blistered skin on her fingers. 'But I'd like to get it more organized, cleared out and whitewashed, perhaps.'

'Well, yes, if you feel that's important. One of your priorities.' He looked doubtfully at the logs again. Typically, he had brought a clean set of overalls with him, he dusted them down where he'd vaguely marked them. 'It'll be one hell of a job. Wouldn't it be better to wait till the summer when the wood's mostly gone?'

'I'd like to get it done now, Mark. You know I can't stand clutter.' She went back to wrestling with her sheets of netting. She could always wheedle him round to her way of thinking, he would do the job without argument, and yet she could be so unkind to him, so short with him, even rude. Why should poor Mark sweat and groan and wear himself out over her woodshed, just because of a whim? She didn't know why. But she knew he would do it.

That evening that old sex question put itself in his eyes again. They brightened in a familiar way after the sun went down and Georgie's irritation grew as she wrenched the cork from the wine bottle and stirred the beef Bourguignonne. It was not a question of whether she'd let him, she knew that she would to save friction, it was the worry over the how and where. And the why, she supposed, she had to be honest. He had asked if she would rather go out for a meal, but she couldn't be bothered to get tidied up, they'd be working

217

again first thing in the morning. No doubt he'd be up at the crack of dawn, pottering, or at the farm.

Remarkably insensitive, it never occurred to him that he, or his advances, might be unwelcome. In his day Mark was known to have gatecrashed the most delicate dinner parties and get away with it. Everyone liked him, that was the trouble, he was so well-meaning and naive. To be unkind to Mark was the same as being beastly to a child.

But Georgie was unkind to him.

In the past they had never talked much about Angie Hopkins because Mark was not really the type you could talk to in any deep sort of way. But every so often he had brought Georgie flowers, and he'd taken to phoning her up every evening to see how she was coping. This forced her into a different mode, she had longed to shriek out the truth, to tell him how hellish it all was, but you couldn't with Mark, so she'd found herself talking about inconsequentials, small talk, nothing important. She used to sigh and sag unkindly when she realized it was only Mark on the phone, Oh no, not him again. But he had always let her know he was there and she knew he would not let her down. Mark was reliable, but then so are most chair legs.

They went to admire the finished hen house as the sun dipped over the hills. There was a night dew. The earth breathed out deeply. Georgie went barefoot and Mark held her hand. It should have been romantic but it wasn't. He showed

Georgie the ramp he had made, with struts to stop the hens from slipping. He slid open the little trap door and showed her the perches inside.

'Oh, that's wonderful, Mark,' Georgie exclaimed, as if to a child home from school with a painting. And Mark's smile was childlike, he beamed because he had pleased her, and she wanted to slap him, she didn't know why. He gave her the piece of wood which he called the front door lock, she fiddled with it, she obliged him. But she wanted to scream and race to the hills.

'Don't be so rough with it, do it more carefully, it's quite delicate and you don't want to smash it,' he said.

The forthcoming intimacy filled her with gloom. She wondered if she should offer herself here on the ground where they stood, among the tall grasses, and if they might do it standing still, like hens did. Georgie's jeans were filthy, her hair tied back with a bit of frayed scarf, but Mark looked impeccable, not one of his sandy hairs was out of place. He had even changed for dinner. He had met the challenge of Stephen's shower. His checked Viyella shirt was new, Georgie suspected, specially bought for a country weekend. His moleskin trousers were perfectly creased, even his belt was on the right hole – not a spare ounce of flesh on Mark, he made sure of that; he played squash too regularly.

So they went back inside, Georgie with that hollow of sadness inside her and Mark feeling it but not knowing why. His dry hand caressed hers. They ate their perfect dinner, profiteroles for

219

pudding, with whipped cream and a chocolate sauce, and they drank their mellow red wine, they listened to some music. She decided to let him do it on the rug before the fire, with Lola locked in the kitchen so she didn't try to join in the fun with licks and wagging tail. He made raucous love to her while she tried desperately to use her imagination. They had it all, didn't they? The firelight, the dim lamps, the beams, soft music, Stilton and biscuits, there were even spring flowers on the table. And Mark was tall and ganglingly handsome in a harmless sort of way. He smelled nice, less of the peppermint than usual, more of his favourite herbal tea.

'I love you, Snuffles.' Ah, yes. So he had drunk sufficient wine.

She played her part with kindness, self-control and patience. She made no complaint at all.

They had coffee watching the news. They shared a packet of chocolate finger biscuits that left Georgie feeling slightly sick.

Afterwards she listened when, flushed and happy, he climbed into the studio bed in his Paisley pyjamas. Georgie sat on her own bed, the three-quarter double, and watched the darkness out of the window until it must have been very late, because a soft white light silvered the horizon and she could hear the Buckpits' cockerel as she slipped under her cover.

The morning brought companionship once again, the sun removed those hopeless yearnings. The sun shone, the stream gurgled, birds sang, and mercifully Mark's eyes were quite clear. They fetched the hens and the materials Georgie would need, they bought the Sunday papers for reading later, after a proper Sunday lunch, because Mark always insisted on that, and began work on the woodshed. It all began to feel rather homely, and the clucking sounds of the plump brown hens were rurally enthralling. How Isla would adore all this. Georgie wouldn't mind whitewashing the woodshed alone, that job was one she looked forward to. She just needed someone to clear it out for her first. *Completely.* Particularly the corner where that macabre doll had been. She hung around outside, watching Mark, feeling guilty for all sorts of reasons and making frequent cups of coffee.

'There's been a fire in here at some point,' Mark called, his voice hollow where it came from the darkness now that the shed was half empty. He backed out to let her in. 'Look, you can see where the smoke has marked the wall.'

Georgie pretended to look. By now Mark's overalls were satisfactorily dirty and there was quite a pile of rubbish outside, alongside the logs. Georgie lugged the rubbish round to the front in the wheelbarrow, ready for the dustmen to collect on their fortnightly visit to the hamlet. A worn-out broom head, the mop bucket with the hole in the bottom, half an iron leg from a missing mangle, a rusty piece of galvanized iron, a set of broken snow chains, an old metal suitcase, badly battered, 'and then there's this,' said Mark, backing out, a line of sweat on his brow and, to

221

Georgie's distress, *a child's make-up case in his hand.*

The sort of cheap and cheerful thing you might buy from Woolworths. Pink plastic with a silvery sheen running through; there was a mirror inlaid in the lid, and various compartments for tubes and jars. Any little girl would adore it. The tiny baby-doll lipstick was tight in its flap, and a powder compact fitted beside it. Mark held it up to Georgie with a baffled frown. 'Rather an odd thing to find underneath all this junk. And used, up until lately, I'd say.' He squeezed a half-empty tube and a blob of brown make-up oozed out. 'Good as new.'

The smell of roasting lamb reached the wood-shed. This was an ordinary Sunday morning. Washing hung on the line in the sun. There was mint sauce in a jug in the kitchen and white wine cooling in the fridge. This was no time to play the neurotic. But Georgie stared, distraught. There was something inexplicably horrible about this latest find, but was that because Georgie knew about the doll? Was that what made her shudder so? Mark was not particularly interested in the unlikely article, he merely put it to one side and went back to his task, good-natured and uncomplaining so long as Georgie was around to bestow some praise every now and then.

But Georgie was repelled by the thing. The plastic was warm when she picked it up to balance on top of her barrow. The heat went out of the sun and she shivered when she asked herself the obvious question, 'Why would this be here?

What would Stephen be doing with something like this?'

She had spoken out loud, but Mark was too busy to hear her. He thought she was asking if he wanted a drink and he called out, 'Yes, something long and cool.' So she left the make-up case where it was and went into the kitchen, where she poured him a large glass of lime juice. She filled the glass with ice. She moved unthinkingly, unseeingly, yet angry to be so badly affected by so innocent a find. Up until then she'd been feeling strong. She was not dreading more time on her own until the next visitors arrived. Not this time. Georgie had decided how she would fill her time. There was plenty for her to do, and now she had the materials at last she could make a proper start.

She wandered back outside and gave Mark his drink. She watched his overlarge Adam's apple bob up and down and wondered weakly if this was the reason she could never feel right about him. She tried to ignore the make-up case as she wheeled the barrow round to the front. She stuffed it deep into the dustbin, trying to avoid handling it too much. She picked it up between finger and thumb and dropped the thing inside, then covered it with the rest of the rubbish and rammed the lid down hard.

That night, Mark's last night, she let him sleep in her bed because she felt so lonely.

'Perhaps we should get married, Snuffles.'

'Yes, Brillo, perhaps we should.'

'We could have a conservatory,' he murmured as he went off to sleep.

It was an uncomfortable night, as well as undignified, and sleepless for Georgie because of his snores and his long dangling legs. She wriggled her feet from under him. Perhaps she ought to have woken him up and told him to turn over, perhaps she should have said something like, 'Are neither of us capable of any serious emotion? Now listen, if you want a relationship with me, a real relationship, then we must be prepared to be honest. We must learn to talk about all sorts of difficult things, like bodies, like hearts. At the moment we are empty together, and I am very frightened by something I can't understand.'

But she didn't say that. What was the point? And Mark would be appalled. She just lay there, feeling like a dead thing beside him, and knowing, suddenly, that a real relationship was the very last thing she or Mark wanted. And Georgie also knew that this was exactly how Stephen had felt when he lay in this same bed. Alone and frightened, craving safety. But Stephen had gone, for love, into the arms of a green bottle of sickly smelling liquid, while Georgie, the whore, searched for the same thing in the arms of a man she could not love.

And they must both have known, as they nuzzled in the darkness for comfort like blind, soily-nosed moles, that they were slowly destroying themselves.

Seventeen

She would never forget that hectic summer. She had never experienced another one like it.

The natural tan suited Georgie, that particular labourer's brown as opposed to the forced tan of the sunbedder. She was brown and sinewy as a navvy, with hard, shiny hands. She kept her hair short and it went very curly. She was lean and weathered. She went round in jeans cut off at the knee.

Of course there was a drought, every day the sun shone, hardly a shower of rain. Mrs Buckpit reported dourly that there was drought here every summer, no matter what the weather did, and Georgie saw the Buckpit brothers labouring away, filling the water troughs in the fields from a tank on the link box. She asked her scowling neighbour, 'But surely there's something that could be done if you suffer like this every summer? Because of the farm I would think a good water supply is essential.'

What a know-all she sounded. Not at all what she meant.

The Buckpit woman gave a hard stare. 'We are only tenants, you know, Mrs Jefferson. It's not up to us.'

So Georgie suggested sensibly, she thought,

that they should put pressure on the Duchy, but Mrs Buckpit's mouth gave a tweak and she stalked away stiffly. It was a surprise to hear that the Buckpits were tenant farmers, Georgie had imagined Wooton Farm to be family owned. The rent they charged Chad Cramer would probably be passed on, or perhaps the Buckpits were entitled to let the cottage as part of the deal.

There was still no sign of Cramer giving up the tenancy, as required, or moving out.

The fierce Mrs Buckpit and Georgie enjoyed these cryptic exchanges when Georgie went to pay for the milk. She knew the farmer's widow would have preferred her to leave the money on the step in a bottle, to save her the bother of conversation, of cracking her face, of polite interaction, but Georgie resolutely refused to behave in this unsociable manner. She was buoyed up in her bravery by her amused guests. She wondered if she'd be quite so careless about confronting the gorgon every week after they had gone. There was something about her quietness that was almost malignant . . . Mrs Buckpit could probably stand still for hours, watching, waiting, ill-wishing.

Communication on any level with the sons, Lot and Silas, was out of the question. Mark kept trying, he even helped bring in the hay in a posh pair of padded dungarees that could well have come from Harrods and quite unsuitable open-toed Jesus sandals. He was obviously unhappy when he was forced to replace these with boots. He took to wandering about with a straw between his teeth and leaning, arms crossed, against gates. He stayed with Georgie on four occasions that summer, and shamefully she slept with him every time. Lot and Silas, that moronic couple, were preoccupied with their work and with their strange, silent, bovinelike watching, while they drew on their bent cigarettes or scratched their heads beneath their caps. When Suzie came to visit she considered them mentally retarded, but Georgie could not agree. There was a depravity about them which had nothing to do with natural affliction.

She lived like a lord, with long periods of forgetfulness and almost well-being. Her fear was hidden behind the full and fresh young green of the orchard trees, and from some of them wisteria hung in garlands like stars of rose, the globes of the trees were overspread with the pink and white of may. Wine every night, rich home-baked fruit cakes, Marks & Spencer chickens and complicated frozen concoctions that visitors felt they owed in exchange for their free vacation. The rent from her flat arrived regularly, but money was not a problem because Isla had managed to sell two of Stephen's paintings to a gallery in Kensington. 'And they'll take more,' she told Georgie, handing over the cheque, thrilled with her achievement. 'The owner's a friend of David's, they went to school together, or something equally odd, and now they have lunch every week. When you need more dosh just tell me.' She twiddled her specs round her finger with pleasure, and the tortoiseshell rims flashed with success.

So that was a nice secure feeling. It took some of the rank taste away.

And Georgie had the most extraordinary communication from Tom Selby, that old Einstein lookalike. Incredibly, another offer had arrived, almost double the first one. Georgie couldn't believe her eyes and nor, it would seem, could Selby. 'You have to accept this offer, Georgina,' he told her sternly when she hurried to Bovey to see him.

'But I'm here now. I can't just pack up and go.'

'Of course you can,' he crackled, the ancient body agitating in rheumatic excitement in a jerky, wavery way. He had made no concessions to summer, like opening the windows or changing his suit, and the smell of cheese and beer in the office was now mixed with pickled onions. 'You intend to sell in the end anyway. What difference would a few months make?'

She peered through the dimness to read the letter. The summer made his office more dusty. Every stick of furniture, every file, every cabinet was faded. 'Who on earth has made this offer? Are we sure they're the same people who made the original one?'

Mr Selby's face crumpled like that of a frustrated child's. 'I don't know. They won't say. But the offer has come through the same firm, still incognito.'

'If it is the same people they'll still be interested six months from now. They can make me another offer then, when the work on Furze Pen is completed.'

He made strangled movements with his head. 'We certainly cannot rely on that.'

But Georgie remained firm. Apart from any other reasons, she and her cottage were fully booked until the end of September. She did not want to let anyone down.

Most of her visitors camped in the garden because of the lack of space in the cottage, and often the nights were balmy enough to allow them to abandon their tents and sleep out under the stars. Often she joined them and they talked for hours around campfires, sang to beginners' guitars, laughed and played silly games while the hens laid their beautiful eggs and some of her straggly, weedy vegetables – mostly lettuce and spring onions – managed to poke their heads above ground and were large enough to include in salads, almost large enough to be seen.

She felt a glow as she bent over the beds, back aching, sweat dripping, a glow akin to the one that comes when a deep ache is stilled. There was pleasure in the feel of powdery, dry soil in her hands, in the touch of the breeze on her damp brow, and in the sense of tingling health in her limbs and in her breathing. The smell of the turned earth was good, and of the bonfire crackling away in the corner, which she could poke and regulate and enlarge for hours. It was good to tread like a country woman on loose soil in heavy boots, and at the end of the day to scrape the caked earth from their soles.

The burned doll and the make-up case began to assume insignificance, after all, all sorts of peculiar things find their way into people's sheds. Georgie was far too busy to be wallowing about in melancholy, nor did she have much time for thought. This physical, active life was obviously the answer to her paranoia, and the tragedy of Angie's death filtered more gently into her mind, the sort of sorrow that came and went, the kind of sadness that could be dealt with.

Wooton-Coney and its inhabitants remained a jumble of scattered impressions. Georgie lived in a shell, she peeped in and out at whim like a cockle. With her friends gathered safely around her she could remain aloof. The Buckpits were up first for the milking, clanking and banging, and the soft-footed cows passed by her window, the dungy smell of them wafting up. Then she would hear the tortured sound of Cramer's Land Rover engine; he would be setting off for God knows where, towing a badly packed, dangerous trailer behind him. Sometimes Donna went with him, but on the days she did not she started to wander across to Furze Pen and join in whatever they happened to be doing. Georgie grew used to her company, she hung around like a lost puppy. Georgie would wave when she saw her coming, but Donna would give a shy little smile as if there was some secret between them. Strange, a little uncomfortable, but then Donna was odd. Donna was needy. Her moods were erratic, sometimes she could be irritatingly rude to Georgie's visitors, at others she couldn't do enough to please them.

Georgie told Suzie that if anyone round here was mentally questionable it must surely be Donna, not Lot or Silas, because of the faraway look in her eye and the way she never followed conversations. But Suzie said she was far from daft, she was clever and manipulative. She had wormed her way into Georgie's affections using a simple sympathy ploy and Georgie had fallen for it. 'She wants more from you than you think,' Suzie warned. 'She's a taker. And she's wound you round her little finger. Watch it, Georgie. That girl is very disturbed and I think you're getting in too deep.'

Poor Donna. She would mentally slip away from all of them, following some unconnected thought of her own. She looked much fitter than the first time Georgie had met her. The warmth must agree with her. But her nose was always a sore red and she could never stop sniffing.

'I am definitely going to leave him,' Donna would creep into the kitchen and confide to Georgie in the middle of some chaotic meal, or after some childish accident which required bandages. These important consultations never came at a good time.

'Well, Donna, that's up to you, of course.' Georgie would try to give her attention while she worked frantically round her.

'It's just that I am obsessed with Chad and I can't seem to break free.'

'You have to think of yourself, Donna,' Georgie told her sensibly. 'And your future. And the way Chad treats you doesn't do much for your self-esteem, does it?'

'I've never thought much of myself,' Donna would moan, listlessly, floating around in her latest foamy arrangement of second-hand scarves. She smelled strongly of dope and Chad's railway carriage. 'I just wish I could be a more positive person, more determined, more like you.'

Like me? If the silly girl only knew. 'Oh, Donna, you're great as you are. You don't need to change. Just like yourself more. It's a pity there aren't any self-assertion courses for women anywhere around here.'

'But you can help me, can't you?' Once she started Donna just wouldn't stop. She would follow Georgie to the loo and carry on behind the door. 'I can't do it without you, Georgie. I've never known anyone like you before. I'd give anything to be more like you, important, intelligent, cultured like.'

Cultured? My God, Mark would snigger at that one.

But Donna always returned obediently to the derelict cottage over the ford before Chad came home. 'He'd be flaming if he knew how much time I spent over here. He knows how much I like you. You like me, too, don't you, Georgie?'

The conversation was getting tricky. 'Well, I'm fond of you, Donna, of course I am. You know that.'

'We're friends, you and me.' She cast down her eyes, embarrassed. For a while they were both silent. Donna stared up under her lashes. 'Chad's jealous, see, and still smarting over that bleeding furniture deal. He hates to be seen off like that and he's the sort of sod who never forgets.'

Georgie thought hard before she asked her, 'But he wouldn't do anything violent, for some kind of misguided revenge?'

'What sort of violence?'

'Oh, I don't know. I just wondered if he might try to frighten me, perhaps by playing some tasteless joke.'

'No. I don't think he'd bleeding bother. But if there was ever a chance he'd screw you up he would. He's like that, you see. And I know exactly what a sod he is, and yet I can't break away from him.'

Sometimes Georgie saw Nancy Horsefield pottering madly in her garden, planting the latest sack of roses she'd sent for by mail order. Georgie would see her staring across into the orchard, and if she could she would go over and talk, because Nancy was mentally imprisoned on her own land. Horace informed her mournfully that his wife had not been out for years. But whenever Georgie put down her spade or removed her gardening gloves to go over it felt like a waste of time, because all Nancy would say, with her little head bobbing over the wall was, 'Wait there, don't move, I'm off to fetch you a nice cup of tea, or would you prefer a cold drink, and I've got some scones fresh out of the oven. Wait right there and I'll bring them out. I'm a drudge to my kitchen, truly I am . . .'

What the loss of a child can do . . .

And Georgie would try to deter her. 'Please don't bother, Nancy. I've just had a drink and something to eat. I only came across for a chat, to see how you are on this lovely day.'

But it was hopeless. Excited and overwrought, Nancy had already gone in. So Georgie would have to wait as instructed, sometimes for longer than twenty minutes, before Nancy returned with a tray all neatly arranged with a cloth, laden with unwanted food. Horace would eye Nancy ruefully from under the shade of his Panama hat. The man worked stolidly behind his wife, his rolled-up sleeves exposing his massive forearms, huge as the hocks of a cow, finishing off the various jobs Nancy had started but would not finish. They were forever digging up old things and replacing them with new, or a hammock would arrive by special delivery and have to be assembled, or a set of pine tables and chairs, or a new garden umbrella, or a complicated lawn-watering system. At the end of the summer they took delivery of hundreds of pastel patio slabs and Georgie watched while poor Horace carted them off the road, over his little private bridge and round into his back garden. No wonder their house was perfect, they were constantly working on it, and clearly, to the Horsefields, money was no object. Happily Horace could afford to pander to Nancy's manic whims.

And Nancy was harmless, wasn't she? There was no malign side to her illness?

*   *   *

But gradually, so gradually it was almost un-
noticeable, Georgie's many visitors retreated to
their tents and pulled up their zips at night. Campfires began to feature as more of an event and folk
started gathering indoors in the evenings. They
began lighting fires inside the cottage again, and
Georgie had time to marvel at how much they had
already accomplished. Furze Pen was almost un-
recognizable. Fresh and clean, neat and tidy, even
the spartan shower room began to look almost
tempting. They'd fitted a new lavatory so that
people felt they could sit on the seat and spend
some time there without getting wet or being
watched by the lurking hairy brown spiders that
used to fill every nook and cranny.

The staunch, sensible fence at the end of the
orchard kept out the Buckpits' sheep. The stream
had been cleared and now ran freely without
slurping over onto the grass. The apple trees had
been pruned and sprayed and the docks had been
dug out of the grass. The brambles and nettles
were all gone. The chickens had broken out of
their run and now they roamed about freely.
Between them they had managed to decorate the
cottage both inside and out, the rotten woodwork
had been replaced and most of the electrics had
been rewired. The old plumbing had been replaced by new plastic piping, and when Georgie
saw the rusty tangle of stuff that came out she
wondered why Stephen had not been poisoned
earlier.

'There'll just be you and me soon,' said Donna
in her soft, fierce voice.

*   *   *

One morning as Georgie walked out she smelled
autumn. She also smelled a rank decay. It came on
sharp little breezes, it came with the most minute
turning of colour and a slight squelchiness of the
ground. The domes of the horse chestnuts were
crimson and amber and green, like the cheeks of
ripened apples, and their nuts littered the grass
beneath them. The tangled hedges were bright
with the scarlet berries of dog rose and thorn and
the blue-black fruit of bramble. As ever it brought
a sadness with it, and a yearning, for Georgie, as it
always did. With a cold shiver she realized that
she had not settled into this small community
at all, she had merely rubbed shoulders with it.
She had watched it go round her for the last
six months, from the safety of a familiar world
which she had deliberately created. And what is
more, it had watched her. It had never ceased
its abominable watching. It was there, a silent
presence over the laughter, over the music, over
the sun. This valley was dark. This valley was
accursed. Once the last of her visitors had left it
would encroach upon her and there would be no
way she could draw herself in tight enough for
protection from it.

Weird and sinister as it was, Wooton-Coney
was Georgie's reality now.

So what? This was her own choice. She could
change her mind at any time, and go back to
London and her flat. There was absolutely no
need to winter here all alone. But she could not
back out now, not now the cottage was so perfect

and everyone had worked so hard to make it comfortable for her. Georgie had convinced all her friends, even if she had failed to convince herself, and now, reluctantly, they'd accepted her decision. They had stopped all attempts at persuasion. So they carried on just the same for as long as they could, working as long as the weather held good. That is how Georgie wanted it and that is how it would be. She was feeling better, saner, freer, she had left the depths of despair behind but was terrified of slipping back down.

'It'll be good when it's just you and me, won't it?' said Donna. 'All those people gone at last. We'll have some fun. We'll have a good laugh. And we'll still drink wine and play cards, won't we?' She sounded quite exultant, but there was something baneful . . .

Could Donna be playing some mischievous game?

And this recurrent fear, this weakness of Georgie's, annoyed her. It frightened her, she had to tackle it and overcome it once and for all, because she was never the nervous type, the weedy, neurotic, self-obsessed sort of person, she'd always been proud of her calm self-assurance.

Isla and Suzie were the last of her visitors and they came for one weekend. Last weekend. They had been lucky. There was nothing too arduous to do so they lazed around in the warm, they could sit and talk and play Scrabble. They could enjoy

237

the fruits of their previous labour with no sense of guilt.

They tried one more time to persuade her. By now custom seemed to demand it. She realized they had been put up to it, probably by the motherly Helen. That was when Georgie kept repeating, '*But I am not alone*. I have neighbours. And in a perverse sort of way I am looking forward to the experience.'

'Oh yes, Donna round here all the time staring at you with adoring eyes, demanding constant attention. She's got you sussed out. She'll be moved in here before you know it.'

She waved this nonsense away. 'No chance. Donna's OK. Donna's no problem.'

Georgie was lying, of course. But she could not bear them to know her need. Donna did not bother her, Donna she could handle, but the fear of loneliness did. The whole Angie Hopkins affair had so undermined her that she had collapsed on her friends, she had shown them a vulnerability that she preferred to deny. Their very concern and kindness had erected a barrier between them which Georgie found hard to deal with. She was the strong, dependable one, she was the one who could cope with anything life threw at her . . . but now look . . .

'I am back to normality now,' she told them, resting her head on her hand with a weary gesture. 'Surely that is obvious. I am back to my old self completely.' It was annoying to have to keep saying it, it felt like they didn't believe her, they were always probing the sorest places, the wounds that were fresh and that she didn't want touching.

Isla pretended the weather concerned her. 'Georgie,' she insisted, stabbing with her spectacles. 'The winters here must be diabolical. The sort of cold we're just not used to with our centrally heated lives, sheltered streets and warm shops . . .'

'If the cold becomes too much for me then I'll jack it in,' Georgie sighed and repeated. 'I am not on an island, you know. And I do have a car and a phone.' It wasn't the cold that worried Georgie, why couldn't they see that? Why couldn't they tell? From the pernicious presence of Mrs Buckpit to the lamentable misery of Horace, from the dull brutality of the Buckpit brothers to the loathsome Chad, all posed an obscure, subconscious threat, all watched, all listened, all speculated in their own way.

Suzie said, 'I'm just bothered that it's your stupid pride that's making you obstinate.'

'Since last December there's not been much of that left.' Georgie poked hard at the innocent fire. 'And you of all people ought to know that.'

'So there's nothing we can say to dissuade you?'

'Nope.' She looked up belligerently. 'I am grateful for your concern. I am grateful for all sorts of things, for so much, but I am determined to stay. *Hell, we're only talking about a few months.*'

'That's that then,' said Isla, swigging down the last of the wine like a hard-drinking boozer and banging the glass down on the table.

'Yep,' Georgie said with her heart in her mouth. *Why oh why did they give up on her so easily?* They ought to know her better by now, she was all mouth, she was all defiance. 'That's that.'

Was she the only one who could smell the maleficence, like a wild beast crouching?

So the following morning she waved them off with that same stiff smile on her face, with Donna standing, grinning beside her, a box of tissues in her hand.

Eighteen

Good. At dear last we arrive at the present. It is so much more immediate.

After Isla leaves, Georgie endures five days on her own, and it's then she sees the figure on the hill, and approaches him, and frightens him away, or at least that is what she thinks she has done.

The devil walking the valley again?

It is only a couple of days after this that this sensible, well-adjusted woman feels she must be losing her wits. The spectre of insanity dogs her in all sorts of nagging ways. She has adopted the habit of taking Lola for a walk over one particular field and, beside the hedgerow of this field, a lane runs down the other side. There's this special oak tree with sofa-like roots and a wonderful view, the tree is the turning point of her twenty-minute walk. She sits there and contemplates airily while the dog goes rabbiting, ears flapping wildly, nose deep in the hedges.

There are times, as she sits here, admiring the changing colours, flaming bracken and chocolate leaves, an earth of red and gold, carried away by the drama of the skies, that she is certain someone is standing on the other side of the hedge, down in the lane behind her.

241

Some silent watcher.

This time the thought is so real she is forced to investigate. She gets up to see, but everyone knows there is nothing more fatal than pandering to this type of imaginary fear. Reaction reinforces it. It is so much wiser to dismiss the irrational and concentrate hard on something real. But anxiety overrides logic. Georgie creeps towards the hedge like a cat stalking a mouse, she creeps behind her oak tree and stands on tiptoe, peering over the straggly hedge and down onto the dusty lane. There is quite a drop in the levels. *Hell, was that a scuffling sound?* Heart stops beating. Ears start pounding. Lola appears, tail wagging, eyes all excited, so Georgie hurries on, careful not to look behind her but whistling the dog to come quickly. Is that an answering whistle? No, she must be mistaken. She blames Lola because it is more convenient, she is furious with the dog for escaping into the lane and causing this unnerving feeling. Was it Lola? It must have been. Dammit, dammit, in future she will take a different route.

Such a feeble, puny fear, caused by nothing but her own paranoia, hardly the kind of thing you can discuss with anyone sensibly.

Somebody out there is watching her.

'I have chopped as much wood as I can but there's nowhere near enough to last me through the winter.' There is no sign that Lot Buckpit hears her as she stands there feeling silly on this chilly October morning. The sound of her own voice

242

seems strange, these days she hears it so little. She carries on, insistent, interspersing her sentences with the falling of the axe, trying to peer into the milking parlour, to check on the rumour of the old man's ashes, but it's no good, the door is closed. When the silver thud is over, when he starts to tug at the wood, that is when Georgie says again, 'I could ring locally and order a couple of loads from town, I'm sure they would deliver them, but I thought I'd ask you first. I thought you might want the work.'

Chop chop chop.

The ignorant pig. OK OK. She is probably being a pain in the arse. We all know what it feels like when you're trying hard to concentrate, fighting for breath, trembling with exertion, and some jerk expects you to speak. You see it when interviewers try to corner athletes, or footballers straight after the game. You experience it yourself while changing the duvet cover. Lot does not glance in Georgie's direction. Perhaps the man is deaf. Maybe Mark is right and he is mentally subnormal. But Georgie can hardly drift away without an answer to her question.

And nor does it seem as if the brute is wrestling with exhaustion. There is not a bead of sweat on his brow and his heavy breath is coming remarkably smoothly. The mighty axe splits the wood as if it's as fluid as water. His pot belly flops with every stroke. He picks up the logs effortlessly and flings them onto the growing pile. Georgie's pile is not growing, Georgie is extravagant with her enormous fires, she has watched her precious

243

stock dwindle to nearly nothing at all. Fires are not just for warmth, they provide some living company with the sounds they make and the moving feeling of another life besides Lola.

'Whaddya want?'

Georgie jumps, so sudden is his hatchet-faced mother's arrival. And so silent. Mrs Buckpit slyly creeps forward in her slippers, somehow making Georgie feel guilty for being discovered in the yard, perhaps she should have gone to the door and approached the woman first, rather than come here behind her back? She almost feels like she's been caught stealing, it really is as awkward as that.

Donna, who loves a gossip, had told her, 'She's a bad-tempered old slag. Just as rude to everyone. And vicious, Christ! She wants to flog and hang, draw and quarter. She won't even speak to me, she thinks I'm a fallen woman. She goes round with that rotten smell under her nose as if you're after jumping in bed with one of her precious boys, as if she believes some slut is going to steal into her filthy yard and screw them. She can't see what slobs they are and that no woman would look at them twice. And anyway, they stink of shit. They're worse than bleeding animals. Someone who knew them when they were little told Chad they used to throw baby rooks in the stream and throw stones at them for a laugh. Baby rooks which fell from their nests. That's the sort of kids they were.'

So startled by the sudden emergence of the venomous Mrs Buckpit, and with Donna's dark stories fresh in her mind, Georgie pulls herself together to explain.

'We will deliver your wood, Mrs Jefferson,' the dragon tells her frostily. 'But it might be damp. It won't be seasoned.'

What is Mrs Buckpit so scared of? Could anything but fear cause such needless aggression? Is it fear of outside influences that frighten the woman so? It is an open secret that she will not allow TV, newspapers, or even radio into her house. If so, how does she think she will cope with letting Chad's cottage to strangers? But hell, it's not as if Georgie is a stranger, she is here at the door every week, has been for months, paying her bill, but the two women are still no closer. Her stare is invariably exactly the same, she acts as if she loathes her neighbour. She is rarely out in the fields with her sons, but stays inside the farm-house like a vixen might stay in its lair, lurking inside shrunken cardigans. Mrs Buckpit deals with the reps who call, but Georgie has seen no other visitors, and Lot and Silas never go out, not even to the Blue Bull of an evening.

At the beginning Georgie had taken a selection of visitors to that local hostelry, but it was basic and depressing, designed for darts and pool, designed for men after work, no carpets, just lino. Mark, a real ale freak, was disgusted. The heavy smell of grease in the air had yellowed the menus which boasted chips with everything, but the Buckpit brothers had never showed up. The only place they visit as a family is the nearby chapel every Sunday, and their only concession to any dress code is a couple of faded jackets over their dungarees, and shoes instead of wellington boots. Their mother disappears once a week in the battered truck to fetch groceries from the cash and carry. She wears a belted old mac, wellies and a headscarf, a selection of string bags over her shoulder reminding Georgie of fairy-tale witches kidnapping children in forests. Georgie longs to ask about Stephen, but Mrs Buckpit remains unapproachable, it is glaringly obvious that the woman dislikes her.

Perhaps, in the past, Stephen had upset her.

Objective achieved and Georgie leaves the oxlike Buckpit to chop away at his wood undisturbed. At the farm gate she passes his spindly brother, small, restless and perky. Silas scratches his head and draws on a battered cigarette. He coughs and spits on the ground behind her as Georgie passes by, and she thinks he is probably leering. Ugh!

The hapless Donna is now in the habit of coming over for coffee each morning, and Georgie is not quite sure if she approves of this arrangement or not. She remembers Suzie's warning. The girl is getting too dependent. Donna stays all day until just before Chad is due home. These endless counselling sessions involve the relaying of every single sad event in Donna's lamentable life, with Georgie encouraging her to put her past behind her. Uneasy in her old social worker role, she is more than frustrated to be thrust back in it by this defeated girl. Apparently Chad picked Donna up in some dowdy second-hand salesroom more than a year ago. Gradually he had acquired, it would seem, complete domination over her. She had run away from home and was homeless, trying to sell some plates she had found while rummaging through a skip. The hackneyed story of step-father abuse. The friends she'd travelled with had abandoned her with no work, no money and nowhere to go, and Chad the masterful offered her a roof and some measure of safety.

'He exploited my needs,' whines Donna, her lanky hair trailing over the marmalade jar, fiddling with a teaspoon as always.

'Poor Donna,' Georgie says wearily, 'I do wish I could do something to help.' The girl smells of damp, of Chad's railway carriage.

'But I needed somebody strong and masterful,' Donna moans in her maudlin manner. 'I needed someone to own me. Don't you ever long to be owned?' She peers at Georgie through watery eyes. 'Don't you ever long to be mastered?'

'Not in the way that I think you mean.'

'But it's horrid to be alone in the world.'

'But lots of us are alone, Donna, aren't we? And I think there are probably more lonely people in relationships than by themselves. But you could find somebody else, Donna, I'm sure you could, if you really tried. Somebody who would respect you for what you really are. You're a pretty girl, you could get a job . . .'

'What job could I do? I've got no bleeding certificates.'

'There must be something.' If Georgie sounds

sharp it's because she's so reluctant to take this voluntary client on board.

'Chad doesn't mean to hurt me, it's only when he comes home sloshed. He's sorry in the morning.' But her bruises are proof, to her, of Chad's love. That same hoary old chestnut. Proof of Chad's ownership of her. 'He shouts at me to get out, he swears he doesn't want me, but I know he does really.' She muses on in silence before going on, probably for Georgie's benefit, 'But one day soon I'm determined to leave him.'

'Yes, Donna. You really ought to, for your own sake.'

It is so easy to know other people's answers.

'And I think I'm in love with somebody else,' says Donna. Mysteriously.

The logs duly arrive. The surly Buckpits stack them neatly in Georgie's newly whitewashed woodshed, completely free of clutter now, but not quite dry because some of the slates on the roof are loose, they don't overlap correctly, if you look up you can see slithers of sky, and when it rains there's a steady drip. Georgie puts down a bucket to catch it.

The woodshed is satisfactorily full. Yet again she attempts to communicate. 'That's wonderful. Now I'll be warm whatever the weather threatens to do.' But the brothers gaze at her steadily as they wipe their hands on their overalls. Lot has the decency to give a kind of a nod, not a friendly nod, of course, more of a crude acknowledgement.

They clearly disapprove of their new neighbour's independence. Of her up-until-now sociable lifestyle. Of her unmarried status. They probably think her a scarlet woman.

Otherwise Georgie is well prepared for the coming winter siege. There are books she has meant to read for years, a stock of good wine in the larder, the freezer is brimming with food. She has made jelly and jam from her apples, although she's not keen on jam. She could live on blackberries for the next ten years, and they slop, frozenly, with the plums across the bottom of the freezer. Her chickens provide her with large brown eggs and there is milk on her step each morning. She has spent many days exploring, driving round the countryside getting to know her way round, stopping at tempting country pubs and taking photos with Stephen's excellent camera. She has been for long walks with Lola, and she knows she is a hundred times fitter than when she first arrived.

So run the days . . .

Sometimes she fiddles with Stephen's paints. She kept a few clean canvases, his brushes and his easel, fingering them and wondering if she could, one day . . . Wondering about his talent and if she ought to try herself. She never has, apart from her childish efforts at school, which were never especially successful, rather apathetic in fact. It would be a way to pass the hours and, who knows, like Donna, she might surprise herself.

She thinks about this so much that it becomes a

worry. Her palms are almost itching with the desire to try and yet she's afraid in case she fails.

But this evening, after Donna's departure, she plucks up courage, she mixes some paints on a palette, sits at the table and tackles the sunset. Ridiculous really, what a daunting subject for an amateur. She makes a total mess of it, and as she obstinately perseveres, trying to correct her mistakes, it gets worse. The whole ugly mess she makes depresses Georgie deeply, for she is a stubborn woman, unable to accept the fact that she cannot be fair at everything. She has to plod doggedly on, in spite of the unlikely odds, she is determined to keep trying.

So it is late when she finally lets Lola out and frustrated goes upstairs to bed. She abandons the ruined canvas crossly and leaves it beside the rubbish bin. She sticks the brushes in jam jars of turps and leaves the paints on the table. There is no need to clear up, what bliss, so different to her life in London. She has no reason to rush off anywhere first thing in the morning and visitors are out of the question. Georgie's got all the time in the world.

She's not in the habit of locking the door, there is no real need to do so. Buried away in Wooton-Coney, such simple security measures would feel quite ridiculous, pandering to needless panic. Even the sighting of the stranger, although it made her uneasy, is not by itself a reason to make her start on the business of locks and bolts. And the foolish suspicion that someone stalks her on her walks is nothing but that, a flight of imagination.

We know she was never the self-indulgent type with an over-active imagination. Georgina Jefferson is multi-steady, her feet are firmly stuck to the ground. She would be most unlikely to see a ghost, and if she did she would deny it, put it down to her state of mind, shadows and effects of the light. The Loch Ness monster could rise and sink before Georgie's eyes and she would turn it into a submarine, a wave, or a floating tree trunk. She quite understands that those who see these manifestations truly believe what they say, but they are poor misguided souls, too naive to be taken seriously. It is a need they have to fulfil, like religion. She does not feel the need for extra drama in her life, or the supernatural. She does not need a god either. She is who she is, and has always been contented with that, able to cope remarkably well without an eternal purpose. You might think these sensible qualities would protect her now.

But a heavy grey blanket comes up from the west. The morning brings a slow, steady drizzle, the sort of condition she will soon get used to. The whole cottage turns dark with it, and water drips depressingly off the edges of the thatch and turns it a mucky brown. Every so often there is a dull thud as a drenched old apple drops onto the grass. She goes to the kitchen to let Lola out. She will have a restoring cup of coffee before she tackles the mess of paints left on the table from last night.

She pauses to inspect the colours and textures,

but only briefly. Her eyes are drawn to the smears of red which now cover the palette. A watery red, not like the oils which bump and wrinkle underneath. This is more like a watercolour.

Frowning, she picks up the palette and holds it to the light. Her oils from last night are almost dry, but this red is still wet and running. New paint? She stares round anxiously with gazing eyes. Is her kitchen undisturbed? And is the palette in the same place as she left it last night? Or has somebody been in here and moved it?

But why?

And who the hell would?

Georgie sits down, not frightened yet, just terribly bewildered. Could she have made those marks herself and forgotten all about them? Had she mixed up some powder paint? No, that was ridiculous. If she had done that she would remember.

Seated at the table with her coffee before her she touches the red paint tentatively with her finger, she rubs it with her thumb. Jesus! *Is it paint?* There is a brackishness about it. She cannot decide. She smells the stain on the end of her finger. Nothing, only hand cream. In her complete bewilderment she is tempted to lick it. She brings her finger towards her mouth, but cannot bring herself to take it further.

It could be the juice of berries, she supposes, sloes perhaps, or blackberries, there are plenty of those about. But the colour is not quite right for either of those, and how would they have reached her palette? The appalling thought that the red could be blood keeps crossing her mind, but then she laughs out loud at such a ludicrously outrageous idea.

She must have left those marks herself, there is no other rational explanation, but she's going to enquire just the same. The whole problem is so bizarre she can find no sensible answer. She tries to dismiss it, but that's not so easy.

As Georgie progresses through the day, not doing much, not doing enough to distract her, her thoughts keep turning morbidly to dwell on that blessed doll, the make-up case, the figure on the hill, the feeling of being spied upon on her favourite walk. Her heart sickens and sinks. All the inexplicable issues come together to worry her, so she finds it quite impossible to concentrate on anything else. She knows that it is illogical, but she is being haunted by neurotic concerns and knows how absurd she would sound if she tried to explain them to anyone else.

The world as she has known it is falling away from her.

In the end she sits, just sits, mute, waiting and frightened, incapable of movement of body or mind.

Dear God, she is not that confused, she is not that blind to reality yet. All that is wrong with Georgie is that she is almost paralysed with terror and apprehension. These marks are not made of paint. Neither are they innocent berries. *They are blood stains put there deliberately*. And she has always had such a horror of insanity.

Right. This is it. This is enough. This is the time

to call it a day. But everyone would naturally conclude that living alone was affecting her mind, that she was seeing danger behind every shadow. They would be proved right after all. They would tell her she wasn't coping, they would advise her to return to London immediately, and Georgie, the successful one, would feel, once again, that she'd failed.

And Georgie doesn't want that. Dammit, she wants her dignity back.

Nineteen

Who are these fat-heads? Heroines who stay in hotels while the tap water splashes with gore, remain loyal to maniacs with axes, wander down into crypts and cellars to investigate some spine-chilling scream, oh no, Georgina Jefferson is certainly not one of those.

So she rarely watches the predictable horrors of mass entertainment, they try her patience too much.

Should she, at this moment in time, leave Furze Pen Cottage and return to London? Would she, if she had been watching a film, have lost sympathy with herself by now and turned off?

Well, all she can say in mitigation is that the situation is not too dire an emergency yet, certainly not dire enough to disrupt all her careful plans. No cause for panic, just unpleasant and rather nasty, so she sets off, true to form, to find some reasonable explanation for the paint, and the only individual she considers remotely suitable, the only house in Wooton-Coney to which she is welcomed, is the eccentric home of the Horsefields.

Back in her bright velour tracksuits after the summer break, this morning Nancy wears pink bottoms and a fluorescent-orange top. Her Hi-Tec boots make her feet look preposterously large under such a small and bustling body. Helpless to refuse her largess, Georgie does not protest as she is ushered to the fire while Nancy rushes off to make proud preparation.

It is not unusual for Georgie to pop round in this casual way. Feeling so sorry for Horace, and having admiration for the manner in which he protects his demented wife who depends on him entirely, she has been known to pop round for a chat. There is no help for poor Horace, no magic agency who will come in and take charge while he has a rest, and he would not consider leaving her anyway. Nancy would not cope left on her own with strangers.

He raises the subject himself in a roundabout way. After Nancy leaves the room, when her slipstream has spun off behind her, he says in his gloomy Eeyoreish style, 'You look strained. You look as if you haven't been sleeping. You must be missing your friends.'

Unsure how she should start without sounding overdramatic, Georgie says, 'It's not that, Horace. But you're right, I am under strain because I've been so worried just lately.' It seems unfair to burden him with more, but hell, he's the only one around her who will listen. He might be miserable and morose, but at least he's fairly normal.

It helps her to go on with her tale when she sees he's not watching. Instead he sits, staring abjectly into the fire with his sunken eyes half closed, his long fingers strumming the arm of his chair and his weary legs crossed. With the minimum of emotion, careful not to overdo it, she tells him how she came downstairs and discovered the wet paint. She is careful to make it abundantly clear that she is no fool, not the kind to be unduly influenced by strange fears and fantasies. 'I know there must be some reasonable explanation,' she says, 'because there always is to these happenings.' And then, because of his continuing silence, because of his comfortable, relaxing breathing, she goes on to tell him about the doll and the make-up case, she even describes her disquieted feelings when taking her favourite walk.

'Dammit, Horace, there was someone there.'

He listens without a word, and Georgie feels as flustered and foolish as Nancy.

Finally, after a good deal of silent thought and strumming, Horace opens his eyes and pronounces, 'There is something about this place.'

Georgie is disappointed in him. She expected something more positive. She says again with more emphasis, '*But someone has actually been inside my cottage at night while I was sleeping upstairs.* And who was the person on the hill – that still disturbs me. Hell, Horace, I walked towards it and it just disappeared, shot into the copse before I could reach it.' She leans forward and clasps her fingers. 'It was as real as you are, believe me. Listen, do you think that some tramp could have come to the hamlet and is living in a deserted barn, visiting woodsheds at night and generally wandering around? Could this be possible? But if there is someone, then how come I

257

am the only person to have seen him?' She shakes her head. 'It doesn't make sense.'

'That is possible, I suppose. Or it might be that odd girl, Donna, she's in the habit of walking at night. I once saw her dancing on the hill. Thought it was a monstrous crow the way the moonlight lit her up. Have you mentioned this to anyone else?'

Georgie sits back, relieved after bearing her soul. 'Well, I'm hardly on speaking terms with Mrs Buckpit, and the brothers have never said one word to me. Chad Cramer's still put out because of Stephen's furniture, and I think if I mentioned these things to Donna she might panic, she can be hysterical. No, I haven't said anything. That's why I'm here. I decided to ask you first.'

Horace lifts his funereal eyes and rests them on Georgie. 'Have you considered the possibility,' he asks, 'that you might be imagining things?'

Her answer is swift. She puts him straight. 'I am definitely not that sort of person. I have even, in my time, been called insensitive.'

Is Horace even listening? Still staring in his hang-dog way, he advises in all seriousness, 'Perhaps it might be wiser if you went back to London.'

'So you think all this is in my head,' Georgie bridles, 'and that I am losing my marbles?'

His answer is slow and ponderous. 'No, not quite. I think it's difficult for anyone to come to terms with somewhere as unique as this from the sort of life you have obviously been used to. This solitary existence could well affect you, I certainly don't believe you are making anything up. Strange things do happen in the country, but you appear to have lumped all sorts of little incidents together and associated them with one man, the figure you saw on the hill.'

'Yes,' says Georgie, 'that's true. I have. So you're saying that all these events could be unconnected?'

'And that most of them are just the sort of silly, odd occurrences that happen every day. When you lead a sociable, busy life, like yours, you don't notice them. But now there's time to sit and think.'

'It's incredible what the effects can do. OK, I give you that a stranger could have been passing through and that Stephen, for some reason, kept a doll and a child's make-up case in his woodshed. They might even belong to Donna, the girl is such a puzzle. I even give you the unlikely possibility that the fire could have started on its own. But how about the paint? *It was blood*, Horace, dammit, and I know how unbelievable that might sound, but I know without doubt, *it was blood*.'

'A bird could have flown in your window that night. It could have wounded itself while trying to escape, banging against the window. It could have left a mess on the table . . .'

Georgie, exasperated, cries, 'But there was no blood anywhere else in the room. My God, I looked, I checked.'

'Or a rodent. There are rats in the country, you know.'

Why is he denying the truth? To protect her? To make her feel better? There is nothing more annoying than this. 'What? *A wounded rat?* A wounded rat managed to climb onto my table, not leaving a trace anywhere else, and stagger about in the paint for a while before wiping its feet and retreating?'

Horace remains patient. 'I am merely attempting to justify . . .'

'But there isn't an answer, Horace, is there? That's what's so alarming. There really is no reasonable answer.' Georgie looks at him sadly, they exchange gloomy glances. 'Perhaps you're right. Perhaps I should go back to London.'

He raises melancholic eyebrows which force hairy question marks on his forehead. 'I think that is probably the answer.'

'But I have nowhere to go in London.' Georgie gives a tired shrug. 'My flat is let. I would have to find somewhere else and start over again.'

'That sounds like an excuse to me, not an insurmountable problem.'

But there's another reason. 'I really don't want to leave the cottage to go to seed again, empty for another winter. The damp would soon break through and destroy all the work we've done.'

'I'd be happy to take care of the cottage. I could light the odd fire, if that's what you wanted.' The poor man sounds so terribly weary.

'I challenged myself to stay here. I told myself I could do it. There are important reasons why I need to be on my own.' She is not prepared to delve any further into her own personal problems. She does not want Wooton-Coney to know what drove her here, or to realize who she is.

'You have to make your own decision,' says Horace, over noises from the kitchen, the preparatory sounds of Nancy's return. 'Of course. But my advice to you is to leave.'

His words are laden with foreboding and gloom.

They go through the familiar performance with the hostess trolley and Nancy's excitement at catering for that rare event, a visitor. This time she sits beside Georgie and shows her some precious catalogues. They encompass everything, from children's toys to bathroom suites, from underwear to garden sheds. 'I am a special, treasured customer,' she says, scurrying off to find the letters where the customer's name is printed in a slot. '*Dear Mrs Horsefield*,' she reads her favourite out to Georgie. '*We know how proud you will be to know you have been awarded our silver shield, a shield only ever presented to those customers whose patronage we particularly treasure.*' And Nancy holds up a cardboard shield she has carefully covered with cling film. 'I am determined to get the gold shield one day,' she tells Georgie excitedly while Horace pours the tea.

Is Nancy Horsefield quite as harmless as she seems?

Georgie tries to avoid Chad Cramer, not only because he's a nasty piece of work, but because she is sure he resents her friendship with Donna. Donna is always telling her so, she seems quite proud of the fact. He is bound to know the kind of confidences Donna is sharing, and it's not hard to guess what Georgie's advice is likely to be – leave him, he's a bastard. But one dark evening she meets him unexpectedly, he on his way to the farm, presumably to pay the rent, and Georgie on her way home having paid her milk bill. Instead of walking on after an exchange of unfriendly grunts, this time she decides to confront him.

'Oh, by the way, I managed to get some good prices for Stephen's paintings. I thought you'd like to know. There was also a rather expensive Jacobean chest and a couple of Turkish rugs. And I've cleaned up the furniture, I kept it all in the end. The cottage is quite a different place.'

'Some folks have got more money,' he growls, 'than they know what to do with.'

'I see you're not out of your cottage yet? You're still holding out?'

'It'll take more than that bleeding lot to budge me.' He's wearing his poacher's cap tonight and a torn brown anorak that comes away from the zip at the front. His skin is an unhealthy blotchy colour. 'And I see you've decided to hang on here now your posh mates have gone back up the line?'

If it is Cramer up to these grim tricks, and Georgie suspects that it is because there is no other answer, if he is trying to frighten her off, then she wants him to know that his plan is not working. 'Of course I'm still here, Chad. I'm like you, a sticker. It'd take more than a few small unpleasantnesses to move me out. No, I'm dug in for good.'

It is hard to gauge his reaction. Georgie can't

stand him. There's an air of unpleasant arrogance about him, and he stretches out an arm and lets it rest on the wall beside her, too close, much too close. In a subtle way this gesture is a threat. She gives him a most superior smile. 'I love it here,' she lies, 'it's a quite remarkable place.'

'You've not experienced real winter yet,' is all he grunts as he strolls away, whistling softly under his breath. 'I'd like to see what you think of that.' Is that the same whistle Georgie heard coming from the figure on the hill? But no, Chad's is a well-known song, the other was on two notes and tuneless. But a cheap, pink make-up case, he could easily have picked one up on the road.

Georgie tackles Donna cautiously the next time she comes over. Donna is nervous enough already, it wouldn't do to scare her. Georgie turns the conversation: 'Years ago, of course, travellers were quite different, gentlemen of the road, respected, even, for their eccentricity, and countryfolk used to give them food and let them sleep in their barns. They were quite harmless, those old tramps, funny, you don't see many these days.'

'No,' says Donna scrabbling around and half emptying Georgie's tissue box. 'Now it's scruffy old vans and dogs, and nobody gives a toss about them.'

'Have you ever seen a tramp round here, Donna? What about when you're out alone at night? Have you noticed anything odd? Do many strangers find their way to the depths of Wooton-Coney, I wonder?'

'Nah. I've never seen one.'

'Or kids?' Georgie goes on hopefully. 'Do the Buckpits have any other family, or friends? It's rather odd how this place lacks children, even visiting children.'

'You never see anyone new round here, that's the bleeding trouble, nobody ever comes and Chad's only got enemies.'

'I'd never have guessed.' But should she quiz Donna further about her nocturnal excursions? Surely, now the weather has turned, she stays safely indoors. This is not the first time it has occurred to Georgie that Donna could easily have let herself into the cottage that night, and for some distorted reason of her own smeared her painting palette with blood. It could have been she who started the fire. Most of her attention-seeking behaviour is pathetically transparent: wearing a bandage when she's not hurt, colouring her hair a dreadful purple, stealing small items she knows will be missed, telling the most un-believable lies. But even more worrying than this, it is now quite apparent that Donna has some kind of schoolgirl crush on her caring neighbour. 'You're a bit old for this sort of thing,' was Georgie's immediate response when Donna tried to air her feelings.

'I know, I can't help it, that's all.' She stood there with her legs crossed, her head hung low like a naughty child. 'I just need to be with you, to be near you . . . I really think that I love you.' She played with her nail-bitten fingers. Tears dripped down her cheeks as she stuttered her eternal devotion. 'I know how silly I sound but, Georgie, I can't get you out of my mind.'

Stranger things than this have happened between clients and their counsellors, and Donna is badly disturbed. 'It will pass,' said Georgie sternly, cutting her off before she went further. Perhaps this transference, although peculiar and most unwelcome, could help Donna eventually in her bid for freedom from Chad.

But now she has to ask the girl. 'Do you ever come in here during the night when I'm upstairs asleep?'

Donna frowns. 'Why do you ask?'

'Out of curiosity. Out of a need to know.'

'Would you care if I did?' Donna asks obstinately.

'I would much rather you asked me first.'

'I never did. Although sometimes I sat on the grass and watched. Wishing I could be in here with you. Safe and happy. Asleep in your spare room. Anyway, I don't go out any more. I only do that in summer when I can see where I'm going. I don't like it in the dark. It's dark in our cottage, dark and dingy.' Poor Donna gazes round Georgie's kitchen, not de luxe by any means, but far more comfortable than her own. 'And it's cold,' she shivers. 'It's always so bleeding freezing in there.'

'So why does Chad choose to make the place so depressing? I can see why he wouldn't bother to do up the house when they want him out, but he

265

could bring in more comfortable furniture, there's plenty of electric fires in that old carriage of his, carpets, lamps, why doesn't he use any of them himself? Couldn't you persuade him, Donna?'

'Oh, I've tried,' Donna whinges, 'over and over again. But he's the sort of bloke who doesn't notice his surroundings. If it's cold he puts his jacket on and sits by the fire in that. He's so sodding mean, that man. I dread another winter here. One more winter in that fridge and I think I might even die of exposure. I really wish I could live here with you. Why can't I live here with you? I wouldn't be a nuisance. I could help in all sorts of ways.'

How often Georgie longs to shake her. 'I've told you why you can't live here. I need to be on my own, that's why I came here in the first place, and anyway, it wouldn't be the answer. Have you tried the social services yet, Donna? Have you explained everything to them?'

Donna sulks. 'It wouldn't do no good, there'd be no sodding point. They'd send me back to Manchester. You don't really care about me at all, do you? Do you? *Tell me the truth!*'

Georgie refuses to get into this. They've been through this so many times before and it only ends in more tears. 'And don't you think that Manchester might be better than another winter here, *with him*? You're not really happy, are you, Donna?' And that is an understatement.

'But I just couldn't bear to be on my own. I'm not ready to make the break.' Poor despondent Donna, waiting for something wonderful, yearning for the impossible. She can't see that if that's what she's after she should damn well go and try for it.

'Well. One day perhaps.'

Just how damaged is Donna? What might she be capable of? Starting a fire? Cutting herself? She's done that before, one look at her wrists gives that secret away.

What other questions can Georgie ask? There are no satisfactory answers. She starts to lock her door at nights. She buys a bolt and chain. She wonders if she should pick some wild garlic to keep the devil at bay.

Twenty

Some hostile force is tampering with time. The days, which ought to be getting shorter, are stretching themselves into endless weeks, endless like the lonely moor, a thousand feet above the sea, which rolls away to left and right, the road just a small rope in the wilderness. This is loneliness, intense and hidden. Huh. How ironic to think that once Georgie truly believed she was getting over Angie's death, after those long summer months helped by a change of scenery, a change of lifestyle. But as winter's metal lid starts to close over the valley and seal it, well, I'm afraid that's how her head is starting to feel.

She cannot get rid of the nightmares – a child clad in a nightie tumbling down the steps at Kurzon Mount Buildings, with huddles of crow-faced women screaming at the burning doll in her arms. Somebody could have saved her, but he was standing on a hillside too far away, a dark figure just watching. Just a dream, only a dream. Trembling and sweating into wakefulness she staggers downstairs, but after finding the blood – was it blood? – she feels uneasy at her own kitchen table. By now she has convinced herself that Cramer is the culprit, that vicious slob broke into her cottage and smeared the blood in a mean act of vengeance. And she starts to dwell on the way she was hounded out of her London flat with bricks and letters and phone calls, that slowly turning cycle seems to be in motion again. *When will her persecutors leave her alone?*

But she is just an ordinary person trying to get on with her life. Never the centre of anyone's interest. Even at her most overwrought Georgie had never before been beset by such dark, astounding happenings as these.

Is it outside the bounds of reason that someone related to Angela Hopkins is conducting their own vendetta against her? Following her down to Dartmoor, stalking her, frightening her, driving her mad, venting his fury in some obsessive bid for justice? To make her pay the ultimate price? And if that is the case, would they be wrong . . . ? And if that is the case, by coming here she has played straight into their hands.

In her mind she sees him in the distance, a tall man, wide-shouldered with thick limbs, a lumbering in his movements and a heaviness in his stance.

With appalled horror Georgie notices how her hands have taken to shaking again.

Stephen remains insubstantial. Only scraps of information occasionally come her way, like how he religiously fed the birds, how he would set off alone with a rucksack and not be seen for days, and Mrs Buckpit unfolds her face enough to reaffirm, with distaste, that Stephen refused all help at the end, insulted the doctor, turned away the ambulance, and the only person he allowed to come near him was the melancholy Horace.

Mrs Buckpit adopts her most menacing tone. She might well prefer to cross herself. 'He got drunk regular. You could hear him, you'd see him performing out there on the road when he got very bad. He was disgusting.' If she considers Stephen disgusting, what does she think of her own two boys? Or doesn't she know that they piss in the parlour in full view of her husband's ashes?

'But what about when he was sober?' Georgie pleads to no avail. Mrs Buckpit, reluctant to give any more away, wipes all expression from her face. 'And surely when Stephen first arrived he couldn't have been as bad as you paint him? After all, he was a young man.'

'He never wanted no-one, not at the end, or the beginning. He should never have painted those naked women. Drove him quite mad in the end.'

And that seems to be that. The real truth at last. Mrs Buckpit had somehow got wind of Stephen's few innocent nudes and considered him pagan thereafter. And the truth about Stephen's life is probably equally simple, he chose his retreat, paid for the cottage – cheap in those days, no doubt, compared to today's standards – by selling his paintings, and refused to abandon it. But had he never felt an urge to move on?

Georgie regularly phones her friends. With a bright and breezy air, she says, 'I am absolutely fine. It's all rather novel, being on my own, but I'm fine.' She turns every problem into a joke and sits and listens as they laugh on the other end of the long, long line. And that is another feature of horror films she has always despised, that abysmal lack of communication, almost deliberate, that strikes the victims and turns them mute so they can't seek the help they so urgently need.

And she tries to remember the useful activities she promised to do with her time.

Helen and Roger Mace and the kids are coming to stay for Christmas, so there is a break to look forward to, if only for three days. But after that there'll be three long months to endure before the tenants are out of her flat and she can sell it, get rid of the cottage and move back to the city.

Should she take up her old job again? She toys with the idea of a brand-new career, in law perhaps, or teaching, but does not progress very far with that.

The days are so long. She can't go for long walks because of the steady, penetrating drizzle. Born on a Dartmoor wind, it breaks through whatever protection you use, you are soaked to the skin by the shattering rain after five minutes' exposure. Drives in the car are nothing but a depressing battle with wipers and demister. 'I want to come. How can you be so mean, driving off and leaving me here?' pleads Donna, struggling with her infatuation, which time only seems to intensify.

'Donna, you can't always be with me. It's not good for either of us. I'm only off for a drive, dammit. Go and find something better to do.'

Concentrating on books is beyond Georgie, life gets so bad that she finds herself looking forward to bedtime, and tries to prolong that longed-for moment. She watches TV until well after midnight, and only then will she release herself and plod up the stairs to try to sleep. When it comes it is balm. More often than not it does not come. She remembers being a child at home, jumping when the door creaked open. She shouted into the terrible silence, '*But I locked the door, you can't get in!*' and wakes to discover she was asleep, having another terrible nightmare. So Georgie lies there tossing and turning, listening to the stream rushing relentlessly under her window, the moaning wind and that infernal rain, ceaseless during this long October. Drip drip drip. It patters off the thatch with such weary regularity it is a Chinese water torture. And so is the fact that Lola, on the floor beside her, sleeps the sleep of the just and feels no need to keep one eye open. Like she does.

Movement, any new undertaking, is a real effort. What the hell did she expect? And what is happening to her mind? Is she turning into a hysteric, the sort she has always despised?

Truly, she is pitiful to see. Georgie is a textbook case. To help herself find sleep she takes to drinking red wine at night. It starts with one glass, but when that fails to work it is two, then three, then the bottle, until the room spins round as she lies there, miserable, wretched, unable to understand what is happening and not knowing how to beat the depression that has gripped her so completely. Georgie never could handle drink. She begins to feel guilty about putting all those empties out, sure that the beady eyes of Mrs Buckpit are watching and counting, marking the results of her failure on some hidden pad to be accounted for afterwards. The cow will think the same boozy weakness runs in the family. She takes to boxing the bottles up, trying to disguise her shameful habits.

Is she heading for a nervous breakdown? This is what frightens her. And no-one would know. Donna, so self-obsessed, probably wouldn't even notice. She'll be too far gone, a screaming wreck by the time they find her, too extreme a case for help.

At last November is almost here. Bonfire night was always a favourite, but there'll be no celebrations in Wooton-Coney. Does anyone here recognize Christmas? That's doubtful, apart from the Buckpits' visit to chapel. Bedtime at last, and Georgie picks up the log basket and trails into the woodshed, one of her little habits by which she has learned to tell the time. She likes to pick out a hefty log to burn on the fire all night so the downstairs is warm in the morning. Earlier, when it wasn't so cold, she let the fire go out, but the stone cottage takes ages to warm through thoroughly. There's a good stack of wood out there to burn, and the fireguard is a sturdy one, so it's safe and well worth it.

She turns on the woodshed light and searches for a suitable log. It has to be flat so it won't roll off. Georgie is fearful of fire, these days she is fearful of just about everything. Something makes her look up, something must have grabbed her attention, and the eye that stares down from the hole in the roof is quite unmistakable.

One horrendous staring eye.

A hideous shock.

Georgie freezes.

Every nerve in her body is screaming.

Bent as she is, arms stretching out towards the log, neck twisted round, her eyes hold to the one that stares back with a glaring intensity. No colour, no blinks, just an eye where the stars should be. Glittering through a hole in her roof. Tense as an animal in a trap she whispers to herself as she backs away, 'It's OK, it's OK.' But she cannot wrench her gaze away. She feels her way blindly from the shed, sobbing softly.

Oh God, where is Lola? It's OK, it's OK, the dog is indoors, asleep by the fire. Georgie slams the kitchen door, fixes the chain and stands there frozen, trying to breathe with her jaw slackly open. She wants to press her weight on the door and not let up for an instant lest the thing, lest the creature with the eye, tries to push its way through and grab her. Licking her lips Georgie slyly tiptoes to the phone, the eye might guess what she's up to and attempt to stop help coming . . . it might slam itself against the door . . .

With a hand that is dead, nothing like her own familiar warm one, Georgie dials 999. The voice that gives her address is steady and, astonishingly, sounds like her own. She is careful to give precise directions. It will not do for the police to get lost. She stresses the need for urgency and watches the night through the windows so hard that her eyes hurt, particularly as the curtains are drawn so she can't see out.

'I'll hold,' she tells the operator sharply. 'I can't put this phone down. It's out there, not yards away, and there's nobody here except me. I'll hold on until somebody gets here.' And she does just that. She grips so hard her hand is a claw, she clings for grim death.

Centuries go by while she waits for the police to arrive. Perhaps it was an animal. Oh my God, and she has mindlessly called the police, of course, it was an animal. What else would climb so soundlessly onto her woodshed roof and wait for her out there, and stare down so vacantly, so totally unblinkingly? The police will arrive and pour scorn on her terror; a Londoner come from up the line, making a fuss over some perfectly natural country occurrence.

Was it an animal? How can she tell? An eye is an eye, she would hardly have the presence of mind to stand there and sort through the possibilities, not in the state she is in, and how many glasses of wine has she had, and will the police smell it and decide she is just pissed?

'Are you all right?' calls the anxious voice on the phone, her lifeline.

'Yes, I'm all right. Just so long as you stay there.'

'Is there anyone I could call who could come and wait with you until we arrive?'

275

No, there is no-one. She can't disturb Horace Horsefield in the middle of the night, he couldn't possibly leave Nancy alone. Mrs Buckpit might come, Georgie supposes, but with such reluctance and bad temper she would be no use at all. Chad would enjoy refusing, and he would never allow Donna to help.

'No,' says Georgie in a pitiful voice. 'There's nobody. Only me.' It sounds as if it's her fault. As if she is unlovable, no friends, no relations. And as if she is one of those difficult neighbours everyone does their best to avoid.

'Not even a neighbour?' The operator will not give up and Georgie wants to shout, *This is Wooton-Coney for Christ's sake. There's neighbours and there's neighbours, and I am a stranger and unwelcome here.*

Eventually the lights of a police car kiss the hem of her curtains. Georgie weeps with relief. 'They're here,' she sobs to her staunch companion of the night. But not until she has let them in, not until the size of them and their sensibleness fills her living room dare she put the phone down, dare she face the click of being cut off.

The two policemen are both locals, both large and reassuring. She makes them tea. She sips her own with shaking hands. Only when they have finished their tea and she has described what happened in detail do they ask to see the woodshed. She cautiously takes the chain from her door and leads them outside. The woodshed light is still on.

'Where exactly did you see this eye?'

276

She points up bravely. Of course it's not there now.

'But you heard nothing when you entered the shed? You think it was already in position?'

'It must have been. There was only one small sound. That's what made me look up. Without that I might have come and gone without noticing anything and he'd probably still be there now.' Georgie shudders.

'We'd better take a look now we're here.'

So Georgie fetches her ladder and stands back and watches as one of the policemen climbs to the sloping roof. It's not high. You have to duck to get through the woodshed door, it's the only part of the roof which is tiled and if you don't duck you could cut your head on the slates. The policeman shines his torch and shouts down, 'Can't see anything here.' They poke about. They chat and look round while the rain damps their uniforms and their shoulders sparkle in the light from the door. Then they are back inside again, sitting by the fire, and the ruddy-faced of the two asks, 'And what makes you think there was a man on your roof? Isn't an animal more likely?'

Oh yes, she had known this was coming. 'It wasn't one of those tiny eyes. It wasn't the eye of a rat, or a mouse.'

'How about an owl?' He's taking notes. The other lights a cigarette and crosses his legs as if he's at home. It's pleasing to see him acting like this, she wants them to stay a while longer.

'It wasn't a round eye like an owl's. It was more slanted than that, more human. That's why I immediately assumed it must be a man.'

'I dunno what a fox's eye would look like from below, d'you, Wilf?'

'Well,' says the comfortably spreadeagled Wilf. 'In car headlights they look red, don't they? But God knows what they'd look like on a roof.' He turns to Georgie. 'What d'you think, Miss? Was it a fox's eye?'

She is nonplussed. This is a ludicrous conversation. 'I don't know what a fox's eye might look like, either.'

'You see, Miss,' and the ruddy-faced man with button nose looks at her kindly and says, 'frankly, it's so improbable that an intruder would be there on your roof, not least in weather like this, just staring down silently with intent, it's so unlikely that we have to discount it. Apart from which, if it was a man, once he'd been spotted he'd be off, wouldn't he? He wasn't to know that you'd hurry indoors, for all he knew you could have picked up a spade and attacked him. So you see, I think we're going to have to discount that possibility, I'm afraid.'

'I thought that's what you'd say.'

Wilf says, 'You disagree with our theory then?'

Georgie pushes at her wet hair frantically. 'No, I can't disagree. How can I disagree when you sound so plausible? I don't know who that eye belonged to, and I admit it seems a bit unlikely that a man would stay there once he'd been seen . . .'

'So, you see, you needn't have been so frightened. I mean, what's he after?' asks Wilf, looking round with a speculative eye.

And then they enquire how long she's been here and where she comes from, and Georgie is terrified something might jog their memories and they'll realize they've heard of her before. Very aware of her boozy breath, she fears they have already decided she's tipsy. But she's sobered up pretty quickly. And she had not been drunk. She's only had two glasses this evening. She tries too hard to sound totally sober, not the sort of neurotic to make up stories for attention on a dark night. A lonely woman who drinks too much. An unloved, unwanted woman with not enough on her mind.

She has a tussle with herself over whether to tell them about the figure, the doll, the make-up case, or the blood, but suspects that if she gets into that they are bound to dismiss her as one more nutter. But she longs to tell them, *she longs to* . . .

They are kindly men, friendly and sympathetic. They see how frightened Georgie is and they give her the time they can. They have no need to linger as long as they do and, of course, they cannot stay here all night, that is just impossible. But there is something so comforting about sitting here, chatting about this and that. Her fears do subside. She tells them some tales about Wooton-Coney and they join in with her laughter.

'Oh yes, there's some strange places round here. Strange folks, too, no doubt about it. Very incestuous, you see. You're just going to have to make sure you fetch that last log in daylight,' says the first cop over a second cup of tea. 'Get that chain on the door early. In the dark it's easy to imagine things. Everyone does it, especially when you're on your own and there's nobody to talk to.'

'It wouldn't have made any difference if there had been anyone else here,' says Georgie in a last bid to convince them. 'I would still have been terrified. I would still have believed there was a man on my roof.'

But would she? *Would she?* She knows just how neurotic she is getting and she knows she drinks too much.

'I tell you what,' says Wilf on leaving. 'Seeing as how you keep late hours, we pass along the top road most nights at about eleven thirty, so why don't we pop in occasionally just to reassure you?'

'Oh yes. Thank you.' She wrings her hands in gratitude, ready to clutch at any straw. 'That would be such a relief.'

But she imagines them in the safety of their car, raising their eyebrows as they drive away. She imagines one of them say to the other, 'Good God, you certainly see 'em all round here. Take that one for a start. Several sandwiches short of a picnic, mark my words.'

Twenty-one

Oh dear. The stuff of a particular horror: impossible to communicate and the overriding fear that nobody is going to believe you. Oh yes, Georgie has been here before, but some devils you know and some you don't, and some you refuse to recognize even when they plonk themselves right down in front of you.

Garlic will not help her now. But the crown of thorns is working well.

How she endured November Georgie will never know, it could be the fact that the Maces were coming, it gave her something positive to dwell on and plan for. She manages to make some sausage rolls and puts them in the freezer. She bakes the cake and sticks it in a tin. She cleans like a mad thing to keep germs at bay, germs, rampant and uncontrollable, and whatever other unseen force might threaten her. She thinks she might change her name and spends pleasant hours doodling around a suitable alternative – Emma, Jessica, Clara? Why not something a little less sensible – Willow, Rain, Anastasia? Will there be enough room in the cottage for her guests, even if Georgie gives up her bedroom? And where will she put the Christmas tree? She sends for her Christmas presents mail order and the postman stretches to pop the parcels in through the bedroom window. They're not as exciting as they looked in the catalogue, in fact, she has chosen badly, and this is the penalty of ordering too early without being in the festive mood. These are worries she can just about cope with. On bonfire night she yearns for a sparkler as a protest against she doesn't know what. With a sparkler in her hand she could sit in the darkened kitchen and write her name in the air in fire. But she doesn't do that, and the long day passes, same as all the others.

Oh the sham of pretending to cope. It sits like a permanent ache in her head. She would wake up fresh in the morning, and then, with first consciousness, the headache would wake too, and from that time it stays all day. From that time the feeling of exhaustion begins, the buried conflict quickly draining off any energy accumulated in sleep. Everything seems to require so great an effort, letters, reading, cooking, any kind of concentration, and she just drifts from hour to hour.

If Georgie can thrust reality aside, just for an instant, she can feel full and tranquil and free. She can only do this by taking time back and pretending that Angie Hopkins lives, that she took immediate action, removed the child from her violent home and found her some kindly foster parents. Then she'd be back in London again with a life of bland contentment, never facing these devils of hers, unaware of their very existence.

There are occasions when she peers from her

window into the gloomy weather outside and imagines she sees the figure again. It is always too far away to make out any details other than the fact that it's padded and menacing, and mostly absolutely still. It disappears in the end, no matter how hard Georgie stares, one minute it's there, the next it's gone, veiled by the mists. Could it be Lot? He is certainly large enough, and has taken to going about muffled up to the eyeballs in a giant army-surplus anorak with the furred hood of an Eskimo, and sometimes a rubber cape over the top of all that. But Lot could never stand still for so long and, besides, the Buckpit brothers don't move an inch without their tractor, and their guns are always over their shoulders. The figure does not carry a gun.

The ratlike Cramer is nowhere near large enough to create this sort of monumental impression and he is rarely around in the day, he leaves home first thing in the morning and comes home long after dark.

How about Horace? Horace is gigantic, but what would possess him to suddenly abandon his precious Nancy and lurk about in such hellish weather? And to what purpose? To put the fear of God into his solitary neighbour? Hardly the most efficient method. What if she failed to look out? How would he know he had been seen?

And what if it's someone she doesn't know, some angry stranger, someone to punish her for her crime?

Donna denies seeing anyone, so does the grim Mrs Buckpit after Georgie plucks up the courage to ask her. Her own imagination must be playing these sinister tricks.

This is no good. She has to start being firmer with herself. She locks and chains the door at teatime. She never ventures out in the dark. In the whole of the south-west Georgie's hens must be the first to be penned up for the night, sometimes she pulls up their ramp and locks their little front door as early as three thirty. There is no effect on their laying, by now most are off-lay anyway.

Not only is it consistently wet, but it's unbelievably cold. Just to slip outside for a moment is to be snapped in the teeth of a raw, burning wind. It sweeps through the valley, hell-bent on escape from the vast frozen wastes of open moorland over the hill and beyond. It might be straight from the arctic. It finds every nook and cranny, it roars down the chimney, seemingly thrilled to have found such a convenient route, and Georgie curses her spartan self for failing to install central heating. She smiles at the memory of her silly high-minded principles. 'It's far healthier. We're such a pampered, lily-livered lot, no wonder we go round with colds all winter. There's nothing wrong with open fires and wearing extra sweaters. People were fitter in the old days.'

Huh! What people?

Because after a certain temperature, struggling round in extra clothes makes not a hoot of difference.

Even Lola is reluctant to leave her fireside position. The ritual now involves thrusting the dog outside, slamming the door behind her and waiting five minutes before relenting. She is always waiting, whining to get back in. Not like the old Lola at all. Perhaps Georgie should knit her one of those poodle tartan coats. Perhaps she ought to take up knitting.

Yes, why not?

Seized with a new and positive hope she jumps in the car and battles her way through flooded roads and over broken branches. The little town, wind-battered and wet, is much quieter; there is an air of normality here, the rows of parked cars, the women with their shopping bags gossiping at the butcher's. There is a reassuring queue at the post office. She buys a pattern and some wool. She will knit poor Donna a long, warm jumper. She chooses a cheerful emerald green. Home again 'cos there's nowhere else, crashing through the mayhem, she sits and knits beside the fire, despite the redness of her hands, the harsh sheen which the cold puts on them, and wonders if she looks like Donna, drooped and raw and listless. She listens to the weather forecasts, but they ignore Dartmoor completely as if it is another world and anyone demented enough to live there deserves all they get, it's hardly worth a mention. The forecasts offer little hope, and if Georgie's cottage is stone cold what on earth must Donna's feel like? The mind boggles. No wonder she visits so frequently and stays for so long, it cannot all be governed by her unfortunate schoolgirl passion.

All too soon she finishes the sweater and starts on a scarf to match. *You see how hard she is trying?* How determined she is? She will not abandon herself to despair, she will not allow her absurd mental state to take over. She can knit away madly like this, pass the hours until winter is over. OK it might be depressing, as are Donna's visits, Donna, with whom she is making no progress. Their conversations rarely vary. Why can't she move in with Georgie? Does Georgie realize how much she loves her? Not in a sexual way, of course, more of a mental fixation. Should she leave Chad or should she stay? What is this need to be mastered? She tells tales of a sad and lonely childhood and harbours desolate fears for the future. Sometimes she brings along her tapes and Georgie would be churlish to refuse to allow her to play them, so Donna sits with her crying songs, swaying sadly before the fire, a vacant look in her bright young eyes, reduced to a morbid state of trance.

All Georgie's spare energy goes into trying to cheer the wretched girl up, and when that is over she sits and commiserates over her bright-green knitting. Quite drained. And when Donna eventually leaves it feels as if she's been no real company at all.

But mercifully Donna has taken to Lola, and it seems that to sit and brush the honey-coloured spaniel gives Donna more comfort than Georgie ever could. Lola can understand anything.

Donna is with her on the deadly day when Georgie lets Lola out and the dog fails to return. Extraordinarily she fails to appear when Georgie opens the door, teeth gritted against the cold, less than five minutes later.

So the huddled Georgie flings the door wider, the cold rushes in on a wave, floods the kitchen and pours through the rest of the cottage, pushes open the unlatched door and gallops on up the stairs. Georgie, shouting desperately, shivers. 'Lola! Lola!' She shuts the door for a moment and waits, gathering strength for another assault. Again she yells at the top of her voice, '*Lola! Lola!*'

As Georgie edges her face out a fraction, it reddens, it burns. But nothing. No dog. No sign.

'Damn and blast. Surely in this she hasn't decided to chase a rabbit.' Frozen stiff in those few short seconds, Georgie retreats to the comparative warmth of the sitting room. 'Lola's not there,' she tells Donna. 'I'll wait a few moments and then I'll have another try.'

But Donna, not up to emotional dramas, is quite the wrong person to have around in an emergency such as this. She pales, instantly fearing the worst. 'Where's she gone then?'

Georgie tries to sound reassuring. 'Probably after some scent. Rabbits. It can only be rabbits, nothing else would keep Lola out in this.'

'But she's never done this before,' cries Donna with her drawn face and her miserable eyes, worse than normal somehow, because now her concerns are for Lola.

'She'll be back in a minute.' But the minutes pass so blasted slowly. She goes to the door half a dozen times, shouts and whistles, but there's still no sign. She fetches her coat, scarf, gloves and hat. 'I'll have to go after her,' says Georgie eventually, not relishing the prospect, but far more anxious than she is showing.

'I'll come with you.'

For the first time there's some life in her voice.

'Right. You'd better wrap up.'

They trudge through the orchard. They scramble over the stream at the end. They start off up the hill. Georgie shouts to Donna, who is only just beside her, but the wind whips her words away and she is forced to repeat them. '*This is ridiculous.*' The wind blows saliva back in her face and she wipes it off with a saturated glove. She acts out her words, pointing. '*You go round the front and check, I'll keep going up here.*'

Donna nods numbly. The girl must be perished, that hopelessly thin coat of hers can't keep a slither of this weather out. Her face is deathly pale and beaten. Cramer is far too mean to provide Donna with sensible clothes, and when Georgie gave her a Mickey Mouse fur, fashionable in its day, thick and cosy, Chad made the tearful girl give it back. 'You're taking nout from that dyke,' he said. The man prefers to keep his women threadbare and miserable as his damn cottage.

So Donna retreats to the road while Georgie carries on up the hill. Although there is no point in calling, she calls anyway, clinging all the while to her hood to keep it up over her ears, and the skin of her face stretches back from her cheeks with the crazed force of the wind. After a futile hour of this – it's hardly possible to see further than a few yards because of the rain – she returns to the cottage with her heart in her mouth. Is there a logical reason for panic? Surely not yet. She must keep a sense of proportion. Lola will come back in her own good time. The dog is probably as bored as Georgie and has seized a brief diversion.

But in this weather? Lola is no fool. Georgie stares out. Lola is renowned for her fondness for creature comforts.

When Donna finally returns, soaked to the skin and shivering, teeth chattering in her skull, her reaction is alarming. 'Something terrible's happened! I know it. I can sense it. Lola's dead, she's dead . . .'

'Donna, calm down, calm down!' They hang their dripping coats in the kitchen, they might as well have left them outside for they are sodden, wringing wet. They attempt to warm themselves by the fire, but there seems to be little warmth in it now and all the time the wind shrieks down the chimney in a wild and mocking cacophony.

'Lola's a wise and sensible animal. There's nothing much can happen to her . . .'

'What if she's swept away in the stream?' Donna is almost hysterical.

'We're talking about a stream, not a torrent, not a raging river. And Lola's a very competent swimmer.'

'A branch might have fallen and knocked her unconscious and she's lying out there, fatally wounded.' Donna's eyes flicker round in her head as she searches for the worst scenario. 'Or what about a trap? One of Chad's traps?'

'What traps? It's illegal to set traps, even Chad

must know that.' It is a relief to feel anger flood through her.

'Since when did that sod give a toss for the law? That's how he catches his rabbits. He sells them to Darren at the butchers, makes a quid or two.'

'Well, I imagine his traps are set well away from the farm, and Lola wouldn't have wandered that far.'

'What about a rabbit hole? Or a badger set? Perhaps she's stuck half in, half out, screaming to get free.'

'Shut up, Donna, for Christ's sake. There's no point in this sort of panic. If Lola's not back in an hour I'll go back out again. I'll ask around, then I'll go to the police.'

Donna's shivering makes her words jerky. 'What good will that do? I've got this awful feeling . . .'

So has Georgie. So has Georgie.

They sit morosely before the fire. This is the worst thing that could happen. If anything happens to Lola . . .

They brave the storm once again. They search. They call. They trail round to the Buckpits to ask, and when hatchet-face opens the door Georgie is not prepared for tolerance. 'Have you seen my dog?' And she feels like pushing past the woman and searching that dark and comfortless house, as if, out of sheer spite, the Buckpits could have kidnapped her dog, another horror deliberately inflicted.

'No, I have not seen your dog,' snaps this venomous woman, still clutching the same tight cardigan. The cowardly Donna shelters behind Georgie. 'And you ought to be more careful. If you're going to let a hunting dog out then you should go with her.'

It is not worth staying to argue. Georgie needs to conserve her energy. To waste it on this heartless woman would be daft.

They almost fall into the Horsefields' hall. They are swept in by the wind. There's a kind of wild excitement in Nancy's flashing eyes, caused, possibly, by the weather.

'Oh, you poor, poor souls,' as she hurries away in the direction of her kitchen. 'What a worry on a day like this. You are badly in need of something hot . . .'

Their anxious calls of, 'No, don't worry,' float uselessly past her.

'We can't stay,' Georgie tells the anxious Horace. 'I just popped in to ask if you'd seen Lola and to tell you to keep an eye open just in case she should turn up here.'

'Of course I will, yes, of course. I'd come and join the hunt except Nancy's a little upset today and I just daren't leave her.'

The poor man never leaves his wife. Like a great spreading chestnut tree he stands, staunch and dependable and sheltering over her.

So they quickly back out of Wooton House and cross the smart little bridge. They continue searching as darkness falls and the lights of Cramer's Land Rover appear, wetly wavering, over the brow of the hill.

'*I must go*,' screams Donna wildly over the top

of the wind, her hair tearing about her face, slapping it cruelly, tangled and wet.

'*I'll ring the police now*,' Georgie shouts back, knowing what a waste of time that will be, but battling to stand up, forcing herself a little bit further.

'*I'll be round first thing in the morning.*' The wind takes Donna like a wisp and she disappears in the direction of a cottage with no friendly lights burning, no warm fire to greet her.

In the comparative silence of Furze Pen, Georgie strips off her sodden clothes. Even her underwear is saturated. She passes through the kitchen and into the converted shower. She lets hot water flow over her, take her and drench her. She rubs herself dry and the feeling comes back to her feet and hands. She changes into warm, dry clothes. Hopefully, she opens the door once more. It is dark, but still she opens it, going against every instinct, the irrational fears which probably have all been imagined. *But this one is horribly real.* Now, this minute, the terror is real, and it is essential that she hold herself together.

She telephones the police, of course, knowing the uselessness of it. But if Lola has strayed too far someone from a neighbouring hamlet might have rung in and reported their find, or taken her in, some isolated farmhouse perhaps, maybe they'd think of phoning the police? The desperate Georgie can't afford to miss chances.

Then, out of need, she calls Isla, trying to keep her voice careful, making light of this awful event, because if she lets herself go she might never find herself again, and what good would that do for Lola?

'Georgie! You must be distraught!'

'I am, yes, but I'm telling myself she's going to come back.'

'Dogs don't just disappear,' says Isla flatly, 'not wise old things like Lola.' How silent the line sounds, no chaos on the other end, no hideously raging wind, no storm, just London. Slightly breezy perhaps . . .

'I'd prop the back door open, but if I did that the cottage would probably lift off . . .'

A joke, but she is glad that Isla doesn't laugh.

Georgie rings Helen. Georgie rings Suzie. In the end she even rings Mark, who blurts out with a desperate honesty, 'God, I wish you'd never gone to that godforsaken place. Let me come and get you, right now! I can be there in five hours.'

But she cannot make that sort of decision, not in the state of chaos she's in. She wishes she'd never come here, too. Anything else she could tolerate, but not this. Who has taken her dog? What are they doing? Is she frightened? Is she being hurt? Lola was a rescue dog. When Lola was a puppy she endured the kind of cruelty you only read about in RSPCA magazines. It took many months of tender love to restore the spaniel's confidence, to take the fear of pain from her eyes. So Georgie sits by herself all night, hugging and rocking and getting up every ten minutes to check the back door. She makes a small bargain with God: if Lola comes back

unharmed, Georgie will return to London at the
first opportunity, no more of these silly heroics.
She has tried, she has failed, now she is ready
to throw in the sponge. Staying here on her own
is achieving absolutely nothing, she should have
gone back with the last of her summer visitors.

For comfort she plays her music softly, trying
to erase the moan of the wind. She avoids the
booze, she must stay sober, she no longer cares
about proving herself, or discovering from what
she is hiding. All this self-analysis is sheer self-
indulgence, and Lola is too high a price to pay for
any such bloody nonsense.

Twenty-two

Fear has a sound – running your finger around the wet rim of a glass.

'Listen to me, Donna,' goes Georgie, 'is it remotely possible that Chad came back during the day, saw Lola, and snatched her on an impulse? Please think very hard about this. Would he hurt her, kill her perhaps, just to get back at me?'

The pained look on her pasty face tells Georgie otherwise. 'No way, Georgie. He's not that much of a bastard. God, I wouldn't bleeding well stay with him if I thought he could do something like that.'

Georgie continues to pummel the pastry. How would Donna know? Too thick, it clings to her fingers, it's stuck under her rings. 'I just thought . . . knowing how he loathes me . . . knowing how jealous you say he is . . .'

'But he wouldn't deliberately injure a dog!'

Oh no? He will hurt human beings, he will abuse women without a second thought, but he'll stop short when it comes to animals. What rubbish, him with his guns and his evil traps. Donna's world is full of such fantasies. There is little point in arguing.

*   *   *

Lola has been missing now for two whole days. Donna and Georgie have searched everywhere. Last night Georgie dragged the mattress downstairs and slept by the fire so she would hear if Lola scratched to get in. When she is not searching she keeps herself busy doing unnecessary tasks, but that is half the trouble, since Lola's curious disappearance nothing seems important in this unreal world. All that is really required of Georgie is that she gets up in the mornings, eats to keep herself alive and goes back to bed at night. She is not required to speak to anyone, love anyone, help anyone . . .

Only Lola.

And now look, she is making pies which nobody wants.

'Seven's an awful lot of people to be coming to stay.' Georgie resents Donna's knack of picking up her negative thoughts and putting them into such worrying words.

'It's only for three days, Donna, and if Lola doesn't come back it probably won't happen at all because I might as well pack my bags and leave.' Donna is watching her work. The girl is a watcher, not a doer, her fascinated face slackens into a kind of mesmerized expression. 'Even if Lola does come back I've decided to move out. If she walked through the door this minute I would bin these bloody pies, pick her up, get straight in the car and leave this ill-wished place for good.'

It is no surprise when Donna's face crumples. 'I knew you wouldn't bleeding well stick it. Nobody in their right mind stays here . . .'

'That's not true. It's amazing how many people do. Look at the Horsefields and the Buckpits, even Stephen. They've all lived here for twenty years or more, quite happily.'

'None of them's happy. It's just a bleeding existence, that's all. Like my life is just an existence.'

'Even your Chad,' Georgie goes on, 'he's no fly-by-night either, there must be something about the place that keeps people here.'

'Well I haven't managed to find out what it is,' whines Donna, her mouth dropping open as she watches Georgie fill the cases with mincemeat.

'*You don't really mean it, Georgie, do you?* You wouldn't really just go like that?'

'Oh yes, I would, I'm afraid. Living here has become intolerable.'

Georgie works on in silence for a while, thinking of Lola, wondering where she might be and whether she should phone the police again, just in case they have heard something.

'I dunno how you can bear it,' moans Donna, sniffing. 'If she was my dog I'd be mad by now.'

But Georgie is mad. Inside she is hysterical, her heart weeps and tears seem to fill every vein, despair adds weight to her limbs. But even now she is covering up, afraid to let Donna see the depths of her desperation. She must think small practical thoughts and keep busy busy busy making mince pies, and she'll go and alter some curtain hems next.

'What you need, Donna,' says Georgie firmly, 'is somebody to look after.'

'I don't. I don't. I want somebody to look after me.' She stops suddenly. 'And now I've got a bun in the oven,' she adds in the most expressionless voice Georgie has ever heard her use.

Oh Lord, no!

Georgie does not answer immediately. She is sticking the pastry lids down. She continues to do so without a pause, in fact, she works more quickly. She starts to crimp the sides with her fingers and then says, 'How far gone are you?'

'Four months.'

'Does Chad know?'

'He'd throw me out if he did.' Her blue eyes are fixed on Georgie's hands.

'How certain are you? Have you seen a doctor?'

'I went last week while Chad was doing the market. I said I was at the dentist. He was good about it, he even paid.'

Georgie continues to crimp the pies, she even holds her head back and pretends to study the effect. She knows that she ought to stop what she's doing, sit down, make a drink, hold poor Donna's hand. *But she doesn't want this!* She honestly does not want to know, or talk about it, or react correctly. She's had it with the caring professions, she's up to here with social work. The whereabouts of a mere dog should take second place to this little drama, of course it should, because how on earth will Donna cope with a baby, or an abortion? But her brain screams back, *Too late for an abortion*.

Careful to keep the slightest hint of accusation

298

from her voice, Georgie says, 'But you must have suspected earlier, Donna. Couldn't you have done something then? When there was a choice to be made?'

Donna looks guilty and says not a word. There is no point in berating the girl, what's done is done. My God, she is so maddeningly simple.

She really is not Georgie's problem.

'You won't be able to hide the fact for much longer.'

'Chad'll throw me out.' Her face is paler than usual, the colour of used white sheets. 'He can't stand kids, or illness, nothing like that.' There's a tremor of terror in her voice.

She is surely not angling to leave here with Georgie?

'You are going to have to go and see someone about this, Donna. You are going to need some professional help.' Careful, Georgie keeps herself distant.

'But you are a social worker, aren't you?'

'How do you know I'm a social worker?'

'You said so, you were talking about it with your friends. All the time. I didn't know it was meant to be secret or something.'

Why so defensive? 'Oh yes, of course, I didn't mean to snap, I'm sorry.'

'*So why can't you help me then?*' And she stares at Georgie defiantly. 'You are supposed to care, so why can't you bleeding well care about me?'

Where is that kind and responsible person? Georgie sits down, they have to sit down. It's no good trying to deny this is happening. It is here and they have to confront it. 'Well, I will help you, Donna, as much as I can. But I'm not in any position to be able to give you the practical help that you're going to need, or the counselling.' She forces herself to be very stern. 'No, I have done all I can to help you, but I'm afraid you're going to have to find professional help elsewhere.'

The silence widens until it engulfs them. Donna's greasy hair droops down and the girl peers miserably through it. 'You're not really my friend, are you? *Not like those others from up the line*. You're only pretending 'cos there's no-one else. You just put up with me, don't you? And I bet you're always glad when I go.' And with this she bursts into paroxysms of violent weeping, howling, drumming her fists on the table so the pastry cases leap in their tins, and Georgie is shocked by the passion in this.

'Donna! *How can you say that?*' Georgie gets up to comfort her. She can feel the girl's misery under her hand in the little hard knobs of backbone and the damp smell of neglect, hot, sticky, shaking and unendurable. 'That's not true at all,' she half lies. Dear God, has it been so cruelly obvious?

Donna chokes, 'Anyway, I'm gonna get rid of it on my own.'

'Now you're just being silly . . .'

'Fuck off, I'm not! I know the ways . . .'

'What ways?'

Phlegm rattles in her wheezy chest. 'Well I'm not going to sodding tell you, am I?'

Georgie lets her cry, it's best. Agonizing jerks

of tears, streams of water pour down her face, and now and then there's a howl of pain. 'Donna! Donna! Come on, my love, it's not as bad as you think. We have got to calm down and start thinking about what is best for you. We have got to start thinking about you and your baby's future.'

The word 'we' is jerked out of Georgie with a terrible reluctance. 'You might even qualify for a flat, Donna, you'll certainly be entitled to some financial support. They can't just turn you away now you're going to have a baby.'

Donna wipes her nose with the sleeve of her jumper. 'Don't say it like that – "going to have a baby" – because I'm not going to have one. I don't want it and I'm not bleeding well having it.'

'Donna,' Georgie says gently, 'I don't think you've got any choice. And that's the first thing we must sort out. Calm down, calm down and tell me why you are so against having this baby. It's not that bad, it's not the end of the world.'

But Donna peers at her fiercely. 'How the hell would you know?'

'Well, look, nobody would ever give birth if it was that bad, now, would they?'

'It is that bad, I know it's that bad and I'm not going to have it. And I can't bear you to go away.'

Not back to that old chestnut. 'But if the child is Chad's, which it is, you are going to have to tell him,' Georgie starts off hopefully. 'Who knows? He might even be thrilled . . .' and she knows immediately she has gone too far, she sounds downright silly, so silly that Donna doesn't deign to answer. 'Is there absolutely nobody else? No family, no relation who might want to help you and take you in, just until after . . . ?'

'You know there isn't! You know that! I've told you all about my life. How can I go back to them, and anyway, they wouldn't have me.'

They sit in silence while Donna shudders. She tears tissue after tissue to shreds, reminding Georgie of her mother. Every so often she gets up to clear the soggy mess off the table.

'Perhaps you secretly wanted a baby, maybe you saw it as a way of challenging Chad, forcing a decision on him, a way of bringing this relationship of yours to a head?'

Donna sobs, but more quietly now, just a gentle shaking of the shoulders. 'Some of your visitors, I noticed, this summer, I watched them with their kids. You were having such a great time and some of them were so sweet, I loved playing with them so much . . .'

'You think it was seeing this that made you decide you might like one of your own?'

Donna shakes her head. 'It's not that simple. It wasn't one thing like that. And anyway, I don't want a kid, it was only a dream and it made me careless.' She makes it sound as if Georgie should know. 'I wish you'd never bleeding well come here.' And Georgie jumps at the suddenness of that.

'What's all this got to do with me?'

'You know what it's got to do with you, but you don't take my feelings seriously. You think I'm playing some sort of game, but I'm not, I can't help it. You came here and everything got right out of hand and I don't know what's going on any more.'

'But you seemed to enjoy yourself last summer, joining in, coming on picnics, sometimes you seemed quite happy.'

'Well, I wasn't happy,' snaps Donna. 'I was jealous, right? And every night I went back to Chad while you sat with your friends and drank and laughed.'

'But you loved Chad. You didn't want to leave him.'

'Well, that's all changed now. Now I want to stay with you.'

Here they are again, going round fruitlessly in the same old circles. There is no way of making progress with Donna. There never has been. It's futile. Georgie makes tea, she makes coffee, she shares some mince pies before she freezes the rest. 'Poor Lola,' sobs Donna every so often. 'Shit. How can things get worse than they are?'

And Georgie doesn't know either.

By the time Donna departs she has been convinced that she ought to tell Chad.

'I don't want to tell him. I don't see the point,' she bursts out.

'The point is, Donna, that if Chad throws you out and you go to the social services, they are bound to give you a home in your vulnerable condition.'

'They'd have to give me one anyway.'

'Not necessarily . . .'

'If I just left him they'd find me somewhere.' And she blows her sore nose vigorously.

'They would say you'd made yourself homeless.'

'I could tell them how he treats me.'

'You don't want a home for battered women,' Georgie pats her hand and mutters. 'And quite apart from all this the child is Chad's, presumably. He has a right to know, he will have to pay maintenance, and the whole thing would be much simpler if you behaved responsibly, acted like an adult for once and faced him with the truth.'

Donna sulks. 'When should I tell him?'

'Now, at once,' Georgie insists.

'Tonight. After tea,' promises Donna. Her eyes are tearless now, though the lids still show red and her face is even paler than usual. 'I might as well. There's no good time. But what will I do if he throws me out?'

'He's not going to throw you out on your ear just like that.'

'You don't know the bastard like I do.'

'No, I don't, but that reaction is very unlikely. Won't he give you a few days' grace, after all, Donna, it's his baby as well as yours, he'll understand that, he's not totally stupid, and then we can go to the social services.'

'He'll go barmy.'

'But he won't kick you out. That would be criminal. In this weather you'd die.'

'So what shall I do if he does?'

'Well, in that unlikely event, you know you can come here. I don't need to tell you that, do I?'

'And you'd take me in?' Donna asks, her dull eyes brightening.

'For the time being,' Georgie tells her, 'until something could be sorted out, yes, of course I would.' And she means it, of course Georgie means it.

'Think of me then,' she whispers as she departs just before dusk. 'Think of me about six o'clock, telling Chad.'

'I will think of you. It's going to be OK, Donna, really it is. Things usually work out in the end, even the worst things we dread the most.'

Huh! Who is Georgie trying to kid?

Georgie sits for a while considering poor Donna's plight and how curious it is how some people seem to attract bad luck. Do they ask for it? On some subconscious level, do they go willingly to their fate, creating their own distress, belittling themselves? It seems to work like that almost every time, and might Donna damage herself in a misguided attempt to get rid of her baby? As a protest? In revenge? Or merely more attention seeking.

Hell. It's late. It is almost dark already and Georgie must close the hen house and stock up with wood. On her hasty way out she trips over Lola.

'*Oh, Lola!*'

Stunned, Georgie can hardly believe it!

Nestling comfortably in a strange blanket, the dog gnaws on a giant ham bone. On seeing Georgie she leaps up, wild-eyed, and tries to lick her to death. Georgie crouches down beside her, staring round in the murky darkness. '*Where have you been all this time?* I've been out of my mind with worry. Where did you get this cosy blanket? And who gave you this smelly old bone?'

Despite shivering in the cold wind, Lola refuses to come into the house if the bone is forbidden. The blanket, a smart tartan rug, has kept her contented and warm. How long has she been out there? Georgie hurries her inside and the dog takes up her favourite position in front of the fire, chewing blissfully on strips of fat, her eyes half closed with pleasure, as if she has never been gone. Georgie examines her carefully. Lifts her ears. Feels her limbs. She even inspects her feet. Lola is absolutely fine, not a scratch on her. Her eyes are bright and her nose is cold, Wherever she has been she was happy and well looked after.

But someone had definitely taken her. And someone decided to bring her back. *They might not have done.* Georgie can hardly bear to confront the dark and close up the hens, it takes all the courage she can muster. She sings out loud for bravery as she visits the woodshed, almost shouting and clattering about with the logs, skinning her knuckles badly, but not even noticing until she gets back inside. She slams the door. Locks it. Chains it.

Oh God, oh God. Along with the surge of relief comes the awful sensation of fear, black and winged, it bats around her head, chilling her spine. She senses the violence somewhere out there. She cannot throw off this sense of foreboding. She must leave Wooton-Coney at once, *this instant*, this very night before it's too late. She could pick up her toothbrush and Lola's bowl and be out of here in ten minutes. Horace Horsefield would feed the hens until she managed to sell them. One simple phone call would organize that. She could send for her things afterwards, pay Pickfords to pack and deliver. She could check into a hotel for the night and organize everything from there.

No time like the present and she'd promised God. So she gets up, eager to start. Let Stephen's hellish cottage burn down. His paintings stare down from the walls, the eyes of his subjects encourage her to go, to leave here at once, while she can . . .

Wait! *What about Donna?* What will she do if, later tonight, she makes her dreadful confession to Chad and the oaf loses his temper and attacks her, throws her out in the darkness with nowhere to go?

Georgie will go and explain to her . . . but what if Chad is still in the dark? What if Georgie goes over and puts her foot straight in it, making matters far worse because Chad would resent her knowing . . .

Well then, she will persuade Donna to come to London with her now. They can sort something temporary out for tomorrow. But Donna is so infatuated, so dependency prone, there'd be nothing worse for her mental state than a deeper involvement with Georgie right now. No, no, Donna is at an important crossroads. She is on the verge of leaving Chad and, in her condition, the social services would be bound to give her a flat. This is Donna's only way out. She must sort matters out with Chad, and then, depending on his reaction, she must face up to her new independence in a responsible and adult way.

Georgie's involvement could wreck all that.

Georgie wrestles with her predicament while Lola lies at her feet, gnawing on her bone and basking in contentment with the logs crackling merrily. Perhaps she can afford to wait and leave first thing in the morning? Mercifully Lola has not been hurt. The door is locked. She has a phone. Surely she can endure one more night for the wretched Donna's sake? The girl has no-one else to take her into town, to help her sort matters out, to take any interest in her welfare. Disapprove of her as Georgie might, the girl needs her, and she's already made enough mistakes without risking one more tragedy . . .

Georgie crouches over the fire and places small pieces of wood on the flames, unable to control her thoughts. She re-enacts all the incidents in her mind, trying to make some sense of them until, at last, she's exhausted and can think no more.

She and Donna have one thing in common, their total isolation.

All that evening she waits for Donna, half hoping she will turn up so they can leave together. The clock ticks on. Perhaps Chad has accepted the news? Doubtful. Far more likely the cowardly Donna has failed to tell him.

So, later on, Georgie and Lola cuddle up by the fire to spend their last night at Furze Pen Cottage. Georgie, of course, cannot sleep, but comforts herself with the sound of Lola's reassuring breathing. There is no doubt in her mind that she is leaving Wooton-Coney tomorrow. She will tell Donna so in the morning, and drop her in town on the way if she's ready.

And this time, after losing Lola, it will take a direct bomb hit to stop her.

Twenty-three

The clock says nine, but outside it looks like night. Georgie, thick and bleary-eyed, wakes with a sense of urgency and, sloughing off the terror of her dreams, crosses the room to turn on the light. Nothing. She clicks the switch again, no result. Donna? Has Chad been told? Where is Donna, *has she survived?*

Today is the day she is leaving Furze Pen. This bright thought brings a new and wonderful sense of relief. But the silent darkness is eerie and all pervasive, especially after the clamour of last week's winds. It has been impossible to get reception on the TV or the radio, and lately she has been far too concerned about Lola to drive the necessary five miles for a paper, so she hasn't a clue what the forecasts are.

She draws back the curtains and peers out. The snow that drifts down forms a moving veil, obscuring even the stream from view. The flakes are thick, fat cotton-wool balls, but, with narrowed eyes, Georgie sees there is some activity through the gloom, the Buckpits' tractor revs its way from the farmyard and, more distantly, there's the dark-grey shape of a snowplough passing silently down the road.

Life, of a sort, goes on.

Shaken and disheartened, Georgie wipes the steam from the windows. Already her car is a humped bump beside the road and the hedge is leaning, groaning, heavy and matted with white. Curse it. A good six inches must have fallen overnight and Georgie, who has always loved snow, feels such an overwhelming bitterness towards this perversity of fate that tears sprout with all the passionate anger of a child's.

Damn damn damn. She will ring the weather forecast at once. Maybe it is clear elsewhere. Maybe it won't last long and, as the snow-clearing truck is here already, there must be a chance of getting out. Her eyes brighten as she lifts the phone, only to confront a stony silence. Damn. Damn. She has been cut off.

Damn the weather. Damn Donna.

She pulls on her boots, still damp from yesterday's fruitless searches, fights with the rarely used front door and rushes outside. Her stepping stones are massive white snowballs, deceptively soft, as if they might collapse on impact. She crouches and scrambles over her stream, followed by an excited Lola, who rolls and delves in riotous joy, shamelessly in love with the stuff. She watches the snowplough disappear into the distance, stares at its tail lights, then down at the road. It has made some small impression, the snow has been churned so it banks the sides, but already the surface is white again. Where has the machine gone now? Perhaps, if Georgie hurries, she could follow it and escape?

But dammit, what about Donna?

If only she could get free. Resentment storms in her head as she stares hopelessly at the road. She herself is already covered, it sticks to her coat like fuzzy white burrs, grim and determined. There's no getting away from it, she cannot attempt to drive in this.

Unable to accept defeat, she struggles across the road to the farmyard, her feet sinking in deep pockets, snow sliding inside her boots, she has to fight hard to keep going. The Buckpit brothers are still busy milking and the glow from the parlour is softer than usual, the sound is different, quieter. She walks straight in, not bothering with platitudes, not caring if the testy Mrs Buckpit should come to wither her with one of her glances. She even forgets about the ashes. Georgie's business is urgent and nothing is going to stop her.

Lot turns round and stares at Georgie inanely, hands on the steaming udders of a cow. He wrings out a grimy cloth. Georgie, ignoring his sullen stare, wades straight in. 'I have to get out today. It is essential that I get out, and I wondered if you could give me a tow up the hill with the tractor.' Not an unreasonable request from one neighbour to another, but seeing the look on his bovine face she quickly amends her request, 'afterwards, of course, when the milking is finished. I'll pay you for your trouble.'

The lout carries on with his work, clanking the metal gate and waiting as another cow obediently sways into position. She will have to repeat her request, although it's quite obvious that he heard her the first time, but just as she is about to speak he turns and proves her wrong, 'And where do you think you'll be going?'

'I just want help to get out of here, it can't be this thick everywhere else.'

'Oh but 'tis. 'Tis everywhere.'

'What?' How does he know? They haven't got a radio, let alone a TV? 'It can't be all over?'

'Mostly.' And he wags his oversized head, it moves rhythmically from side to side, like the tails of his cows, and his hair is equally black and tufted. 'They said so on the CB before the aerial snapped.' A CB radio? Ah yes, that's the reason for the outsized aerial on the top of the Land Rover. *Could he be her adversary*, this burly brute of a man, could it be he who stood so unnervingly, the figure in the fields, staring in such sinister fashion? Stalking? Skulking around her woodshed at night? No, not Lot. He wouldn't have the wit for a start . . .

'If it wuz remotely possible for either of my sons to help you this morning, d'you honestly think they'd have the time?'

Georgie turns round wearily. So the shrew has been keeping watch, huddled at her kitchen window. Does nothing get past her?

'I realize this weather must cause extra problems . . .'

'*Extra problems?*' And the Buckpit bitch gives a keen-eyed, skeletal smile. 'We're on a generator already as it is, we can't get the milk out. We'll have to throw the lot away. I'd have thought, if you were planning a journey, it might have been wise to check the forecast before you went.'

313

Georgie shrugs her shoulders desperately. 'I have been far too worried about my dog to be taking notice of ordinary things, as you know. And anyway, this is an emergency.' But the numbness in her cold feet is slowly spreading throughout her body, leaving her wooden, empty, the fight frozen out of her.

'I see the dog came back then. Of its own accord.'

And Lola gazes up at the woman, willing to be friendly, even with this charmless character, so forgiving is she.

Georgie protests, 'She was brought back, Mrs Buckpit, by the person who took her away.'

'Well, we wouldn't know anything about that. And now, if you don't mind, God willing, we've more to be getting on with . . .'

But she just can't leave it at this. Georgie attempts to persevere by attracting Lot's attention again. The thin and weedy Silas, with cow manure all over his hands, is watching and picking his teeth with the needle end of a syringe. 'So you don't think there is any chance, not even later when things have calmed down?'

The woman answers for her sons. 'What makes you think anything's going to calm down? There's wuss to come, midear. They say it's gonna be bad, real bad, wuss than we've had it before. Luckily,' and she stares coldly at Georgie, 'we have made preparations, I suggest you go back home and do the same yesself. While you can.'

While she can? Mrs B. seems to be prophesying the end of the world as we know it, and her thin voice crackles with triumphant foreboding.

There is no way to vent her indignation. There is nothing to do but accept. On her unsteady way back to the cottage Georgie strains to see Chad Cramer's place, but all there is is a distant shape, she cannot even tell if the Land Rover has gone. The snow is deeper already, in those last few short minutes. She rubs angrily on the windscreen of her car, but no colour, no metal shows, just the odd piece of black tyre tells her it is still there under the mound of white.

It would be impossible to drive it down the few feet to the ford, let alone up either of the inclines which lead out of Wooton-Coney.

So be it. Sod's law. But if Georgie is truly as helpless as she feels, she reminds herself that so is her evil protagonist. She will keep her door locked and chained. She will keep Lola in sight at all times.

She calls the dog to her side as she goes to free the chickens. Even this job proves difficult, because Mark's intricate home-made lock has frozen up and she has to work hard to shift the tiny sliding door, wiping her face free of snow as she goes, and seeing the corn she so recently scattered disappearing under the thick white covers. It might be kinder to keep the fowls inside this morning, warm and comfortable on their perches. They, too, are uneasy, the unusual silence must have shocked them, she misses their contented clucking sounds.

It's no good, dammit, she can't shift the bloody

315

door, so she takes off her gloves and works on the small flap window with frozen fingers. With a sudden snap it opens, and Georgie peers inside. Where are they? They should be roosting. Instead they are on the floor of the hut, but wait, there's something horribly wrong. She brings her eye to the hole and stares in.

They don't have heads any more.

That's all. Do you understand what I'm saying? They have no heads. Just raw stumps with sticky red bones ending at the neck, and their beautiful russet feathers are clogged with blood. They lie, quite still, on the floor of the house in a neat, plump row, as if on a slab in a butcher's shop. Placed there neatly. Where the slaughterer put them.

Last night all was hope, now there is nothing but horror. Now, for some desperate reason connected to keeping her sanity, she has to open the door, even if it means breaking the blasted thing down. She tramps determinedly through the snow, through the deep orchard grass, to the woodshed for a spade. She carries it back to the chicken house and bashes the spade against the flimsy construction again and again until it splinters and gives way. She flings down the spade and stares in breathless terror, thrusting her arm inside and pulling out bodies, one at a time, every one identical, every pretty head chopped off in exactly the same place. But there aren't any heads to be seen, just bodies, and she lays them down in a row on the snow and regards them with dismay.

A total revulsion.

A wreath of scarlet carnations.

Where are the heads? Oh, dear God. What has he done with the heads? She starts searching.

While Georgie is out there dealing with death the wind begins to whine. It starts on a whistle of just two notes. The whine turns into a snarl, gusting the snow into her face and stinging her skin in a series of vicious slaps. It tears down the valley like a cartoon wind, a tatty grey streamer with evil intent. With its sharp teeth it is almost smiling.

Useless to question who or why. Georgie wants to be far away, she wants to nurse her frightened sickness, but inside her cottage is the furthest she can go. There is nothing can be done for the chickens, so she leaves them and the holes in their necks, red and searing in the snow. Whoever is doing this hates her, for some unknown reason this is the truth, although she can offer no explanation, she can't apologize or make things right because she doesn't know who he is, or what the hell he wants from her. But his perfect hatred drums in her ears and turns her blood to ice.

With a shuddering certainty Georgie knows that this is the work of the figure on the hill. And now she has seen the violence.

From her small cottage she watches, face white, staring and horrified, a prisoner held against her will, wanting to beat her head on the wall, longing to scream for help. But there is no-one. It is only Lola's comforting presence that keeps her sane

317

and steady. Perfectly still within her house she watches the snow accumulate, she sees the wind take it away and build shapes of a crazy structure, no rhyme, no reason, just madness all around her. Never before in her life has Georgie been closer to something so mindless or so completely wild. Now it whistles down the chimney, invading her sanctuary and cutting her off from the rest of the world. Her hands shake. Her body jerks. She can no longer see the rest of the hamlet and it is doubtful that anyone could make it from one house to the other. Even Donna, in her desperation, could not reach Georgie now, her own garden has disappeared. And inside the cottage it is dark, some endless night has descended. They have the firelight, they have the weak glow from the candles, and that is all.

Suddenly, without warning, the last vestige of security has been gutted around her and Georgie knows she is waiting, in a scene set by some hostile hand, and all she can do is wait like a puppet for destiny to unfold.

She eats. But does not remember eating. She remembers nothing for the rest of this endless day, it disappears in a haze of horror, and she comes out of her self-induced trance when she hears a frenzied knocking at her door.

Her fright leaps inside her. No-one has ever knocked there before.

It has to be Donna. Someone to talk to, thank God. Somehow the girl has made her escape, but she hasn't been able to reach the back.

318

So now it has come to this. At first Georgie stares at the banging, unable to move in her terror. The whole cottage appears to shake. Menace is everywhere. Above the wind comes the voice of a man. '*For God's sake*, Jesus, is there nobody in this fucking place?' BANG. SLAM. BANG. SLAM. Lola cocks her ears, she walks to the door and sniffs underneath it. She wags her ridiculous tiny tail and looks back at Georgie expectantly.

Not Donna. *Then who?*

There is no chain for the front door. With its massive lock and its dungeonlike key it is too staunch to need one. Like a sacrifice attuned to her doom, Georgie steps forward mechanically and turns the key, and at her movement the candles flicker and dim. Once again she pauses to listen, licking her lips like a threatened beast, and she might well be snarling.

It is open a fraction when the body falls in with a whump. It must have been leaning against it. In a second her bulky visitor is back on his feet and shouting.

'*For God's sake hurry up*. The lad's over there. The snowplough went over his foot and this was the nearest place to get help. I'm going to have to carry him here, but I had to make sure there was someone . . .'

All the candles blow out in the wind. Georgie can smell their deadness. The stranger clutches her arm without really looking at her. *Is this a trap?* Does a grisly fate lie in this man's hands? Does he want Georgie out there so he can murder

319

her? Cut off her head and lay her out on the snow, neatly, with the chickens?

But now she sees that his eyes are sincere, with nothing in them except concern. 'Come on, he's in agony. We've got to hurry, get him into the warm before . . .'

Something automatic takes over. 'Just a sec, I'll get the torch if someone's injured.' Can this be her own voice, coming from nowhere and sounding so firm, her old sensible, capable self emerging from the depths of her terror? She even has the presence of mind to shut Lola in the kitchen before she follows her agitated visitor out.

'It's going to take two, I can't move him alone.'

They hang together in order to move. Speech is impossible, although he tries to mutter his explanations. Breathing is difficult enough. The wind howls like a banshee, there is nothing to see except snow. They move like blind men, one arm feeling in front and the other linked together. He seems to know where he's going, his old tracks are just about visible. What is the time? It must be almost seven o'clock, back in her London life she might be having a drink after work, cooling off before an evening at the ballet, soaking in a perfumed bath.

Thank God it's not far. No more than fifty yards. The great shape of the snowplough looms out of the greyness while, at the same time, the torchlight illuminates the ashen face of the man on the ground. 'The bloody thing's broken down on us. It slipped back on him while he was underneath.'

How bright the boy's blond curls are, and what an odd thing to notice at a time like this. Nervously Georgie adjusts the beam and takes it down over his thick donkey jacket, down his navy overalls towards the ankle that has been hurt. The older man is bent down already, reassuring, she supposes, trying to strengthen his friend in his pain.

'Dave! Dave! Come on, wake up! We're back now, we'll soon have you inside and strapped up.'

But wait.

There is something else.

Something unspeakable. *Dear God, no*. Rigidly she keeps the torch directed in the same place. She does not move it because she can't. That torch beam and Georgie's arm are in such terrible communication, she feels they can never be parted.

If this young man has hurt his ankle, if the snowplough rolled over and crushed his ankle, then everything is all right now. She will touch his friend on the back in a moment, she will touch him on the back and show him. Everything's fine. No need to worry. She feels her frozen face crack into a rictus smile. He does not have a foot any more. His foot has gone, you see. It is chopped off neatly right at the ankle, as if by an axe or a cutlass, and there is nothing but splintered bone.

Twenty-four

She has always craved for safety in life, for when she is safe she is loved.

Donna, of course, holds the opposite view.

But now poor Georgie has never felt more unsafe.

If the accident had been any further away they would not have made it back. But they manage. There is no alternative. They have to get Dave to safety. It's just no good sobbing and trying not to look at the awful wound or the pulsing blood, the gore. Georgie tries, but fails, to lift the heavy shoulder end, so she takes the legs instead. Black blood pumps, they staunch it, they tie it, they shove a spare clean overall around it, which the man fetches down from the cab.

Wildly they fight their way back through the frenzied teeth of the gale, but this seems normal now, as if Georgie makes a habit of this, bent like this, muttering, slipping, cursing like this, not minding the warm feel of fresh blood as it slops through her gloves, her sleeves.

Back at the cottage she yells at Lola, '*Get back! Get back!*' and doesn't stop to figure out how the dog escaped from the kitchen. After their hurried departure she had left the front door open and now there's a pile of snow in the hall, so that after they drag their burden inside Georgie has to use a shovel to lever the door closed again. They both feel, having seen the butchery, that it is essential to close the door. *And lock it.*

And now, still grunting and sweating, they cart the unconscious Dave to the sofa and lay him there. The blood pumps from his severed right leg and the exposed bone is bluey white, like a lamb bone fresh from the freezer.

The difficulty lies in facing the facts, and Georgie can't bring herself to do that. 'The lorry must have done this . . . it must have rolled back over his leg after you'd gone to fetch help . . .'

The dark weathered man glances back at Georgie, and his eyes are so full of knowledge that she wants to put out her hand and close them.

'That must be what happened to your friend.' Georgie can hardly force the words through her chattering teeth, and the words knock together like enamel. 'The snowplough must have moved again somehow . . .' Georgie sobs, knowing otherwise, 'perhaps some sharp piece of metal . . .'

'Don't talk rot! *Somebody has cut off his foot.* When I left Dave his ankle was broken. Jesus Christ Almighty. The machine ran over his ankle, but now he has lost his whole sodding foot . . . God God God.' There are tears of fury in his eyes and he looks at Georgie as if she's not there, as if none of this can be real. 'Build up the fire,' he says ominously.

And she cries, fearing the worst, looking into his eyes for an answer, '*Oh no, oh no*, we can't do that, not that . . .'

323

But he says, 'Well, I don't sodding know what else to do . . . we have to staunch the bleeding . . .'

'But the shock, my God, it'll kill him.'

'Well, what the hell do you suggest?'

The fire is a hot one, having burned solidly for several weeks now. The ashes underneath are white hot, so hot you can't get near them without stretching your arm and turning your face away. But Georgie banks it up just the same.

'Or the cooker perhaps,' says the tall, wide-shouldered man looking round, unaware, it would seem, of the darkness or the reason behind it.

'The electric's off.'

His eyes close with an awful weariness. 'Of course. Shit, I knew that. No telephone either? Is there anyone else round here who might know what we should do?'

She thinks hard at first, Georgie has to concentrate to remember exactly where she is . . . who her neighbours are . . . reality is hard to pinpoint. Eventually she shakes her head, 'No. Nobody. No-one at all.'

While she is building up the fire he is kneeling on the floor at the injured end of his dormant companion. 'Can you find some newspaper for all this blood? And we ought to raise the leg up somehow. Should I relax this tourniquet now, isn't that what they do, release it every so often . . . Jesus Christ, and he's only eighteen.'

'I don't think we ought to relax it. We should keep it tight until we've . . . after all . . . we're not worried about gangrene yet, gangrene wouldn't happen that fast . . .' For several seconds she thinks she might faint.

And the man looks as if he might cry when he groans, 'I know fuck all about gangrene.'

All those courses she could have gone on, all that blasted basic first aid that you owe to yourself and others. Everyone should have some bloody idea about how to cope with an accident. Why stay dependent on others? But she's never been on a first-aid course, she was never remotely interested.

But they seem to share the same lack of knowledge, God knows where it comes from . . . fiction, probably, mixed with the fag ends of life-saving programmes missed on TV. There is something reassuring in this. They do not argue over what they believe should be done.

He joins Georgie to search the kitchen. The only suitable knife, the knife she shows him, is stainless steel. The blade is wide, but wide enough?

'We might have to sear it several times,' he says, terribly drawn, his teeth gritted against the thought.

She mutters miserably, 'You better get your coat off.' Partly because his coat is wet and partly because she wants him to know that if anyone is going to cauterize anything round here, it's him, not her. They return to the roaring fire, where Georgie thrusts the knife in the flames, willing herself to calmness while he watches anxiously over her shoulder. 'I'd better get some towels, some sheets, I'd better look for some antiseptic.'

And all the while she dreads the chance that David might wake up, groan, show some signs of life which will make hurting him and the sealing of his wounds all the more ghastly. Because what they are planning to do is monstrously preposterous, there is no getting away from that.

She tries to distance herself, to be practical.

She stares at the boy's deathlike face. 'D'you think we should try some alcohol? Whisky?'

'We might have to do that later, but I don't think we should try that yet, and alcohol's bad for shock, they say. Don't they?'

'But fluids! He has to have fluids!'

'Yes, but not now. For Christ's sake, not yet.'

When will the blade be hot enough and how will they tell? Georgie bustles about the cottage gathering armfuls of towels and sheets that her nervous companion rips up and neither of them really knows why. Perhaps this is a practical method of delaying the awful moment of truth. Her inadequate first-aid kit is discovered underneath the sink and the Dettol is on the top shelf in the kitchen. Dettol, surely, rather than the childlike Germoline in its silly little pot, enough for one scraped knee, not a massively serious injury. The finger-sized bandages laugh at her. The tin of Band Aid is a mirthless joke, ditto the eyepatch, the Dispirin, the Rennies and the half-squeezed tubes of God knows what. These, presumably, have had their day, but they are not going to save Georgie now.

'I don't even know your name.'

'Oliver. And yours?'

'Georgie Jefferson. This is ludicrous. Here we are dealing in conventional introductions . . .'

'Listen. Georgie, you're going to have to hold the leg firmly in case Dave wakes up or tries to move, the knife mustn't slip . . .'

'*Shit*.'

Dave can't be cold, that's one blessing. Only his face and legs are exposed, the rest is under a duvet and blankets. Oliver begins to untie the laces on the one boot that is still here, but his hands are shaking badly.

'Yes, I'll hang on for dear life, I'll try.'

'The sodding snowplough broke down. We were on our way out. We knew it was a dead loss. We were on our way out when it broke down and Dave crawled underneath to see if the bugger was leaking again. That's when it slid back. His fucking ankle was right there. I had to let the snowplough slip further before I could free him to pull him out. God, he was screaming blue murder . . .' he shudders. 'I'll never forget those screams. Perhaps someone else's phone is working?'

Georgie shakes her head hopelessly. There is no point in playing games, it is far too late for that. There is no outside help to be had. There's only Georgie and Oliver. The man, Oliver, has crinkly black hair, he's a medium-sized, stocky bloke who looks capable and serious. His face is pleasant, his hands are large, with no accent it isn't possible to guess if he's local or not.

He asks, 'This is your house then?'

'Yes, but not for much longer.' They are try-ing to pass the awful minutes with safe, sane conversation. 'In fact, I'd planned to leave this morning. I've had quite enough of Wooton-Coney.'

They need this kind of mindless talk that requires no concentration. Their eyes are riveted on Dave's face, both terrified that the boy might wake and they'll have to cope with his anguish. Georgie, holding her breath for long periods of time, allows it to shudder on its way out.

Oliver slaps his head with his hand. '*For Christ's sake, how did this happen?* God almighty, come on, come on, let's face it, some tosser's chopped off Dave's sodding foot. I was only gone for ten minutes and look? *How else could this have happened?* Shit, who the hell could do this?'

Georgie does not answer. She squeezes her hot hands more tightly together. She checks the look of the knife in the fire, it is red hot and glowing, while Oliver goes on, hysteria rising. 'Some axe, bloody sharp, a bloody strong bastard. *What else could have happened?* How else does somebody's foot get sliced off . . . ?'

'The snowplough . . .' starts Georgie, thinking of Lot and his woodpile.

'Damn it! *Dave was out of the snowplough!* I wouldn't have left him underneath! And it would fucking well crush his foot, not actually chop it off! By the time I left him he wasn't anywhere near the snowplough. Oh, *Jesus Christ.*' And Oliver says again, as if she didn't hear him at first, 'the kid is only eighteen!'

'The kettle's boiling. D'you want a drink now – or later?'

But now Oliver sets his face as if he's going to war, there is no expression upon it and it suddenly feels that they've done this before and know exactly what to do. It is extraordinary. Some inner strength, her mother would call it. Well, Sylvia would faint if she were here now. With determined hands Georgie unwraps the bleeding stump and raises it onto the pile of books that are covered with several towels. There's newspaper all over the floor as if Georgie is houseproud, as if she cares a damn at this stage what the blood will do to the carpet. She rolls up her sleeves like a dull, conscienceless automaton. With a terrible solemnity, that of a ritual, Oliver dons the oven glove to grasp the handle of the now white-hot knife. He swings it from the fire very quickly and, as sweat pours down his face, gaunt in the candlelight, he lays it firmly against the pumping, raw and awful wound – holds it . . . holds it – he could be holding the sizzling steel against his own flesh by the horrified look on his face, and after counting to ten he replaces it swiftly back on the fire.

Then sags. And screws up his face in agony.

Burning pork. Singeing in the soupy air. Georgie has the leg gripped above the knee, and when it's over it is hard to let go. She is locked there, locked in combat with every nerve in her body. She has to ask if it's time to let go, and Oliver says, 'Yes, let go now. But we're going to have to do it again.'

With horrified awe they inspect the result. Half the wound has gone quite black. A layer of charred skin has formed, bubbling and blistering around it. Thank Christ it seems to have stopped the bleeding.

There is no reaction from Dave. Not a flicker. No movement.

After the longest five minutes of her life Georgie and Oliver repeat the whole abominable process, laying the knife on the other, untreated half of the stump.

'OK. Now. Should we cover it, or will it stick?'

'Perhaps we should lie clean sheets over it and leave it.'

'What about antiseptic?' And her fingers play stupidly with her mouth.

'Don't let's do anything else for now. I don't think I can do any more,' Oliver admits with a groan. 'Let's not disturb it. I don't reckon we should wet it with anything.'

'No.' Just put it away and cover it up. But they decide to keep the leg raised. They feel they ought to do that.

The atmosphere in the room is so stifling that by now they are both gasping for breath. 'That's some fire,' says Oliver, rolling down shirtsleeves covered in blood and not even noticing. Georgie sits beside him where he has sunk down on the floor. They rest their backs against a chair so they have a good view of the comatose Dave. And then Oliver puts out his hand and takes Georgie's. She feels her face going, slipping away into tears of tension, she shakes, she jerks, and, still sobbing, she creeps into his arms and he holds her.

The pair hold each other, sitting there, listening to the wind wailing down the chimney, watching the snowflakes land on the logs and spit, as aware of Dave's breathing as they are of their own. They make a gory sight, both smeared copiously with blood, and Oliver has a smear of crimson slicing his cheek like a scar. They don't talk. They can't talk. They just try to comfort each other until the violent shivering stops.

He turns and pushes her hair away, where it has stuck to her forehead. Eventually he smiles and sighs. 'You were great.'

Her wide eyes stare into his. 'So were you.'

'I don't think we could do any more.'

'I think the less we do now the better. As neither of us has a clue.'

'You must love me for bringing this to your door. It's strange, when I first saw you, when you opened the door, it looked as if you were expecting me.'

And so, sitting there watching their patient, too weak to rise if they wanted to and unconcerned with the mess, then and there Georgie tells him all of it, every intolerable detail, right from Angie Hopkins's death to her first visit to Wooton-Coney. At first, too disorganized to find words, she finds it hard to begin. But soon she is almost babbling, doesn't hide a thing, they are too close to separate one from another and their trauma would make trivial conversation obscene. There is no point in pretending.

And Oliver is the kind of man who listens without interrupting.

In the middle of all this Dave groans and tries to turn over. Georgie and Oliver leap to their feet, energized by fear, but his eyes remain closed, thank God, and he does not try to move his leg. She leaves Oliver watching over the patient and staggers to the kitchen to make some coffee. Lola is safely upstairs in her room. No doubt the dog will be sleeping.

'I could do with a tad of Scotch in that.'

So she pours in a tot of Teacher's, and they go back to their place on the floor because they can be closer that way, and Dave has the sofa. The coffee gives them strength, it is so comfortingly normal. As the colour returns to Oliver's face Georgie resumes her curious tale, the burning doll, the make-up case, the feeling of being stalked on her walks, the figure on the hill, the paint which was blood, the peering eye in the woodshed roof, the strange disappearance of Lola, the decapitated hens and how Donna's plight kept her here against her better instincts.

'Donna was lying, of course,' says Oliver 'Given everything else you've said, it's pretty obvious she was trying it on.'

My God. My God. In all the chaos this simple truth had never occurred to Georgie. Of course the girl isn't pregnant. Donna could not have been pregnant for four whole months without confiding the fact to Georgie, without milking her sympathy. The news was announced right out of the blue when Georgie threatened to leave, and Georgie fell for it, like a fool. Despite all her experience she fell for it!

'It just proves how affected I've been, by loneliness and fear.'

'And guilt. Don't forget guilt.' Oliver's face grows more and more serious. 'It all adds up.'

She answers his questions, all she knows about the Buckpits, the Horsefields, Chad and Donna. She rambles on about Stephen and his paintings, the good and the bad, the ones she has disposed of because nobody liked them.

'Hell, I'm unstoppable,' she actually manages a laugh. 'It's nerves, of course, I'm sorry. What a bore.'

'I think it's pretty essential that you go on talking,' Oliver says thoughtfully. 'There's somebody out there causing all this. There's some kind of monster out there on the prowl, and whoever it is, it's not just you they're after. That man you saw on the hill did this to Dave, and if any human being can do this . . .'

'It's madness, isn't it?' Georgie whispers, looking steadily at Oliver, wanting an honest answer at last, someone to tell her she's not paranoid. Eager to face the truth herself.

'Yes. It is madness.'

'And we can't get out of here?'

'Not for the moment we can't. And they say this weather's in for a week.'

'What the hell are we going to do?' And, oh God, it's such a relief to be able to ask someone else this question.

'We are going to keep the doors locked and we are going to try to look after Dave. You know, don't you, you're not under any illusions, I hope, Dave will probably die.'

'Yes, I know that.'

'No matter how hard we try, whatever we do he probably won't even come round.'

Georgie nods sadly.

'But at least you're not alone any more enduring this hellish nightmare. And surely, whoever's out there must know there are two of us now. Nobody's going to try anything when they know they are outnumbered.'

'If he hadn't gone after poor Dave tonight the pig would probably have come after me. Whoever it is totally insane, a terrible, violent kind of sickness with a psychopathic strength behind it.'

So they sit in each other's arms like two frightened children not knowing what to do next. And they hold each other this way all night until a pale daylight pierces the darkness.

Twenty-five

In her overwrought mind, every sound, every breath, symbolizes the terror that now surrounds and threatens them. The massive and overwhelming force of madness seems too great for the strength of the two who huddle beside the fire, helpless as rabbits. The steamy heat of the room smells of bodies and burning and pain, dreadful pain, but at least Georgie is no longer alone, despite the additional horror that her two new companions brought with them. Surely she is more secure tonight than she was only yesterday.

If she's going to die there's a very good chance that she might not die alone, like Stephen.

Now Dave tosses and turns and shakes in a demented fever. His teeth chatter and grate together, and occasionally he moans like a man in torment. He had felt so very cold at first, cold like a long-dead fish, with skin dry and scaley, but now, with the blankets piled on top of him, the heat burns from inside him like a smouldering autumn bonfire. A yellow sheen appears on his skin, a noxious sweat as the sour smell of pain comes and goes, fetid with fear. Georgie and Oliver take turns cooling his face with a damp flannel, clucking motherly words of reassurance that sound idiotic when you bear the situation in mind, but they mouth their platitudes just the same. For their own sakes as much as for his.

They don't look at his leg. There's no point in looking. They have done all they can, so they drip water on his parched lips instead, hoping that some of the drops might find their way into his mouth.

And they carry on reassuring him as the candle-light casts shadows across the ceiling and into the corners, and the carriage clock on the mantelpiece ticks the grinding minutes away. Oh, the inaptness of ordinary words. But talking to Dave, who is deaf to the world, is an easy way of talking to each other, and they need to keep doing this. They exist within a circle, and somewhere outside that circle a homicidal maniac waits and breathes and watches, and it is essential that the three in the cottage are all included, that nobody be left out in the cold.

There is menace out there in the moving darkness. Somewhere between the snow and wind the devil still walks in this valley.

There's nothing like fear for loosening the tongue. Already Georgie and Oliver feel like old, old friends. They know more about one another, trapped as they are in this bloody hell, than if they shared a lifetime of memories. She told him her story, not giving a damn if he believed her or not, nor in what light she appeared, and it sounded simple, quite straightforward, not the symptoms of some lonely hysteric. Talking like that has been a release.

'Dave's a student. He was only doing the bloody job to fill in during the holidays.'

'Holidays?'

'Four weeks off for Christmas. He only started yesterday.'

She's forgotten Christmas is nearly here. The Maces were supposed to be coming, she was actually worried about lack of space and where she might buy decorations. 'And you?'

'A private contractor, we work for the council, but so many men couldn't make it because of the bloody weather that I stepped in at the last minute like a goddamn fool . . .'

It is comforting, talking like this to a stranger in the gloom, almost a confessional situation, and their voices are quiet and respectful, as if they are sitting in church and Dave is laid out on the altar. A sacrifice to be washed and pampered to satisfy the gods. If he dies there will be no mercy. If he dies it will all have been in vain. They manage to communicate even though their exhausted eyes rarely leave their patient's face. 'So you're used to driving these huge wagons?'

'I'll have you know I have driven lumber wagons in the Canadian backwoods in my time.'

Yes, he looks as if he might have done that. 'A logger, how romantic. So what made you come back here?'

'To start my own business,' he shrugs. 'To see my wife. We're divorced, but we're friends. I share the business with my brother-in-law.'

'I didn't know it was possible to divorce and stay friends.'

'Well, Jess and I have proved that it is.'

They have to pause because Dave starts one of his terrible shivering fits. They have to stop and cool him. Georgie finds some wet-wipes in the kitchen. Her mind shies away from thoughts of the wound and what Dave might feel if he comes round properly. *Will he come round?* Oliver thinks not. Will death be gentle if it comes to claim this golden-haired boy who lies shaking and steaming on her sofa? Or will it come with a screaming agony? And what the hell can they do to prevent it? There are no painkillers here.

But what about the farm?

Veterinary remedies are often similar, or the same, as the medications for humans, and Mark had commented on the jars and lotions laid out on the shelves in the parlour next to the ashes. Georgie doubts the Buckpits would think to lock any powerful drugs away, partly because they are daft and partly because of the lack of need. She herself has seen Silas picking his teeth with the needle end of some outsized syringe.

All they want is something for pain, and some strong antiseptic would come in handy. But neither she nor Oliver know a thing about drugs, although Georgie possesses a drug dictionary given to her by her mother along with a book of symptoms, essential reading in Sylvia's eyes. Georgie tries to think how out of date they would be. How long has she had them and where in God's name are they?

At no time does Oliver let the poker out of his hand. It is a heavy brass antique, at least three feet long and a useful weapon. Despite their inept ministrations, at no time does either one stop listening for any unusual sound from outside, something that might not be part of the storm. 'Now the business is off the ground I'm preparing for the journey of a lifetime, a journey I always promised myself. I'm taking off round the world with a camp bed and a jeep. Or that's what I thought I was doing.' Thoughts of this ambition light his pleasant face with a smile.

Isn't he, middle-aged as he is, rather old to be off round the world? Is he planning to go on his own? To Georgie, who craves safety, the idea holds little appeal.

'So you're prepared to give everything up on a whim?'

'The business won't fold without me. I missed my chance to travel as a kid, so I'm taking it now instead. It's that simple.'

'And your children? I presume you've got children?'

'Two boys. Saul and Daniel. Both at college in the USA. There's nothing to hold me here.'

Georgie gives a wry smile. 'How strange that you should end up here, bang in the middle of nowhere, driving a council snowplough, and now sitting here talking to me like this.'

'Not so strange. The whole of life is dependent on fate.'

'Oh, one of those.' She gazes at Dave's poor leg. It works for some, this fatalism. Rather bad luck on the third world.'

'But nothing that's ever happened to me is

quite as improbable as your last few months.'

She has to admit, 'Till you came along I truly believed I was losing my mind.'

'Why the hell didn't you tell someone? Why didn't you get out earlier? You knew something was badly wrong . . .'

'I thought no-one would believe me. I've had rather a lot of attention just lately, people might have thought it was getting to be a habit. I did call the police after the eye in the woodshed roof, but they thought I was barmy, they said it was some animal. And any of those other odd happenings could be the product of an overwrought imagination.'

'Not the paint, though. Your pallet was covered with blood for God's sake.'

'But I wasn't sure it was blood.'

'You were determined to overcome, to stay here until the spring, to prove them all wrong. Too damn stubborn for your own good.'

'It's true. After Angie died I lost most of my confidence and I wanted to get it back somehow. I hated the sort of person I was, dependent on other people, so needy. If they were around I would lean on them, I needed to be alone. Or that's what I thought. Maybe I could be self sufficient, more like my brother . . .'

'And now?' His smile was rueful.

'Now I wish I'd never heard of the blasted place.'

'It's laden with atmosphere, I'll give you that.'

'It's not quite so spooky as this when the electric's on. You should see it in the sunshine.

During the summer, surrounded by friends, this cottage felt so totally different. But then there were no monsters.'

'Weren't there? I thought that's why you came away. Because of Angie?'

'Well, yes. There was Angie. There still is Angie. She will always be with me.' But Georgie clams up after that, not wanting to open up any further, and slightly annoyed by his attitude, too canny, too invasive.

Reluctantly, because of the danger of any such action, she mentions the drugs at the farm. She is well aware, if Lot really is the axeman of Wooton-Coney, of the risks involved in any such pillaging operation. Getting across would be bad enough, although Wooton Farm is the building nearest the cottage, let alone the awful danger of being seen.

'I know there's a chance we'd find nothing to help us, but farmers do use their own anaesthetics for small jobs, like dehorning and castrating calves. Knowing the Buckpits they'd rather do everything themselves than pay out for a vet . . .'

'Why didn't I think of that?' Oliver slams his fist into his hand. 'Of course, it's so obvious, you're right . . .'

Georgie freezes, wishing she hadn't mentioned it, she had hoped for more of a rational discussion rather than this impulsive response. 'He'll be out there . . .'

'No doubt . . .'

'If it's Lot, he might even be there in the parlour . . .'

'Not at night he won't.'

Georgie trembles. 'It's pitch-black out there at night . . .'

'Night or day, in this weather it's all the same . . .'

'So you think we should . . . ?'

'There's no doubt about it.'

'Oliver, I really don't think I can stand it. What if anything happens to one of us? I just don't think I can cope with the thought of being here alone again with all this madness going on,' Georgie shudders, tears sprout in her eyes. Death rustles against the windows. 'Damn Stephen, damn Dave, damn Donna, damn everything. I've just had enough.'

Oliver takes her hand and presses it, his brown eyes crinkling. He is a kind man. 'I know. I know. Well just try and forget it for now. We won't mention it any more until nearer the time.' Sensing Georgie's terror Oliver moves the subject to more future matters. To her it seems a terrible horizon. 'When it's light it might be better to call on the others, I know they don't sound very hopeful, but somebody has to help us out here. And we're going to need the Buckpits' tractor the minute the weather calms down. Somebody has to get to a phone, a helicopter will get through even if nobody else can make it. Dave has to get to hospital, if he lives, and then there's the bastard who did this.'

They listen to the row outside. The wind shows no sign of abating. 'That means there's going to be two occasions when one of us must stay here alone with Dave. Tonight as well as the morning.

We said we wouldn't split up, Oliver, and I don't like the idea.'

'I realize that. But we have to try to get the drugs, and it's imperative we find some help.'

'Huh! And to think I dreamed of a leisurely old age. I wonder if Donna's told Chad she's pregnant or whether that little drama was reserved uniquely for me. I'd almost forgotten, it's strange, that seems like another world after this.'

'After this we can cope with anything,' Oliver says, looking round dismally. 'Compared to all this your friend Donna doesn't know what real problems are.'

'It didn't seem like that yesterday.' Good God, was it only yesterday that they had sat in the kitchen while Donna told her tale of woe? How are they coping in that spartan house without electricity? It is most unlikely they would have candles. Nothing so organized.

Each time the wind gusts from another direction, each time there is a creak from the stairs or a deeper, hollower sound from the chimney, the chill of horror sweeps over Georgie and Oliver's expression, his hold on the poker, tells her he is equally afraid.

'The bastard's already been here in the cottage,' Oliver reminds Georgie needlessly while they wait for night to fall. 'He got inside somehow to daub that blood on your pallet. There's no chance, is there, that he might have a key?'

'The door was open that night, I remember. I never used to bother to lock it.'

'And what about the woodshed? Do you bother to lock that? Is there any other possible way this fiend might enter your house?'

Georgie does not need to think, she already knows the answer. 'There's no way. Both doors are locked. The stable door has a chain, too. The upstairs windows are far too small, even for a child to get through, let alone a large man, and he is large, remember, I've seen him.'

'But only from a distance. Think, Georgie, think, what the hell did he really look like? It has to be one of your oddball neighbours. It can't possibly be anyone else.'

Even to conjure that dark silent figure in her mind is repellent. But Georgie tries all the same. 'He was big, I am quite certain of that. And bulky, almost fat . . .'

'But could his clothes give that impression?'

She waits a moment before answering, thinking hard. 'Yes, yes, I suppose the width of him could be his clothes. There was always something on his head, some hat, or his collar was up because I couldn't see any neck, and he wore a dark knee-length coat, and trousers.'

Oliver looks at her closely. 'Never any different?'

'Never.'

'And he didn't move at all?'

'Well, he must have moved to get there. And he managed to move very fast when he did his disappearing act. But no, when I was watching he just stood there. Still.'

'He must be quite an agile sod to climb onto your woodshed roof.'

'You think that was definitely him? You think he is behind it all?'

'Don't you, Georgie?'

'I wish I didn't.'

Oliver shakes his head. 'But where does the burning doll come in, and that unlikely make-up bag?'

'They could be unconnected.'

'If we're going to take this at face value then your lunatic has to be Horace Horsefield or Lot Buckpit, doesn't it? Neither Cramer or Silas fit the bill. Which is the most likely contender? Think, Georgie, *for God's sake think!*'

And she knows that their lives might depend upon it.

'Horace wouldn't. He couldn't. He is a gentle, kindly man, slow and ponderous and worn out with responsibilities. All his time is taken up looking after Nancy. He never leaves his wife, never.'

Oliver says unpleasantly, 'Or that's the impression he's given to you. And you've swallowed it like you swallowed Donna's unlikely story.'

'Yes, I swallowed it. I can only tell you what I believe. Lot Buckpit seems the most likely. He's dim-witted, ruled by his mother, but he's fit and strong and I've seen the way he wields an axe.'

'It has to be him. And it is possible that his mother knows and is protecting her mutant offspring, that's why she doesn't want you near. That's why she's so aggressive towards you.'

345

'But why would Lot Buckpit want to do all those odd things?'

'When it comes to madness you don't need a motive. There's a lot of in-breeding goes on in these obscure places. It could be that the man's driven mad by the arrival of a strange woman. You say the brothers go nowhere, see no-one. They've never lived anywhere else and their mother is obviously some kind of religious fanatic. You can understand their fascination for anyone different, and if one of them is unhinged to the point . . .'

'Of murder? *To the point of murder?*'

'My money's on Lot Buckpit, Georgie.'

And that makes this coming nocturnal sortie all the more frightening. Is it Lot? Is it? So she puts the farmer's head on the shoulders of the figure she can never make out and yes, it fits. It suits him. She shudders and moves closer to Oliver.

On the sofa the boy twists convulsively. Then comes a bout of dreadful shaking, but for now, thank God, Dave's eyes stay closed. Oliver is right. Whatever the dangers, for Dave's sake, they have to try to find something to relieve his pain.

And Georgie agrees with Oliver when he says, '*Sod this fucking bastard phone.*'

Twenty-six

What a knight. His armour is a three-quarter
Barbour, his breastplate a long-sleeved thermal
vest, and the poker serves as his trusty sword and
shield combined. With his blood-encrusted face
and his hair scruffy with dried sweat, he looks as if
he is back from the fray already well beaten.

'Shit. Shit. I do not want to do this. I do not
want to go out there.' He takes in Georgie's ashen
face and grimaces again. 'Show me one more time
on the plan.'

She spreads the vital piece of paper. Oliver is
determined to go and she has come to accept it.
'This is us, and this is them. It's out of the front
door, over the stream, turn left on the road.
Follow it for a hundred yards and Wooton Farm is
right opposite. If you reach the ford you've gone
too far. You might be able to make out some
lights. At least they have a generator.'

'I doubt they'll be wasting that at five o'clock in
the morning.' He bends over her shoulder to
peruse her basic drawing. She can feel the tension
coming off him, it meets with hers and creates an
aura almost electric. 'Then I go through the cowshed, which presumably will be full, and through a
corrugated door to the parlour.'

'And you try not to use your torch at all until

you get right there. You've got the string bag. You either fill it and get the hell out of there and we have to hope you've hit the jackpot, or you try to read some of the labels, be a little selective, but I don't think you'll feel much like doing that.'

'One day,' says Oliver, 'we will look back and laugh.'

'No chance,' says Georgie. 'And it's all got to be done so fast that anyone waiting out there will be caught off guard. You'll be back here before they know where you've gone.'

Oliver takes her hand. 'Thanks.'

'For what?'

'For trying to be positive.'

'If you only knew what I feel like inside.'

'Ditto,' says Oliver. 'I'm no bloody hero.'

'I am so glad,' says Georgie. 'I never could stand heroes.'

'Lock up behind me for Christ's sake.'

He is gone, into a blast of whiteness, into a howling frenzy of cold. Georgie locks the door behind him, it's no good trying to follow his progress, you can't see a foot in front of your face, and she retreats back into the sick room where Dave's prone and mutilated body lies in awful state on the sofa. After checking him over – he seems to be dreaming tonight, under his eyelids there's rapid movement, and every so often he emits a chilling groan – Georgie paces backwards and forwards in front of the fire. Selfishly she wills him not to wake up while she's here on her own. She doesn't know how she could cope with such agony, a screaming, thrashing chaos of pain, so yes, Oliver's expedition really is imperative. Dave can't stay unconscious for ever.

It's funny how some people inspire confidence, her friend Helen Mace for one, and Oliver is a natural. In his public school way Toby would have strutted out there like a boy playing some Death-watch computer game, in the same way that his predecessors must have strutted off into their various wars, programmed to show no fear, for God, country and the womenfolk back home. When Georgie married Toby she preferred it like that, she craved to be looked after, to be championed by somebody stronger. Pathetically, she quite understands Donna's need to be mastered.

Mark, on the other hand, although from the same kind of background as Toby, is more the intellectual, more into peace, he would be more likely to insist on discussing all this with the Buckpits man to man. He would no more dream of dashing off into the void to purloin some imaginary medicine than sell his beloved old MG to some common collector.

But neither Toby nor Mark would inspire the same sort of confidence that Oliver, with all his misgivings, inspires in Georgie. So far he has shown himself capable of the most incredible bravery, strong and gentle, funny and sad. She has sworn not to look at her watch, but now she looks at it. The hand has hardly moved since he left, she must give him time.

Now she leaves the muttering Dave and, by the

light of a candle, she goes upstairs to search for the dictionary of drugs that she knows is around somewhere. She shields the candle with her hand, remembering the spooky melodramas she's seen, those dark Victorian houses where the wind gusts round every corner. Well, in Furze Pen Cottage it gusts through the cracks in all the tiny-paned windows. Many of her books are still boxed, there's a scarcity of shelf space in the cottage, but surely she saw this one recently in the blanket box at the end of her bed.

Georgie puts down the candle and kneels at the foot of her bed like Christopher Robin, only her hands are not together. Her prayers for Oliver's safety are all in her head. She heaves up the lid of the box and peers inside. She is prepared to empty the whole thing out, sod's law, the book she wants is bound to be right at the bottom, but no, it's only three layers down. She retrieves it triumphantly and turns to pick up the candle when she sees the light approaching through the darkness of the cottage window.

Oliver! Oh, thank God. Thank God. And it didn't take too long after all. She should have had more faith in Oliver, she shouldn't have been quite so frightened. Any would-be attacker eyeing up Oliver's stocky size and strength would think twice before picking on him. No, the monster they face is a coward, preferring women and wounded boys on which to vent his fury.

Georgie stands up and moves to the window, a smile of relief all over her face. One small success at last, perhaps now fortune will change and they will overcome. But why is Oliver moving so slowly? My God, has he been hurt? And now the light is perfectly still, directed on the cottage, three steps forward, three steps back, now it shines on the sky and now it is a pool of light illuminating the snowy ground.

Georgie blows out the candle quickly. Teeth already chattering she stands behind the curtain and peeps out. Slowly the beam of light approaches, she can make out nothing at all behind it, it's as if it moves of its own accord, at its own pace, in its own carefully chosen direction. *Does it know where she is?* Did it notice the candle flame?

As if in answer the light approaches, slowly, methodically, wavering as it traverses the uneven hillocks of snow, and then it comes forward again. It flickers against the fantastic patterns of frost on the window and gives it a strange perfection, like the stained-glass window of a church, deliberately positioned to catch the brightest light. This can't be Oliver. Oliver would know how nervous this sort of approach would make her – unless he really is badly injured and is signalling for help, the psychopath close behind him. Lola might know, but Lola is shut in the kitchen in case she should feel like sharing the sofa with Dave, or, God forbid, licking his stump, thinking it charcoaled meat. Should she go down and open the door? Should she open the window and call from here? She releases the catch and pushes. The frame is badly iced up under the heavy folds of snow. She pushes again, with both hands this time, the hammering of her own heart overtaking the buffeting roar of the wind as, in her urgency, she calls upon God or whoever else might be up there, 'Help me, please help me, please.'

She thumps. She curses. She calls out wildly in her terror.

If the light didn't know before, it has her whereabouts pinpointed now. All of a sudden the approach quickens, concentrates on one direction, the beam directed straight at the window so that Georgie is forced to narrow her eyes against the aching brightness. And still it comes, nearer, nearer. This is the window through which the postman used to post parcels in the autumn to save her having to open her door, so low-built is the cottage, and now there's an extra layer of snow to bring it within easier reach.

The sinister light floods the little square bed-room, but Georgie doesn't wait any longer. This is not a friendly light, somebody come to see to their welfare at five o'clock in the morning. This is not Oliver. She stampedes down the stairs, slamming the door at the bottom and pushing the table in front of it, she dashes into the kitchen and grabs the cauterizing knife, wrenching the kitchen door closed behind her, and then she takes up her position as defender of the helpless, rigidly at attention beside the slumbering form of Dave. Georgie hardly breathes. She is a tablet of stone.

And if the creature is on the prowl, *what has happened to Oliver?*

She wishes she had closed the curtains as Oliver

had advised her to do. She had foolishly said, 'If I keep them open at least the windows give you some little glow of light to direct you.'

'Oh, Dave, Dave,' Georgie's voice quivers. She licks her lips which are as dry as his. 'What the hell do I do?'

Dave's bloodshot eyes only flicker.

Lola barks loudly, hackles raised, staring intently at the window.

Gradually, with palpitating heart, Georgie makes out the unutterable horror of the face at the window, the face which presses against the window forming it into some ghoulish mask, some diabolical carnival mask evoking some unspeakable hell, spread nose, flattened lips in a grotesque grin, eyes stretched into slits of hatred. Aghast, she can only stare as the creature's breath accumulates on the pane and melts the ice patterns there, so that they slide in an awful watery glaze down the features of the demon, giving them another dimension, a pulpy, rubbery sheen.

Lola jumps up uselessly, her lip curled, a blood-curdling growl issuing from somewhere deep in her throat. But Lola is a softie at heart. Plenty of bark but no bite.

So this is it. This is the end. At least Dave is well out of it. No-one in their worst nightmares could imagine a death as terrible as this . . .

It's a crashing against the door, the hammering of a man at the end of his tether, it hardly reaches Georgie as she stands, awed by the horrible nature of her own imminent demise.

'Shit! *Where the hell are you?* Open this sodding door . . .'

Like a bird hypnotized by a snake, still she stares at the idiot face.

Lola, excited, yelps behind her. The battering on the door attains the decibels of heavy metal. 'Georgie, GEORGIE COME ON . . .'

She jumps to life at the sound of her name but it sounds as if somebody is calling from some half forgotten other world. She turns from the face at the window towards the echoing sound, by the time she turns back the face has gone, and along with it the light that preceded it. There is nothing there now, just snow-swept darkness, and the hammering on the door is increasing.

'*Oliver!*' She must reach him before the face . . .

'Hell, what are you trying to do . . .' he says as he falls in, a figure entirely encased in white.

But Georgie is on the floor, collapsed in a trembling heap at his feet, under attack from Lola who thinks this is a game.

'What the shit is going on here? What sort of crazy are we dealing with? Pushing his face against the window, pulling faces, hanging about in this sort of weather, Jesus, it's unreal, it's infantile, it's incredulous, outrageous . . .'

'There's no point going on,' says Georgie wearily, 'it happened. But I'm so relieved you're back safely I seem to have ceased to care about him.'

'I thought you were dead,' pants Oliver, still out of breath. 'Shit. I thought he must have been in and got you both, and the dog, while I was gone.'

'Just let me cling a little bit longer.' Georgie has not let go of his arm since he lifted her firmly and moved her to a comparative place of safety, on the floor in front of the fire. 'I'm not ready to let go yet.'

'I don't want you to let go.'

'I want to hear what happened to you.'

'Nothing compared with what happened to you,' he strokes her arm, she's still clinging. 'I'm surprised you're still coherent, surprised you haven't cracked up completely. Obviously it's more dangerous to be in here than outside. Next time . . .'

But Georgie shudders. 'Believe me, there's never going to be one of those.'

'I found the cowshed, more by luck than judgement, and then I had to fight my way through nosy cows wandering around between cubicles. Christ, it was so bloody dark in there, and all the while I was trying to listen for Lot – impossible with the blizzard. I had to give up in the end and just press on, told myself the quicker the better . . .'

'. . . and there was no sign of anyone with a light? No new footprints?'

'Nothing like that. I turned on the torch in the parlour, and managed to clear one bottom shelf before I chickened out and turned and legged it . . .' Oliver opens the string bag to reveal an odd assortment of rusty tins, slimy jars, several rolls of coloured tape, boxes of vials containing mostly colourless liquids, syringes, some disposable needles, cans and a spray of WD40, tractor grease. 'Mostly rubbish. Sod it! I should have taken more time, but I told you before, I'm no hero. I don't suppose for a minute you found your drug book . . .'

Her smile is still a nervous one. 'Well, I did, actually.'

'I'll get it.'

'No, don't leave me. We'll go upstairs together.'

Settling back on the floor Oliver holds up a jar full of grey granules. 'God knows what use these are . . . looks like some cure for indigestion.'

'Oh no,' Georgie blanches. 'Don't tell me. This is too much. You've fetched old Buckpit's ashes.'

The sudden silence, the incredulous look on Oliver's face, reduces Georgie to a kind of sobbing, hysterical laughter. Between bursts she manages to hiccup an explanation for his grisly find, and soon he joins her, the tension is released for one whole manic, marvellous minute. 'Perhaps we should sprinkle them on the stump . . .'

'Oh no, old man Buckpit's black soul might be introduced to Dave's body, a kind of incubus—'

'Or we could throw them into Lot's eyes and blind him—'

'Stop it. Stop it. Perhaps if we rub the jar the genie of old man Buckpit might rise up and offer us a wish—'

'We could hold the ashes for ransom, demand a tractor in return . . .' and Oliver wipes his eyes.

They cackle and crow with this disrespectful, macabre stuff until they realize how juvenile they sound, how responsible they still have to be and how vulnerable they are . . . but it is a moment of blessed release and both feel better after it.

And after a serious study of Oliver's haul they come across two items which might well be of use – one is a spray which contains Tetracycline, and from what they can gather from the rusted instructions it is used for disinfecting wounds, and the other is a box of capsules labelled Lignocaine, used in the farming profession as a local anaesthetic administered by injection.

This find poses the next problem: dare they use the drugs on a human? And when?

'We could use the spray now,' says Oliver, 'that can't possibly do any harm and it must be stronger than anything you've got in your kitchen. But I think we'll leave the local anaesthetic until it seems necessary . . .'

'You mean until Dave wakes up screaming?'

'Exactly.'

'Yes. I agree.' Georgie is also reluctant to start sticking needles in Dave, especially anywhere near the vicinity of that ghastly wound.

Dave's stump is a lurid purple.

'That's done, thank God. The colour alone would scare off infection. Now let's try and relax until dawn.'

Relax? Some hope. But at last she has stopped shaking. They spread a rug on the floor, two large cushions for pillows and lie down next to each other until Lola spies them and, a jealous creature by nature, inserts herself rudely between them. All the curtains are firmly drawn. There is no chance of sleep, even if either one felt like it. Four eyes are better than two. Two weapons better than one. 'Lola,' groans Georgie, trying to shift the dog over, 'why aren't you a pit bull?'

'She's lovely,' says Oliver, stroking her, 'just the sort of dog I would choose. They say stroking dogs is good for the heart, reduces blood pressure, too, so we ought to stroke her for dear life because my heart, for one, is about to give out.'

She rests her head on his shoulder, and while he strokes her cheek and neck she keeps her eyes closed and her lips slightly smiling. 'Are we going to get out of this alive, Oliver?' Suddenly she turns deadly serious. 'Tell me what you truly think.'

They both gaze ahead of them, staring at nothing. 'If we do, you and I ought to spend some time together, sane time, calm time, get to unknow each other a bit.'

'With our defences up, you mean?'

The laughter lines crinkle beside his brown eyes. 'Certainly. I'm a much more acceptable person when I can hide the shit underneath. You should see me at parties. We can't have a decent relationship based so disgustingly on truth.'

'You are absolutely right,' says Georgie, encouraged to hear that, all being well, this will not be the end between them. It's a long time since she felt such pleasure. These close and tender feelings must have something to do with fear. Maybe if they had bungee jumped together it would have produced the same chemistry, the secret and perilous games of children. How ironic that these are the terrible circumstances in which, for the first time in almost a year, Georgie feels expectant and alive.

'Perhaps we should share a bottle of wine together right now, just in case we don't get another chance,' says Oliver, picking up Georgie's hand. 'I don't see why we should be done out of that by some sick bastard staggering around the hillsides with an axe.'

'Hardly the most ideal situation.' Georgie smiles as she brings in two glasses and a bottle of Nuit St Georges and stands it beside the fireplace. 'This is my favourite. I was saving it for something special. But look at us both. Anyone would think . . . This is madness.'

'This is the only right thing that has happened since I arrived,' says Oliver, bringing his lips down onto hers.

And Lola gives a deafening fart.

Twenty-seven

Oh, please let it be morning. Either let it be morning or let this closeness go on for ever. Take away all the tomorrows.

It's hard to tell the difference for the light has only slightly changed with the black turning a pale shade of grey. The candles have less effect on the gloom, and yet whenever one of the flames goes out, Georgie replaces it with another. It is a little positive act, some small achievement, and Oliver, for much the same reasons, tours the cottage now and then, poker firmly in hand while he tests the windows and checks the doors. In the end it seems sensible to drag Stephen's sideboard into the hall to make a firm barrier behind the front door.

'Hell, but we can't stay stuck in here for much longer. At some point we must get more wood or agree to freeze to death. And that poor dog of yours needs to go out.'

'I'm not worried about that. What's a few lumps of dog shit?'

But Oliver is right. Keeping themselves warm is essential, especially poor Dave, so at some point they must open the back door and venture out into no man's land. They are OK for food. Even with the freezer kaput the frozen stuff will last for a few days. Somehow it will have to be cooked on the fire, but that's no big deal, it will give Georgie a chance to test the little bread oven tucked inside the chimney.

The nearness of the stream means they need never worry about lack of water, and luckily the fire heats the water, so there is no shortage of that.

With the slightly brighter light it is all too horribly clear just what a mess they are both in, blood-smeared clothing gone crispy brown, nails rimmed with the stuff which has settled into the creases in their hands, and it's in Oliver's hair, so it must be in Georgie's. Each assesses the other, both covered with far more blood than Dave, who is relatively clean after their gentle attempts at hygiene. Yes, Oliver and Georgie make a grizzly pair in the pale morning light.

'What I'd give for a bath, to lie steaming in the blissful heat and soak some of this crap away,' Georgie says.

'Have one. You might as well. We ought to sort ourselves out, and there's nothing else to be done at the moment.'

There's no change in Dave's condition. Still burning hot, every so often he writhes and contorts and starts to lick his dry, flaky lips. His golden hair has changed colour in the night, and now it is dark, drenched with sweat, his curls turned into tendrils. Occasionally he cries out, as if from some hideous nightmare, but although his eyelids flicker, thank God they stay closed. They have anaesthetic at the ready.

'I can't have a bath because I don't possess one.

There's no space in the bathroom, as you must have noticed. It's hard to turn round in there. No, I'll have to have a shower.' Georgie stares at Oliver. 'So will you. You look disgusting.'

'Let's venture out first.' Oliver's expression is stoic. 'Shit, let's get it over with. We could fetch a couple of baskets of logs and fill some buckets from the stream.'

In any other circumstances these would be simple tasks, and the suggestion is casually made, with an air of resignation. But to actually carry out these chores feels like climbing a mountain. If Georgie had been alone she would have let the fire go out rather than take one step into such a sinister unknown. She would have stayed in bed with the doors firmly locked, for water she would use snow from the windowsill. They both know that simply the movement of opening the door will sap all the courage they have.

But, realistically, it has to be done. After last night's fiasco Georgie refuses to stay behind. They decide to go together so that one can defend them both with the poker, should the need arise, and for extra protection Georgie thrusts her carving knife through the bottom of her pocket. With one constantly keeping watch they will see if anyone approaches the door and they'll never be too far away to leave Dave unguarded. Yes, it is essential that Georgie and Oliver keep together.

Before the moment of truth arrives they peer out of the bedroom windows to see if anything moves out there apart from the storm itself. Pale and spiky icicles sprout from the overhang of thatch, suspended at the window like broken bars. Heavy snow, slanting, chasing in a roaring wind, blows across their line of vision and blurs it. Any footprints left by the devil have been well and truly covered. 'Well, good luck to anyone waiting out there, the crazy bastard, he'll have frozen to death by now,' says Oliver, 'and it wouldn't matter how padded he was. Nobody could survive.'

'He managed OK last night.'

Only half satisfied by their own reassurances, armed, and muffled to the teeth with sweaters and coats, they finally open the door. Lola creeps out behind with her half-tail between her legs. The woodshed is their goal. Georgie stands guard at the door while Oliver disappears in its darkened depths, she can hear him cursing and shouting as he feels his way forward. She hears him filling the basket. She watches as he staggers back to the kitchen door, dumps the first load on the step and staggers back for a second. Her eyes feel sore from staring so sightlessly. She can see no further than three or four yards, and she curses the screaming wind because it cuts out most other sound. Blind and deaf, and yet she is on guard for her life, hopping from one foot to the other, willing Oliver to hurry, hurry, hurry . . .

In a moment that seems like hours the second basket arrives inside, and Lola creeps in with it, happy to be out of the excruciating cold. They close the door firmly behind her, and then they are on their way to the stream, each with a bucket that has to be filled. Of Georgie's poor hens there is no sign. The weather has either whipped them away or conducted their funerals for her. This is the most incredible journey, Oliver must have made light of last night's endeavours. The snow is deep, and frozen to a dangerous crust on top. Down one hedge it has taken the shape of an immense tidal wave, foaming and towering above their heads, threatening to fall and wipe everything out. In places the snow is waist deep, so they have to pick their way with care, and it's still impossible to see more than a few yards ahead. The apple trees are twisted monsters that loom in the half-light as they stumble blindly past them. Every so often, with a gasp of cold air, they swing round suddenly in case they are being approached from behind. But nothing. Nobody's there. They try to keep an eye on the door, but the whole cottage is swallowed up into the mist of white. It's a struggle to keep a sense of direction. Never has Georgie's orchard felt so long, never has that stream seemed so distant.

With intense concentration – not a second can be wasted – they fill their buckets and tramp back, fighting to keep going, with no other thought than the desperate need to keep each other in sight. In the cottage they both collapse, chain the door and hurry to the sitting room to check on Dave, hearts in their mouths. No change. Their charge has not been disturbed. Nobody has been in the cottage while they've been gone. The floors are quite dry. Nevertheless, they search every room, upstairs and down, Oliver with his poker and Georgie with her carving knife, before they return to the kitchen, exhausted.

Georgie's heart is still hammering. Where her face has been exposed to the wind the skin feels flayed. The stillness indoors is palpable. They stand there dripping in the kitchen, examining each other with watering eyes before falling together, clinging. Now they are almost laughing. Incredibly, laughing and crying. Either will do, either comes with such relief.

No-one could miss the irony in Georgie's voice when she cries, 'And you are seriously suggesting that one of us venture out there later to try to find help?' The very idea is absurd.

'Give us a chance to recover,' gasps Oliver. 'Let's see how it goes. Let's just wait and see.'

While the feeling returns to her body, after Oliver makes up the fire, Georgie cooks bacon and egg carefully, the frying pan balanced on an ashy log. They dare not leave Dave for too long, let him out of sight for a second and there's a wild sense of panic, although they both know there's little they can do. They drink too many cups of coffee. They keep lifting the phone to check. Gingerly, they raise the mutilated limb and attempt to clear up around it, laying strips of clean sheet down, and fresh towels. Oliver gives it another spray with the Tetracycline, in which he seems to have great faith. Dave's teeth start grinding together. Should they cover the wound or not? What about a pad smeared with Germoline? But might that stick and get matted in the stump? They decide to leave it alone. They are terrified of doing the wrong thing, of causing more agony, or instant death from shock.

Georgie sees how gently Oliver wipes the boy's face and attempts to drip more water into his mouth. His expression is all concern. There's tenderness there, a complicated criss-cross of laughter lines, and a firm, honest mouth with a way of tweaking before smiling. She feels closer to this stranger than to anyone else in her life, no secrets. It is the bizarre situation, of course, the horror they are sharing. Only something so calamitous could draw two such strangers together so closely and so quickly. When it's over, dear God, if this is ever over, they will each go their separate ways . . . forgetting the promises made?

Why does this thought pain her so?

'Why don't you go and have your shower?' Oliver looks up and catches her glance before she can turn away. There's a kind of answer in his baleful smile. 'And then I'll have mine. If you've got some gear which might fit me I wouldn't mind a change.' He looks down ruefully at his blood-spattered self. 'I won't ever wear these again. I'd rather burn them.'

She has only Mark's overalls, which he left behind after his last visit. 'For the next time,' he had told her. 'I won't be needing them anywhere else.' And some of her own sweaters are man-size.

Georgie fetches clean clothes from upstairs and rests them on the loo seat while she plucks up the courage to undress in the cold. She stretches through the curtain to turn on the shower, and gives it a chance to run hot first. She bundles her clothes in a tight parcel, she won't wear hers again either.

The water hisses. Steam cloys the air and slides down the white-tiled walls. With her eyes half closed Georgie steps into the shallow square base and reaches for the shampoo. Though not as relaxing as a bath, the water is gorgeous all the same. For a while she lets it splash over her, basking in the pleasure as the jetting water warms and stimulates. When her hair is soaking wet she leans forward and soaps it, scrubs it until pieces of foam fall at her feet and down the pinkness of her wet skin, and when she has finished she flings back her head to wash the soap from her face.

She feels the smile come.

She hears the laugh and knows her teeth to be clenched.

The severed foot makes her laugh again.

It is hung on one of the meat hooks, a piece of loose skin hooks it there.

Above the shower, high on the ceiling. It appears to be quite dry, not dripping. Not bleeding.

Still laughing inanely Georgie passes through the plastic curtain, picks up the waiting towel and half crawls, half crashes through the hazy kitchen and into the sitting room. Oliver is still there beside Dave, stroking his forehead gently. Georgie crouches on the floor at his feet, dripping wet, huddled in her towel, giggling, sobbing, shouting and crying all at the same time.

He grips her hard by the shoulders. 'Jesus Christ! *What the hell . . . ?*'

But Georgie can't stop laughing. Tears blind her eyes, but still she laughs, the cracked, broken witchy sound of total hysteria. She attempts to point behind her, she must show him where, *she must show him*, but she has no strength to hold up her arm, and anyway, what direction? *She's forgotten.* She keeps attempting to speak and Oliver is shouting at her now, panic in his own eyes, 'What is it? *What the fuck is it?*'

Clutching the poker, his face tightened grimly he shouts, 'Where? Is it back in there?' He nudges Georgie with his foot, unable to move his eyes from the doorway, but she keeps on laughing desperately wanting to tell him. 'No, he's not here, he's not here . . .'

'Then what? Who? *Tell me, damn you!*' and his voice is at screaming pitch.

'In the shower.' At last she finds words, clipped and precise. 'It is there, in the shower.'

'What's in the shower, for Christ's sake?'

But it's no use. She can't remember. She can remember getting in and washing her hair, the familiar smell of shampoo and steam, but she cannot remember what she saw that brought her scurrying back here crouched by the fire with a towel around her. Oliver should not go in there. No-one should ever go in there. So when he walks towards the kitchen and the sound of running water she screams, 'Don't! Stop! Come back! *Oh God, please don't leave me.*'

But she is powerless to prevent him. He is

determined to go. Georgie crouches and shivers, unable to look in that direction. 'Oh don't, oh don't,' she continues to sob, unaware of the presence of Dave or of Lola's wary eyes as she stares from her place at the hearth.

Oliver is gone for a very long time. The water is turned off. Now she hears the door closing firmly. What the hell is he doing in there? *What is in there?* What has he found? Terrified by her lack of memory . . . perhaps the man is in there, with his axe . . . is that it? *Is that what she saw?* If that was it she is going to die, they are all about to die, painfully and bloodily, and there's not a damn thing they can do about it.

A poker is no defence against a madman wielding an axe.

The look on Oliver's face is harrowing. He looks like Dave, colourless and hardly alive. He comes and sits on the chair beside Georgie and he feels squeezed out and empty. He rests his head in his hands. 'What was it?' she asks him, panic rising. 'Oliver? What did you see?'

Finally Oliver raises his head. 'When the hell did that bastard get in there?'

She wants to help. She's determined to help. 'When we were out for the wood and the water?'

But Oliver shakes his head. 'No way. He wouldn't have had time. To do that must have taken some time, it can't be that simple to get up there and . . .'

'I can't think,' Georgie sobs. 'Dammit, I can't think of anything. I hardly know my own name.

369

And I don't want to remember. I want to get away from here, I want you to take me away.'

Ignoring her hysteria and fighting his own, Oliver's words come slowly and clearly. He gazes into the fire as he speaks. 'You left the front door open when you came to help me the night I arrived, didn't you, Georgie? I know you left it open because the hall was full of snow when we arrived back here with Dave. There was time for the sod to get in here then, if he was around, if he was watching. And he must have been around at that time because of Dave's foot.'

Now Georgie remembers exactly what she saw hanging from the meat hook in the bathroom not inches from her head. She had seen it, ivory white, veins swollen and gently oozing. She had seen the elastic-stretching skin and the hole where the rusting hook had pierced it. There had been a slight swinging movement, hardly noticeable at all. They should never have left those hooks in the ceiling, Isla had even joked about their handiness for towels. And she opens her mouth and begins to scream, and Oliver leans towards her, takes her face roughly into his two large hands and says, 'Stay with me, Georgie, you must stay with me. I'm sorry, I have to do this.' Then he slaps her. Hard. She moans. She shivers like a beaten dog. Then he holds her.

'I thought you said whisky was no good for shock.' Her teeth chatter on the edge of the glass as she feels the fire of it burn its way down, bringing her senses back to life.

But Oliver's smile is a cold one and he holds his own glass in two hands. He tips it slightly and watches as the colour rolls up the side of the glass.

'Everyone in this valley is in danger.' His voice is quiet but resolute. 'We should all be together in one place. It's the only way we will survive. And God only knows how long we're going to be cut off from the rest of the world with this repulsive thing out there. Who knows what might have happened to the others by now? They could be dead for all we know. This monstrous beast will stop at nothing. This is madness beyond all control. Sick. Twisted. And if Mrs fucking Buckpit, if anyone out there knows about this and is concealing the bastard, then God help them. We're facing a thing here, not animal, not human.'

'So what do we do?'

He swallows more whisky. He muses on it. Savours the taste in his mouth before he swallows, and rolls the glass between his hands. 'We've got to warn everyone for a start, in case they don't already know. We've got to band together. It's no good trying to sit this out, each in our individual cages, alone. No one man has the kind of strength it's going to take to destroy this monster.'

Georgie shivers again. 'But we don't know for sure it's Lot Buckpit.'

'It looks pretty much like it. But we've got to take some action now, we can't just sit around here suspecting everyone. It has to be Lot, sod it, there's no way it can be anyone else but Lot.'

'So we've got to warn the Horsefields.'

'And Chad and Donna. They'll have to come

back here with us because there's no way we can move Dave.'

'So who's going? Who's staying?' The thought is unendurable.

'I'm going. While you stay in here with the doors locked.'

'Oh no. Oh no. Not after last night. And it's me who knows them, it's me who knows the lie of the land. You nearly got lost in my orchard. You can't see a thing out there, you'd soon lose your bearings.'

'Georgie, you can't go out there alone.'

'Well then, we'll stay here and stick it out.'

Oliver stares at her seriously. 'We can't do that, Georgie. Not knowing what we know. Not knowing that others are at risk.'

Self-righteous prat. Such heroics. Georgie doesn't care about others, she cares about herself. And Oliver. And Dave. And Lola. She doesn't want to go and fetch the others. She doesn't even like them much. She attempts to argue with Oliver, she puts every obstacle in the way, but he remains determined that something must be done, that they will be safer gathered together.

'But perhaps he won't try anything else. Perhaps his madness has worn itself out on Dave. Perhaps we'd be wiser to stay indoors and wait.' Oh God, if only they could, if only she could make Oliver see sense.

They argue for most of the morning but still Georgie fails to convince him. 'We'll wait for a couple of hours to see what the weather does,' is all he will agree to. So Georgie watches and listens and detests this snow and wind with such a burning ferocity it is all consuming. She wants to rage at it, fight it, defeat it. Peace. Dear God, she wants peace and quiet and normality. She wants Dave to be well and she wants the sight of that dangling foot out of her mind for ever.

Where is the safety she's craved and sought after most of her life? What the hell is happening here? And why can't she ride out the rest of the storm safe and secure in Oliver's strong arms with her eyes tightly closed.

Why not?

Why not?

Twenty-eight

They opt for four in the afternoon, the time of the Buckpits' milking, a ritual so deeply ingrained that even a hurricane is unlikely to change it.

Hopefully Lot will be out of the way.

Oliver's plan is now inevitable. They can no longer stay here like terrified rats. Georgie's brain races like an engine. She tries to still her heart by telling herself that nothing, no matter how evil, could be waiting out there in all this mayhem, in the loneliest spot in the world. She glances around the familiar room, probably for the last time. 'So. This is it.'

'Don't go, Georgie. You were right. We should stay here . . .'

'What crap. We both know that's crap.'

'But to lose you now would be . . .'

She bites her lip hard. 'Oh, come on, be fair, don't make this any harder, Oliver.'

'You know how I feel . . .'

'Yes, I think I do.' Abruptly, and with a shiver, Georgie says, 'I must go.'

Oliver kisses Georgie goodbye, a gesture so normal, so infinitely tender, so alien in this hellish chaos that, for the seconds it takes, it brings with it all the warmth in the world, and all the safety. And she, noting his grey, drawn face, brings her hand gently down it as if to keep the memory there.

The storm outside enfolds her in a swirling haze of white sound. Her feet alone are commanding her movements in this infinite waste. Only once, in a blinding flash, does Georgie allow herself to think of the terrible nature of her unknown adversary, the fear of his watching eyes, his face pressed on glass, distorted, hideous, but she instantly cuts it off. She thinks instead about Dave and his anguish, his needs.

All the muscles of her face tauten with the pain of the cold, and her head is a wooden block that aches. Grimly Georgie trudges on, dimly aware that the Horsefields' warm living room will mark the end of this riot and disorder. The cottage lights have long disappeared, along with the smell of woodsmoke. Over her stream she goes and up to the field that leads round the back of the Horsefields' house.

Dimly and palely Georgie sees that there has been a violent alteration in the pattern of her life, and if she can change to meet this pattern she might find harmony again. Could she start to love again? But this time as someone better, stronger? The day before yesterday she had been a poor and desolate thing, only wanting to fly from the world, but look at her now, alone and going out to face the demon against all the fears of a lifetime.

Hell, *how long will this take?* Has she lost all sense of direction? She used to be able to see old Nancy pottering about in her garden from the edge of her own fence. It's no good, she can't see, her eyes are blinded by the absolute whiteness all around her.

Although the carving knife rests in her pocket, stuck through the lining, she begins to wonder, what does it matter? What does she care for the world and its wiles? How lovely to reverse her tracks and stumble back into Oliver's waiting arms . . .

A sob like a child's storms up in her and then sinks, perishes and gives place to a sigh.

Dear God. *He is here.*

He has always been here in Georgie's head.

It is over. He is covered with snow, like the abominable snowman, and vast, he could be a gorilla with his small unlaughing eyes. Strangely, he is welcome. Wait long enough for the blow and you will want it to come, and when it comes relief will mingle with the pain.

Georgie remains quite still. There is nothing else to do. Somewhere in her terror the thought emerges that this is all very different from what she has imagined. She'd imagined he would attack from behind.

The indrawing of breath is an agony, the cold makes it painful to gasp. Weakly, she stares at her nightmare. His clothes form the bulk of him, but the height she'd imagined is correct. He wears a balaclava helmet so only his eyes show, but she's seen one of them before, close up, closer than this, and she knows what his pudgy face looks like. The collar of his donkey jacket is pulled up so there is no discernible neck. His trousers, a thick brown corduroy, are tucked into fur-lined, zipped-up boots, and the axe hangs loose in his right hand, the metal edge resting in the snow. The leather biker's gloves make his hands seem huge, in-human.

But then everything about him is huge, and he has been standing here, watching her coming, and whistling. Horrible. Horrible. She cannot hear the whistle, but the bulge of his lips under the wool makes the shape of a mouth blowing air.

Slowly she starts to back down the slope. If she doesn't take care she is likely to toboggan down and end up in her stream at the bottom. After the first mind-blowing shock it's extraordinary how little fear there is, nothing so bad as the foot in the shower, but Georgie's brain has gone numb, frozen, just like her hands and her feet.

In a voice incredibly normal she asks very care-fully, 'What are you doing?'

At this he inclines his furry head like a bear, pretending to listen. Her words do not reach him, of course, the wind just whips them over her shoulder. She fights for balance. He is higher up the slope than she, in the stronger position, tower-ing above her, and his thick legs are set apart.

'What do you want?'

Jesus. Is he about to come nearer? Can he reach her from there if he swings his axe full circle?

'Tell me what you want me to do. I'll go back if that's what you want.' She must not panic or fall, she wants to prepare him for her flight. This fiendish savage is mad, a psychopath on the rampage, quite lethal, and any sudden movement will be likely to trigger him off.

With immense care and courage, weakened by cold and terror, Georgie takes one step backwards, feels her foot slide, and fights for balance. He comes one step towards her and she stays stock-still. He doesn't like that. 'OK. OK.' She moves her hand towards her pocket, nearer the handle of the knife, she can feel the point of the cardboard sheath where it rests against her leg.

'It's so cold,' she might be chatting at a bus stop. 'I've seen you standing out here before.' Well, they advise you to talk to them, don't they? Keep calm, engage them in conversation, make them see you as a person, cauterize a leg when the foot has gone, hang on to your pride, honour your father and mother, do your best, work hard, say your prayers. *They say they say they say*. She knows the maniac cannot hear her, he can only watch her moving lips, and they are probably contorted by fear and cold. If she screams from here Oliver won't hear her. Perhaps she can somehow lure this living abomination nearer to the cottage – if he'll give her time, if he'll stay the axe.

He didn't give Dave much time. He didn't give Dave five minutes. He chopped off Dave's foot and he slaughtered Georgie's pretty brown hens.

Her horrified eyes stare straight into those of the demon. There is nothing human about them, nothing with which to answer her pleas, nothing with which to recognize her fear. Her own bleary eyes, rimmed with snow and exhaustion, meet his

378

implacable gaze, the mindless gaze of a shark, set deep in his head, quick and restless and cruel. Staring through the slits in the black balaclava. But some sense drives him. *What sense?* Is he mute? Is he insensitive to the cold? It would seem so. But, dear God, even a mammoth would suffer from cold if it stayed motionless much longer. Georgie herself will freeze to death.

Time. Be gentle and slow, take your time. He won't allow her to step backwards, so what if she tries stepping forwards? But time holds no reality, it could be seconds, it could be hours that go by while she makes her rapid calculations, exploring every option minutely for this, the most dangerous, the most complicated manoeuvre she has ever undertaken in her life. What if she attempts to go forwards, what if she makes it clear she's not interested remotely in him, that she merely wants to complete her journey? But oh, it is hard to take a step further away from home when she yearns to run back like a fox to its layer in this most murderous hunt.

Sweat soaks her body and freezes it as she holds her breath for this fatal step. My God. It is done. But no response. Just watching.

Georgie doesn't think any more, or hesitate before making a second brave move, then another. Right. So this direction's OK by him? But then the ogre sways slightly before raising one boot to the side, leaving a dark-black hole in the snow. The axe slices the snow as he goes, dragging a trail behind its own weight like the thin, meandering tracks of a bird. Sweet Jesus, will he allow her to pass? Helpless as Georgie is, the hope that she feels now is cruel, it's this hope that brings tears to her eyes so that she almost flounders. What she needs is despair, no hope whatsoever, the fear of this is what drives her.

Oh God oh God oh God help me.

With the same bursting lungs and dreamlike sensation of moving underwater, she continues along this passage of hell, aware of his impossible strength and her own abysmal weakness. She will soon be beside him, with him several paces to her right, eight paces to be precise because now he has moved eight times, there are eight deep holes in the snow just to the right of her pathway.

'It's all right. I'm going past you. I swear to God I won't look at you, only please let me get past.'

He lunges. With no warning he raises the axe and lunges at Georgie. The wind and the snow whip together in one concentrated fury as she goes down beneath him, buried alive. Struggling for air, for light. Clawing for breath. Her lungs searing with pain, she gasps for breath in this dark underworld of snow and inhuman pressure. She is facing upwards, but she cannot tell because his awful weight and the overflowing mattress of white is in her mouth and nose and eyes, and is suffocating. He must have slipped because *where is the axe*, her fingernails scrape at the all engulfing vileness of his coat. He will have to get up to use the axe, unless he decides to stay here like this, lying on top of her, squeezing the life from her this way.

And the rank smell that comes off him can only

be the stench of the grave, dark old soil, a crumbly coffin-brown and the wet stems of churchyard flowers, scummy green water and mildewed urns, tarnished, rotten. The decay of the soul into madness.

Then – a flash on metal, as he raises himself slightly and Georgie can grip the knife's handle in the split second she has to cut herself out of her silver coffin. She wrenches it free. She lunges upwards; the mistake she makes is in using one hand, not enough strength to force the knife through the padding, and her hand slips down the ivory handle onto the steel of her own blade. There's a lick of scarlet flame from wrist to fingers, pulsing steadily, seeping life.

Unharmed, the monstrosity regains its balance and stands above her in the storm, gazing at her like a zombie through those impenetrable slits of eyes. He raises his axe using both hands, and the killing edge disappears into the gun-metal sky. Georgie senses the blade's descent, whistling on one screaming note. In the delicate manner of the dying, she crosses her arms across her chest. But his stance was always precarious, the wind tears against his great body, the snow is deep and drifting just here, and she watches him slowly lose control. A century passes while she watches and braces herself for his weight once again. His total weight. She has split seconds to raise the knife. This time she grips with both hands, the handle braced against her chest. This time she aims at the creature's throat. The face of black wool comes hurtling towards her, no surprise in his eyes even

now, neither pain nor anger as the axe falls helplessly by his side and his weight crashes down on
the tip of her blade.

It pierces the base of his throat. But, Jesus, it's
rammed a hole in her chest.

The slain colossus lies still while she waits. They
lie there silently, connected by Georgie's kitchen
knife, and still they wait, and she thinks that he
breathes . . .

Weary, so terribly weary, her right hand pulsing
with fiery pain, she edges him off her and struggles slowly to her knees. Kneeling, she pushes
him over so he lies in the snow on his back. His
torn throat is a terrible sight, blood foams out like
pink froth on the sea, the white edges of the skin
are pulled back to make way for the steel of the
blade, which disappears neatly up to the handle.
Garrotted. Repelled, she's hardly able to touch
him, yet she has to see the giant's face. Individual
fingers fail to respond, so it is with a frozen wedge
of hand that Georgie slides the balaclava clumsily
over the chin and up.

By now she is crying, her red-hot tears freeze to
her face but she cannot stop, she cannot stop
crying.

Bubbles frothing at his lips, frothing like that
hot-chocolate machine she had seen at the motorway services, but this froth is of pink scum.

There is no doubt that he is a woman and her
hair is long and black like an American Indian's,
but to Georgina Jefferson this revelation is not so
shocking. The monsters are often the women. Her
mother was a woman. She knows her victim is

female long before she runs her hands over the front of the donkey jacket to discover if there are breasts. There are. Braless breasts, uncared for breasts that no-one has ever touched with love, breasts, like Georgie's own, which have never suckled a child.

She kneels by the devil of Wooton-Coney and knows that they walk in many valleys, over shippen and stable, stone wall and stile, up stairs and along ordinary landings. They go disguised as men, clicking along in high heels and lipstick smeared on their faces and purple slanting eyes. They rarely get themselves into the news. They carry green raffia bags with green bottles inside them, which chink beside dining room chairs.

And she hears herself screaming, '*No, Mummy, no!*'

Twenty-nine

And she might well stay here for ever, until the snow covers her, resting there with her hands on the breasts of the slobbering devil. Georgie has forgotten there might be a new reason for living. Her spirit moves in a desolate waste. For a long time, for hours it seems, she can only sit there and moan, '*Oh God, help me.*' But now a man's voice calls through the void, and she thinks it might be Oliver but, oddly, it comes from above, not below.

She can't bear to look at the monster again. Despite its lethal injury it is probably still living because the bubbles round its mouth are sucked in and out in irregular rushes, flotsam on the edge of a wave. How very strange it is that she and this freak should have converged along their life-journeys to this meeting, to this terribly intimate moment, and that now they are parting again, she to live and it, most probably, to eventual death. Georgie leaves the knife where it is, plunged to its hilt in her victim's throat, but unconsciously she has pulled down her sleeve to cover the pain in her sliced right hand. She stands up carefully, trusting to trembling rubber legs, and attempts to locate the voice, starts to stumble desperately towards it.

Georgie the conqueror falls many times as she

drags her way up the slope of the field, mostly on hands and knees and sobbing like a beaten child. When the calling stops she stands and listens. She knows she was heading for the Horsefields' house before she met her Goliath and the voice is coming from that direction. Perhaps Oliver, desperately anxious, left Dave alone to come after her, perhaps he went the front way and is now, in frantic despair, struggling back to find her.

'I'm OK, Oliver, I'm OK,' she sobs, her breath rasping in the badly bruised chest which took the brunt of the plunging knife. 'She's almost dead. She can't hurt us now.' In her confusion she calls out to Stephen. 'You can come home now, Mummy's gone.'

She slides her hand from her sleeve and stares at it when sheer exhaustion forces her to pause. She cradles it in her other arm as if it's a wounded kitten, pathetic and sorry for itself. The slice is a neat one, although it cuts her lifeline in half, and the blood wells up through the wound in a vicious red line before flooding her hand in crimson waves.

She doesn't bother to glance behind her, she doubts that the heinous thing on the ground is strong enough to follow her and, strangely, she has ceased to care. All she feels now is the animal need to find Oliver and the shelter of his arms. She wants to tell him what she's discovered . . . what she has done . . . murder, she has murdered. She is afraid that he might not forgive her. Perhaps it is already too late.

She stops when she sees the figure calling

beside the Horsefields' back gate. Is that Horace standing there, staunch as a beacon against the storm, calling out into the gale? Seeing Georgie, the figure fights its way forward, and she rushes to meet it in a shambling run, heaving for breath and gasping her last, forcing a way through the damnable snow.

He catches her as she falls into his arms.

'Good God, girl, *what has happened?*'

She holds out her hand as a child would, as if he might kiss it and make it better. As if this is all that is wrong.

It is Horace's vast strength that gets Georgie the rest of the way as he half carries, half drags her through his back garden and into his perfect English rose kitchen. She collapses on the red floor tiles, conscious, but only just. Her legs give way beneath her and the closing door completes a silence that leaves only her own heartbeat. She huddles there in the corner beside the sink, curled up like a comma.

Nancy rushes in, her face a wrinkled mask of anxiety, there is not one smooth area of skin, not one unworried part of her face. She springs round the room in useless concern while Horace fills a basin with water and disinfectant and rests Georgie's hand in it. The water turns a brilliant red.

'*I was coming to warn you . . .*' Is this Georgie's voice, this hollow echo that comes up from the floor, up from the very cellars of the house? She attempts to lick her lips, but her tongue is so swollen and dry it bulges, out of control.

'What could she be doing outside in this, Horace? What could the girl be thinking of?'

'But I had to come out because . . .' The thick wad of gauze which Horace lays across her hand stings with a red-hot agony.

'It'll stop in a minute,' the big man reassures her, bending in half to reach her on the floor. 'You haven't cut any tendons. It's nasty, very nasty indeed, but superficial, luckily. We'll have to get you to hospital as soon as this lessens a little and we can find a way out. You need a few stitches.'

The heat from the Horsefields' Scandinavian woodburner is quickly dulling Georgie's senses. Every bone aches as if she's been under a steamroller and is now quite flat. Gradually she feels herself filling out.

'Get her to the fire, Horace, and we must get something hot inside her.'

'I must let Oliver know I'm safe.'

'Oliver?' Horace enquires, neatly applying a sensible bandage with quite surprising skill. His enormous hands are deft and gentle, but his eyes show a tortured sorrow when he stares into Georgie's and asks, 'How's it feeling now?'

'A little easier. Not quite so stiff.' She tries to move her fingers but they are still frozen. They seem to be gripped in a glove of ice.

'Yes, we'll move her to the fire, and why don't you put the kettle on, Nancy?' This is his way of calming his wife.

'Shall I heat up some peanut brownies?'

Georgie appeals to Horace, finding it hard to find the words. 'She's out there.'

He stares at her intently. '*Who is out there?*'

'I stabbed her. She was killing me so I stabbed her.'

'And a nice little silver doily, I think, as it's getting near to Christmas.'

'*Who was killing you?* What are you saying?' And Horace's white unhappy fingers feel the stubble on his chin.

Georgie babbles, 'The person who's been stalking me, the watcher I told you about, the owner of the doll and the make-up case, the same one who came to my kitchen and covered my pallet with blood. She's out there in the snow where I left her. There was a terrible accident – there's a man at our house with his foot cut off, and we think he might die if he doesn't get help. *She cut it off with an axe.*'

Georgie is crying properly now and her body shudders, quite out of control as she tries to explain the awfulness of it to someone who doesn't yet know. To someone who can't possibly imagine . . . He will think her quite insane. Driven mad by the snow. But it's so essential that Horace believes her so she can get a message through to Oliver. He looks as if he does believe her, and a terrible knowledge crosses his eyes. Is he concerned for Nancy's welfare? Nancy, who even now is balancing on some kitchen steps reaching for a cake tin?

No, Nancy's not on his mind right now.

'Where is she?' asks Horace.

'Halfway down the slope, where I left her, and my kitchen knife is in her throat because i wouldn't go through the padding.' Georgie tries to demonstrate how it happened with her hands, but the violence is too impossible. 'She tried to kill me with an axe, but she fell on me and I had this knife . . . and I don't know what we should do about her because she might still be alive . . .'

Where are his disbelieving questions? She is crying out these unspeakable things, and he is merely staring back with sadness in his troubled eyes when he ought to be shaking her to her senses.

At last the bandaging is finished. There's a slight trembling of Horace's hands as he clips the tiny safety pin, but that might be because of his concentration. He has done a professional job. A doctor would be proud of it. Georgie can bear to lift the hand now and inspect it properly, the wad of gauze must be thick because there is no blood seeping through.

'Let's get her into the sitting room, Nancy.' And Horace steps behind her and helps Georgie up with all the gentleness in the world. 'D'you think you can stand, or walk on your own?'

She can hardly speak through her tears, but she whispers, 'I'll try.'

She wobbles along unsteadily, leaning heavily on Horace's arm like an invalid. Nancy puffs up the cushions of Horace's overlarge armchair, brand new, by the looks of it, the triangular label attached to the corner of the seat declares it to be flameproof.

'Somebody has to go . . .'

'I am going,' says Horace, 'just as soon as you're comfortable.'

'You'll have to be terribly careful,' Georgie insists. 'She might have got up again. She might have crawled away.'

'With your knife inside her?' asks Horace sombrely.

'Yes, it is possible, with my knife inside her.'

Throughout all this Nancy acts as if she is not remotely involved, or as though she's unaware of the drama that's going on around her. She is aware that Georgie needs help, that much is obvious, but she betrays no emotions, not horror, fear, or shock. She carries on in her familiar fashion, scuttling around her visitor, making her guest comfortable. She even fetches the hostess trolley, and Georgie lies back and hears that ridiculous article squeaking its way into the room and thinks how bizarre it is that she should be offered cake while all the time . . .

And still she can't stop crying. Her hands shake and her head pounds. Every bone in her body is aching.

'I'm off now.' Horace brings good news. 'The wind seems to be dying down and the snow has almost stopped.'

'Oh, Horace, tell Oliver I'm OK. Tell him I'm coming back just as soon as I know it's dead . . .'

'Don't worry, I'll tell him.'

'And you'll take a look at Dave's leg just in case there's anything more . . . ?'

'I'll look at his leg, but I'm sure you've done all that can be done.'

'Now be sure to wrap up warmly, Horace, you know how easily you catch colds.'

Nancy reaches on tiptoe and fiddles with his scarf. Colds? *Colds for God's sake?* But it's good that Nancy is unaware; she is lucky her illness provides this protection. Perhaps Georgie used the same device when she refused to see the devil as a woman, when she refused to accept Gail Hopkins's guilt – yes, of course, Gail killed Angela – but for the first time she can see it all clearly, she never dreamed Gail would kill her own daughter. There truly was nothing Georgie could do . . . hindsight and guilt can be so confusing.

Georgie tries to concentrate on controlling her shaking. Please make Horace come back soon, this waiting is unendurable. The poor man won't be prepared for such a terrible bloody find. Nancy removes the cup from her patient's uselessly shaking hands and lifts it to Georgie's lips, but her hands tremble more than Georgie's, so the exercise is hopeless. Somehow it must be possible to relax this body of hers, there are classes where you can learn to do it. Georgie allows her eyes to close, she cradles her burning hand. Nancy's small talk is comforting. It rocks her brain like rippling water. Now the monster is wounded, now the storm has abated, they'll have a chance to get Dave to hospital . . .

You hate to think that the monsters could possibly be women like you, because women are gentle and caring.

If they give you a key to your own room they are cunning enough to keep one for themselves, and you can always hear them coming, crawling along brown landings at night with curses on their breaths and boozy, unfocused eyes. You can hear your door being unlocked, and it doesn't matter how deeply you snuggle down under your covers. They come in, these women, just the same.

The eyes of every dwarf on her bedside light were different, Dopey, Happy, Grumpy, Sleepy, they bordered Snow White in her blue dress, all marvellously indifferent. Georgie would watch the dwarfs' eyes and wonder which ones Mummy would be wearing. Oh yes, she had seven sets of eyes.

Mummy would snip on the light and Georgie would know that all the dwarfs were lit up and staring. She would sit on the chair beside Georgie's bed, Georgie could smell her, she could hear her tugging her hanky. Ripping and grasping her hanky. She had to get the venom out, it had gone inside her with the drink and Daddy wouldn't let her do it to him, although she used to try, yes she did. So when all the screaming downstairs was over Mummy would come up, pulling herself by the fat brown banisters and then along the landing slippery with brown rugs.

Oh, Georgie has always craved safety. If she is safe she is loved.

Mummy hissed like a snake, 'Don't you damn well make out you're asleep. Sly bitch. Crafty cow! Just like your bloody father.'

And Georgie would breathe in deeply in a heavily sleeping way.

'Oh no, you don't fool me, you fucking little tart.'

It was like being stabbed with a knife.

'You! Get out of that bleeding bed!'

And Georgie, shivering, would obey. They rarely put the heating on, especially at night, and in winter the ice made patterns on the windows just like it did in Wooton-Coney, and their light switches were brown and round. 'Don't you move a fucking inch! Stand right there where I can see you! Oh yes, Georgina, I know your dirty tricks.'

She would stand there and stare at the brown patterned carpet while Mummy looked straight into her head. She tried not to see which eyes she wore. She knew Mummy's face would be twisted, twisted like her handkerchief hands, and Mummy would twist Georgie, too, until she turned into small threads that could be hoovered away.

'Get under that bed and stay there! Don't you dare come out!'

Georgie's small face touched the carpet, it felt damp and stale under her bed and it smelled of dust and crumbs. There were bits of carpet where the threads were worn, and she played with these with her fingers, twanging on them like strings. Sometimes Mummy would keep guard all night and Georgie guessed she had gone to sleep. But, oh no, she never protested, she had been too young when it started and she didn't know how to protest. She grew up believing that this was normal. It could be happening to all little girls.

But she knew she could never invite her friends home and thought Mummy wicked to even suggest it.

But in the daytime the let's pretend was that such events never happened. Daddy played the same game, too. So when the dawn of childhood was over and Georgie reached the daytime of life, she still pretended it had never happened. That women did not do it. That mothers did not do it.

That Gail Hopkins did not do it. While all the time, deep down, she suspected the violence was hers. While Ray Hopkins, just like Daddy, pretended to be a protector of women, protecting his violent wife even now as he languished in his prison cell. A hopeless, despairing kind of love, like that of the white knights of old, who would disappear for years at a time never knowing what went on at home.

And if Georgie had known it was Gail who'd killed Angie, who had finally gone too far with her scolding, her screaming, her angry smacking, if she'd known it was Gail who killed her daughter, *why had she denied this mother's violence?* Why was she still playing let's pretend whenever the morning came?

A sensible woman like Georgie? A plodder, wise and capable?

Oh yes, she knew why Stephen had gone, and she understood his paintings. If Georgie had been able to paint perhaps she would have told on Gail Hopkins.

Maybe she would have done her job properly and saved little Angie's life.

She opens her eyes to Stephen's picture, the gift he gave the Horsefields. It hangs on the opposite wall inside its gaudy frame, and the child's face stares straight at her.

Georgie's mouth goes dry again, and she feels her tongue starting to swell. She wishes she could sip that tea. 'Who is the girl in the picture, Nancy?'

Almost invisible, confused against the dark background, yet Georgie suddenly notices that among the toys on the tartan rug there is a doll with missing hair, and a pink, childish make-up case that could have come from Woolworths.

Nancy smiles broadly. 'That's our June.'

'June?'

'You know June. Everybody knows June. Stephen was very fond of June. Such a pretty child, isn't she? So very appealing. He used to let her visit him and she'd help him paint some pictures. June was very fond of Stephen. She used to play in his woodshed when he was too busy to let her in. Oh yes, poor June was devastated when Stephen passed away. Too young to understand about death, that was the trouble. We tried to explain that he wasn't coming back, but it was all too much for a child to take in. Too cruel, don't you think?'

Georgie's brain whirls slowly round, creaking like a rusty cog while Nancy offers her a peanut brownie. She cannot take it in. She hasn't the strength to assimilate this. Stephen passed away and Georgie came to his cottage instead. She had filled June's playroom with logs. She'd cleaned it out, whitewashed it. Thoughtlessly thrown out the make-up case. June tried to remind her she wanted to paint, but having no oils had used blood instead . . . no wonder June was hurt and angry.

'*Where is June now, Nancy?*'

'June's a naughty girl. She's upstairs in her room. Horace had to be firm with her.'

Georgie's voice is soft. 'In her room? Here? *In this house?*'

'Of course. Where else? This is her home. June has her own special place upstairs, the whole of the attic. Horace converted it when we first came. Oh, he did a lovely job, and I chose the furniture and fittings, mail order.'

'And Stephen painted that picture of June?'

'Yes. She was very good. She sat for it under the tree in the garden. I remember we had a lovely summer that particular year, rather like the last one. There was a drought. Stephen had all the time in the world for June.' Nancy smiles and her face lights up. 'She used to dance for him sometimes. She was always a very good girl when Stephen was around, she loved it when he let her paint her own pictures.'

Georgie's words are slow and careful. 'Does June often go out on her own, Nancy?'

'She shouldn't go out alone, of course, not these days, with the dangerous roads and dirty men, but she has her little ways. She hasn't been allowed outside for a long, long time now. Horace has had to get very strict. She discovered a way of opening the shutters and climbing onto the roof. We had it rethatched a few years ago and the little monkey hangs onto the netting.'

'She must be a very brave girl to crawl across the roof like that. How old is June now, can you remember?'

A quick flash of annoyance passes over Nancy's face. 'Of course I know the age of my daughter! She will be seven next birthday. I always bake her a special cake, June loves the way I ice them. The last was in the shape of a little log hut, I built it up with chocolate fingers. Stephen liked to come to June's parties when he wasn't too busy, when he wasn't too sulky. Your brother was never a sociable man, and, of course, he missed the last one. Poor June. Poor Stephen.'

Given Nancy and Horace's ages their daughter has to be over thirty.

When she speaks of her fantasy child Nancy's face becomes sweet, pink and healthy, all the sickness gone out of it. 'Loves animals, you know especially dogs. We did get her a dog once, gorgeous little thing, but Horace said she killed it with kindness. I never knew what he meant.' The hands that are always plucking become suddenly still. There's a faraway look in Nancy's eyes as they both gaze at Stephen's picture.

Georgie forces herself from her chair when she hears the back door open. She limps across the room, through the hall, and stands there, too shocked to go any further.

Horace Horsefield, this giant of a man, holds his monstrous child in his arms. His eyes hold

397

Georgie's for a moment before he moves them to his wife. Nancy is right behind her. Horace pushes his way past with all that heavy weight in his arms, and it seems as if he carries a feather. He goes into the sitting room, where he lies his daughter gently on the sofa. The knife is still lodged in her throat and pink bubbles still flake her lips, but now they are dry. The girl is not moving.

At once Nancy flies to her side. She kneels before her grotesque baby. She strokes the huge frozen face with the side of her own birdlike hand. 'June! June! What's happened to you, my darling? *Where have you been?* And you are a naughty, naughty girl when Daddy told you not to go out, he told you to stay in the playroom, and I bought you all those new toys.'

'June is dead.'

Horace stands perfectly still, watching his wife's desperate ministrations with anguish in his patient eyes. He repeats those three hopeless words, 'June is dead, Nancy, my sweet. I'm sorry, so sorry, but June is dead.'

'Tut. And what's that horrid, horrid sharp thing doing there in her throat? Take it out, Horace, do, before it starts to hurt.'

Horace crosses the room, picks up a blanket and begins to cover the body of the creature. 'We couldn't abandon her in some heartless hospital, even when they told us how bad things would get.' Georgie stands, watching, shivering, and although she was their daughter's victim, some measure of the couple's torment touches her heart and wrenches it. 'It's the drugs, they affected her size

398

and her senses. They never said she'd get dangerous. To leave her would have killed Nancy. We had to choose our home very carefully. But in the end, you see, even Wooton-Coney proved too sociable a place.' Horace adores his wife. And now Georgie sees to what lengths this kind man, this decent man, has gone in order to protect his family, even making huge offers for Furze Pen Cottage when he noticed the change in June's behaviour, advising Georgie to leave the hamlet . . . He did what he could, so far as he knew his child was just playing naughty tricks . . .

Cramer must have known about June and suspected, how the man must have revelled in Georgie's blatant distress. Donna, a newcomer to the hamlet, had never seen the girl, who has obviously been kept a prisoner since Stephen's untimely death and the dreadful effect this event had on her unstable behaviour. The hideous Buckpits must have known, too, but considered it none of their business. After all, until June's savage attack on Dave, the only person affected was Georgie.

Nancy reaches to pull down the cover. 'Not over her face, Horace, please, you know how afraid she is of the dark. You know that she needs her night light on, even in summer when the nights are quite bright.'

'I know, dear. I know.'

Mother love. How can one mother love so obsessively while another can kill her own child?

Nancy continues her gentle stroking before she tuts with a shake of the head. 'She must have been fighting again. That's what must have happened this time, and it got out of hand. She's such a sweet child, really, but she's always had a temper, a very nasty temper. And now she's gone and hurt herself. Perhaps, at dear last, she'll have learned her lesson.'

THE END